Also by Merrill Markoe

IT'S MY F---ING BIRTHDAY
WHAT THE DOGS HAVE TAUGHT ME
HOW TO BE HAP HAP HAPPY LIKE ME
MERRILL MARKOE'S GUIDE TO LOVE
THE DAY MY DOGS BECAME GUYS

Recordings by Andy Prieboy

SEVEN DAYS IN SAMMYSTOWN (with Wall of Voodoo)
HAPPY PLANET (with Wall of Voodoo)
UGLY AMERICANS IN AUSTRALIA (AND BULLHEAD CITY, AZ)
    (with Wall of Voodoo)
UPON MY WICKED SON
MONTEZUMA WAS A MAN OF FAITH
SINS OF OUR FATHERS

THE PSYCHO EX GAME

Villard New York

The Psycho Ex Game

A NOVEL

MERRILL MARKOE *and* **ANDY PRIEBOY**

Copyright © 2004 by Merrill Markoe and Andy Prieboy

All rights reserved under International and Pan-American Copyright Conventions. Published in the United States by Villard Books, an imprint of The Random House Publishing Group, a division of Random House, Inc., New York, and simultaneously in Canada by Random House of Canada Limited, Toronto.

VILLARD and "V" CIRCLED Design are registered trademarks of Random House, Inc.

LIBRARY OF CONGRESS CATALOGING-IN-PUBLICATION DATA

Markoe, Merrill.
The psycho ex game: a novel / Merrill Markoe and
Andy Prieboy.
p. cm.
ISBN 1-4000-6076-1
1. Rejection (Psychology)—Fiction.   2. Mate selection—
Fiction. I. Prieboy, Andy.   II. Title.
PS3563.A6652P74 2004
813'54—dc22   2004043011

Villard Books website address: www.villard.com

Printed in the United States of America on acid-free paper

1 2 3 4 5 6 7 8 9

FIRST EDITION

Book design by Dana Leigh Treglia

To the Memory *of* Marc Moreland

THE PSYCHO EX GAME

Chapter 1

LISA

When I went out to the driveway to pick up the paper, a Starline Tours bus pulled up.

"This is Nick Blake's house," I could hear a nasal tour guide say into a primitive bus microphone. "Looks like we're in luck, folks. I believe the woman in the driveway is his girlfriend, Leona." Reflexively, I licked my forefingers and tried to remove the chunks of black crud from the corners of my eyes as I heard him lead the assorted bus simpletons in a wan greeting. "Come on, everybody . . . Let's all say good morning, and maybe she'll come talk to us. Come on over, Leona! Come say hello!!"

"G'mornin', Leona!" said a bunch of people, not quite all at once.

First thing in the morning I like to pretend that each new day is awash in infinite possibilities. Being

stared at blithely by a busload of asymmetrically featured people did nothing to enhance this already shaky premise. Even if
it had been a busful of handicapped children, I would not have
acknowledged them. Well, maybe only then.

"Nick around?" the driver asked.

"Sorry. You missed him," I said, still looking at the ground.
"He just left eight years ago." Like he would have played along
had he been here. For a brief moment, I could see Nick's compact but chunky form facedown in our bed, unmovable, like a
bulldog under anesthesia: his blanket kicked off, a pillow pulled
tightly over his head as he angrily waved off all attempts to
wake him before two in the afternoon. In response to "Nick,
there's a tour bus in the driveway! Come out and say hello!," he
would have screamed, "What, are you out of your fucking
mind?," his black hair sticking out in all directions as though he
had fallen asleep during a monsoon. "Tell them you haven't
seen me in weeks. You heard I was flattened by an asphalt
spreader." That would have been if he was in a good mood. If
he wasn't, he would have just glared at me, too furious at being
awakened to even remove his earplugs.

"Everywhere you take us is either not home or dead," I
heard a woman on the bus whine as I caught a distorted
glimpse of myself in a hubcap, dressed in the T-shirt I'd slept
in. Silly me, not remembering to dress up for paper retrieval.

"Leona! Please! Can we talk with *you* for a minute?" the
driver shouted.

"My name's not Leona," I said, tripping over absolutely
nothing as I sprinted back to the house, demoralized, no idea
what to do with all the anger except phone in sick to work. It
was ridiculous that I still let the happy bus people affect me.
Though it was once a daily occurrence, the tour organizers had
started losing interest a few years back. I'd been so delighted
with this sign that my life was now my own again that I'd considered sending the management a bouquet of Mylar balloons

that said THANKS A BUNCH!!, thereby expressing gratitude, but in the most annoying way possible.

By afternoon I'd been sitting immobile for hours, sprawled on the couch, in the room I had designated as my office, surrounded by piles of catalogs. I was wasting time circling things in red pen that I might like to buy one day. For instance, monkey candleholders, sixty-five dollars. Then wasting even more time debating with myself whether monkeys were still an iconoclastic, offbeat decorating choice or if they had now become an adorable housewife fad that would mark me as cutesy. As if what my big dark underfurnished house needed was more whimsical pointless medium-priced crap.

By evening I had put down the catalogs and begun to go through the giant shoe box of recipe cards from the seventies that I had purchased at a thrift store for two dollars the previous weekend. None of the food photos looked particularly tempting as meal suggestions, but there had been something about the enormous quantity of cards for so little money that had made them irresistible. I hadn't known what I would do with them until today, when, while studying the brightly colored photo of the cauldron of Lamb Chops with Vegetables, I took out my Wite-Out pen and added one eyeball to each of the two protruding lamb-chop bones. This instantly turned the adjacent string beans into eyebrows and the cherry tomato at the bottom of the pan into a mouth. The furious snarling face that emerged was, in my opinion, so successful, and such an accurate depiction of the essence of Lamb Chops with Vegetables, that I began to go through the rest of the cards looking for the appropriate face in every one. Next thing I knew, it was evening and I had been making faces out of photographs of food for almost five hours. Berry Ring with Creamy Fruit had become a surprised guy with mandarin-orange eyebrows and a raspberry mouth. Chicken Liver Timbales were crying out in agony from their resting place between a tomato and sprig of parsley, looking not unlike those paintings of the screaming popes by Francis Bacon. Veal Cordon Bleu was three different faces in a row: the Pep Boys, only on a bed of noodles.

I got so lost in my new hobby that I took the cards with me when I decided to move to the couch in the front room, where it didn't seem so isolated. I planned to settle in for the rest of the evening. The front room was what the real estate salesperson who showed the house referred to as the Living Room, even though relatively few of the things the real estate person would think of as "living" had been taking place there since I took occupancy. The biggest room in the house, it was kind of cavernous and drafty because of what that same real estate person referred to as the Cathedral Ceilings—certainly the only cathedral-like thing in any proximity to my life.

Before I got too settled, I walked over to the unused fireplace and held a match to both ends of the paper wrapping on the artificial log I had deposited there weeks before. Instantly the room had a happier, cheerier, cozier, more magnetic center. A perfect environment for discovering the miserable grimace hidden somewhere in Steamed Cranberry Pudding, I thought as I sat back down on the couch with the recipe cards in my lap. I looked over at the crackling fire with satisfaction. "People might like it here," I told myself with a burst of optimism as I moved on to a pan of Pepper Steak, easily transforming it into a happy gathering of irritable and arrogant sliced-meat men. "Or maybe at least they wouldn't completely hate it if I served enough booze, so they didn't have the ability to scrutinize things too closely."

I was only too aware that if I was going to become someone who entertained, a lot more attention to detail would be necessary. My living room was decorated with other people's discarded things: matching nautical brass lamps that I took from my father's apartment after he died, not because I liked them but because no one else wanted them. Weird mismatched end tables and chairs left over from past relationships in which I was stupid enough not to know that agreeing to a piece of bad furniture was not a symbol of a lasting emotional bond. My whole life I had been very good at tuning out details I feared I couldn't control by ignoring them and escaping instead into fantasy. Which was why the fact that I had hundreds of recipe cards still needing faces offered me such comfort. There were things about my life that I wanted to forget. For instance, I needed to make my brand-new unhappy workplace situation disappear. After promising myself never to take this kind of job again, I had agreed to "consult" on a television show. My last experience had been so upsetting that on New Year's Eve I had made a special trip to the Psychic Eye bookstore to purchase Fiery Wall of Protection incense, which I burned while I chanted, "Nicely you shall put my heart back into its former condition again. Pleasant again it has become" from a Navajo Indian prayer book. I was counting on the Navajos to help me harness natural forces bigger than my own will, to keep me from being lured back to a mind-numbing job by a large pay-check. What I really should have looked for was an incense and a prayer designed to protect me from expensive home-maintenance bills. The cracks in my walls, the sinking founda-tion, and my near-empty bank account had all recently formed a guerrilla alliance that was holding the Navajo forces of nature hostage.

It was very disheartening how quickly I succumbed to the praise of the team of guys who created the show, Mark Eden and Steve Rosen. They had begged me to come on board be-cause they needed to add "a smart, funny female point of view." And they said this right when I was feeling overwhelmed by the spooky isolation of writing at home alone.

So there I was, on the staff of a midseason replacement called *You Go, Girl!*, a sitcom set in a gym. It involved the theoretically hilarious misadventures of genetically superior

spandex-clad Hitler Youth coulda-beens whose sarcastic dialogue made them sound more like Catskill comics than any
gym rats on *this* planet. Ten doughy white boys made up the
rest of the writing staff. Not one of them had ever actually set
foot in a gym.

I wanted very much to convince myself that there was a way
I could work on this project, collect some money, and not let
the ham-fisted written material get under my skin. It would be-
hoove me to learn how to compartmentalize troublesome feelings, like rage and humiliation. Plenty of other people were
able to do this. For example, everyone else in the city of Los
Angeles.

In fact, once work began, I was able to maintain an aloof,
businesslike attitude. For about two hours. From that point on,
when I was supposed to be thinking of ways to help the script,
I was actually silently reciting an ever lengthening prayer that
began, "Dear Lord. Please let the show be canceled prema-
turely and the stars be possessed by the desire to leave television for movies, thus causing them to be cast into the pit of
oblivion forever and ever, world without end, amen."

The worst thing about it all was that when I got home at
night, I felt so whiplashed and stained by bad comedy that I
had started to refuse to leave my house. Right now I was once
again thinking of backing out of the plans I had made for the
evening. Plans, I might add, that I had made a few days before,
expressly to force myself out of seclusion. I had patiently
worked my way through a lengthy dissertation on hipster
nightlife in the *L.A. Weekly*, then combed through the weekend
listings before deciding to purchase a ticket to see the only
thing that really caught my interest: a live show called *Tommy!
(Lee!) The Musical*, playing at a small hipster club called the
Empire. The review said that even though the play was based
on the doomed, overpublicized, and ill-considered love of
Tommy Lee for Pamela Anderson, it defied all logic by still

being delightful. The only other thing I knew about the show was that my musician friend Kat had seen it and liked it. And though Kat's taste in men was nightmarish, her taste in music was solid. So I forked over the ticket money by offering myself the secret proviso that if, at the last minute, I was too depressed to get up off the couch, I did not have to attend.

But as I lay there resisting, I also knew that if I stayed home, I might be looking at another no-speak weekend: two big long days and nights when I might have to phone people at random just to hear my own voice interact with another human being.

That was the hardest thing about living alone: the amount of work required to constantly jump-start a social life. How many clubs and bars and restaurants and concerts and street fairs and art openings and novelty balls and one-person shows and poetry readings and heavy-handed little plays and evenings of new comedians and readings at bookstores was a person supposed to attend on a monthly basis to prove to her friends that she wasn't deteriorating mentally?

And then the phone rang. "Honey, you are still going tonight, right?" drawled Kat. "Because Jake and I decided we're going. So if you want, we can save you a seat at our table."

"I don't know," I said flatly, feeling tired just visualizing the amount of work a "yes" was going to require: the grooming, the driving.

"Don't you dare talk yourself out of it. You're spending way too much time out there in the Cathedral alone," said Kat. She sounded relieved when I said I'd meet her there. What the hell. I actually did want to see the show. I was also vaguely curious to find out who Jake was.

Which was how I came to be walking into the Empire at nine-thirty at night, wearing a serene yet amused expression that I hoped effectively covered up my fear of being over-dressed in the pin-striped suit that I always wore when I had no idea what to wear. I strode purposefully into the darkened, candlelit room, past table after table of couples, trying to appear too preoccupied with weightier matters to have noticed my own lack of an escort.

And not a moment too soon. The show started thirty seconds after I hunch-walked to the empty chair at the table up front where Kat and a guy I assumed was Jake were seated. Even before I turned to look up at the stage, I liked what I was hearing: great, elaborate, baroque melodies with complex vocal harmonies. The singing was beautiful: a loud cross between rock and operetta. But the lyrics were what really caught my attention. Good word usage, I thought, immediately sitting up straighter. Good word usage got me hot.

"Who wrote this?" I asked Kat, scanning the large group of theatrically dressed people on the tiny stage. She pointed to a tall, skinny, long-haired guy in a black coat, stage right.

"Hmmm," I said, raising my eyebrows.

Kat looked at me and shook her head. "No, no, honey. Trouble," she mouthed in the softest whisper that could still be heard above the singing. I raised my eyebrows again, to ask what she meant. When I couldn't hear her over the music, she wrote it on a napkin that she passed to me. "Porno addict," it said.

Porno addict, I thought, looking at the bleeding ink of the letters. That is a little grim. Not as specifically horrendous as a heroin addict or an alcoholic. But maybe no worse than a computer-game fanatic or a gambler. At least watching dirty movies can be kind of fascinating if they aren't too horribly strange. And even the horribly strange ones are still more interesting than televised sports.

For a brief second, a scenario of my date with the porno addict went flashing before me. There we were on a Sunday morning, messy in last night's clothes. Light was streaming into his elaborate rock-star living quarters: part Gothic castle, part psychedelic pad. A reel of porno played on his large-screen TV as we sat side by side on his red velvet couch, staring expressionless at a close-up of a lipsticky blonde with a mouthful of somebody's dick. "I hope you don't mind watching porno at ten o'clock on a Sunday morning," he said pleasantly, offhandedly, the bad jazz porno sound track playing behind him. He took a big handful of popcorn from a greasy aluminum bowl before passing it to me. "No, no, not at all," I lied with fake enthusiasm, taking a handful of popcorn and then putting the bowl between us on the couch. "I can't remember a Sunday morning when I didn't watch porno. It goes way back to when I was a kid!" After which we both munched in an uncomfortable silence, punctuated only by the sounds of porno orgasms. How I longed to be teleported home to the cozy comfort of my bed and back to a more innocent time when I was still unexposed to whatever frightening contagious things a musician picks up from God knows whom when they tour.

My reverie was broken by a nudge from Kat, knocking me back into the present. "Girlfriend," whispered Kat, pointing to the tall, busty Rocker Barbie creature who was singing the part of Pamela Anderson. Her lips were so spackled with glittering lipstick that the glare was almost blinding. "Ah," I said, understanding, "I get it."

My fantasies decimated, I tuned back to the content of the show and listened, with awe, to the impassioned aria Tommy Lee sang to his prospective bride the night before their big beach wedding as they both got tattooed with each other's names. It was a song of love, of longing, of egomania, and of narcissism as "their hearts were hot-glued together." Even weirder was the fact that I was moved. I found myself thinking, Will I ever know such love? That anyone had bothered to write a work of beauty and merit based on the lives of these show-business miscreants was as astonishing as the fact that it was bringing tears to my eyes. It was also exciting to see that I knew some of the cast: Brian Reynolds and Kevin Beezer, two comedians who were playing members of Mötley Crüe (among other things).

After the standing ovation wore itself out, I got up and ran over to Kevin, grabbing him by the arm as he headed back to the dressing room.

"Kevin! Great show!" I said, giving him a hug.

"Wow. Lisa! Thanks. It was fun," he said, pleased.

"Do me a favor and tell the guy who wrote it that I really enjoyed it," I added.

"You should tell him yourself," he said, "I'm sure he'd like to hear it."

"No, no, no, no," I said, backing off, thinking that no porno-addicted hipster musician with ratted hair wanted to endure the pointless gushing of a stranger in a rumpled pinstriped suit.

"He's going to be down here in a minute," said Kevin, not hearing me. "Stay here. I'll be right back."

"Well, honey, me and Jake, we're taking off," said Kat, coming up behind me. Jake nodded and didn't say a word. Knowing Kat and her romantic track record, I gave him two more weeks, tops.

"I guess I'll probably take off, too," I said. "Thanks for talking me into leaving my house. I'm glad you don't take the things I say too seriously." I had started to follow them toward the door when Kevin came up behind me.

"Come with me," he said, taking my arm in his and leading me toward a growing cluster of people.

Chapter 2

GRANT

Y our adoring fans are waiting for you, jackass." Sylvia strode into the dressing room,
her many bracelets jangling as she handed me a cup
of coffee. Sylvia was letting me know I had hidden
backstage long enough. Time to go downstairs,
greet the fans, grip and grin with the music-biz executives. Do it so Sylvia could boot them out of her
club for the night and let the after-hours party
begin.

She was giving me a hard time to let me know
she loved my show but that I shouldn't let it all go to
my head. Sylvia: loving her artists in the grand tradition of all club owners by following a big hug with
a hard punch. Famous for having slept with members of the Clash, Liquid Liquid, and of course Iggy,
to name just a few, Sylvia Warren had created the

Empire, "The East Village of West Hollywood," a place where musicians could be not only heard but listened to. Although Sylvia was a gossip who could be creative with fact, she was also a lot of fun. But more important, she knew musicians and she loved music. The Empire was Sylvia's universe, and she ruled it in an Old Testament manner. We, her devoted subjects, tried never to mention that we all knew she'd won it in a divorce settlement; we preferred to let her think we believed she had created it on the seventh day.

She sat down next to me. "By the way, great, great fucking show tonight, Grant."

I gulped the coffee, feeling it kick, then lighting another cig to complete the rush. "Yeah?" Careful. Don't let her know you know how good it was, or she'll pop your balloon. "It was okay," I sniffed.

"Fuck that," she said. "Best show yet."

I barely nodded, resisting her gravitational pull by staring at her bracelets. There were thirty years of rock history in those bracelets, starting with the spiky ones near her wrist that she got as a homeless punk and ending with the gold and emerald ones up by her elbow that were presents from her ex, with a whole lot of junk in between.

"Is Winn takin' care of business?" I asked, switching gears.

"Last I saw, she was talking to two fucks from MCA. There's a whole shitload of 'em out there. Your girlfriend can't keep their attention forever, push-up bra or not." This was Sylvia's way of saying that Jack, my manager, was sleeping on the job. Sylvia jovially sowing discord, cheerfully casting doubt, doing her job as a club owner. "You also got three film companies down there . . ."

"Huh," I snorted. I was hoping it sounded like a jaded snort. Winnie and I had learned not to exhibit too much enthusiasm around Sylvia.

"Better get down there."

"Shit," I whined. "I just did the show. My show's over. I can't even talk anymore. I just talked for ninety minutes. I—"

Sylvia pulled the cig out of my mouth, stood, and grabbed me by the back of the neck. "Knock it off. You're finally hot. So go do your fucking job."

I walked into the Empire's kitchen, with its familiar blast of Mexican music and clatter of pots and pans, through the wet steamy air, pushing open the doors that led to the back of the club. Suddenly the universe was transformed as I was slapped by a frosty blast of AC. The club room was dark. Candles glowed on the tables like red stars. As my eyes adjusted I made out about seventy heads, all murmuring over the strains of that recording of Elvis Costello crooning Burt Bacharach on the sound system. The whole swanky Empire crowd: musicians, rock journos, comedians, and TV writers talking record deals, TV production deals, and guitars, and drinking Guinness, lots of Guinness.

A knot of fans took a step toward me as one. Not a rush, just a polite step. To their immediate left were two suits from CAA and Fox. Shit, here was where it got hard. I always hated this part of the job. I wished I was sufficiently narcissistic to spread my arms and bask in the attention of people who needed more me. However, my head was woolly from being onstage talking, playing, singing for ninety minutes. I was easily confused and exhausted from five weeks' rehearsal. Now I had to juggle the needs of the fans while making nice with suits. The demands of both canceled each other out. At that moment, a guy who could get me a movie deal for my ridiculous musical was standing next to the pie-eyed girl who bought every record I ever made. He was cocky and anxious to chat. He could lead me to millions and change my life. She was polite and loyal. I would never play to an empty room because of people like her. This current upswing in my career was built on these few fans.

So not only was I caught between gratitude and opportunity, I also felt guilt. She had battled cancer and said she listened to my albums the whole time. My music—my bleak, dark, depressing old smudgy work that I couldn't stand to listen to anymore—had carried her through cancer, for God's sake, cancer! Had I known, I certainly would have worked on it harder.

The Fox guy stepped right in front of her, cutting her off. What was his fucking name? The girl looked at me with hurt eyes, obviously feeling undercut by the suits.

"Great show, Grant. Amazing. Where you wanna eat on Tuesday? We were thinking someplace funky?" said the Fox guy.

What a dork, I thought. They always want to go someplace funky. Two, three hundred thou a year, with stock options, and they want to eat at some trendy shithole. Doesn't he understand that my life is a trendy shithole? I was about to go into this spiel when I glanced over at a thin, ghostly Goth girl who looked at him with disgust. Deep ruby hair, pouty mouth.

For a second, time stopped. The suits smiled. The fans eyed me cautiously, waiting to see what I would do. Who was I now? I wondered. The long-suffering poet musician? Pure of heart and incorruptible? Or had I turned into the hot-shit wheeler-dealer Hollywood whore, batting my eyes at the suits? Was it possible to be both? I decided it was. After years of obscurity, poverty, and lame low-budget indie deals, I was going to charge the suits an astronomical price to remain untainted.

"Funky?" I said, looking at the fans for support. "Man, I live, eat, and sleep funky. How about expensive? Starched tablecloths and waiters with gloves, and guys selling cologne in the john. Let's do that!" The fans all giggled and took a step closer, clutching their albums, posters, and magazines. "Hey, why don't ya let me catch up with these folks here, and I'll meet up with you at the bar?" I told the guy from Fox, placing my

hand on his shoulder and hoping my attempt at manly cama-
raderie was convincing.

I looked toward the bar and found Winnie. Who could miss
her? Almost six feet tall, red-and-black custom-made bustier,
false eyelashes, fire-engine red hair piled high on top of her
head. She caught my eye and smiled. I felt warm inside. Winnie Veenstra: my champion, my girlfriend, my backup singer,
and the brains behind the outfit. Her Dutch background provided her with a no-nonsense approach to business, even
though the only Dutch Winnie really knew was *"Godverdomme!"* It would occasionally surface when she was riled. Not
for the first time, and certainly not for the last, I marveled at
how far I had come. Ten—no, twelve—years ago I was sitting
at a funeral in a chapel alongside Jane Gray, my junkie girlfriend, thinking this was as bad as things could ever get. Wondering what another year with Jane might bring. Her death?
My death? As I looked at Winnie, I realized she was a sign that
life didn't have to get worse every year. It could actually get
better. Maybe I had finally made some real progress, learned
from my mistakes. "She's the balls and I'm the dick," I always
told folks. Tonight, when this was all over, she and I would go
over every nuance, pause, hint, and inconsistency of every busi-
nessman, cast member, and esteemed club member, and every
joke, ominous giggle, and probable lie of Sylvia's. Winnie
jerked her head to the left, signaling me that she was talking to
MCA's prez. She flashed me an overstated smile to let me know
he was mentioning a possible deal. I looked at her and nodded.

"Are you ever going to do your music again?" asked Goth
Girl, breaking the spell.

"I *am* doing my music," I told her.

Looking hurt and Keane-eyed, she shrugged and handed
me a copy of the first album I did with Slowly I Turn, backside
photo up. There I was in my cowboy boots, tight pants, concho

belt, and a pile of blue-black hair sprayed and teased to storm-cloud height. I recalled that moment on Hollywood Boulevard, 1985, feeling the whole world was at my feet, wanting to face it with dignity and self-assurance. But having so little of either, I had overcompensated and ended up looking like a stiff, stuck-up, overdressed prick. I recalled how, a year later, promoting the album, I had walked into the San Francisco State University radio station for a victory interview. The hero returns. There I was, recording! Touring! Doing interviews in my adopted hometown! I sat down to the mike, and as the DJ began his intro spiel, I picked up the station's copy of the album and flipped it over. In ballpoint pen, someone had drawn an arrow, pointing at me. "IDIOT," it said. "Asshole," someone else had written with a different pen, presumably on a different day.

Goth Girl wanted a signature. I flipped the album back over. There was only one place to sign, as there was so much black on the front cover. I inked my name across the Wild West R in the title, *Rah Mith Nith Nith*, and felt a pang. We chose that title thinking it would be funny to make the radio ads and DJs sound stupid. "Rock Out on the Dark Side with Slowly I Turn's *Rah Mith Nith Nith*!" A great idea provided, of course, that the album was a hit and there were commercials for it, which never happened. Instead, we spent the better part of the eighties explaining *Rah Mith Nith Nith* to the European press, who looked at us with dead, unamused eyes and accused us of pretension.

"Not the musical. *Your* music," Goth Girl repeated.

I could have explained that if she listened to these albums from fifteen years ago, she'd hear that what I was doing now was itching to get out even then. A flourish here, a hint there. Sift through all the fucking gloom and you could find a nineteenth-century white man who wanted to write Gilbert and Sullivan light operetta. "Well, I'm going to be doing a regular concert-type show here in November," I told her.

"Thank Christ," she sighed, a little too relieved. As I handed back the ancient album, I also recalled why it was I never took as much advantage of groupies as I might have. They were often cranky, demanding people.

Behind her in line was a tall, very fat fellow who handed me *In My Night*, the hit album by Slowly I Turn. The album I wasn't on. The album that had convinced Arvin Petro to go solo, leaving my boys stranded without a star and singer. He was compared to Raymond Chandler, Charles Bukowski, Tom Waits, and every other literate who crossed the line into art rock. I was compared only to him. Once I got the job, for the next eight years it was Arvin! Arvin! Arvin!, morning noon and night.

"I hope you don't mind," the heavy guy said. I didn't understand what he meant until my eyes landed on Arvin's signature. Of course he had asked Arvin first. No other Slowlys' names on the record. With guys like him it was still Arvin Arvin Arvin.

"I don't mind at all. It's an honor to be associated with the early band," I said, repeating the lie I always told, figuring these guys might snitch to Arvin. "I'll just sign it on the back, out of respect to Mr. Petro. Your name?"

"Oh, just your signature. . . ."

That meant eBay. A collector/seller. Arvin Petro's signature *and* mine? Wow. Probably increased the value by a whole five dollars for some decrepit middle-aged new waver. Suddenly fed up after twelve years of Arvin! Arvin! Arvin!, I flipped the album over to the front. Hell, my career was on track and I was riding high. Fuck that shit. So, right underneath Arvin Petro, I wrote, "loves Grant Repka." It could go for maybe ten bucks on eBay now. I'd made this guy's night.

As the fans began dwindling down, Sylvia turned up the

sound system to drive the paying customers out. It was after hours at the Empire, and only the select, gifted, and/or famous could stay behind. As I took a final eBay-purchased poster from a last Goth girl, up walked Kevin: one of the comics in my cast, the guy who played the dim-witted road manager. He was waiting with a tall woman. I smiled. Kevin smiled, winked. She had her hands clasped together and seemed to be glaring. Intense dark eyes. Pin-striped suit. Exotic, striking face. Long nose, slanted eyes. Egyptian? Armenian?

They stepped forward. "Grant? I have somebody very special to introduce you to. Grant Repka? Ms. Lisa Roberty."

As she extended her hand, my other star, Brian Reynolds, stood behind her making an expression of openmouthed awe. He pointed to Lisa, doing an elaborate "okay" signal. Then he slapped both hands to his cheeks, shaking his head, and walked away. Gripping my hand, Lisa fixed her eyes on mine. Large, strong hands. She let loose a flow of praise that was all but drowned out by Elvis Costello doing Burt fucking Bacharach. I heard her say "lyrics" and "great" and "really" and something about being a writer. I noticed that she shook, vibrated, like my grandfather. Still, as she shouted over the music, I wondered why Kevin was standing there beaming at her, then looking at me and saying, "See?" Nodding proudly. I also wondered why Reynolds gave the big knock-out sign. What was the big deal?

I nodded, and smiled when she smiled, which wasn't often, so I knit my brows to match hers, agreeing with everything I couldn't hear her saying. There was something familiar about her. The mental Rolodex began flipping, trying to match face with year and place. A groupie? A hundred one-night stands flipped by: the coked-up girl from Phoenix? No. The weeping woman from Berlin? "I don't like sex, Grant; just hit me." No. Italian three-way? "Kees me, Grant! Kees me!" No. My God, is it Dawn Mazella, the girl I secretly loved in high school? No. But I know her. Where? Wait! There it is, the memory comes

into focus; Winn and I are going out. The TV is on. I'm but-
toning a shirt. I see a woman on the screen with a disdainful
yet comedic rubber-faced expression in a group discussion.
"Winn? Who is this woman?"

Winn enters, in the fifth stage of getting her hair ready, and
looks at the TV. "Oh! That's Lisa Roberty. I think she's an author now. She used to write Nick Blake's movies. They were an
item for a long time."

As I stared at the television, I thought absently about
women of letters—poets, critics, writers, journalists—wondering why a whole artistic subgroup had ignored me. I'd never
scored with a writer. At that moment I worried about my lyrics
the way some guys worry about their breath. I blinked it away
and looked back at the face of the woman on the television.
"She's hot," I mused.

"Eu hink evverubby's hoot," said Winnie through a mouth
full of bobby pins. And then I surfaced and found Lisa Roberty
staring at me, waiting for a response to something else I hadn't
heard.

"I know who you are!" I blurted out. If she appeared pissed
off and intense before, she now looked mostly disgusted. No
wonder literary women never went for me.

Chapter 3

LISA

I felt like an idiot standing there waiting for Kevin to introduce me to this guy. "Where'd you get this?" Grant was saying to a little Goth girl as he signed an old poster with the same Sharpie that it looked like she had used to outline her eyes. "You're too young to have been a fan in 1987."

"EBay," she answered a little too theatrically, trying to make some kind of a lasting impression on him, I thought.

"How much?"

"Five dollars."

"There, now it's worth four-fifty," he said, signing it and handing it back, smiling, handling it all much more gracefully than Nick ever did.

"Thanks for coming. Glad you enjoyed the show," he said sweetly to a tall obese guy, handing him an old signed album.

"Grant, this is Lisa Roberty," Kevin said suddenly. "Lisa and I worked together on a terrible sitcom pilot called *Mr. and Mrs. Ed* a couple of years ago." Then he left a quiet space for me to interject my compliments.

"I just wanted to say how much I enjoyed the show," I said, embarrassed, feeling like my arms now reached the floor and my head had inflated to a parade-sized balloon. Grant Repka looked at me with a blank face. No reaction at all. None. So I kept going. "It was really funny. Really nicely phrased. Great. Really, really great."

I was hoping that someone would interrupt and offer me a way to make my mouth stop running like a pair of those windup chattering teeth. Even worse, the loud music on the club's speaker system was forcing me to lean in and yell everything right into his face. His expression was distant and exhausted, hopefully because he was tired and not because he found my breath offensive. It seemed the best thing I could do was make the moment brief.

"So, uh, summing up, then . . . great. It was really, really great." I turned to go. But in my several seconds of downtime, I had a thought: That was hardly even a compliment. He doesn't know enough about me to value my opinion. If I were flashier-looking, wearing something besides an inexpensive rumpled suit, I could have grabbed his interest and had a certain amount of credibility just from being a hottie. Then I wouldn't have had to be so concerned about the content of my sparkling repartée. But as it now stood, the only chance I had for making this moment register was to repackage myself as a person of substance. So I turned back and started the engine again. "It was really nicely written," I resumed. "I really like how you pick words. I'm a writer. Which I guess you could probably sense from the way I used the word 'really' eight times in under two minutes."

Now I was tap-dancing on my own tongue. I should've quit while I was ahead and left in blessed anonymity. What was this pathetic need to be known?

"I know who you are," he said, with no real change of expression, signaling to his girlfriend, the glittering, towering, now red-haired Pamela Anderson, on the other side of the room. "Winnie," he shouted, "come meet Lisa Roberty." As Winnie crossed the room to join us, I slid into a time-delayed slow-motion replay of the moment. I realized he'd just said, "I know who you are."

"Yeah, yeah. You're probably going to say something about Nick Blake," I said. "And since I'm giving you my résumé, I might as well throw in that I also wrote a couple of books that no one read and some memorable speeches for the governor that no one knows I wrote. Blah blah blah. Ain't I something. Wheee." I listened to myself trying to impress him. I was making myself sick.

"No," he said, confusing me further, "that's not it."

Now I went into a stall. I was too nervous to ask follow-up questions. Was there a problem between us of which I wasn't aware? Had I overstayed my welcome? Had he called the glamorous centerfold girlfriend over to help move things along because he feared he was never going to get rid of me?

Now that she had joined us, I felt like a German shepherd by way of Tijuana who was accidentally being evaluated for Best in Show by the Westminster Kennel Club. "Well, nice to meet you," I said, turning to leave. "Congratulations to you both. And good luck with everything. I'm going to go right out now and buy all your CDs." I threw that in as an afterthought, a way to make him feel more kindly disposed by offering to contribute to his income.

"I doubt you'll be able to find them. I don't think they're even for sale anymore," he said without prompting. "How about this? You send me your books, I'll send you my CDs. Fair exchange."

"Wow. Sure!" I said, looking at the glittering girlfriend and finding her impossible to read beneath the perfect glossy surface. It was almost as if she'd decided that her look made such a strong statement, adding anything more would just be gilding the lily. I was riveted by the way she was able to keep both lips completely coated with glitter gloss and at the same time talk and drink liquids. How? Some kind of polymer coating or facial shellac? Before I could draw any conclusions, she excused herself, shook my hand, and sashayed back to the center of the storm.

"Well, guess I'll be going, too," I said, figuring it was wise to follow her lead, even though I suddenly wanted to stay. "Where do you want me to send the books?"

"You can just send them to my house," he said, graciously writing his address on a tiny wet piece of napkin. Big ego, I thought. Assumes he's important enough to make a person keep track of a torn napkin scrap. "Thanks so much for coming. It was good to meet you," he said as a group of guys in very hip-looking suits enveloped him and started talking all at once.

I walked out into the night, heading down the street to the parking lot, aware of the shaky sense of nervous awe that came from having met someone new whose work I admired. Good for me, I heard myself thinking. Nice evening after all. But as I drove toward the freeway and began examining the interaction with Grant in more detail, paralyzing anxiety began to set in. It had all started out okay, when I was giving him compliments. Of course that always worked. But then I had started pushing, trying to seem important. From then on I was talking too loudly and too quickly, until I was standing there red-faced and bleating like a sheep. I had even started to do that anxiety-loosed neck twitch that I always hoped everyone mistook for simple hair maintenance and not one more symptom of my terror of socializing.

By the time I walked in the door of my dark, cold house, I was sorry I had allowed Kat and Kevin to force their agendas on me. Maybe I should have just stayed home and finished up the wistful face on the Braised Short Ribs, like I had originally planned.

As always, my dogs were happy to see me. I was consistently delightful, even mesmerizing, to them. Maybe it was the minimum definition of positive reinforcement, but it was also the only positive reinforcement I could count on. "Hello, boys," I said as they followed me to the kitchen and stared at me intently while I heated a container of sake. I couldn't wait to get that warm blanket of fuzzy fog pouring into my brain. Nothing like hot sake to put some pleasant perceptual difficulties in between me and my ability to comprehend and analyze. God bless sake time.

Chapter 4

GRANT

I knew it was the wrong thing to say the second it came out of my mouth. Her eyes did a slight roll. "Yeah, right, yeah, yeah. You probably know my name from when I used to work with Nick Blake, I wrote a couple books that no one read, blah blah blah." She was Nick Blake's ex. She wrote *Macaroni and Cheese Club I* and *II*. My first thought was to rush in with an apology, explaining that all I was remembering was that she looked hot on TV. Then I realized you can't say something like that to a woman you just met in a bar. Then again, did her exasperated tone indicate that I'd just been dressed down for referencing her career? Which was when I realized that I hadn't mentioned her career in the first place. I panicked a little; I had inadvertently stumbled into the minefield we lesser-knowns in

Hollywood encounter when meeting the better-known. It works like this: In her world, which meant the *whole* world, her success and prestige were common knowledge. So the rules dictated that she could talk about my show, whereas I would be considered rude if, from my lowly position, I commented on her work. The rules said I should just shut up and listen with silent reverence as she deigned to speak to me. Fucking A-listers, slumming. What a burden to be so fucking successful. Everything anyone does in Hollywood is generally within a few degrees of Adam West in *Batman*, anyway. Why don't they all do what he does and wear their outfits at the opening of the new Target, and be a little goddamn grateful that the showbiz God smiled on them at one time. Then I remembered that Winnie had said Lisa and Nick Blake ended badly.

Oh, that's right, be a gent, I cautioned myself. She's been hurt. You don't like it when people bring up your work. You were hiding upstairs. Make up for it quick. Tap-dance. Say something brainy.

I said, "I'm glad you liked the show. But you know . . . it takes months to write this kind of song. Rock tunes and sad little ballads are easy. This stuff? Hard, very hard. I throw out a lot. Most of it's crap." Good. I hoped that smoothed everything out.

I noticed she clicked her head again, tossing her hair out of her eyes. Was she camouflaging a twitch?

"Don't sell yourself short," she shot back, not smiling. Didn't she smile? I wondered about her head-toss twitch. Was this some sort of Nick Blake neuro damage? Did he, like, fry her?

Elvis Costello singing "Do You Know the Way to San Jose?" blasted on the speaker system. I didn't care if it was Elvis Costello, it was still a song my mom would like. Awful, I thought. Does a great singer singing shit make shit great? I looked over to the bar and caught eyes with Winnie. She immediately sized up Lisa's back and, cocking her head, teased me by dropping her jaw and raising her brows. I shook my head in a manner Winnie knew to mean "Knock it off—get over here." So she broke from the group of which she was the center, and headed toward us.

"Ahh, here she is," I said, as if I'd just seen her. "Winnie, this is Lisa Roberty."

Winnie beamed in recognition. "Oh my, how nice to meet you," she said. I watched Lisa's eyes as Winnie spoke. Predictably, they registered surprise at just how tall Winnie was. In her platforms and her red fall, she was as imposing as a Masai warrior. Winnie flashed a smile way too big for her own face. I put my arm around her, just in case either one of them was getting any ideas.

"You guys were really great!" said Lisa, shaking the hair away hard. Definitely a twitch. "So, you two wrote this together?" she hammered on.

"Oh no," said Winnie. "He did all that. I'm the organizer. And I do the accounting. The grunt work."

"Well, you two do great work together. It was fantastic."

"That means a lot coming from you, Lisa." Winnie beamed.

Lisa ignored the compliment neatly tucked away in the thanks. "Where can I get some of your albums?" she blurted. Lisa was all business! Nick Blake must be made of steel if this was his former second banana.

"Oh, I'm sorry," Winnie said. "Excuse me. I have to talk to Jack and Earl before they go."

"Manager and lawyer," I said to Lisa, who I sensed felt left out.

"Oh, I'm sorry. Don't let me keep you," she said apologetically to Winnie.

"Oh no no, it's great meeting you, Lisa, it's just that I . . ." Winnie made nervous hand movements that said "What can I do?"

I was surprised she made those particular moves. She got

the gestures from a wonderfully bad/filthy Italian porno film, *Rx for Sex*. In it, a waiter too busy boffing a woman whose boob job has made her suddenly insatiable keeps ignoring a hungry patron. With a bad overdub, the starving diner exclaims, "Waiter! My food!," the words coming a beat later than his tormented hand gestures. Fingernails to mouth, then fingers up, fingernails back to mouth, then fingers back up again. It had become a thing between Winnie and me. Any minor frustration or trivial indecision had one of us doing "Waiter! My food!" Right now it was Winnie's way of apologizing for an awkward departure. She probably didn't realize that Lisa, for all her cultural endeavors, had most likely missed *Rx for Sex*.

"So, where can I buy your records?" Lisa asked again, watching Winnie glide away.

"You can't," I said. "The Slowly I Turn stuff is, thankfully, out of print. My solo stuff you can find on eBay and in some used-record stores."

She wanted to know if I had any extra copies. No, I needed to hold on to the few I had. I could make her copies, but it would take time.

"Great!" she said. "I'll swap you my books for your CDs. Fair exchange. What's your address?" She opened her purse, displacing handfuls of junk. And no asking permission. No sir. Cut to the chase. "I will swap you books for your records." Period. Is she focused and driven, or just klutzy and clueless? I wondered, writing my address on a napkin scrap and feeling odd. Rock stars, big or small, local or international, didn't give out home addresses or home phone numbers. And men with girlfriends didn't do that when the girlfriend had just walked away. At least not men who were caught in an affair six years ago. And even though getting caught had made way for a strengthening of the relationship between Winnie and me, even though I had filled journals on why I had ever done such a stupid thing to Winnie, dragging in my mother and father and the first thirteen years of my life as an explanation . . . and even though Winnie and I had spoken endlessly about the matter until the hurt was healed and my soul laid bare, as I gave my address to Lisa, I realized this was the first time in six years that I had allowed a woman to enter my life without Winnie's approval first. I felt an urge to ask Winnie's permission. Was it because I was whipped?

No. The fact of the matter was that I never wanted to see that look on Winnie's face again—hurt beyond description, and utterly disappointed in me. I had been a rake with many women in my life, but I'd never been caught before, never seen the effect on someone's face. Once was enough.

Lisa folded up the paper and pushed it in her purse. The deed was done. And I felt guilty.

"So, it's a deal," said Lisa. "Books for records."

"Great," I said, forcing a smile. "I can't wait."

"Well, don't get your hopes up too high," she snapped, flicking the hair again. She obviously never smiled. She seemed to be in a hurry. Pissed off? Arrogant?

"I guess I should say my goodbyes. It's a long ride home. Nice meeting you. And congratulations on the show," she said. When she walked off, I was strangely relieved, as if a quiz had ended.

My cast and the rest of the Empire regulars all hung around for a few more hours, the musicians swapping stories with the comedians, who, as always, tried out their new bits packaged to sound like casual conversation. Not that anyone was complaining.

By four A.M., everyone was exhausted. They all pitched in and helped us load the gear into our car.

As usual, Winnie was behind the wheel. I watched, terrified, as she backed the huge Electra out of the parking lot by looking only through three inches of cracked rearview mirror, arguing with me that she was doing it the right way, plus, *she* was driving. Oh well, fuck it. At least there weren't any kids playing in the alley at four A.M. I propped my knees up against the dash and glove compartment and lit another cig. "So, was that any good?"

"Yes. The show was great," said Winnie matter-of-factly.

"Really? But was I any good?" I asked, worried.

"Yeah . . . you know you were," she chided.

Come on, be a fucking girlfriend and gush a little, I thought.

"I could have killed Najette," she spat. "Did you see her special curtain call?"

"No. What'd she do now?" I asked.

"Oh, nothing aside from refusing to get offstage, eating up all my time, your time, and then vying to be the last one off. She nearly knocked Justine in the mouth waving to her friends."

"Ai yi yi yi," I sighed. "Okay, I'll talk to her."

The fact that I would have to have another fatherly heart-to-heart with Najette about overt attention grabbing was indicative of the fact that this musical, once a lark, had now become serious business.

"So, not to change the subject . . ."

"Please do," moped Winnie.

"Lisa Roberty was nice, wasn't she? That's not such bad shooting, is it? The woman who brought you Nick Blake thinking our show was fantastic."

"She thought *your* show was fantastic."

"Nay, my dear. She thought *our* show was. She said so to you. You didn't like her?"

"No, no . . . She was nice. I liked her just fine. I think it's very nice that someone like that enjoys your writing."

"She's gonna send us some of her books. In exchange for some records," I chirped.

"She's gonna send *you* books for some of *your* records."

I laughed. I enjoyed this stuff with her. We were musicians. We overdressed. Getting hit on was part of the job. On tour, I would wink at her and get a wink back as some Tom Fool fan asked her or me out on a date backstage. "Is that a problem?"

"No. I think that's great. I'm really glad someone like her likes your work. Just be careful of her."

"Why?"

Winnie made bird noises. With her free hand, she fluttered her fingers around the crown of her head. Another one of her gestures: singing birds circling the skull. The Warner Bros. cartoon symbol of someone with a crush.

Chapter 5

LISA

E ven after sake, I was still too wired to sleep. All three dogs took it as a sign that an unscheduled additional mealtime was close at hand. Turned out they were right. By three A.M. they had weaseled an extra meal out of me.

I spent the rest of the night drinking sake and thinking of things to say in the short letter that I would enclose in the manila envelope in which I would send Grant Repka one of my books. It always made me nervous to show my work to anyone. But the fact that he had asked me to send him a book was kind of touching. Maybe after he read it, he would find me intriguing and want to be my friend. Although it could certainly be argued that since he had a girlfriend, what did he really need with a friend like me? Still, before he was completely emptied of the gnatlike attention span that he, like all show-business males, almost definitely possessed, perhaps I could grab a moment or two of entertaining platonic friendship. Socially speaking, times were hard. I had to gather my moments where I could. So I would just stop making such a big deal out of everything and send him the damn book and hope he liked it. Then, as the Navajos suggested, I would nicely put my heart back into its former condition again, so pleasant again I could become.

I'd send the book of humorous travel pieces, including my mind-numbing cruise-ship adventures and the pieces I wrote at the nerve-racking singles resorts. Those made me look brave and were good for a few laughs. And the cover picture of me in a rowboat full of dogs was not too awful. My legs looked okay, my face not that great, but the picture was cute because the dogs looked so happy. It would all be fine. Especially since there was almost no chance that he would actually read the book. Not a single member of my immediate family had. And then I could look forward to getting a CD in exchange, specially copied for me by a semifamous rock personage. Whom I had never heard of before tonight, but there were tons of accomplished people in all areas I had never heard of. He was in good company. It was a very all-inclusive group.

All I had to do was write a short, polite, but slightly amusing note that he probably would only hear about from some former record-company chick turned personal assistant who opened his mail. If I even made the cut, since she probably kept the cool stuff to give as Christmas presents and threw the rest in the garbage. No point in being too coy or cute or funny. I deleted the one that went, "Dear Grant, I am still singing the songs from your show. Unfortunately, I don't sing that well. Please hurry and send a CD before I ruin your career."

Ultimately, I composed a note that I felt was inoffensive but to the point, pleasant yet businesslike. It went, "Dear Grant,

Here is the book you requested. Best wishes, Lisa Roberty."
Then I worried that it might appear excessively abrupt so I
added a P.S. "My e-mail is snarlingirl@yahoo.com, in case you
ever need it." Hopefully, this made things a little less brusque,
a bit more genial, but still not pandering. Although, in the final
analysis, it all looked a bit plain. So finally, to add a touch of in-
dividuality, I decided to replace the computer paper with a
piece from my funny stationery collection, acquired during
that singles cruise to Japan for *Girl Traveler*. One of the things
I loved most about that visit was the Japanese stationery decorated with poorly translated, indecipherable English phrases. I
selected something from a pack that featured strange little
pairs of unnamed lima-bean-shaped people I had to assume
were beloved by the Japanese. Across the top of each bright
turquoise page was a puzzling but cheery message in red block
letters: "When you wants to make friends with someone Mr.
Friendly will becomes a great messenger who brings such
wishes to him." The matching envelope was even more cryptic:
"None of your joke don't go well with us! Listen, we're perfectly well matched couple."

I put the whole works in a standard manila envelope with a
few stickers featuring lima-bean people pasted where a return
address would ordinarily go, in order to make the package look
intriguing enough for a bored, antsy, porn-addicted musician
who might be on some kind of drugs to want to open it.

Coincidentally, right when I finished, I saw the postal truck
pulling up.

A wave of panic and insecurity washed over me. And then I
thought, Oh fuck it. I make such a big deal out of everything.
All I'm doing is being neighborly.

I handed the package to the postman and headed back inside to begin the harder-than-it-appeared task of nicely putting
my heart back into its former condition again, so pleasant again
I could become.

Chapter 6

GRANT

We're a perfectly well matched couple'!?"

Winnie looked up from the letter, jaw open, doing a Warner Bros. double take for emphasis. "Did she forget that *we're* a couple?"

"Yeah," I said, "I saw that."

Winnie looked over the note again, brows knitting, preparing her case. "The stickers are the giveaway. She just can't suppress her schoolgirl crush," she spat. "Rich artsy chicks substitute crap like this for hearts and big loopy flowers."

I tried to hide a grin from her when I heard "schoolgirl crush." Looking at the letter more objectively, I took on the tone of a fellow scientist dispassionately discussing the speed of an approaching giant asteroid. "So, where do you see evidence of this crush?" I asked.

"Look at this!" said Winnie, mounting her soapbox. Her voice went up a half-step. "You meet this woman on Thursday, and the package is postmarked Friday. That means she rushed home and wrote you that night. She bombards you with everything she's got: 'Here is my book! See my nutty stationery? Now that I've done all this, you must reciprocate. Now! Send me your CD. Now! Oh! Here's my e-mail address, in case you need to talk with me right now! Don't forget, we're a perfectly well-matched couple!' "

I reminded Winnie that the line had two parts, the first being "None of your joke don't go well with us!" How did that work into all of this? Besides, Lisa didn't write the line, some stationery designer in Japan did.

Winnie looked at me, then blinked. "Grant, if you were writing to a woman and she had a boyfriend, and you wanted to just be friendly, would you send something that said, 'We're a perfectly well matched couple'? What would you think if I got something like that with no mention of you at all?" Brown eyes turning black. "A single good-looking successful man sends me a bag of books and a letter festooned with cute stickers?"

"Guess I wouldn't like it," I said.

"Thank you! No. You wouldn't like it. You would know better than to cross that line with a couple. You'd also make sure to mention the spouse."

"So, what do you make of her?" I asked, getting the subject off me.

Winnie took the letter from me, scanned it again. "She's either a big show-off, or she's got a crush that's making her that way. You have to be extremely careful writing her back. Don't encourage her."

I was shocked by what Winnie had just said. "You trust me to write her back?" I asked. If, after six long years, trust was no longer a problem, that was news to me. It was Winnie's job to guard the gates like this. I gave her that job, or she took it. Or both. When she'd shown up as one of three backup singers at a recording session seven years ago, not only was my career a mess, but my life was populated by a gang of emotional layabouts and ne'er-do-wells. Nutsy, manipulative, inconsistent guitarists, singers, ex–band members, and former groupies turned lovers turned embittered friends, living off the small trust fund of sanity I possessed. "Vampiric" might be too strong a word for them; more like "fruit bats slurping pulp." I forgave. I forgot . . . well, that is, I ignored and begrudgingly accepted their shortcomings, because music came first. They might drop out of gigs at the last second, or leave abusive phone messages in which they shrieked "Don't you dare psychoanalyze me!" They might throw deli plates backstage, or invite me on a European tour and then cancel the whole shebang because of a bad dream. They might vanish during a session and call up weeks later like nothing was wrong, drawling, "Hey, man, how ya been?" They might be so drunk that they put the capo on the wrong fret and played the big encore in C sharp against my C natural. But what the hell, they were musicians. They were an ethereal bunch. Music first, personality third or fourth.

But that was before Winnie came in and shooed them away, one by one. Things got better and ran smoother. Winnie had no patience with dreamy, manipulative little-boy/girl-lost musicians. No matter who or how successful a muso was, how well he dressed, or how beautifully he scrunched up his face during his hard-bitten C-to-E-minor ballad, a dipshit was always a dipshit, and dipshits wasted time. To her way of thinking, talent did not justify bad behavior unless you could produce a *Guernica* or a *La Traviata*. Don't have one? Then screw you and your jangly coffeehouse crap. Winnie wasn't AA, or Al-Anon, or twelve steps, or in therapy. If someone was a problem, get rid of him, fast. Winnie didn't believe in confrontation. According to her, confrontation only served to give the wicked tips on how they might improve their game. Therefore, don't explain. Ice 'em. Perhaps the vacuum of silence might inspire reflection and remorse.

Winnie's world was filled with books on Fabergé eggs and Greek mythology. She'd recite the lineage of all the gods on Mount Olympus to pass the time at the DMV. She also collected costumes; she wore them and with great effect, mixing and matching decades, nations, and styles. The world seemed to flow through her, but for all the input, Winnie's world was a black-and-white one, a world of simple equations and simpler solutions. Certain cultures were simply better than others. "We put a man on the moon. They put a worm in a bottle." And no one was spared. "God, I hate crazy people!" she would rasp, watching a video of Brian Wilson babbling. Winnie might have been supermodel beautiful, but she was no wan peacenik. She detested chicks with acoustic guitars and their so-called women's issues. She ate red meat, smoked, and didn't give a fig about healing or nurturing. You want a better world? Stop whining. Learn the language. Stop having so many kids. Learn to dress right.

Ultimately, Winnie was a fascist. And I liked it. The old adage about trains and fascism was true. Before Winnie, my career had stalled. It was a rusting hulk that had never arrived, and now here it was, shiny, right on time, and steaming along at speed, on track. But fascism could be unpredictable. The trick was to keep it right at the point where the trains ran on time, but not toward extermination camps.

Still, nobody handed over the reins of power without a good reason. Not a nation of millions or one love-struck boyfriend. Unless, of course, there was a clear threat to domestic security. And there *was* such a threat to our happiness. It was I.

Listening to Winnie point out the suspicious aspects of Lisa's letter, I knew it wasn't Lisa's crush that was the issue. Flirtation from the public, after all, was part of the job of being a musician. Fan letters drifted in. Women made cow eyes at me in the crowd. Guys leered at her, and vice versa. It was all in a night's work. Winnie was stunning, and me? Well, I fit the mold, sort of. Tall, thin, dark, I got that much right. On the assembly line of rock gods, I came from the Nikki Sixx/Keith Richards division. Physically, I was a knockoff of a knockoff. There was something inferior about the mold into which I was poured, like I was manufactured on hangover Monday. I had high cheekbones, but they weren't chiseled. I had a strong jawline, but I'd get a turkey neck when I sang vowels. There was one angle where I looked all right, provided the light was correct, but get it wrong and there was a shadow where my father had broken my nose. A tooth that had grown in behind the others appeared as a black spot in photos, giving me an Alfred E. Newman grin, inhibiting toothy smiles. I tried lippy smiles for a while, but they made my cheeks look big. I had a good side to my face—and I tried to make an easy-to-remember adage for photo sessions: "Left is right, right is wrong." Or was it "Left is wrong, right is right"? I always forgot and would have to wait for the proof sheets, when I would find out too late that the other way around was, alas, correct. Thus was my career documented by thirty years of the same stiff, serious pose in which I tried and generally failed to find my good side. Still, under the stage lights, or in the dimness of after hours, or hiding behind the classic Keith mirrored aviators, I looked okay. In fact, I looked like Tommy Tune portraying Keith Richards when he stood trial in Ottawa. I had gotten my share of attention over the years.

So the idea that a woman had written a slightly gushy letter was no real threat or surprise. However, Winnie was concerned about what I might do with it. Unlike most rock men of my rock age and rock station, I didn't have a weakness for dim-witted, adoring child brides. Lord no. Winnie knew that I harbored a crush on *The Mikado*'s Katisha and that I had shipwrecked my life before on slightly older tragic women. There was something about a fallen angel and her patina of middle-aged sorrow that got me hot.

Winnie wouldn't have cared much if it had been in my past. It would have been another long tale she tuned out. But in the end of our first year together, when she caught me red-handed with a tragic ex . . . that was it.

Now, after six years of reconstruction, here she was again: the brilliant, single, successful woman with a damaged romantic past.

"You think it's right that I write her back?" I asked.

"I've thought about this. Sooner or later, we're going to have to test this trust you've rebuilt," she said. "Might as well be now."

"Well, I'll write her a letter and send her a CD. I'll let you read it, and you tell me if you think I'm playing into anything," I said, knowing that my natural inclination to show off could create the wrong impression.

The letter was a bitch to write. I wrote it in pencil because I can't spell too well, and pencil allowed me to erase the hard ones. By the end of the week, the wastepaper basket was full, and my chest was sore from chain-smoking. When I finished, I walked out of the studio to the house, where Winnie was at the computer.

"I'm done with that letter, Winn. Can I read it to you?"

Winnie didn't look up, eyes glued to the screen: eBay. "I got two more minutes before it goes off. It's up to two hundred bucks."

"I thought we agreed the limit was a hundred," I said.

She made the "Waiter! My food!" motion, explaining by gesture that she was caught in the undertow of a guilty pleasure.

"It's okay. Go 'head." I felt good saying that. I liked spending money on her.

"Here we go," she said, making her bid and holding her breath. Then: "I got it! I won. Suckers! Ha ha ha!"

I loved making her happy.

After she paid on eBay for the red and black dress Uschi Digard wore hitchhiking in *Stud Service*, she turned in her seat to face me and said, "Okay. What do you got?"

I had about half a page. "Dear Lisa," I read, "I enjoyed your first book so much I smoked three packs of rich, tarry Winstons in one night finishing it. I now am recuperating in bed with a heating pad on my chest—"

"Don't say 'chest,' " interrupted Winnie. "Don't refer to any part of your anatomy. Don't get her thinking."

"I didn't say 'my big strong hairy chest.' "

"I'm trying to help you here, *Godverdomme*. Don't mention body parts. She's single. She doesn't need those details."

"What details?!" I said, a little too strong, a hint of exasperation.

"Details like you laying in bed and heating your chest, Grant. Details like you being so enthralled by her, you hurt yourself, poor lamb. Don't you dare start showing off to this woman."

"Showing off?!" I was getting steamed. "It was just a fucking letter."

"There is no such thing as a simple letter to a single woman with a crush on you," Winnie shot, suddenly fierce. We glowered at each other, eye to eye, will to will. The words "showing off" had doused the flame of my rage. Shame took over. Winnie had struck the proper nerve. She was right. I had spent a week trying to really knock Lisa out. Why?

"You're right," I said to Winnie finally. "I'm sorry. I don't know people like her. TV people, book people. Nick Blake's fucking ex. I guess I was overcompensating—"

"Grant. She already said she likes your work. You don't have to try so hard."

I went back upstairs to my office and pulled out another sheet. I started again:

Dear Lisa,
Find enclosed a "best of my recorded work" CD. It's the stuff I can still stand to listen to. Thank you so much for your book. At the rate I read, I won't need to speak with you for another three years.

"Perfect!" said Winnie. "Now, don't send it off right away. Let her wait."

Chapter 7

LISA

I didn't hear anything from Grant for a couple of weeks. Big deal. Who cared? Well, I guess I kind of did. I was certainly checking the mail a lot more often than back in the olden days, when all I could reasonably expect was the newest Pottery Barn catalog. The frustration I felt about my job was causing me to desperately seek distraction. Six days a week, and sometimes seven, the ten-boy writing staff of *You Go, Girl!*, dressed in hockey shirts, football jerseys, baseball jackets, and backward baseball caps, sat around an oval table under a fluorescent light in an unadorned and windowless conference room known as "The Room," usually until three or four in the morning. At forty-one, I was the oldest person in The Room, and the only female. All around me, pale, chubby men in their twenties and thirties competed with one another for the theoretical honor of getting the most jokes into the script. The moment a joke left one mouth, it was aggressively group-attacked like a piece of meat in a shark tank, then annihilated and digested by every other guy at what they called "The Table."

The more manic and boisterous the rest of the writers at The Table behaved in The Room, the quieter and more sullen I became. A couple of days before, I had ventured forth with a joke about a female bodybuilder working out on the elliptical trainer next to an attractive weight lifter. The point of the joke was that she became terrified when she looked in the mirror and saw that sweating had caused her mascara to melt down her face, transforming her into the inverse version of Pagliacci. I watched without expression or reaction as the pudgy white boys turned it first into a joke about itchy testicles, and then I sat for another hour and listened as it morphed into a joke about an embarrassing erection. Just another piece of that great female point of view that I'd been hired to bring to the show.

But I didn't protest. Instead, as the other writers were pitching their jokes and voraciously snacking on handfuls of trail mix and taco chips, I took out my Wite-Out pen and the twenty or so recipe cards I had brought with me from home. And while everyone around me was accumulating a thin layer of salt-and-crumb coating on their lips and fingers to match the grease spots on their shirts and pants, I was turning a pail of Chuck Wagon Beans into a furious screaming lunatic. The puddle of red sauce in the center already looked like an angry mouth. After that, a tray of Cheesy Bacon Baked Potatoes couldn't wait to become an angry mob. Shrimp Creole looked like a death-row inmate. It was very nice to have someplace to escape to in my brain, because in addition to everything else, the first draft of the script being pulverized at The Table had been written by me. Writing first drafts was a fool's mission. The "written by" credit on the title page would continue to bear my name, even though every single word would be group-rewritten any number of times.

We had all just gotten another set of rewrite notes from Mark Eden and Steve Rosen, notes that were so dunderheaded and self-canceling that when I tried to make logical sense of them, I momentarily got hysterical blindness. Instead of getting upset, I lost myself in a successful attempt to transform the red ellipse of meat peeking out between the chunks of cabbage and carrots in a New England Boiled Dinner into a scowling furious guy. The peppercorns worked out perfectly for his eyes, and the slice of meat at the bottom with the shadow under it made a great angry mouth. I think the intensity with which I was focusing on this project might have been the reason that Mark Eden called me into his office to "talk."

"Is there something wrong?" he asked me. "Everything okay?" He pulled his chair a little closer. "You having a good time here with us? What do you think of the show?"

I paused. Should I say something honest? Was there any point?

"Well," I said, tucking my recipe cards deep inside my script, "sure, everything's great. But permission to speak freely?"

"Yes, absolutely," he said, looking at me earnestly, staring right into my eyes. "I welcome your input."

What was that expression he was doing? It was so paternal and yet so sexually charged that it looked a little bit like Perverted Daddy. "Well, I was thinking that a lot of the characters at the gym sound too much like each other. That we should try to vary their voices and their points of view a little more," I said.

He held his hand up, palm out, and shook his head. "I tried

that in an earlier draft of the show. Never works in The Room," he said, unbothered by the fact that he had just dismissed as impossible the tools of literature and drama.

Immediately, I started a new prayer. Please, God in heaven above, I began, if you will give me the inner strength to resign from this job and return to my drafty, dark, underdecorated home and my containers of heated sake, I will not only never again complain about feeling isolated or unfulfilled, I will also throw in a promise to give the whole religion thing more careful consideration in the future. World without end. Amen.

The next time I looked up, Eden was beaming a very intense look my way. Oh my God, was he hitting on me? It was riveting enough that I ended up saying nothing about resigning. Hey, I was compromised artistically, but I was also lonely. It felt good to be kind of swept into that electrical current.

Of course, this new connection complicated things. And the more insidious and complex my situation became at work, the more I found myself searching for something unconnected to my job to care about. Maybe that was why, when I got home and found in my mailbox a padded manila envelope with Grant Repka's name and return address in the left-hand corner, I felt my insides leap around like I was a winner of a contest.

Inside was a CD he had compiled for me. This made me disgustingly happy: that someone had done something for me and me alone, not collaborated with dozens of other people in the hope of pleasing millions, but just compiled something for me to hear. Well, Jesus Christ, how fantastic.

In addition to the CD, there was also a short, illegible note from him, written in frequently erased pencil. It was a real challenge to decipher. Every sentence required reading out loud two or three times, accompanied by a good deal of improvising. "Dear Lisa, Fire . . . Final . . . Find endorsed . . . encased . . . enclosed a beat . . . a best of my rental . . . receded . . . recouped . . .

recorded word . . . world . . . work LP. CD. It's the soup . . .
the stiff . . . the staff . . . the stuff I can slit . . . I can still . . .
stamp . . . stand to listen to. Thank you so much for year-
book . . . your book. At the race . . . the rape . . . the rake I
reap . . . The rake I reap? The rate I real, ream . . . read! At the
rate I read I want . . . went . . . won't needle . . . to take . . . need
to talk to you . . . Geez . . . for another three years?"

Once I'd translated them, I reread the words with shock.
That Grant would actually read the book had never occurred
to me. My own brother had never gotten past the title page. I
raced to scan through the contents to find out what he had
seen, because I couldn't quite remember what I had written.
When I did, I was truly mortified. I had said many more
embarrassing things than I wanted a new friend to know.
Throughout the pieces describing the awkward, unpleasant
goings-on during terrible vacation packages, there were also
mentions of humiliating sexual encounters. Like the graphic
detailing of a one-night stand with a university tour guide on
one ship who had actually complained that I made too much
noise administering oral sex. Was that story the reason behind
the following kiss-off? "At the rate I read, I won't need to speak
with you for another three years." Kind of a demoralizing response.

I decided to hold off on getting depressed, because I was
anxious to hear Grant's CD. The songs on it were dark, interesting, musically layered, literate tales of weird love and bad
behavior that I was not always sure I understood. A lot of them
seemed to be about obsession, pain, and revenge. Perfect for
Goth girls with raccoon eyes, I thought.

What more nightmarish pit of quicksand than a cute guy
who comes with his own compelling sound track? I thought, I
am so lucky he is spoken for. Still, I couldn't help but feel
thrilled about getting personal attention from two attractive,

potentially dangerous males in one day. Which was when the song "My Psycho Ex" began.

Here was a set of lyrics I understood perfectly. It contained themes of panic, revenge, and violence. It was a tale of the Wagnerian emotions that accompany every sick relationship. Now I knew what to talk to Grant about when I wrote back to him in three years. I noticed that he had enclosed his e-mail address, probably out of reciprocal politeness. I thought, Fuck it, an e-mail isn't a very big deal. It's the perfect semipersonal way to say thanks for the CD without getting on anyone's nerves.

I sat down to write.

Dear Grant,

Thank you for sending the CD. I can't tell you how much I enjoyed it. Well, I guess actually I could, but it would take a lot of time, and that might be pushing my luck, since you asked me not to write to you for three years.

I especially liked the song "My Psycho Ex," because I could relate to it so strongly. I don't know what happened to you, but where the topic of a sick-insane-long-term-dysfunctional relationship is concerned, I could drink anyone, and I do mean anyone, under the table. Well, thanks again for the CD, and continued success with your show.

Best wishes, Lisa Roberty

I read the letter over a few times to make sure I hadn't said anything that would make him regret hearing from me three years too soon. Seeing nothing inflammatory, I pushed "send" and immediately broke into a cold sweat. The fucking guy *asked* me not to write to him for three years. But I compulsively wrote to him anyway. Well, so what? If he couldn't at least allow me to do the polite thing and thank him, then fuck him. I had Meatballs and Cheesy Shells that still needed faces. The meatballs were perfect eyes, and the cheesy shells were all lined up like teeth. It took only seconds to help them peek out of their tomato sauce in terror. Add to that a little sake, and before I knew it, my heart was restored to its former condition, and pleasant again I had become.

Chapter 8

GRANT

I was being pulled along by the current of partyers in the dark hallway at Beer Can Eggy's. Through the rehearsal hall, one line of hipster humanity smelling of armpits and patchouli moved north toward the homemade bar for beer, as the other whiffy hipsters, now bearing beers, inched south to the backyard for pot. This was a big event in many Silver Lake circles. Beer Can Eggy ran a very cheap, if dingy, rehearsal hall, and everyone used it. Hundreds of people were here.

Winnie was hanging out, gossiping with her friends from the Drag Hags, the amateur burlesque revue they put on for the hell of it. She and I didn't spend an awful lot of time together at parties. "Apart-ies" was more like it. She was great with a group. I liked one-on-one. She liked big shindigs. I liked small dinners. She liked to dance. I liked to smoke. We'd worked out this general-to-specific system over the last seven years. So I wandered, nodding at familiar faces.

Somewhere in that clump of people ahead, I could hear Jamie, my other singer. The yip of his coyote laugh gave him away. As I passed, pushed along by the crush, our eyes met. He had his arms around Mitchell French. He hated Mitchell French. He rolled his eyes and made an "I smell poo" face at me while apparently telling Mitchell how good it was to see him.

I emptied out into the rehearsal section, as DeeJay L'argent let loose a roaring go-go tune from the sixties cult classic *Vampiros Lesbos*, one of Winnie's faves. She and the girls leaped out on the dance floor squealing as the crowd pushed me closer to the street. They were cackling, dancing, and having a ball. The nine and occasionally ten years that separated Winn and me really made itself felt at scenes like this.

To tell the truth, I had seen this same party in a million different ways since high school and those dim years at college, followed by those blurry years of punk, then Goth, then glam, to say nothing of all those parties on the road: chips, beer, pot. Somebody's place packed with hipsters, old records, and Salvation Army crap.

I walked outside. Although it was L.A. summer, the night air stung like fall. Soaked, I parked my back against a wall and pulled out a cig. Why did I always overdress? As I cooled, a shaggy rock kid came up and begged a cigarette. He called me Mr. Repka and explained he was "fresh out." I liked that. I hadn't heard "fresh out" since *Perry Mason*. I gave him two. He thanked me, and had his own lighter, a real smoker. His politeness was refreshing. It reminded me that people weren't usually so sweet anymore when they bummed cigs, a trait of the new century of healthy Americans. Now L.A.-tians in general don't smoke, except socially, and then they smoke yours. And they don't say thanks, because why should they? Who thanks the cig machine, or the Coke machine, or any dispenser of small pleasures on the edges of the room they are working?

The door flung open, and out came a wet, sweaty, laughing crowd. Inside, "Fly, Robin, Fly" came on, and the disco-hating rockers screamed with delight. I could imagine Winnie and girlfriends jumping in with Jamie, Ollie, and Dan, three gay men, all expertly doing the hustle in perfectly arranged seventies fashions. I rolled my eyes.

When did food change into garbage? Bad taste into irony? When did shit become art? My age group was dead. Most of my seventies punk-rock/new-wave compatriots had either OD'd, died of AIDS, or become dental hygienists. This party seemed to be populated by the ABBA and *Scooby-Doo* generation, like Winnie and Jamie. No. That was wrong. As far as this demographic was concerned, Winnie and company were old people, too. The *Scooby-Doo*ers had peaked some time ago. Which generation was in control now? Shit. As a musician, I was supposed to know this stuff. Bowie would have known this. Who followed *Scooby-Doo*? I realized, to my horror, that we were actually on the generation after the generation that followed *Scooby-Doo*. Or was I missing a generation somewhere?

So who was I writing music for? People my age, I thought optimistically. I had to keep reminding myself that old people were not as old as they once were. The Sansabelt/white-shoe/pastel-dressed/blue-haired old ladies of my youth were as dead as the matriarch in the black Victorian dress with a cameo. The current bunch of old crows would get plastic surgery and enjoy oral sex and swap, just like they did in their youth. They would continue to listen to rock and its derivatives. That's why it stood to reason that they'd want the view of a forty-something songwriter, right? Sadly, no. The older folks wanted what these post-post-*Scooby-Doo*ers wanted: love and nasty sex with a wafting of poetry to give it oomph.

This vague feeling I'd been carrying all night suddenly jelled, then hardened, and I knew I'd had enough. Not just of this party, but all parties like it. Somebody's place packed with the smart set, damp in vintage clothes. Enough! I felt old. I *was* old. The bangs over my eyes might have obscured the fact that I was twenty years older physically, but they couldn't hide my soul. I fluffed my hair and hid a little harder.

No use. I must look like a college senior crashing a high school prom, was what I was thinking. I was that sad product of rock and roll; without real fame I was Peter Panic, lost in Never-Was Land. Past forty. Jeesus.

Where I really wanted to be was at a reception like the kind they throw for Diane von Furstenberg and her husband Whoosy-whats. Or maybe celebrating a quiet New Year's Eve at the Seychelles with the Jaggers and the Stings. I ached to be photographed in *W* magazine or *Interview*, looking leathery, healthy, laughing with perfect white teeth alongside Princess Ann of Anhalt-Zerbst and Fran Liebowitz. My skin would glow from applying the unguents of the wealthy as I was photographed—gotcha!—in the act of grabbing a bacon-wrapped date, made of really good bacon and a really expensive date. It was high time I became a part of odd celebrity photo pairings: Steven Tyler, Henry Kissinger, Louis Vuitton. I wanted to find out what the fuck those people said to each other. "Steven! Loved *Toys in the Attic*." "Henry! Loved the Paris/Hanoi peace accord!"

I didn't want to see dirty rehearsal-room parties with black lights anymore. I'd already heard all these songs, already seen all the colors of dyed hair. Maybe I hadn't been the most rabid punk in the mid-seventies, but at least I had stayed true. Disco sucked then, and it would always suck. I looked around me at the shaggy heads, the unshaved faces, the rumpled clothes. Why was I still with the people who just woke up?

And it all jelled right here, outside of Eggy's. I wasn't bitter. I didn't think I was better than these people. They weren't clueless or Philistines. It was just that this was a door they were going in, and one that I was revolving around. It wasn't my time now, it was their time, and it was long past the time for me to go.

I went back in and found Winnie and her girlfriends in a post-dance cluster, dewy with sweat. Her face gleamed. "You going home?" she asked, knowing I was.

"Awwwwww!" her group teased me.

"Call me if you're going to be late," I said, knowing she wouldn't. We smooched goodbye and I walked off. I didn't know how to feel, exactly. Should I feel guilty for leaving when my girlfriend was having a great time without me?

I said my goodbyes to Eggy. "Yeah. Gotta go to work," I said, turning and goodbye-ing my way through the crowd and out on the sidewalk. I got into my Lincoln and rolled down the windows, turned on CD six and found track nine of *Die Zauberflöte*—the conclusion, where the entire choir kicks in with Masonic majesty—pressed "play," and turned it up as loud as it would go as I drove past the rock clot on the sidewalk. "Goodbye, kiddies," I muttered.

I could hear the dogs whining as soon as I pulled up in front of my tiny house. I was going through my collection of keys when my neighbor Cole ran toward me from the peeling shacks next door.

"Yo! Dude!" she said. "Check this out!" Cole was a wiry, aggressive, sharp-faced woman who talked like a biker, but fast, and kept her eyes out for the few people she liked. I was one of them.

"Dude—hey, I saw that T-shirt guy again, and he was lookin' over your gate." This was in reference to a mentally challenged man who often would stand for quarter hours on the sidewalk, arms and face slack, staring vacantly into various dwellings. We all hoped he was harmless. Cole continued, "I told him, 'Dude, I don't know what your fuckin' trip is, but you got to get the fuck out of here.' He's cool if you just talk to him." This was the entirety of our friendship: keeping our eyes out for each other. I knew not to get too close, as I had over-heard too many microwave-throwing catfights between her and her stripper girlfriend. Still, I was eternally grateful for Cole having once chased, tackled, and pinned down some flee-ing rich kid who had driven his daddy's Acura into my parked Lincoln.

"Thanks, Cole! I'll keep an eye out," I said.

"Just lookin' out for you, bro'." She smiled, walking back-ward like a gunslinger. "You better get in there. I didn't want to say anything, but your dogs are going fuckin' nuts and my old lady is sick."

When I opened the door, the smell hit me. Cat box with a wafting of dog pee, old grease, cigs, old coffee. Did it always smell like this? We used the living room as a bedroom. Even though it was the biggest room in the house, it was more than a mess. This was a Dark Ages kind of filth, a hothouse for TB. It hurt my eyes to look at it.

There was a charming bachelor pad underneath all of this, or there used to be before Winn, before the pets, before The Musical, when there was still time to tidy up. All too often, our schedules would be so full, we'd forget to secure the dogs when we left. We'd come home to a floor piled with coffee grounds, bread bags, and cat-food cans. The bed would be full of un-eaten food clumps and cat grit, forks, spoons, and God knows what else hidden between the stale sheets and Winnie's dirty clothes.

That was the biggest problem: Winnie. She was so bad at keeping her things in order, there was no way to tell what awaited you in that bed until you crawled in under her dirty jeans, boas, sixties faux-fur coats, soiled panties, socks, stacks of magazines, thick-bristle brushes, and lost lip-liner tubes. She made a pungent nest of her personal belongings. With her, one paid a small but annoying price for a wonderful life. There was no getting around it: Winnie was a slob.

Worse, with the growing cast of my musical, we had between ten and fifteen people here almost every night. Add to that two dogs and two cats in a three-room cottage, plus Winnie's careless attitude, and the result was disastrous. This was why, when I got home, after I let the dogs out, I always went next door to my studio. This was my sanctuary: an old desk, an old French walnut bed, books. And it was clean. Well, cleanish. The walls were painted a rich cranberry, and combined with the amber wood, the place glowed warmly. Seated at my desk, I opened my laptop and sang along with the ping-pongy dial-up sequence. Three ads came up . . . and then an e-mail from Snarlingirl. I got a swift stab in my gut and stopped before opening it. Better wait for Winn to get home.

■ ■ ■

"Allie just found out that Tim's a cokehead," said Winnie, coming in the door, flush with fresh gossip about her friends. She dropped her coat on the bed on her way into the kitchen, and it slid to the floor. "Some surprise, huh? What's going on? Anything?"

"Well, she wrote," I said.

I didn't have to tell Winn who. "She did? Lemme! Lemme! Lemme!" She pushed me off the chair, put her already chewed nails to her mouth, and peeled as she read. I watched her brows knit. I lit a cig.

"Ah!" she yelped before she read it back. " 'Dear Grant, thank you for sending the CD. I can't tell you how much I enjoyed it.' Well, maybe you should tell him how much, cunt. He only made you a special CD of his goddamn work." She continued, reading the next line in a snotty singsong. " 'Well, I guess actually I could, but it would take a lot of time, and that might be pushing my luck, since you asked me not to write to you for three years.' Oh boo-fucking-hoo. 'I especially liked the song "My Psycho Ex," because I could relate to it so strongly. I don't know what happened to you, but where the topic of a sick-insane-long-term-dysfunctional relationship is concerned, I can drink anyone, and I do mean anyone, under the table.' Of course! How could anyone compare to Nick Blake?" Winn let out an exasperated gust. "Fuck her. You could kick her ass. That's what gets me here. What does she know about you? For all she knows, your ex could have been Aileen Wuornos."

"Close," I said.

"Well, you ought to give her a story and let her know what she's up against. Somebody should remind TV Chick there's a whole other world out there." Winn turned back to the screen, adding, "You'd fucking kick her ass."

"Which story should I tell to start?" I said gleefully.

And everything went still. The world stopped. Time stopped. The heavens shut down. Winnie stared at me, creating a void I was to fill. Her brown eyes glinted, cold, almost black. Time then started up again, but slowly. Fish crawled out of the swamps and became lizards, lizards became dinosaurs, and they in turn became mammals. The mammals stood upright and, over time, built the Pyramids and the Great Wall of China and, ultimately, destroyed the World Trade Center.

I knew what she was thinking. Though she sat in front of me, she was back six years, intercepting the twelve nutsy lovesick messages Claudia had left on my voice mail. I didn't know that Winnie had learned my secret access code, and obviously neither did Claudia as she laid her soul bare. "When I give my body to you, it's a gift": a line that Winnie took great pleasure taunting me with that morning.

"You should go with her, Grant. She sounds great!" she'd say, twisting the knife.

Claudia was no unmentionable shadow in our home. Winnie had discussed her and our affair until only a carcass of the poor woman remained. Along with my motivations and methods, Claudia had been dissected, analyzed, and sucked dry of any redeeming features. Just as Hitler is synonymous with the big-band era, the name Claudia summoned up an entire dark epoch in our life.

"Well . . . little Lisa Roberty is very impressed by you. And she's alone. And now she wants to tell you all her secrets about Nick Blake. I don't know if she realizes what she's proposing here."

"Proposing what?" I asked.

"Listen, Grant, I want you to write her back. I'd love to read some dirt on Nick Blake. Who wouldn't? But you have to be careful. Lay down some rules. No sex talk. No talk about problems in the bedroom. Don't start up a dialogue about sex, or it will open up all kinds of crap. Next thing you know, she's writing 'I'm sitting here in my white cotton panties . . .' "

"Okay. That's real smart. So the rules are . . . ?"

"One story per day," said Winnie, "so you don't seem so available."

"Good!" I replied, typing it onto a blank e-mail. "And no sex talk."

"No, no, don't say 'sex talk.' It's too graphic." Winnie shook her head. "It means you're already thinking of her sexually."

"Oh Jesus," I said, suddenly realizing the potential complications of this correspondence. "How about I call it . . . marital relations! I've always liked that phrase. It's so sweet and antiquated, as if sex was something that could occur between a man

and a woman only within the bonds of holy matrimony as recognized by the state and the church."

"Perfect," said Winn.

"Okay, listen, Winn," I added. "If I write this woman back,
you read everything that goes out and comes in. You tell me
when I'm going too far. That's the only way this will work."

"Oh, I'm way ahead of you on that," said Winnie.

Chapter 9

LISA

I stayed up all that night drinking sake, afraid to go to sleep, because if I did, I knew I would have to wake up and return to *You Go, Girl!* I know this sounds desperate, but I was trying to reclaim my life. I wanted to listen to how my brain sounded, uncluttered by the cacophony of poorly conceived, constantly interrupted and then slightly changed one-liners. I wanted to remember what I ever liked about waking up in the morning.

I got out of bed and paced around, and when that got old, I decided to try and work my way through the pile of *New York Times Book Review*s that I had been saving all year. But my brain wasn't allowing me to input any more words. I was worried that reading would make the night disappear too quickly. Instead, I put on the CD Grant made me while I played with the search engine on LoveAtLast.com. Brent from work had met his wife through this service, which had, as its claim to fame, a questionnaire that covered "the twenty-seven dimensions of a compatibility essential for true love." Kind of impressive for LoveAtLast to contain sixteen more dimensions than the eleven they were boasting about in string theory. Although it was hard to detect them in the context of what the website actually offered, a road map to your soul mate through short lists of likes and dislikes. Learning that someone else liked the Zombies but hated corn bread didn't seem to lay the groundwork for much.

Before I turned off my computer, I reread the e-mail I'd sent Grant, making sure I hadn't said anything to embarrass myself. Since I would probably never hear from him again, I wanted my last impression to be a good one.

Of course I had no other e-mail to speak of, except from my good friends in the Penis Extender Bureau. And one from my friend Marc Robinson, full of information about getting a digital camera. My computer, my television, my VCR, my DVD player, all were purchased only because Robinson had nagged and shamed me into them. Such were the perks of platonic male friends.

Just as I was about to put the computer to sleep, I heard a little brriiing, then the voice of the "You've Got Mail" Irritant announcing a new piece of mail.

From Danton1789. I stared at it, surprised.

Dear Lisa,
You're on.
Grant

I continued staring for a minute, not understanding. Then I heard a second brriiing, and there it was: another piece of mail from Danton1789. He's somewhere, right now, writing to me, I thought, suddenly full of new energy.

PSYCHO EX CONTEST: Rules of competition

1. Not for public consumption.

2. No more than one entry per e-mail.

3. Only one destructive, long-term, psychologically challenged significant other permitted per competitor.

4. No details regarding marital relations.*

*"Marital relations" is loosely defined as any act of sexual congress between a principal player and the human object of his/her affections.

Seconds later, a third piece of e-mail.

PSYCHO EX STORY #1

I had twenty-five dollars in my pocket. Psycho Ex demanded that I give it to her for drugs. I argued that we wouldn't be able to eat or take the bus or anything. When my arguments failed, I shouted, "I won't give you my twenty-five dollars because it's MINE." She screamed, "You think I need your money? I'll go out right now and suck some dick!"

What a nasty little anecdote, was my first thought. But as ghastly as the story was, I was thrilled to be suddenly thrust into the middle of an official contest, with actual rules. The first three rules seemed fine. The fourth one puzzled me. "No details regarding marital relations." What a weird rule to make. Especially before sending a story in which a drug addict threatens to suck dick. Didn't the phrase "suck dick" violate the rules of the game in the very first entry? Or was it okay because sucking dick for money didn't technically fall into the category of "marital relations," though it was an act of sexual congress? I was tempted to point this out, but I figured I wouldn't get things rolling by being a nitpicker. And since I didn't have any dick-sucking stories with very good punch lines, I figured I'd follow his lead.

"Dear Grant," I wrote. "At the onset, I would like to acknowledge that my stories have a different texture than yours. You will find that they are not nearly as lowbrow."

That was an understatement. But it sounded a little cruel, so I changed "lowbrow" to "down and dirty." His ex sounded like the kind of person I'd move away from at a restaurant counter. My ex was a very different type, but in his way, possibly less rational than a dick-sucking junkie. This woman at least operated with a certain amount of logic. She wanted drugs. She would do anything in her apparently limited repertoire to get them. Nick rarely made that much logical sense. "However, I believe that my stories may, at their core, be even more truly, clinically psychotic," I added.

Nick's irrational actions were the weapons in my arsenal, though I shuddered as I realized that a dick-sucking junkie, like a terrorist, would probably not observe the rules of war as laid down by the Geneva convention. Which was how I developed my battle strategy, based around the one book I'd read about success in business negotiating: No matter the evidence, always maintain a winning posture. Claim victory regardless. So I wrote:

> I will retaliate with the story of a lovely winter vacation where my Psycho Ex and I decided to fly to Telluride to go skiing. We had first-class tickets, which I always loved, because for some reason sitting on the other side of that curtained partition in the plane and being served small bowls of warm mixed nuts with your choice of after-dinner drinks does a lot to provide the illusion of safety. Everything seemed fine until I noticed, as I ate my cashews, that I had a big bump on the inside of my lip. As I was giving it the once-over with my tongue, Psycho Ex noticed my discomfort and asked what was wrong. I showed it to him, and rather than offer me sympathy, he surprised me by pronouncing

that I had syphilis. And if I had it, now he had it. He began to interrogate me endlessly on the extramarital relations that had caused me to contract this horrifying, deadly STD. I explained emphatically there had been *no* extramarital relations, but that did not matter in the least. His behavior continued to escalate. Later that afternoon, in Telluride, as we were about to board a tram up a mountain that looked like a spread in *National Geographic,* he announced that he was developing a similar sore on his lip. Since we were now both syphilitic, there was no sense in continuing with the charade of this vacation. He was going home. I followed him back down the hill, arguing that this was silly, that I didn't even *know* any syphilitic men. But he ignored me. Instead, he returned to the hotel, and we booked an early flight home.

When we got back, I immediately went to the dermatologist, who took a brief glance at my lip, identified what I had as a water cyst, and removed it in under a minute. When I explained this to Psycho Ex, he said nothing. He just never mentioned it again. Or apologized.

After I wrote the thing, I lay on the couch in my office for the rest of what was left of the night, visualizing Nick, remembering how he had regarded my every misstep and imperfection as part of a plot against him. He knew my schedule. He knew the people I knew. If I'd even *wanted* to fuck syphilitic guys, where would I have met them?

I also started fretting about how hard it would be to win this game. A heroin addict might be capable of anything. Then it occurred to me: If that scary junkie of his upped the ante too much, what was to stop me from making up a story that Nick had forced me to help him kill a man one summer in Winnipeg? How could Grant prove me wrong? "You want to see the graves?" I'd say. "Fine. I'll book us plane tickets right now.

Just be ready for a long plane flight, followed by a fourteen-hour drive."

By the time I finally pushed "send," birds were chirping outside. The sight of the beautiful sunrise made my heart sink. It signaled the beginning of another drive to the office of *You Go, Girl!* One that might best be described by a picture of me with steam shooting out of my ears, because the show we were about to tape was laughingly referred to as my script. On top of that, as the painful endless rewrite sessions wore on, it became clear to me that my boss, Mark Eden, wanted to have marital relations.

Chapter 10

GRANT

W innie was getting ready to go out, one towel wrapped around her head, another wrapped around her body. The air in the tiny bathroom was steamy as we talked. I sat behind her, on top of a low counter that was opposite the sink, and we looked at each other's reflections in the mirror as I smoked and she applied makeup. My legs were propped on either side of her. Next to the kitchen, the bathroom was the most common location for many of our discussions, as that was where Winnie spent a large amount of time.

"What did you think of her story?" I asked.

"I don't know," said Winnie. "I guess she thinks having a canker sore is the same as loving a heroin addict."

"Did you read that bit about mixed nuts in first

class creating an illusion of safety? It's taken right out of her book. Word for fucking word."

"Gross. You think she copied it?"

"I think she's like any professional humorist. On autopilot. They don't talk. They recite."

Winnie had placed a spongy ring on top of her head, and I knew it was time to skedaddle. She was going to attach a red fall, and if her freshly dyed red hair did not match the fall, it could get real ugly in here. "I'll leave you be," I said.

"Hank hugh," she said with a mouth full of bobby pins.

I sat back in front of the computer and reread Lisa's note. A poor desperate dope-sick Jane Gray had inspired a story of a water cyst and a skiing trip? Was she mocking me? Her indifferent attitude rankled. She had not acknowledged my story in any other way than to say "down and dirty." Her story was full of holes and misfires. Nick Blake's behavior was pretty awful, I'll admit. And the repeated airline story was disappointing. Still, who hasn't gotten panicky about the bumps and blisters that pop up on our bodies from time to time? "At the onset, I would like to acknowledge that my stories have a different texture than yours." That's all I get? Did she even read my story, or just rush in to tell hers? Was she just a yakkety screwball?

I lit a cigarette and held my breath as I went to my "sent" folder and reread my letter. "You think I need your money? I'll go out right now and suck some dick!" "Down and dirty," huh? Lisa didn't know the half of it. Two years before the story, I'd had a song on the charts, but by then I was clinging to twenty-five bucks I had borrowed from my manager for food and the bus. From tour buses to the city bus, for chrissakes. When Jane spat out that foul threat, I'd felt like I'd been punched. I saw stars. And here was what I didn't tell Lisa: The big man had opened his wallet and muttered, "You win. Here. Take it. Go." Defeated. Beyond lost. And how could I explain to Lisa that it was hush money? I was paying Jane to stop short of the god-awful truth.

I inhaled again. Sucked in the smoke and kept it in, kicking around the old questions that followed in sequence. If Jane would have whored herself on the street for drugs, would she have whored herself to me for the same price? If I could have debased myself to demand it, would she have debased herself and done it? When I told Winnie this story, she shrugged and said, "At least then you would have gotten something for your money." Everybody talks big like that when it comes to junkies. "I woulda," "You shoulda." Add the word "junkie," and your lover is immediately void of rights. Friends and family think of movie junkies or book-of-the-month junkies. They think of addlepated zombies stealing car stereos. They imagine that you're living with a Sterno bum. They don't know the woman who, more than all the smart, sane women you dated, let you know in big, if not childish, ways that she needed you, desperately. You have never meant this much to anybody before in your life.

"I'm going," said Winn.

"Oh my God!" I said, jarred. Winnie was radiant. "You look fantastic."

"I look like I'm getting old," she said. I wondered if Winnie could ever take a compliment. "I'll be at the wrap party till ten," she said, flexing her arm-length glove.

"Call me if you're gonna be late," I said, again knowing she wouldn't. "Hey," I added, pointing to my lips, a cartoon gesture I had learned from her.

She did her "Waiter! My food!" gesture, then pointed to where she had lined and glittered her mouth. So I kissed her cheek and smelled the coconut oil of hair straightener, the perfume of color enhancer, and the mule kick of recent bleach. After seven years, I still didn't know what Winnie's hair smelled like. Then I waved as the Electra chugged off.

Once she was gone, I sat back down and reread Lisa's letter. Funny, but without Winnie there, Lisa didn't sound so arrogant. Now it read like someone having fun, posturing a little. And now I could see Lisa's tactic. If I played dumb and fed her pride, this could work to my advantage, points-wise. So I wrote:

Dear Lisa,
There is no way I can lose. No way. Down and dirty or not, I face your advantages calmly.

1. You are a professional writer. I take you on with the five hundred words I can spell correctly. I still will win.
2. Your ex is a big shot in the movie business, mine an unknown rock moll. I still will win. I can cite similar historic contests: the glittering British whupped by the starving Yankees. Bonaparte's disaster in Spain. Need I mention Vietnam? You will win tactical victories with your ex's egocentrism and cruel intelligence. I accept that. However, I will win the war. I have the atom bomb.

Grant

In the meantime I'd send her a trifle. I would do as Moe Howard advised and "give the champ another cream puff."

Chapter 11

LISA

ear Lisa,
I move forward onto the battlefield with this volley:

DRAGON HEAD

One of the women I dated before Psycho Ex was named Lorraine. It didn't last long, but she did give me a swell birthday gift: an intricate Chinese dragon's face fashioned into an earring from the nineteenth century. It was made of thin brass, had whiskers, long fangs, and a little red ball in its mouth. It was beautiful. I kept it on my desk long after Lorraine was history.

Now let's move the story up three years. I was living with Jane Gray and working with Slowly I

Turn. In 1986 I was on a world tour. I spoke with P.E. every night. One news item was her new guitar player. His name was Kip Kinches, and yes, it was the same Kip she had dated a short time before we met. "No, don't be silly," she said. "He's a gentleman. And he's got a girlfriend."

As the tour dragged on month after month, I noticed she didn't call as much. When she did, Kip was often the subject. "Kip says . . . Kip bought me . . . Kip went to . . . Kip, Kip, Kip . . . Kip works at his father's firm. Kip has a nice car. Kip is on a very expensive methadone program."

Eventually I got home, and now P.E. wanted to go to the clubs and wanted to introduce me to, you guessed it, Kip. So I went.

"Grant, this is Kip." My jaw dropped. This guy wasn't handsome, he was stunning. He was a god. Everything was chiseled, sharp, pointy. He oozed the sex and cool I could never master. But what gave? I noticed Kip was really nervous, upset. He wouldn't make eye contact with me. Psycho Ex was forcing loud phony laughs. For just a howdy-do, it was deadly. He clearly did not want to meet me, or to be there. My third eye kicked in: They're having an affair. She didn't tell him I'd be here. She's making fools of us both.

What happened next was awful. As I shook his hand, I looked down at the rock jewelry on his perfect rock-god chest: a cunning rope made out of about thirty necklaces. It looked pagan and gaudy, yet this excessive self-adornment only enhanced the Dionysian radiance of Kip Kinches. And then I noticed that the glittering strands were very familiar. They were Jane's. I'd given them all to her. Those were three years' worth of my gifts on his chest. My mouth went dry. My hands shook. Why, there was her Christmas present! And that string of jet pearls I brought back from England. My eyes sorted through a blur of twenty or more pieces of jewelry that I recognized as hers. And, there . . . grinning at me dead center, was my intricate antique Chinese dragon earring.

I took P.E. aside. "What's he doing with all the stuff I got you?" I hissed.

"We were looking at my stuff one night, and I just gave him what I don't wear," she said dismissively. Enraged, I demanded she get my earring back. "But that's just from Crazy Lorraine," she said.

"But it's mine," I said.

"But you never wear it," she said.

"Get it OFF HIS CHEST. GET IT BACK NOW."

She glared at me, shook her head, and trotted over to the god Kip. They conferred and then giggled. She walked back, holding the earring in her fist. She punched it hard into my chest.

"Here you go, ya big baby," she sneered.

I felt a little electric shock. Another letter from Grant! And much sooner than I'd expected! I couldn't wait to retaliate. I immediately began to make a list of all the stories in my inventory, and as I did, a new battle strategy began to emerge. Initially I had planned to win by hammering him with a lot of big awful incidents: the ones that had made me cry and caused me to pack my suitcase. But the more I thought about it, the more I was taken by the way he detailed a small humiliating moment. Maybe the smarter strategy was to mirror him. Striking with lots of littler traumas, the kind that used to make me go numb and gave me the shakes, left me with more ammunition.

The phone rang. I heard Mark Eden's voice on my answering machine. I made no attempt to listen. The previous week I had started having an affair with him, just to add some drama to the time I felt I was bludgeoning. And now, as I saw myself screen his call, I wondered if maybe the secrecy wasn't the only thing that made the affair appealing. That and the fact that I hadn't had any sexual contact with a warm-blooded mammal of any kind in two years. I missed sex. It was kind of like an old friend I never heard from anymore.

When Eden started coming on to me, I could actually hear the guitar chords from the beginning of "The Last Time" by the Rolling Stones. "Maybe the last time, I don't know," I sang along. If it worked out badly, I told myself, what sort of loss was Eden? I hated the giant loopholes of logic in his right-wing political views, and the way he used them to rationalize his self-absorption. He wasn't even particularly good in bed. He never made it past my Three-Hump Law. (First time: Evaluation suspended, as awkwardness a given. Second time: All details logged in the name of research. Third time: Clear evidence of a learning curve and at least the hope of an orgasm, or else, game over.) But during encounter three, when I was unable to direct Eden to a place where something might happen for me aside from the burning of calories, I started thinking, What's the point? By the time he learns the road map, I'll have relocated. As a result, sex with Eden was so quiet it could have happened in the stacks at the library and never disturbed any research. On the plus side, I was fascinated by the absolute sordid dirtiness of the whole affair. The time he reached up under my skirt at The Table in The Room during one of those endless and completely pointless rewrite nights that went on until four in the morning provided my only motivation for not phoning in sick with pneumonia the following day.

Our routine was that during lunchtime, while the other writers moaned about how much they wanted another bucket of chili cheese fries, Eden would say he had to go run the script changes by the network. Then he and I would sneak off to an editing bay and fuck noiselessly, leaning against a door, so no one could accidentally walk in on us. The first two days, I was so pleased about the affair's effectiveness as a distraction from the frustration the show was causing me professionally that I guess I tuned out the disappointment it was causing me personally. But earlier today, as Eden was groping and fumbling with my clothes, I had noticed I was distancing myself, drifting, preoccupied, composing letters to Grant.

Dear Grant,

My God do I love this contest. While I want to acknowledge how impressed I am by your individual sorties (which I am hoping is a word that means battles), I would like to remind you that I hung in with Nick for eight years. Not unlike my model, the Viet Cong, I can just keep on coming long after your arguably flashier bombing raids have ended. You may win many battles, but I will win the war. And now I go to prepare.

Lisa

P.S. By the way, if I am not being too presumptuous, what is it that you ever liked about your P.E.? That little junkie broad is really a piece of work.

When I got home from work, I sat down and wrote up a draft of the story I'd thought of while Eden was huffing and puffing away. It seemed to have a similar level of anguish and discomfort to the one Grant had sent. His story was titled this time, so mine would be, too. I thought of calling it "The Parable of the Mysterious Unfixed Car."

We had only been living together for a couple of months when my Psycho Ex agreed to speak for one night to a freshman filmmaking class that his friend was teaching at a college in Oregon for one night only. I drove him to the airport, and on the way, we dropped my car off at a repair place for its sixty-thousand-mile tune-up, then took his Mercedes the rest of the way.

That night a huge El Niño storm blew in, causing floods and mud slides. When I went out to run a few errands the next day, the Mercedes, which was parked in the driveway, would not start. Knowing that I had to pick Psycho Ex up at the airport pretty soon, I went back into the house to call AAA. However, the phones were dead. Water was coursing through the streets like a river as it dawned on me that I had no way to pick P.E. up, unless I could get my car back. But how? Panicky and desperate, I went out into the pouring rain and began to hitchhike. Almost immediately, a neighbor took pity on my rain-drenched ass and gave me a ride to the car repair, where they took my car down off the rack, unfixed, so I could get to the airport on time.

As I drove, I was thinking, Whew. That was close. What a good girlfriend am I! This ought to win me some kind of bonus points for extreme devotion.

However, as we were walking to where I'd parked the car, and I was maniacally recounting my horrible day, Psycho Ex was eerily quiet. When he finally spoke, he explained that this unfixed-car-and-dead-phone story was very suspicious. Did I expect him to believe his Mercedes suddenly wouldn't start when it had been fine yesterday? Did I think he was stupid? Obviously I was hiding something. Was I fucking around on him? Was that it? By the time we got home, all of my "No! No! No . . . you don't understand"s were going unheard. As soon as we got into the house, he said to me, "So, the Mercedes doesn't start, huh? Well, let's just see . . ." Smirking, he picked up the keys to his car, jangled them at me, and then made a slow, deliberate walk out to the driveway, to start the car. My heart was pounding. Oh my God, I was thinking. What if the fucking

Mercedes decides to start? I will be totally screwed. And I didn't even do anything. I felt light-headed, almost faint, as I sat in the house waiting. I was too tense to go watch. About ten minutes later, Psycho Ex came back into the room and threw his keys down on the dining room table. And, saying nothing, went to the refrigerator, got a beer, and then took it into his office to call a tow truck.

Lisa

I felt very strange after I finished writing. Why was I confiding in Grant Repka? Who was he, and was this a good idea? I shrugged it off. Our budding friendship was helping to nicely put my heart back into its former condition. After all, he was confiding honestly in me. It was tit for tat. It all felt safe.

I reread my letter before pushing "send." Then I checked my e-mail every fifteen minutes until I fell asleep. At five o'clock in the morning, when I got up to pee, it occurred to me that I could check e-mail again, something I had never done in the middle of the night. And there it was, almost like magic. An answer, written just a half hour ago. He was always writing at four in the morning. What was going on in their house? Late-night rehearsals? All-night drug-and-drinking binges? Orgies with the Pamela Anderson girlfriend and her centerfold friends? I couldn't really imagine what his life looked like. Maybe it was for the best that I didn't know.

Dear Lisa,
Great story. And to think we are only watching the opening act.

Why did I like Psycho Ex? Well, she was a woman, as opposed to the twentyish girls I met and dated while working on Melrose. Her "former addiction" had given her a sedate kind of maturity as well as a deadpan gallows humor. She had been married, made records, been in bands, had a kid and dabbled in motherhood. She was calm, affection-ate, and if anybody ever gave you trouble on the street, she'd more than have your back and their throats. She pre-sented herself to me as someone who had survived a hard life and a lengthy heroin habit and kicked. Someone who, for all her rock-jiggery-pokery, desired nothing so much as a little domestic tranquillity with the man she loved. She was easy to get along with, and the bonus was folded laundry, great dinners, and a clean house. That's who I thought she was: a wounded rock veteran who found her safe haven, at last.

As for sorties: Thank you for the compliment. I suspect that you are trying to make me overconfident through flat-tery. As it says in *The Art of War,* "When the enemy's envoy speaks in humble terms but continues preparations, he will advance." And regarding your Vietnam analogy, listen: They were at war for almost a hundred years. The Chinese, the French, and don't forget the Japanese, took 'em over in WWII. Those people were pros by the time we got there.

I have eight years, too. Two with F.P.E. (French Psycho Ex) followed by six with plain old P.E. With F.P.E. I revisited the rage, the violence, and the verbal abuse of my child-hood. Speaking of which, I attack you now with a quick commando raid entitled:

KNOCK KNOCK KNOCK

It's around eleven A.M. Psycho Ex and I are asleep. We are suddenly jolted awake by someone knocking at the door. A woman's voice is calling out P.E.'s name.

"Hello? Jane? Hello?" Knock, knock, knock . . . "Helllllooooo?"

P.E. grabs me and motions "Sshhhhhh." Her eyes are wide and full of fear.

I hear a child's voice, a boy, say, "This is where she

lives?" There is another series of knocks. "Is she in there?" he asks.

"Guess not," says the woman, and we listen to them walk away.

"Who was that?" I whisper.

"It's my sister-in-law and my fuckin' kid," hisses Psycho Ex. Sitting up in frozen silence, listening to the footsteps retreat. "That was close, huh," Jane says.

I reread the story a number of times. Fuck. If Grant was going to bring P.E.'s kid into the game, I was doomed. Nick didn't even have kids. I considered inventing a couple of poor beleaguered grade-schoolers to have at the ready. Poor, sad, overlooked, and asthmatic little Jimmy and Pammy, their grades suffering from the unpredictability of Dad's moods.

Story aside, I was also kind of touched by the part where Grant called this the "opening act." He seemed to be saying he intended to keep writing. It was kind of the minimum definition of a commitment.

Dear Grant,
At what portal of hell did you find this nightmarish woman? And you mentioned another, even crazier one. This makes me wonder about your childhood. What did your dad do for a living? After you realized your P.E. was avoiding her kid, did you say anything to her about it? How did you rationalize her behavior? Did you meet the kid?

Well, truce over. Back to war. Just because some of your tactics are really brutal doesn't mean I can't retaliate using more classic methods. This living-in-the-past stuff is very disquieting. Which is not an indication that I'm planning to surrender. You mistake my contemplative remarks for weakness at your own risk.

It was seven in the morning by the time I sent the reply. No point in trying to go back to sleep now, so I went into the kitchen and made coffee. There was just enough time to shower and maybe skim through the paper before leaving for work. But instead I found myself back at the computer, shuffling through my files, figuring out my next entry. I was thrilled to see another letter had come while I had been working on answering his last one. It was written at five-thirty. Had he just gotten up, or never gone to sleep?

Dear Lisa,

In war, our opponents should be contemplative. We don't go to war willy-nilly. We go to war only when we assess our opponents and believe we can win. Therefore I perceive where I may attack.

What did my dad do for a living? High school phys. ed. teacher and football coach: A job custom-made for sadists. Thank God he didn't teach at my high school.

Re: P.E.: Of course I said something to her about avoiding her own child. It was the key topic at breakfast. That is, over coffee and cigarettes. She explained that the kid was being raised by his aunt while Jane got on her feet. When I tried to ask more, she just got defensive. "What do ya want? I had a fucking heroin habit, okay? He's with his aunt, and Aunt Dorothy loves him, okay? You don't think it kills me? Is that what you want? To see me ripped up?" Breakfast talk! Try interrogating a mother on her deepest regrets and shame first thing in the morning, and see how far you get. I wish I could tell you I ran heroically down the street looking for the kid, brought him back, and fed him good warm bread and soup. Unfortunately, I'm a rock scumbag. I lay there sucking smoke, chugging joe, thinking, Well, it's their thing. Ain't none of my beeswax. She'll work it out when she gets on her feet. The kid sounded okay. I figured she would call him later in the day. But she didn't. Nor the next day. Or the next, till the issue was forgotten. The incident added a new dimension to my mysterious, sphinxlike beauty: something dark, sinister, and cruel. Not only was I repelled, I was intrigued and drawn even closer. I thought maybe I could help.

Grant

I had to leave for work. No time to shower. I looked pretty bad, but I didn't really care. What was there to be gained from dressing up? The final draft of "my script" that was about to go into production contained only two complete sentences by me, both having to do with a gym regular always pouring his energy drinks into a dying plant. Otherwise, even little details I had tried to slip in under the radar had disappeared. Like a dyspeptic receptionist named Andrea Saperstein, who had been changed for no real reason into a thuglike janitor named Adrian Saperman. Simple exclamatory greetings I had added, such as "Hey! I'm here" had mutated into "Yo! It's me!"

I could have repressed my feelings about this more effectively if people hadn't been coming up to me all week long, saying things like "Hey, Lisa! Great script!" as though I hadn't noticed that it contained just two of my sentences. On this kind of show, no one else considered that a problem. The others all thrilled to their "written by" credit when it was televised, whether the show contained any words by them or not.

Since I had no outlet for my frustration, short of breaking my contract, I was half thinking that maybe my poor personal hygiene would get me fired. But no such luck. It didn't even turn off the sexual advances of Mark Eden, who was starting to get on my nerves. This wouldn't have posed a problem that antidepressants couldn't cure if not for the fact that Mark Eden was my boss.

Chapter 12

GRANT

W inn and I had a dark secret in our relationship. We didn't sleep together. We did sleep
together, euphemistically. However, definitively, we
didn't. We had separate rooms. My room wasn't
down the hall but across the patio, along the flag-
stone path, through the garden, and up the back
stairs behind the garage.

To look at Winnie, you might think I was nuts.
But the fact was, to have sex in Winnie's room, one
had to put away the shoes, books, bags, dirty jeans,
piles of dirty clothes, hair-care products, and magazines, and yes, sweep the floor. If we ever engaged in
a sex act that insisted knees be on the floor, that act
concluded with one dusting off one's dog-and-cat-
fur-covered knees. Winn's bedroom was almost custom-made to discourage the act.

My office above the studio/garage was nicer. Here's where we'd have sex—away from the animals, the phone, the mess. I also tended to sleep during the day; Winnie got up early and needed the house. That's why I once again opened my eyes in near-blackness, upstairs in my studio. I smelled the air and listened. The birdsongs and traffic were scant, so I put it at two-thirty P.M. Counting backward to my six A.M. bedtime, yep, I'd managed eight hours' sleep. I struggled up, put my boots on, and weaved out the door. I only had to put my boots on because, well, I sleep in my clothes. The big earthquake of '92 cured me of sleeping nude. I swore that when the next big one came, as the camera panned past the crowd of stunned L.A.-tians, there would be one guy not caught bottomless in his T-shirt and flip-flops to represent the dignity of the human race.

I pulled out the house key as I got near the house, but found the door open. "Winnie?" I said as I went in. No answer. Winn was out. She never left a note or phone message.

Recently, my habits had changed. Between making coffee and the morning pee, I now downloaded e-mail. I would light the first cig at the same time, getting a huge payload of tobacco, caffeine, and Lisa's stories.

Just before I flushed, I heard the chipper ringing of fresh e-mails.

I went over to the computer and sat down, readying the coffee and the cig as I opened Lisa's response.

Dear Grant,
As my constant mentor Wang Xi says, "When an army has the force of momentum, even the timid become brave. Nothing is fixed in the laws of warfare. They develop based on momenta." And so, as I gain some momenta and simultaneously develop a few warfare laws, we march forward.

THE CONSEQUENCES OF THE VANISHING CAT

Psycho Ex and I had rented a house in Woodland Hills after his first movie came out but before it got any attention. He had a lot of free time and wasn't handling it well. On this particular evening, he was looking for his cat, Kenny. Kenny was the kind of cat who would hide: in closets, in cupboards, under furniture. Like her dad, she was a contrarian who did not mind keeping you waiting. "She's around," I said. "She shows up when she hears food being served." So I opened a can of cat food and put on a big show, but the cat still didn't appear. Next I walked around the house, offering meals, snacks, cash, prizes . . . still nothing. This evolved over time into more intense kitty searching, until Nick and I were both out in the yard, using flashlights, rummaging through the bushes. Somehow, as this escalated, the fact that the cat was missing started to become my fault. "Are you sure you didn't leave a door or window open?" he began to ask me repeatedly. "You know how careless you are." I said I felt sure that I hadn't. But by about eight at night, when the cat still had not put in an appearance, P.E. had become convinced that I did something negligent. By about nine, he was sure the cat was dead and I was to blame. I tried to remain calm. I said I would continue looking for her in the yard, and on our block, and then tomorrow I would put up signs and call all the vets and animal shelters in the area to see if anyone had brought her in. "Cats don't go too far," I told him, trying to be reassuring, "and even if they are gone for a day or two, they usually turn up unexpectedly." I felt sure we would find her. This further enraged P.E., who now claimed that I knew I was guilty, and that was why I was so nonchalant. I explained that I was not acting more upset because I didn't see what good that was going to do. This enraged him more, until he was in a spiral of fury, attacking me for my every personality flaw. He was throwing in things I once said to him that irritated him years ago, as well as hurling at me every cruel thing he could think of to say about my crazy mother and how I was exactly like her. He was recycling a mind-boggling set of ir-relevant data that built to an accusation that I was fucking around on him. I told him I did not want him to talk to me like this, and if he continued, I was going to leave. Naturally he continued. So I headed for the door. He jumped in front of the door to block my exit. Shocked, I turned and headed for the back door. He jumped in front of that door, too, taunting me for thinking I was going anywhere. I started to panic. No one had ever kept me from leaving a place like this. It was scary. As was the amused demonic expression on his face, which, combined with his rage, was really fright-ening. Once again, I charged the front door. He blocked my way, and put his big red face so close to mine that when he screamed, his spit was hitting me.

I didn't know what to do. So I went into the living room and sat down on the couch. I would wait for him to give up his door guarding. Sooner or later he would have to go to the bathroom, and when he missed a beat, I would leave. Meanwhile, he resumed taunting me.

I sat quietly until I saw him move away. Then I raced for the door, but he sprang back in front of it. So I sat down. This time I had my purse with me. This cat-and-mouse game he was playing was not just nerve-racking but infuriating. Finally, a long and horrible hour of screaming later, he turned his back just long enough for me to see my chance to escape. I made a beeline for the door, opened it, and ran out of the house. I headed for the garage and made it all the way to my car. I got the garage door open. I got the car started and began to back it out. All the while, I was also wondering where the fuck I thought I was going, because it was the middle of the night. At least I have my purse, I remember thinking. Then I heard a giant thud. Did I hit something? Had the muffler come loose? No, while I was pulling out onto the street, P.E. had thrown himself on the hood of my car and was now swearing at me, glaring in at me from the other side of the windshield. "Get back in the fucking house," he was yelling. This was embarrassing and dangerous on a couple of levels. Furious though I was, I did not want to endanger his life. Although, as I tell you this story, I must confess I wish I would have just driven onto the highway. Instead I pulled back into the garage and we both went back in the house. This time he walked in the bedroom and shut the door. Not really sure what to do, I slept on the couch. Around sunrise, I awoke to see the cat tiptoeing out from the top shelf of the coat closet and over to her bowl to check out today's entrée. So, I picked her up and put her in the bedroom where Nick was sleeping. And then I got dressed and went to work. The entire incident was never mentioned again.

Lisa

I liked the image of Nick Blake lying on the hood of a car, screaming through the windshield. What a great place for an aria, I thought, and began to imagine one for Nick. I sat at the piano and began to sing:

> *You fucking bitch, you fucking whore, you fucking cunt,*
> *   you fucking twat!*
> *I hurt again I hurt again I hurt again I hurt a lot!*
> *Bitch! Whore! Twat!*

I pulled out my thesaurus and soon had a second verse.

Courtesan! Cyprian! Demi-mondainian!
A fornicating harridan who, hurting me again,
   hurt me a lot!

Before I finished, I heard the low rumble of Winn's Electra throbbing up to the house. Putting my aria aside, I wound the animals up, exclaiming, "It's Winnie! It's Winnie!" in a high voice. As she walked in gripping many Trader Joe's plastic bags in her hands, the wound-up dogs danced around her, yelping. I admonished her for not calling me to help unload the car. She admonished me back that she hadn't known if I was awake.

"Well, next time blow the horn or something," I said. "Besides, you've got to read this one from Lisa. You're going to love it."

After putting the groceries away, she sat down and chewed her fingernails as she quickly read Lisa's story, making a high cartoonish shriek just where I thought she would. "What a nutcase!" she said. "But I wonder how she feeds into this. What did she say that she forgot to mention? She certainly has the ability to piss *me* off. God knows what it's like to live with her."

"Maybe, Winn," I said. "But it's the escalating reaction that pushes this story. He goes from mad to madness."

"Right!" she said. "But what buttons was she pushing? He gets madder and madder, and she's just sitting there?" Winnie mimicked a wolf from early Warner Bros.: "Dere I was, officer, just mindin' my own beeswax."

I shrugged. I more than understood how someone could just be minding beeswax. Winnie didn't. I had been through it a million times, and she never once.

She continued, "I also wonder if Lisa maybe wasn't getting off on playing victim in some sort of S-and-M game."

"You want me I should ask her?"

"I'd love to hear her answer." Winn got up and walked into

the bedroom to put on her exercise clothes. In our place, that meant she took five steps to the right. "While you're at it, ask her why she stayed. Battered-wife syndrome? Or did she stick around because he's Nick fuckin' Blake, and trillions of dollars buy a lot of Christian forbearance?"

As she headed out to meet up with some friends for a hike, I poured another coffee and lit a cigarette. My lungs were already feeling soggy. When I visualized Lisa in her story, on the couch, waiting for a chance to run out the door, she was blond and pretty, and her hair was modestly teased and sprayed. She was wearing a nurse's uniform. It was 1966, and I had blurred Lisa with my mother. Both sat there, eyes fixed mid-distance yet defiant, enduring a bombardment of nonsense and rage. Lisa from Nick, my mom from Coach Repka. I felt something stir inside me. I admired that expression. That look reminded me of all the battle paintings I had stared at in my war books as a kid. Be it *Bunker Hill*, *The Death of General Wolfe*, *The British Infantry Squares Repel Ney's Cavalry Charge at Waterloo*, or *Mom Silently Endures Another Irrational Verbal Assault from the Deeply Disturbed Coach Repka*, the expression was always grim, thin-lipped, dignified. Calm reserve as death approached on a thundering tide of fury. Small wonder I'd sought out the relationships I had; I wore my mother's frontline expression throughout 90 percent of them.

So why *had* Lisa stayed? She was either acting on some sort of parental conditioning, or she was taking the bumps in exchange for the bucks. Was Nick daddy or sugar daddy? Could a gentleman ask a woman these things directly? I lit a cig and thought, No, but he can, however, do so indirectly; if I ask about his motives, she may inadvertently reveal hers.

Dear Lisa,
Have I mentioned how shaken I am by your stories? Well, I am. I wonder, and you don't have to tell me, but where does

all this come from? Was P.E. acting out his traumas or just keeping his nails sharp?

Grant

After sending it off, I got up to begin the day's business. But hell, I smoked five packs of cigarettes a day. When did I ever ignore my impulses? Ten minutes later, when I heard the arrival of another e-mail, I sat right down and opened it.

Dear Grant,

I think both. But like any good narcissistic character-disordered borderline overachiever, he was so un-self-examined that I could never get a fix on the cause. My shrink used to say, "With Nick, you are either part of the pillar of support or part of the abyss around it." She must have said, "He cannot stand for you to be separate" five hundred times before I understood what that meant. Apparently, when you live in the world of a narcissist, if he sees you as a separate person, with separate interests and reactions, he also sees you as a threat. Or, to put it in terms you will prefer, a relationship with a narcissist is like being annexed by a larger country regardless of previous treaties.

The Nicks of the world are angry for reasons they don't understand. They live in a pressure cooker that is seeking a vent. They live in a world of last straws. Maybe I am boring you with this crap. If you want, I can explain it to you someday in greater detail. The point I am trying to make is that, back then, it seemed to me that Nick was the second person I loved who was accusing me of causing their problems. My mother used to constantly say that all I cared about was myself. She liked to let me know how perfect her life had been before I came along and started putting cups down on tables without coasters. How could she, after all, be expected to exercise any kind of restraint in the face of that kind of unmitigated gall? Ultimately, I figured that since I caused all these problems for two people I loved, it was also my job to cure them. So I hung around in the name of showing them both that I could make them happy, never suspecting that what I was actually doing was waiting for hell to freeze over.

Lisa

P.S. Once, I was trying to figure out what about my mother's childhood caused her to be so volatile. I thought I'd ask her a few questions. "What kind of a personality did your mother have?" I asked her. "Personality?" she said dismissively. "Grandma didn't really have a personality. No one had them in those days."

This was encouraging. The mention of a shrink indicated a whiff of self-examination. If Lisa was a nut, she at least had supervision. This was an argument against Winnie's sugar-daddy theory.

Still, anyone could use psychology as a smoke screen. For strategic reasons, I thought it wise to get an idea of just how screwed-up her family had been. That kind of a repeating pattern might predict her relationship with Nick. I baited my hook:

Dear Lisa,
I like this. Families keep everything in tightly wrapped boxes, don't they? Let me tell you about my uncle Crazy Gintares Repka. Old Gintares lived alone in squalor. A Lithuanian immigrant, he worked at the Shell Oil refinery from the day it opened, when he was in his teens, until he died in the sixties. He owned a home: that is, a shack with no lights and no running water after the city shut them off. Just some clothes, dirt, a bed. He only possessed five things:

two religious pictures, seventy-five thousand dollars' worth of Shell Oil stock, seventy-five thousand dollars he kept pinned to his pockets—and sixty years of dirt.

About ten years ago, I asked Good Coach Repka about Old Gintares. "I remember you all said Old Gintares was punishing himself. Why? What did he do to feel so guilty about?" As if it was nothing, my dad said, "Ahh, he murdered Grandma's brother back in Lithuania." Oh. Is that all? Last year I ran this past my mom, and she got snippy. "Your father is so dramatic," she said, exasperated. "Old Gintares didn't kill Grandma's brother." She shook her head, disgusted at my father's cheap theatricality, adding, "Gintares didn't even know Grandma back then." Then, as an afterthought, she added, "He murdered somebody else."

Grant

Just as I pressed "send," I heard the key go into the door, and Winn entered, damp and glowing from her walk. Christ. Had another hour gone by?

"Are you still online with her?" she asked. "That's some letter."

"Two, actually."

"Ohhh!" she teased, school-yard fashion.

Right then, the four cups of coffee and fifteen cigs hit me in a nasty, pukey sort of way. I was full of smoke, caffeine, sugar, and Coffee-mate, a poisonous high. It was the wrong moment for Winn to say, "You really shouldn't always be there for this woman." I don't know why—perhaps it was the caffeine, perhaps I was genuinely angry that I was suspected, even a little, but whatever the reason, I blew up in the way that only a nine-year-old brat or a caffeine-addled adult can do. "Ahhh, for fuck's sake!" I said.

At that, Winn arched a brow and stared at me, shock mated with surprise, giving birth to the monstrous twins Indignant and Amused. Winnie knew "Ahhh, for fuck's sake" quite well. She heard me say it in traffic, when it slowed to a standstill, or when someone canceled rehearsal at the last second, or about vanishing band members and bad news from the IRS. I said, "Ahhh, for fuck's sake" to my horny sister, who went trolling through my few fans to fuck and then fuck over, and at that five-minute mark when a movie goes from a brilliant idea by a writer to a version "improved" by executives and focus groups. I had said, "Ahhh, for fuck's sake" to just about everything that chafed, irritated, or grossly disappointed, and about everybody and everything at one time or another, except one. I had never said it to Winnie. When the firecracker smoke in my head cleared, it dawned on me that where I thought I had been admonished for wasting time writing, I had actually been accused of paying too much attention to another woman. Any overreaction would appear as guilt and denial. The last thing the situation called for was an angry, defensive response.

She stood there like Madame Pompadour observing the rabid peasant through a lorgnette. Mildly shocked, mildly amused. She cocked her head to the side and squinted. "Did you eat today?"

No, I hadn't.

"Well, for fuck's sake, eat something," she scolded.

Thank Christ, she was playing along, I hoped. "I'm sorry . . ." I stammered. "I just got carried away with writing."

"Yeah, but to her, it's not writing, it's writing to *her*," Winn said. "Go eat."

There was no bread in the house. We didn't eat bread. We didn't care about our hearts or colons. We cared about our waistlines. I found half a hunk of Brie left over from last night's dinner, and I soon felt my entire system weep with relief as the protein entered my bloodstream, quelling the rioting nerve endings with soothing cheese atoms, or however the fuck it worked.

Calmer, I apologized again. She nodded. She always nodded

at an apology. Is acknowledging an apology the same as accepting one?

"Go take your shower," she said. I think that was her way of saying, "Forget it. It's okay."

I shaved and showered at the same time. The bathroom was dark, because I liked it dark when I showered. I knew where all the parts were. I could shower by feel.

Suddenly the bathroom lights came on. Winnie charged in, her tone high-pitched and furious.

"Well, once again she doesn't seem to have read your letters," she said.

Handle this one better, Grant, I thought. "Whaddya mean?" I said.

"I was reading your story about Crazy Old Gintares, and a new one came in from her. She barely acknowledged yours. You told her about an uncle who might have killed your grandmother's brother. Your family is abusive. Violent. And you and your sister are fucking wrecks because of it. This cow barely blinked and wants to tell you all about her new carpet."

"Aww, Gawd," I said, which was good. Winn would know that "Aww, Gawd" meant "What are we going to do with these people?"

Winnie put a towel over the shower door to give herself a little privacy. I heard the toilet seat clank down, and she continued, "That's what worries me about her. If she's not reading your stories, then why is she writing back? You go through everything she sends, and discuss it. But her? Nothing. When she can't compete with you, she reminds you how rich she is."

I put my hand to my hair. I could feel that it was at the right point, clean enough to pass inspection, but with enough air pollution, hair gel, and personal grease to be extremely manageable. Wash it tomorrow, I thought. "That's not really true. Look at that last response. I ask her a little question, and she sends me a whole dissertation."

" 'Maybe I am boring you with this crap. If you want, I can explain it to you someday in greater detail,' " Winnie said in a singsong voice. "I'll bet she would just looove to explain it all to you one day."

"Did you memorize this?" I asked her, my voice echoing in the shower.

"I printed it out. I have the response that just came in. You wanna hear it?"

Before I could say no, I heard the toilet flush. She pulled the towel off the shower door and began to read:

Dear Grant,

Gintares Repka sure sounds like a pip. I guess the good news is that no matter how much you fuck up, you never have to worry about being the black sheep in your family.

On a happier note, they installed a new carpet in my living room today, since the doggy plan to spread a fine layer of mud on every inch of the existing carpet was a complete success. I took the adventurous step of getting the exact same carpet as before, in the exact same color, so it looks the same, only cleaner. Now I am trying to bask in the glow, since it will only be a matter of hours until all that remains of my redecorating effort will be a canceled check. By the way . . . couldn't help but notice there was no P.E. Game entry in your last letter. Do I sense that perhaps you are getting ready to surrender, much as we did at Bunker Hill or the beach at Normandy or Gettysburg? We must have surrendered at one of them.

Lisa

"Okay, look. Thirty-eight words to you and . . . ninety-five about her. I love how she drops this bit about 'No matter how you fuck up.' Very nice. And then it's all about her carpets and her money and those goddamn dogs."

While she was slamming Lisa's latest, I stepped out of the shower and draped a towel around my neck, gripping it with both hands. I then twisted my face into a very manly insincere smile. I was posing à la *Playgirl*, my flaccid cock dangling pointlessly. I froze in the position, waiting for Winn to look up.

"She ends the thing, 'By the way . . . I couldn't help but notice there was no P.E. Game entry in your last letter.' For Chrissakes, Grant. You were responding to her dissertation on narcissism. But that's not good enough for her. No." Winnie squawked in a low croak, " 'Where's my story? I want my story.' Then all this supposedly hilarious stuff about *surrender*? She doesn't know she's whipped, because she only skims your stories."

She looked up at me finally and, as I expected, let go a squeal of thoroughly amused revulsion. She liked my creepy *Playgirl* Model man, more than any other girlfriend I ever pulled it on.

"I think she's just excitable," I said. "Though I'm disappointed that she doesn't have more to say about Crazy Old Gintares. I thought it said a lot about my mom and my dad, as well as my family."

"Yeah, she doesn't understand how much you put into these stories."

"I got to pee," I said, and she left. Winnie was right. Fuck Lisa. I lost two hours today just being friendly, and I barely got acknowledged. I turned to the mirror and drew a '68 Buick Skylark with my finger on the steamed glass. And as I did this, it all came to me: how I would make Ms. Roberty see the finer points of the stories I was sending. My cast would be here in an hour. I wouldn't be able to write Lisa back until after that. Later, one A.M. or so. "You want a story now, Lisa? You wait."

Chapter 13

LISA

Dear Lisa,

I attack: With regard to my surrender; when you say "Bunker Hill" are you referring to Breed's Hill? Hey, we didn't win. But we sure as hell didn't surrender! And as for Gettysburg, the good thing about the American Civil War is that everybody is both a winner and a loser, since a case can be made that America lost, but since they lost to the Americans, they also won. Hence, it is beloved by all.

THE OLD FOLKS

Opening scene—1965. A field in northwest Indiana. My young chums and I have discovered a weathered copy of *True Police Stories*. Toward the back of the magazine is an ad that reads, "Exotic Lingerie from the sinful world of April LeMay." There's a small, pouty picture of April, looking sleepy and sexy. Below her are black-and-white illustrations of leggy gals in bewitching lacy things. The boys laugh at the push-up bras and the special girdle with the exposed butt cheeks. Who'd want a woman's butt to stick out that way? Well, we did. But we didn't quite understand why.

Cut to 1983.

An old couple lived in our apartment complex. Carlos and April were in their late sixties, married, but kept separate apartments near each other. He was a large fat lummox who was in bed all day. Frostbite from Korea had chewed his legs up bad. The VA hospital said they should be amputated.

April was a thickset gray old woman who shuffled around between her place, Carlos's, and the corner liquor store in her bathrobe and slippers. I tried to say hello a few times as we passed on the street, but she never said boo. I noticed, however, that in this old, wrinkled, flabby face, two clear baby-blue eyes glowed like proverbial diamonds.

Now, this takes place later on in the tale. At this time P.E. wasn't working, just hanging around the apartment building. There was very little money, just what I brought in from Slowly gigs and working retail. One day she said, "Ya know, Carlos is a strange guy. We were talking, and I swear I noticed track marks on his arm."

Uh-oh.

"No," I said, "he's sick. He's old. It's probably from treatments he gets from the VA hospital. He's too poor to be a junkie."

"I don't know," she said.

That evening she came home with all the news:

"I was talking to Carlos, and you'll never believe this. He used to be a big-time magician in the fifties, and his wife used to be a famous stripper. She was in movies, too. She makes all her money now selling her old photos by mail." I don't know why this clicked, but I was rocketed back to that field in Indiana, then rocketed back to my living room.

"April is April LeMay?" I said. "That old woman is April LeMay?"

"Yeah, that's the name," said P.E. "How do you know her? Was she like really big?"

I told her what I knew. A burly-que star in the forties, thought of as "classy." Appeared as herself in *Hell or High Water*. She later started the lingerie line that started me on the road to perdition.

"Yeah, that's it," Jane said. "Carlos told me they used to live in a mansion, and he'd tour with her and stay in first-class hotels. But they shot away everything on dope."

Uh-oh. I had a bad feeling about this.

"I found out something else, too. Carlos DOES have track marks. See?" she said proudly, "I told ya. You can't fool me! When his VA check comes in, he goes down the street and cops, but those fuckin' Mexicans on Van Ness always rip him off because he's so old and slow. I know those fucking guys. Weird, huh?"

Oh God, no.

"I know the place he goes. They sell him shit. I told him so."

Soon after, I came home very early. Four P.M. instead of late evening. I let myself in and sat down at the table near the door. Lighting a smoke, I heard someone walk past my apartment and knock on Carlos's door. I heard Jane's voice say, "It's me, Carlos."

"You got it?" I heard him ask from inside as she let herself in, leaving the door open so I could hear the whole conversation about how many balloons of dope his money bought and how many more balloons of dope she'd charged him to score for him. She mentioned a couple of names I'd never heard before. Carlos was grateful to the point of fawning.

I sat there listening, going numb with disbelief, awestruck by the amorality: that she would be willing to get an old man with lame legs hooked so she could get high. Had I heard her right? My mind was searching for an alternative explanation. Surely the woman I loved could not be such a degenerate. Then I heard Carlos's door close, and followed by a few footsteps, and in she walked.

"Oh, hi," she said, startled. "I gotta go use the bathroom."

I nodded, waited. I couldn't imagine what she was going to say. When she came out, she paused, sighed, then spoke. "I need to talk to you," she said, all business.

"Okay," I said, all business back.

A look of serious contemplation crossed her face. It was one of those expressions easily learned off TV. Sheriff Taylor figures out how to explain it all to Opie. Slowly nodding, she exhaled and said, "Well, I've decided that Carlos is in such bad pain from his legs that I should buy dope for him."

I looked at her, deadpan. Then I smiled. And then I laughed out loud. She smiled, like we were playing "Caught ya inna fib."

We sat there smiling at each other for a moment. Then my fist came down on the table, causing her to literally jump out of her seat. "Have you no fucking fear of God?" I screamed.

SCORE	Points
P.E. button-busting proud at being able to spot another junkie	5
P.E. thinking it was a bonus that both old people were old addicts	15
P.E. getting caught in an abominable transaction and deciding to bluff her way through it	10
P.E. justifying the deed as an act of compassion and supplemental health care	20
P.E. thinking I was stupid enough to buy it	15
Not booting P.E. out on her ass and calling the cops on her because I believed the drug demanded she be amoral, but if we removed the drug, the wonderful girl underneath it all would emerge, and that I was stupid enough to buy that	10
Getting two old people hooked on heroin in order to utilize their pension/Social Security checks for her own habit	50
TOTAL pain, shock, and humiliation suffered:	125

The Official P.E. Game Rule Book states that all points in P.E. game are self-awarded by the narrator. Points are given based on a personal value system of humiliation, horror, self-debasement, and pain endured.

The story recipient may contend these points, having only the follow-up e-mail to do so. Failure to contend story points indicates the recipient has accepted these points as valid.

In the case of contention, the narrator must explain his/her reasons for awarding the particular amount of points in question.

Debating is allowed, if not encouraged. The exchange of stories must stop until an agreement is made.

Grant

Brand-new rules! I was so excited, it was almost a Christmas-morning moment. It was three-thirty A.M., and not only had I bagged a fresh e-mail, I had me some brand-new rules! So I made myself a cup of tea and sat down in my dark office to read the whole thing again by the glow of the computer. Since the game had started, I had been filling notebooks with rough drafts of stories and ideas for upcoming battles. I had also made a special trip to Barnes & Noble to buy *The Art of War* in order to compile a more extensive compendium of hostile military remarks for enhanced warmongering.

However, I found this story about April and Carlos particularly grim. Nick and I had been many strange, unfortunate things, but down and out were not two of them. Almost from the beginning, things got busy when his first movie, *The Valedictorian*, was picked up by a big distributor, and with the money we got paid, we—well, Nick—bought the house in Santa Monica Canyon. On many occasions over the years, I regretted that I hadn't done as he asked and gotten the fuck out that very first night instead of living with a partially packed suitcase for the next eight years. But now, for the first time, it all seemed worth it. I couldn't wait to move through my own painful details and get points for them. I returned Grant's e-mail at five A.M.

Dear Grant,
Once again you have achieved a truly hideous portrait of a really high-quality P.E. My compliments to you on a very nicely fought ground skirmish.

In keeping with your theme of the elderly, I was tempted to counter with the story of an early trip to Acapulco, where a group of old ladies on the beach asked my Psycho Ex to take their picture together. He said, "Sure," and, taking their camera, posed them for several shots by the ocean. That's so sweet of him, I was thinking, genuinely moved. When he came back, he was laughing. "I took every picture so their heads were cut off," he told me.

Yet, as a war offensive, this is obviously too insignificant. I will choose my next move very carefully. I am in a good position. I am calm. My inventory is massive. As Sun Tzu reminds us, "Those who are good on the attack maneuver in the heights of the skies thus making it impossible for opponents to prepare for them. If you are unfathomable then what you guard is not attacked by opponents."

This makes me think it might be time for something unfathomable.

Look out behind you!

THE PIZZA STORY

It is 1992, just after Psycho Ex's first movie, *The Valedictorian,* has been released to very strong ticket sales for a low-budget independent film. And every day since it opened, I had been listening to him yell, "They hate me. They hate the fucking movie. They're all snickering at me behind my back because I'm such a fucking failure," despite a lot of evidence to the contrary. If I would counter with "Well, you got a great review in the *Chicago Tribune,*" he would scream, "Everybody knows that guy is a fucking cunt. I'm sick of you and your Pollyanna bullshit," and punch the wall.

In my uncomprehending naïveté, it occurred to me that maybe we were just spending too much time together. So I took a job at Paramount. Another plum assignment: trying to rewrite Elvis's movie *Clambake* for a younger audience.

The producers envisioned it as a vehicle for someone like Sebastian Bach, even though they had no indication that he was remotely interested. Still, I hoped that bringing a new set of people and influences into my life would take the pressure off my relationship with P.E.

The Friday night after my first full week of work, I picked up Psycho Ex at his office so we could drive home together. This was the night that he always liked to stop at Gondolier Pizza in Brentwood for a specially ordered, very specific extra-thick-crust pizza with these toppings and no others: pesto, olives, pepperoni, and sun-dried tomatoes. A P.O.P.S. pizza, was how I remembered it. He had his assistant, Jason, phone in the order before we left. Then, upon arrival, P.E. sat in the idling car while I ran into the busy restaurant to claim the order. When I finally returned to the car with the pizza box, he was so antsy to get out of there that he practically stepped on the gas before I closed the car door. As we drove, I lifted a corner of the box to make sure everything was as it should be. Horror-music sting as it was revealed, for the first time, that where the sun-dried tomatoes were supposed to be was a standard kind of canned tomato. Uh-oh. "Stop the car. I'll go right back in there and get them to change the tomatoes," I volunteered, bracing for trouble.

"Forget it. It's fucking ruined," he screamed, "it's totally fucking ruined. Why am I always the one who gets fucked?" All the while we were continuing to drive farther from the restaurant.

"Turn the car around and go back there," I said, "it'll only take a second. I can get them to fix it. I know the guy behind the counter."

"It will not take a second. It will take forever," he screamed. "Didn't you see that mob? You are not going back in there. I am just fucked." He stepped on the gas and made the brakes squeal as he angrily drove toward home. He was swearing with rage, railing against that fucking moron Jason who had fucked him over again, probably on purpose. As I always did in such situations, I got very calm. "Well," I suggested, "if you stop at Trader Joe's, I can run in and buy a jar of sun-dried tomatoes, and we can fix it ourselves."

"I am not stopping at no Trader fucking Joe's," he said as we drove past it. "I am just completely fucked, as usual," and he punched the roof of the car. Again. I was very quiet now, as I sat wondering whether I had an alternative other than leaving, wondering if I should pack my things as soon as I got home or wait until he went to bed. And of course my silence only made him angrier. Soon he had his big red face right in mine, screaming at me, wet bullets of spit shooting out of his mouth as he scrolled through the laundry list of all my shortcomings: my crazy fucking mother, how I didn't care about him, only about myself, how I was a cold castrating cunt who didn't respect his needs. The screaming went on and on as we headed up dark and winding Topanga Canyon Boulevard toward the house we were renting. Finally, I said, "If you don't stop screaming at me like this, I am getting out of the car."

He pulled the car over at the next turnout. "You want to get out? Then get out. Be my guest."

Seeing no other card to play, I got out.

"Get back in the fucking car," he screamed at me.

"Not if you keep yelling at me. I can't take any more screaming," I said.

"Get back in the fucking car," he repeated, furious. And when I just stood there, he said, "Fine. Have it your way," and he drove off.

Now I was alone, at about ten at night, on a rural twisty pitch-black section of Topanga Canyon, full of hairpin turns and switchbacks, invisible to the speeding traffic, and miles from anything in either direction. Should I turn around and walk back down to the Pacific Coast Highway? If I did, then what would I do when I got there? Take a bus to Santa Monica and rent a car? Find a hotel room and buy some clothes? I was panicky until I realized that I didn't really need to worry. He would definitely come looking for me. He wouldn't just leave me alone in the dark in Topanga Canyon. It was too dangerous. So I decided to continue walking up the hill toward what is laughingly thought of as downtown Topanga. Maybe a bar in one of the little restaurants would be open. If I even got that far before he returned.

I walked for about two miles on the dark woodsy road. When I finally reached the not-much-business district, everything was closed except for one crowded bar at a seafood place. I took the only seat available, in between two surfer guys drinking tequila shots and a single white-wine-guzzling woman who turned out to work for an airline. I ordered a gin and tonic and stared straight ahead, even after it came. Then I glugged it down in a couple of gulps and ordered another. All the while keeping an eye on the door, because I knew P.E. would soon appear and he would gesture irritably. And when he did, I might just refuse to go with him. Maybe I'd make him sweet-talk me into leaving.

At some point, one of the surfer guys to my left offered to buy me a drink. "You know, it's okay if you take off your jacket and stay awhile," he said with a wink. I nodded pleasantly, refusing both offers, careful not to make eye contact. I was too upset and too uncomfortable to be genial. At some other point, the flight attendant on my right began an endless conversation with me, babbling on about her career and her trouble with men, totally not perceiving my de-

pression or anxiety. But after we exchanged names, she realized something. "I know who you are," she started gushing, "I read all about you. You're Nick Blake's girlfriend!
He's totally adorable and sexy. You are soo lucky!"

By now it was about quarter to twelve, and there was still
no sign of Mr. Totally Adorable. So I hastily called the only
cab service in the area. Thank God I was able to catch the
lone cabdriver before he went home for the night.

When I entered our dark quiet house, the embers of a
recently built fire were still glowing. There was an empty
pizza box on the coffee table in front of the fireplace. Psycho Ex was in the bedroom asleep.

I sat alone in the living room, staring into space, until I
fell asleep in my clothes on the couch. On Monday, when I
went back in to my new job, I told this story to a couple of
people in the office as though it were an amusing and col-
orful anecdote. I remember being a little surprised by how
they all just stared at me with concern.

I eagerly tallied up my scores, trying to duplicate Grant's scoring system. When they only added up to ninety, I went back and
raised a few of them by five extra points, especially the fifteen-
pointer. I wanted to best his top score. A good general doesn't
accept his enemy's limitations.

SCORE	Points
List of my personal shortcomings screamed for hours due to pizza-topping blunder	10
Forced into job rewriting *Clambake* to help relationship	5
While P.E. is thinking that pizza-topping neglect is affront to his dignity	15

Further punished for suggesting that the topping problem was fixable	15
Put in physically dangerous situation because of pizza-topping blunder	20
Having to pay for two drinks in bar alone over same topping blunder	10
And interact with the idiotic drunken babbling flight attendant	5
Who tells me I am lucky	5
While I stare at the door, waiting for P.E. to rescue me	10
Having to pay for a cab ride home	10
Not even getting a piece of the pizza after paying for it	10
Being stupid enough to accept not even getting any kind of apology	15
TOTAL:	130

Well, how do you like that? It looks to me like I am winning. Winning winning winning. If you would like to surrender at this point, I won't think less of you.

Lisa

I pushed "send" and then sat there, amused by my saber rattling. Maybe I was fated to go down in flames, wounded in battle by a junkie, but I would do it defiantly, demanding a recount, never acknowledging defeat. I was only too conscious that the accumulating details about Grant's P.E. seemed to indicate that I was in way over my head. Chances were that her drug addiction came complete with the usual complimentary add-ons that God throws in free, like floor mats when you buy a new sociopath: lying, theft, prostitution, contagious diseases, violent outbursts. She was an embarrassment of riches.

I shored up my confidence by remembering the many world-class bullies who were, in fact, white-collar. I had O. J. Simpson, Robert Blake, and Joan Crawford in my corner. I had Louis XIV, Richard Nixon, the Enron guys, Pablo Picasso. My P.E. was linked to the time-honored grotesqueries committed by people of social rank and accomplishment throughout history. I could at least give that junkie a run for her money.

At six o'clock in the morning, I checked my e-mail again.

Dear Lisa,
I am so sorry. That is a sad story. Over pizza. All about pizza. I have to tell you, I am suspicious of finicky eaters. They look for trouble. What's heartbreaking is how long you believed he would come to get you. Sad. Tragic. Unfair. Inexplicable. Cruel. Unjust. Psychotic. Undeniably unique. A brilliant move, yes. But am I willing to give in? Oh no. Not by a long shot.

Grant

I was beginning to love the way this e-mail thing was offering me an intimate connection to a man, unpoisoned by the vagaries of romance. It was better than an affair. No expectations meant no disappointments. No boyfriend, in my experience, had ever been this communicative or playful.

Sometimes I found myself thinking that it was too bad Grant wasn't single. But in the same breath, I would remember that I was lucky he wasn't. There was no way it could ever have worked out between us. I knew other musicians. The behavior they expected women to deal with amicably was even more brain-scrambling than the murky fluid in the cocktail that was

Nick. Who did you have to be to slough off information about the girls on the road, and the girls off the road, and the rest of the girls who were more or less road-adjacent? It was good that Grant and his behemoth centerfoldlike girlfriend had found each other and were in love. Women who looked like she did were immune to ordinary jealousy. And it was comforting to know that things had worked out well for at least a couple of people. Hopefully, that made my own odds a little better.

> Dear Grant,
> As for your comment of "brilliant move," I don't for one second trust your so-called compliment. Know that what you expect me to do, I definitely will not do. I have every intention of winning this game . . .

I was scrolling through the Internet, looking for war analogies, when my posturing was cut short by the voice of the "You've Got Mail" Irritant.

Chapter 14

LISA

D ear Lisa,

IGNORING THE OBVIOUS

It was summer 1984. I was twenty-nine, and there was a spring in my step. I had just been asked to replace Arvin Petro, the much loved, respected, often imitated, and, according to most, irreplaceable lead singer, lyricist, and front man of Slowly I Turn. It was a suicide mission, but I took it nonetheless.

By doing so, I had just zoomed out of the world of retail rockers. I was no longer a member of that class of musicians who are gonna do, who stay at home making tapes, who mooch along looking for something. I was now signed. I was in a well-known band, and as it was a controversial move, I was controversial. At last the dark days were over. Life was good. Best of all, I was single.

So, there I was with a big Slowly I Turn meeting coming up. I had a few bucks in my pocket, and I decided to treat myself to a haircut and a dye. At around four-thirty I strolled down Melrose Avenue to Zuzu, the place to get a haircut.

Melrose, Melrose, Melrose. Back then it was still a small collection of humble hipster stores that had just moved in and replaced the Jewish middle-class restaurant-supply, dry-cleaning, and plumbing-fixture shops. Rents were low, and its workforce was mainly musicians, a small army of male and female dyed-and-mousse-haired, black-lipstick-wearing Goths, punks, cowpunks, and early glam boys. It was an in-between period. The next big thing hadn't happened yet, and therefore any one of us might be it. The music world seemed alive with excitement and expectation. I recall this period happily now. In my memory, it seems as if the earth had achieved an equilibrium long since lost. Actually, this was the last day before all the unholy shit hit the fan. For the want of a trim, my youth was lost.

She was sphinxlike and stunning, a little older, tough. A thirtyish rocker who was shampooing hair at Zuzu. She looked a little like a starved and sinister Anjelica Huston, if Anjelica Huston had an odd accent and a disarming overbite and had cut her hair into a short blue-black fuzz. She told me she was a singer heading back to Manhattan, where a new band was forming, in a week. As we talked for a while, she mentioned that she was going to a party the next night and asked if I'd like to come.

So the following evening I got dressed up in my finest: a long dove-gray vintage seventies morning coat with a black velvet collar. When the party was a drag, there was nowhere to go but back to my place: a one-room apartment full of beat-up furniture, historical art reproductions, and my Oedipal but fun drawings. At first it was awkward.

"Can I get you some coffee?" I asked her as she looked at me blankly. "Would you care to look at some books on Napoleon? I just got a great new book on furniture from the First Empire." After I offered all available refreshments and literary distractions, she crossed her arms, blinked once or twice, and said abruptly, "Can I use your bathroom?"

"Sure," I said, and then gave her elaborate directions on how to get to the other side of my one-room apartment. "Go all the way to the wall, take a hard right, and then look for the door by the chair."

She walked the three steps to the bathroom and closed the door. While she was gone, I stood there nervously, smoking, fluffing my hair, trying to ignore the usual mysterious girl-in-the-bathroom noises. I heard the faucet turn on, the toilet flush, and the faucet get turned off. She opened the door, stepped out, closed it behind her, and cocked her head to the side. "You're drivin' me fuckin' nuts," she said, walking toward me. "Will you just shut up and kiss me?" We kissed. Then we kissed some more. And then somehow the lights got turned off and marital relations ensued.

During the act, she surprised me. To look at her, I would have expected whips, spit, and even a little blood for spice. But she was surprisingly tender, endearingly affectionate and gentle. True, in bed she was knowing as advertised. But when she climaxed, she wept big hot tears. Then she regained her composure and waved it away, going back into character as tough, inscrutable.

Afterward, as we lay there on my single-bed mattress and naked box springs by candlelight, I noticed something. Her arms were crisscrossed with slash scars and tiger-striped razor slashes all the way up to the elbow and beyond. "What are these?" I asked her.

"These?" she said very casually. "What's it look like? I tried to kill myself."

"Why?" I asked her.

"I dunno," she said offhandedly. "Things were bad. I'll tell ya one thing," she went on wryly as she lit up a cigarette, "it takes a long fuckin' time to die. And it hurts like hell."

She told me the story of how, after she had slashed her wrists and arms, she ran down the hall of her apartment house to the door of her gay Brazilian neighbor. "When he opened the door, there I was, both arms bleeding. When he started to scream, his lover ran in to see what was wrong, saw me, and started to scream too." She laughed. "Then they called an ambulance."

"Those neighbor guys take care of you?" I asked her.

"No," she said, low-key.

"They wait to see if you were okay? Anybody at the hospital? Counseling or anything?"

"No," she said, shaking her head.

"They just stitched you up and sent you home all alone?" I asked her.

"Yep," she said.

I looked at her arms again, and this time I noticed a different type of scar, deep divots on her inner elbows.

"What are these?" I asked her, touching them lightly with my fingertips.

"Heroin," she said, shrugging again. "I finally kicked in January."

"That's good," I said. She nodded, followed by a silence. There was so much to ask. We sat there quietly, smoking. "So you feel okay about going back to New York City? With the drugs and all?"

"Well, they sell heroin here, too," she said.

I'd never met anyone like this before. On top of that she was leaving town and had no one to see her off. Nobody who cared. So I leaned down and kissed her arms, scars and all. And with that Oscar-winning performance, I had sold my soul.

End of story.

SCORE	Points
Faux Christlike gesture	50
Rewarding suicidal impulses with affection	50
Putting lips to junkie scar tissue and junkie abscess wounds without first prepping the area with Phisohex	25
Not calling a taxi and then fumigating the place when she left	50
Not using a condom	100
Assuming that someone sane enough to want to sleep with me could NOT be crazy, despite all evidence to the contrary	100
TOTAL:	375

Dear Grant,

You said we are allowed to challenge points, so I am going to give that rule a trial run. I don't exactly get what moved you to kiss her scars. You were in a rock band and therefore familiar with the world of overdosing musicians. And presumably you are not a drunk or an addict. So why that sort of over-the-top chivalrous reinforcing gesture with regard to a piece of behavior you knew to be not just terrifying but also a very bad sign of things to come?

Dear Lisa,

I look back on my life and am horrified by the number of stupid symbolic acts that I have committed. This, of course, like my big brown eyes and long lashes, I inherited from my mother and father. Nobody knows this, but my folks are two fantastic movie stars, or at least that's how they appeared in our home movies and family photos. Both were great-looking: handsome and beautiful, perfect genes, athletic and graceful, more than well dressed. He was snazzy. She was snazzy. My father popped bennies, goofballs, drove a black Imperial sedan and changed his name from Hank to Henri. He told everyone he was French instead of Lithuanian. The only difference between my folks and movie stars was the incidental fact that they had no actual movie careers and lived two thousand miles away from Hollywood.

To my folks, life was a series of scenes, but, as is often the case when a movie is made, the scenes were not shot in any kind of sequential order. God would take care of all that later in editing. My father might occasionally put his hand on my head and call me "son," but only if the scene was so scripted. Otherwise, he might slap my skull and scream "goddamn kid," if it was a dark seventies drama. Or spin the chamber of a .45 and say "mudduhfuckah," if it was a Mafioso Movie Moment.

I was never admonished if some moral had been defied or rule broken. However, I was slapped, kicked, chided, mocked, or bullied if the dramatic arc of the scene called for it. My father didn't have a conscience, he had an inner director. There's a story where Good Coach Repka is pounding his fist on the roof of his car, crying "They're arresting my kid! They're arresting my kid!" A neighbor is saying "Easy, Hank." Even though the truth was, nobody had to arrest me. I hadn't done anything. Some neighbor had called the cops because she'd seen teenage boys standing around, lurking and smoking. The cops showed up and Coach Repka was notified. Fearing that the moment where he had to actually witness his son being dragged off to jail might never be written, his inner director advised him to "go off book." So he improvised the scene for the cops, the neighbors, my mother, and myself, who stood there agog if not aghast. Cue the music and exit. That's a wrap! Lunch!

It's a proven fact that under battlefield conditions, without thinking, we act like our parents. When facing a difficult moment, some of us drink, like our moms. Some of us get in the Volvo and flee our troubles at ninety mph, like their Dad. Me? I was trained to look for the right dramatic tone and the biggest socko ending. "When confronted by something that ignites a strong emotional reaction, son, don't do what is right, do what plays." So you see, Lisa, at that moment where Jane's arms were first revealed to me in the light, my inner director stepped in to prep me.

"Grant, in this scene, you have just made love by candlelight to a rock veteran like yourself. She is about to start a new life, this time drug-free. She faces New York City alone, older, impoverished, sober, vulnerable. Only selfless love can heal her. You will never see this mysterious stranger again . . . Moved, you kiss her scars. And . . . action!"

Mind you, somewhere in all this, an honest, dissatisfied persona was able to form and break off. This clump, this dermoid cyst, developed into the clod writing you now. This relatively sane side of me was the part that would watch his parents' dailies and yell, "This movie stinks."

Grant

After digesting Grant's scar-kissing epic, I thought to counterattack with the story of meeting Nick. But next to heroin addiction and attempted suicide, it all seemed a little pale. Nick and I met at a job interview in an agent's office. As I walked in, wearing my usual job-interview uniform of a T-shirt, a short skirt, a sport coat, and boots, I walked past Nick on his way out. He was dressed in his usual uniform of black jeans and a vintage bowling shirt that came to his knees. What I remembered most were his intensely focused light blue eyes. And of course his sly grin. He was shorter than I was by a couple of inches and about twenty-five pounds too heavy, but something about his mischievous, confident expression made even extra weight look appealing. After Nick left, the rodentlike agent, who had about him that too-slick-too-oily thing that always makes me wonder who he would be in the regular world (a Porsche salesman? A maître d' at a steak house?), talked Nick up enthusiastically. He had been a child actor since the sixth grade, but by high school he was almost washed up, getting only little parts in movies and on TV, playing surfer dudes or dumb frat boys. So he had gone back to college, gotten a film-school diploma, and now was starting to make a name for himself as a hyphenate: an actor who developed and directed his own projects. He was going to be hot, said the agent.

As I drove home, for some odd reason, I kept thinking about Nick's smile. There was something about that playful grin that had made him seem immediately familiar to me. Years later, I figured it out. My father, a man with the interpersonal skills of a carjacker, had that same sweet, self-effacing grin. And Nick's vibe, the essence that drew me to him instantly, was almost identical to the one that had pulled me toward my dog Juicy when I picked him out of a cluster of dogs at the pound. As the other dogs were barking and jumping up against the chain-link fence, Juicy remained near the back, his tail barely wagging. He broke my heart by staring intently with a sad, sweet, self-effacing expression, as if to say, "I hate to bother you, but if it's not too much trouble, before they put me to

death, I think you should know that I love you very much."
And lo and behold, those sweet sad eyes that reminded me of
my dad's masked a homicidal rage against members of his own
species. My instincts had led me to rescue the one dog in the
pen who was offering me nothing except my own fantasies
about being needed.

The more thought I gave this story, the more I decided I
might as well fight the battle of the early-warning signs with
Grant on his own turf.

> Dear Grant,
>
> Okay. I think I understand. You can keep your 100 points
> for chivalry.
>
> It's an interesting coincidence that your parents were
> imaginary movie stars, because, oddly enough, mine were
> imaginary movie producers. The Robertys were primarily
> preoccupied with exercising script approval over the movie
> in which I was starring. They were also doing everything
> they could to keep it from being released until they got a
> page-one rewrite, because not only didn't they understand
> the plot, they had big problems with the casting and thought
> the wardrobe was awful and the hair and makeup even
> worse. All of which is just camouflage for the fact that now
> I return your attack.

MORE EARLY-WARNING SIGNS UNHEEDED

I met Nick outside an agent's office, where we both went for
a job interview. Neither one of us got the job, but not too
long after that, he phoned me. He'd gotten my number from
the folks who were doing the hiring. I couldn't tell if his motive was friendship or networking. Nevertheless, we had a
long pleasant conversation during which he told me all
about his many girlfriends in other cities. One wanted to

move in with him, one wanted to get married. I didn't think too much about it, because after all Nick and I weren't dating. The more I talked to him, the less I thought he was my type. However, pretty soon he was calling every night and making me laugh. I found myself looking forward to talking to him. About a month into all this, we decided to get together, though it still wasn't defined as a date. He said he would come pick me up and take me to lunch after his ten-thirty meeting. So I got all dressed up and then sat watching the clock as it turned one, then two, then two-thirty, then three. By the time it had turned three-fifteen I was concerned that maybe I had heard him wrong. By three-thirty, I was living my life in five-minute increments, each with its own individual panicky explanation. What had I not heard him say? Or had a catastrophe befallen him? Was it possible he had fallen off a ladder and severed his spinal cord? Was he somewhere writhing in agony, waiting for me to call for help? By five, I was willing to shoulder all the blame for having screwed up everything. It had happened before with female friends, but we always forgave each other. By six, I had given up and was on my way to the gym when the phone rang. It was Nick, sounding very humble, insecure, and apologetic. "I'm so sorry," he said. "The meeting just kept going and going. They ordered in lunch, but I didn't eat. I thought I would leave any minute. When they told me it was five-thirty, I totally freaked. I had no clue. I was really looking forward to having lunch with you."

"No, no, it's fine," I said. "These things happen. I'm just glad you're okay. I was kind of worried."

"Can we please reschedule? You know, I'd come over now, but I'm not sure you still want me to."

"Well, sure. Come on over, if you still feel like it," I replied, since I had no plans for the evening except working out.

"You're sure it's not too inconvenient?" Nick said. "If I leave right now, I can be there by quarter to seven, although I would understand if you'd just rather do it some other time."

He got there at eight-fifteen, a mere seven hours after he said he would. By then I had taken a second shower, changed clothes a third time, and started completely over again on my hair and makeup. Looking back, I wonder why I wasn't more pissed off when it turned out he had no actual excuse for not calling to say he was running late. But this was part of the genius of Nick. He had this way of seeming like an overwhelmed little boy whose utterly pure intentions had been hijacked by unfortunate circumstances. He and my mother both were great at repositioning a completely selfish act so they appeared to be its victim.

Then again, maybe it was all connected to the reason I found it so amusing when he walked into my house for the first time, walked over to my action-figure collection, and said, "Nice place you have here. But you know what it needs? A little more cheap plastic crap." Then he sat down on my couch, stretched out, and said, "Ah. Lovely couch. What's in these cushions? Ball bearings?"

"No," I said, laughing, but feeling my face redden and my stomach tighten from embarrassment. "The package said human teeth."

He barely acknowledged my joke.

Over the years, I've often thought about that moment. How I kind of liked it when he insulted my house. Since I'd grown up in a family where tactless remarks and insults were explained away as expressions of care and concern, an attack felt like an indication that he was both onto me and one step ahead of me. He could see through my bullshit, and cared enough to know I should be ridiculed. Had he arrived ten minutes early and told me how lovely everything looked, the crazy truth is that I might not have liked him nearly as much.

He ended up taking me to a loud greasy coffee shop on Van Nuys Boulevard, where we shouted at each other over the cacophony of a wall of pinball machines. P.E. loved that kind of diner, populated by irritable employees and full of Formica tabletops so coated in hardened condiments that my silk blouse stuck to it when I leaned on my arm. After our waitress delivered our food, Nick looked at me, smiled, and said, "She hates us."

The weirdest thing of all was that we had a very nice time. I remember coming back from the ladies' room and seeing Nick alone at our table. I was so enamored, I thought he glowed like an angel.

I was mesmerized by the hurt but sweet little kid I could see on his face when he smiled. The words he spoke were anything but sweet. "Over there. The woman at the table by the window who looks like a stuffed pork roast with shoes . . . look at her inhaling those chili fries like she thinks her extra two hundred pounds are water retention." Still, that sad little boy I saw in him killed me.

We sat for a couple of hours, drinking beer, sniping at people. Later, it occurred to me that though we had talked and talked, he never asked me any questions. I think I kind of liked that he was so preoccupied with himself, because it let me off the hook. If he was focused on his own craziness, he might not have the time to notice or criticize mine.

The evening ended awkwardly. We left at about eleven o'clock, and when he pulled into my driveway, he patted me on the arm and said, "Well, good seeing you, kiddo. Have a nice week." Kiddo? Have a nice week? So I shouldn't expect to hear from him? Why not? Was there something I missed?

Turned out, he did call, the very next night. And the night after that. He would always end his calls by saying that he "might drop by later." Because I was eager to see him, I would hold the evening open. I would find myself sitting there for hours, only to hear at one A.M. that it looked like he couldn't make it, after all. Finally, the following Sunday at two A.M., just as I had abandoned all hope, he showed up. I still didn't know if this was dating or just pals hanging out. We sat up all night, talking, and drinking beer, and at about six A.M., when he got up to leave, I was drunk and in the throes of a big crush. "Do you want to spend the night?," I heard myself blurt out. He replied, "I think I already did." He was standing in my doorway with his arms dangling like they were attached by rubber bands. I went over to hug him, but he didn't hug back. My face went hot with embarrassment. Had I breached the boundaries of our friendship? Which was when he said, "Well, I'd like to stay, but I don't know if you really want me to."

"Of course I do," I said emphatically, having no idea if I did. But I didn't feel it was polite to back out at this point, despite the complete absence of sexual or even personal chemistry between us. The excruciatingly slow walk to the bedroom that followed was like a walk to the gas chamber. No one said a word. What is this mission I am on to screw every cold and distant man in the world? I was thinking as we lay down on my bed. Take me now, God, and open up a space on the planet for someone with a tiny shred of sense. Which is when, magically, everything changed. Suddenly Psycho Ex was wonderful, vulnerable, even emotional. And in a single instant, I changed from one kind of victim to another. Now I was overcome by love. Now I was overwhelmed and terrified, adrift without moorings. P.E. was so brilliant, so desirable, so incredible, so handsome and sexy. He could have anyone. What did he want with me?

SCORE	Points
Knowing about several significant women being fucked over ahead of me in line from get-go	25
And buying Nick as the confused innocent victim of this situation	25
Trying to help him feel comfortable about having stood me up for hours on first date	50
Then not going to the gym in order to stay home and continue waiting	25
While buying Nick's show of humility as a cover for arrogance	50
And finding comfort and security in being insulted	25
Turned on by the fact that he exhibited no interest in me	25
Ruined silk blouse	25
Trying to have appealing flirtatious conversation over pinball machines	25
Liking the idea that he was so preoccupied with his own craziness, he might not have the time to criticize me	25
"Have a nice week"	25
Unreturned hug at door but still asking him to spend the night	125

Going from one kind of terrifying delusion to another in seconds, by now believing in the

cloud of ecstasy I was feeling, only to immediately
punish myself for not deserving even a cloud of
ecstasy   150

TOTAL: 600
NEW TOTALS: Grant 500   Lisa 730

Chapter 15

LISA

B y the time I got up and took a shower, it was seven in the morning. I'd been sitting in front of the computer for two hours, focusing and refocusing my stories with an eye toward trying to accumulate the highest number of awful details and therefore points. As I did, I kept seeing Nick across the room from me, stretched out on the floor, legs arched up the wall, glaring at me with one raised eyebrow, chewing gum, as always. "You sell me down the river for a chance to flirt with some rock fuck in Silver Lake?" he was taunting me. "Where in this stupid game do we hear *my* side of the story? As usual, I'm the asshole. You're the queen. I'm the Psycho Ex, but you're just perfect. Just like your fucking mother."

I got up and made myself an English muffin.

When the clock said nine o'clock, I picked up the phone and called my friend Kat.

"What's up?" I said, when what I really wanted was for her to ask that of me. "How's it going with Jake?" I had a pretty good idea that what was up with her and Jake was a deep, monumental love, etched in the sands of time and written upon the wind. But no. I had guessed correctly about Jake at the Empire. He had been replaced already with Miguel, an amazing percussionist, a genius who made his own instruments out of everything from hubcaps and Rubbermaid dish racks to Tupperware containers and saw blades. Divorced for only a month, and currently living in his van, he was, she said, "magical and brilliant."

"Well, be careful," I said, knowing that would never happen. Finally, she said the words I longed to hear: "What's going on with you, honey?"

"Did I tell you about my correspondence with Grant Repka?" I said.

"Grant Repka? What do you mean, 'correspondence'?"

"Well, e-mail. We write to each other four and five times a day."

"Honey! You're having Internet sex with Grant Repka?" she gasped.

"No. Not sex. Not sexual in any way. In fact, any mention of marital relations is forbidden by the rules."

"Marital relations? What do you mean? What rules?"

"We've been playing a game to see who's had the more hideous love life. Grant laid out some rules when we started," I said.

"What does whoosywhats-the-girlfriend think of all this?" she asked.

"Well, I don't know. My guess is she doesn't care," I said. "Though I don't really know. Who the fuck knows what goes on around there."

"We're all better off not knowing, I think," said Kat.

"Anyway, I think we're becoming good friends. He's very open with me. His stories are full of all kinds of personal details."

"Like what? I always wondered about him. Tell me, tell me," she said.

"Well, I don't think I can," I said. "One of our rules is 'not for public consumption.' So I'm not saying anything, and I assume neither is he. But you know what's the part of it all that amazes me? The way he asks me questions. He actually listens. And the fact that he listens makes this one of the most personal relationships I've ever had."

"Okay, can I say something here? First of all, honey, he isn't listening. He's reading. There might be an hour, a fuck, and a full meal in between sentences. And a word of caution," she said. "Everybody knows e-mail is deceptive. It gives the impression of intimacy where none exists. Remember that glassblower I met online? We had this incredibly close relationship until we spent time together. You trot out the good stuff when you write an e-mail."

"Well, yours was online dating," I said. "This is more of a literary thing. Like Anaïs Nin and Albert Camus or Henry Miller or Jean-Paul Sartre, or whoever it was she wrote to. Not that I think Grant Repka is Jean-Paul Sartre. And not that I really know anything about Anaïs Nin. She was the diaries, right?"

"Honey," said Kat, "Anaïs Nin was a slut."

"Then I'm probably thinking of Colette," I said.

"She was a slut, too," said Kat.

"Then Eleanor Roosevelt. She must have written some letters."

"One biography called her a lesbian, but no one ever called her a slut," Kat said, "I'll give you that. Just don't get all wrapped up in e-mail. You need to save some of that energy for going out and meeting three-dimensional people."

"I don't think I'm tapping out those precious energy re-

serves. A great deal of this correspondence takes place at four
A.M.," I said. "I don't generally meet that many new people at
four A.M."

"Honey, I'm just saying that sometimes when you get comfy
with an e-mail thing, it's nothing but an empty shell. It's air. It's
not anything, really," said Kat. "At least, that's what happened
to me."

"Okay. I will bear that in mind next time it seems remotely
applicable," I said, realizing with a little disappointment that
Kat had nailed it. My plans for tonight, in fact, were to wait
around for new e-mail. "What are you doing this evening?" I
asked her.

"Well, we're going to the Empire to see Randy Randall's
Rock Filibuster," she said. "Miguel wanted to go, so I got us on
the list. It's pretty great. You wanna join us?"

"Yes," I was surprised to hear myself say. Fuck this e-mail
shit, I thought. I need to have a life that involves three dimensions. If only to accumulate fresh anecdotes for future e-mails.

"Okay, we'll be there at ten," said Kat, "and we'll save you a
seat."

And so it came to pass that I again agreed to go out at nine
o'clock at night, an hour after I wanted to be in bed reading.
Oh, I am not claiming that the whole drive in I didn't berate
myself for being an idiot. But I thought, Kat is right. Sitting at
a computer waiting for e-mail is a pretty hollow pursuit. I also
knew that I wouldn't get any more e-mails until about three in
the morning. I would be home by then.

I was one of the last to arrive at Randy Randall's Rock Filibuster. Randy Randall was legendary. "A musician's musician.
Like a snowflake, every show is different. And like a Christmas
present, the fun is that you never know what you're going to
get," said the big blow-up of the *L.A. Times* review in the front
window. As the audience member's audience member, I was
pumped.

To my amazement and delight, as soon as I walked into the dark, crowded room, Sylvia, the club owner, recognized me and escorted me to where Kat and her new one true love, Miguel, were awaiting my presence.

"You're going to love Randy R.," Sylvia said to me with such warmth that I felt very honored to think she saw me as that kind of person. She seemed so hip, so connected, so powerful in her world that when she spoke to me, I felt like I had been knighted. "Bobby Snuggs is almost done," she went on, referring to a slight guy in his mid-twenties in a Weezer shirt and cargo pants who was at the mike doing stand-up. His act seemed to consist mainly of other people's overused and now unfunny comedy clichés, repackaged as ironically hilarious because of their very lack of humor. Much less risky to be intentionally unfunny than accidentally unfunny, I thought, surveying the well-dressed young and middle-aged crowd before the club went dark for a few minutes. The appetizer portion of the evening's entertainment was clearing out while the entrée was being readied.

A handsome, angular, long-haired guy with a gray forelock, wearing a long dark trench coat and a purple scarf, pulled a chair up to our table. He was missing part of his left eyebrow, which I thought looked rather dashing. "Lisa, you remember my friend Ethan?" said Kat. "He used to play bass for me. And this, of course, is Miguel." She gestured toward the man around whose neck she was now hanging: also handsome, also fortyish, which was old for Kat. My impression was that he was a little too serious, too self-important in his faded denim, leather, and braids. When he and Ethan stepped outside to have a cigarette, Kat looked at me with eyes full of love beams. I gave him another month, tops.

And then out onto the stage came Sylvia to introduce the pièce de résistance. "Ladies and gentlemen, it's a dark night out," she mumbled cryptically. As theatrical-looking as she was, onstage she became shy and seemed to vanish. "Here is your Rock Filibuster, with Randy Randall!" Before I could unravel what she meant by "dark night," on came the plumhaired Randy R., in a shiny green-tinted sport coat. He took the stage alone, saying nothing, his back turned to the crowd, and began to play a series of shifting tones on an electric dulcimer. Sometimes he pressed a device to make patterns that sounded like "Furshwanga wanga wanga wanga" repeated endlessly.

I heard someone at a table up ahead yell, "Yeah!," and that triggered a scattered round of applause. "Yeah? Yeah what?" I wanted to shout as I scanned the stage, which was littered with a group of electric instruments. Assuming he was going to play them all, I figured we were in for a long night. Settling into my chair, I ordered another beer as Randy R., with his back still turned, picked up an electric guitar. He proceeded to layer a bluesy riff that sang "Badoinga bee badoinga bee" over the aforementioned "Furshwanga wanga." Soon, "Boodle am fah fah voo" joined the other musical onomatopoeias as Randy, smiling blissfully, began to crank a tiny music box, his eyes glittering with inspiration. The crowd purred with a murmur of approval. I was good and fucking lost.

I looked at my watch. Randy Randall had been going for an hour and fifteen minutes, and still not a melody in sight. Finally there was silence. And then the crowd stood and cheered. Peer pressure and a desire for aerobic exercise caused me to join them. This music made me feel like I did the day I laid off marijuana forever because I felt like I had entered a time warp where a minute and an hour were the same thing. Well, okay, I thought. Not my cup of tea. But fine. It's over.

Which was when, to my grave disappointment, Sylvia walked back onstage. She had made a costume change and was wearing a different coat. "Randy's gonna take a quick break. Stick around for the second half . . . we got some great guests," she said. I felt every cell in my body droop. "There's more?" I blurted. Miguel looked at me and said, "Of course there's more. You know he's improvising, right? Making it all up as he goes along?"

"I know what improvising is," I said, revising his Kat-love timetable downward to two weeks, tops.

Okay. So I was a music moron. All I knew was I needed to go home. I was seconds from leaving when Sylvia, happy and beaming, sat down at our table. I wondered how deep her relationship with Randy Randall really went. Was she in love with him, or was this just the giddiness of a fan?

"He started rough, but he saved it. He was having a tough night. He's at war with his label," Sylvia explained as Kat and Miguel commiserated. I nodded empathetically as I reviewed my excuses: toothache? Deadline? A sick dog?

"What are you drinking?" Sylvia asked me, as the bartender brought her a tumbler full of Scotch.

"She's drinking beer," said Ethan, nursing an unlit cigarette.

"Done," said Sylvia, calling to the bartender. "Next round on the house. I'm glad you folks are having a good time. It's nice to have you all here."

"Thank you," I said, politely accepting a beer I did not need. "You run a great club. I loved the *Tommy! (Lee!)* musical the other night."

"Oh yes," she said. "Grant's really found his voice. I'm so proud of him. I mean, he was always a good writer, but . . ."

"I know. We've been having a lot of fun e-mailing," I said, thrilled to have something seemingly relevant to add.

"You and Grant are e-mailing?" Sylvia asked, eyebrows raised.

"Look at her face. You can see she's got a crush," Kat teased, while massaging Miguel's beefy neck and shoulders. "Even though her good friend Kat already warned her that he's not available."

"Ah. Yes. I can see what you mean," said Miguel, who had never laid eyes on me before tonight.

"Will you two knock it off?" I said, looking over at Ethan to see if this was turning him off and noticing, with some delight, that he seemed to be intrigued.

Enjoying the tease, Kat continued to needle. "I keep telling her, 'You're wasting your time, honey. Grant's taken. He's spoken for.' But Ethan's not."

"Stop it," I said, first embarrassed, then pleased, because Ethan grinned playfully. I wondered if I could get him to leave with me.

"Grant and Winnie are a great team," said Sylvia, getting up from our table and looking around. "They're usually here tonight. Might still come by later." She looked to the back of the room. "Oh Jesus, Randy wants to go back on. Stick around. This is just getting started." She rose from our table, gave a little nod, and disappeared into the kitchen. A minute later, Randy and Bobby Snuggs got back onstage, took the mike, and began singing "I Dream of Jeannie with the Light Brown Hair."

That was it. I wasn't in the mood to try to find anything else ironically funny. "I'm so sorry," I said to the group, "but my dog Juicy has been sick." Everyone nodded and muttered in sympathy. Before I left I made the usual arrangements to have dinner with Kat that she would completely forget. And as I gathered my things, Ethan gave me a shy smile. "I don't blame you. I'd leave, too, if Sylvia wouldn't kill me," he whispered.

He's cute, I thought. There must be something wrong with him. Then, pretending to head for the restroom, I sneaked out the back entrance, thrilled to be leaving the musician's musician to the musicians.

Chapter 16

GRANT

There was nobody in the alley behind the Empire. This meant something was cooking inside. I pulled open the back door for Winnie. We were part of the Empire's A list, and letting yourself in free through the kitchen was one of the perks. We said hello to Edgar, the dishwasher, waved to the cooks, and peeked through the window into the club. Sylvia saw me and burst in. "Ya gotta come see this!" So we nestled in the back by the sound booth, shoulder to shoulder with a klatch of comics who guffawed conspiratorially. Onstage was Bobby Snuggs, singing Stephen Foster's "Jeannie with the Light Brown Hair" as though it were a funeral dirge, accompanied by Randy Randall on the harmonium. Bobby was mocking Jeannie, his ex-girlfriend who had not only dumped him but was already living with another comedian. Jeannie had been on the A list when we first started playing there. Recently, Sylvia had informed us that Jeannie was driving Bobby crazy. Bit by bit, people stepped back from her. Some sort of silent club order had gone out. Then the fix was in. Jeannie was politely ignored out of the club. There was a price to be paid for back-door privileges.

I got a Coke and whispered hello to the barman as Snuggs finished to a big hand. He was the darling now, the undisputed comedy master of the Empire.

"I love Randy's jacket, Winnie," said Sylvia.

"Thank you," Winnie answered. I beamed. Randy had asked Winn to assist him in upgrading his T-shirt-and-tennis-shoe-packed wardrobe. Tonight he was wearing a vintage lime-green silk double-breasted sixties jacket off Carnaby Street that Winnie had originally bought for me.

"Yeah," Winnie chided, "Grant pussed out on the color."

Sylvia giggled and elbowed me. "Your loss, Grant," she said. "Randy's got you beat tonight."

Before I could think of a comeback, Randy surprised us all by calling Kat to the stage. I perked up. I didn't even know Kat was in town.

Randy moved over to the mellotron. The eerie warped bowing of long-dead violinists filled the club with a haunting familiar melody. The crowd applauded, catching it before I did. Randy was playing Kat's 1986 new-wave hit, "Flight Grounded." Only Randy played it slow and somber as Kat sauntered up to join him. The quirky new-wave words took on a new meaning as the nagging playground melody turned mournful, exposing the lyrics for what they always were: the scattered confused thoughts of a woman about to break down. Eighty-six, she was top of the world. Eighty-seven, a breakdown and suicide attempts. Eighty-eight, vanished. I hated this song eighteen years ago. Now it was stunning. It was for moments like these that we came to Randy's nights.

I applauded, then answered the call of another cig. Out in back, Winnie and I joined a clot of comics who were clustered around Bobby Snuggs, listening to him riff on his breakup. I slipped my arm around Winnie, as I smoked and chuckled at their banter. Then the back door flew open, and there stood Sylvia with an uncharacteristic scowl on her face. "Hey," she said, "these people onstage come out to *your* shows. Get in there and give your friends some goddamn support." The comedians sheepishly filed back into the club. Winnie and I were the last ones back in.

"Sorry," I said to Sylvia.

"Ah, forget it," she said as soon as the others were out of earshot. "Those fucking comedians. All they care about is their eight minutes onstage."

"Is Kat still up?" I asked her.

"Oh yeah. She's doing fucking great. You know who she came here with tonight? Lisa Roberty!"

"Really? Lisa's here?" I said.

"No, she skedaddled the second you two walked in." She shook her head and grinned. "She's a little nuts. Nice harmless nuts, but nuts nonetheless. You wanna hear something hilarious? She was going on and on about Grant and her e-mailing." She giggled mischeviously.

"Sylvia, it's a harmless correspondence," I said, seeing where she was going.

Sylvia looked at Winnie. "Yeah. Whatever, Grant," she said, rolling her eyes. "Maybe to you. But Kat told me Lisa's crazy about you." Sylvia was clearly enjoying this. "Kat said she tells her over and over that you've got a girlfriend, but she refuses to listen. She just keeps saying, 'I know . . . I know.' " Sylvia ham-acted a woman in painful denial.

Winnie shrugged, knowing better than to fall for the bait. "Of course she has a crush on him. He's hot. Everybody's got a crush on Grant," she said, locking eyes with Sylvia.

"Well, the pickings are pretty slim here on a Thursday night." Sylvia laughed and went back into the bar.

Later, as Winnie pulled the car out of the lot, I asked for her thoughts on the Lisa Love Bomb that Sylvia had dropped. "Probably some of it's true," said Winnie. "But you know how Sylvia is. She loves to stick the knife in. She takes a grain of truth and elaborates on it."

"Like *The National Enquirer*," I said. "I loved you throwing it back in her face like that." I laughed.

"Yeah, but she didn't even blink," said Winnie. "She's too good."

"Suggesting that Sylvia has a crush on me. Man! You've got balls of brass. But you gotta be really careful. You don't want to light that powder keg." I waited a beat, lighting another cig. "And what about that grain of truth? You think Lisa's a problem?"

"Well, sure, Grant. She's in her, ahem, middle years. She's alone, and along comes this dashing rocker who's good with words and who listens to her every secret. I told you this would happen."

"Yeah, but I haven't encouraged it."

"You have. By always being there for her."

"Oh, come on! We're playing a game! You've read all this stuff."

"Grant. She's creating a little world for you two where I don't belong. Just like Claudia did. You play along because you like to be needed by needy fucking people."

"I am playing a game, Winnie," I stressed defensively, "with your permission and supervision. A game that wasn't causing any problems until awhile ago when Sylvia put the boot in."

"Right," she said, even hotter. "Exactly! And now Sylvia

knows all about a correspondence between my man and another woman. Wonderful! So now Sylvia has a rock to throw at me. Lovely! And who gave that rock to her? Who, Grant? Your good friend Lisa Roberty."

"I'm sure she didn't do it on purpose," I said.

"No. I'm sure she didn't," Winnie said. "I'm sure good old Lisa just blundered and stumbled into it like every fucking thing she does. So right now, as we drive away, everyone within earshot of Sylvia is being told that there's something brewing between you and Lisa Roberty. That I'm standing by helplessly and letting it happen. They'll all chew it up and pass it around and come up with their own nasty conclusions. It's the Empire way, Grant."

"Aw come on, Winnie. Sylvia talks shit about everybody."

Winnie was going fifty in a thirty-five zone when she suddenly swung the car, nearly fishtailing it into another. With a lunge and a lurch, she pulled it over to the side of the road, slammed it into park, stomped on the emergency brake, and turned to me.

"Do you fucking know what goes on there?" Winnie screamed. "No! Because I don't fucking tell you, Grant. You say, 'Don't tell me who's out in the crowd. I don't want to think about it during the show.' So I don't tell you that the head of Universal's live events and five Paramount bigwigs and every fucking record company in town is out there. And the *Weekly*, the *Times*, and some snot from *The New Yorker*." I tried to interject, but she continued charging. "And each one of these people wants a table, so I finesse this weeks in fucking advance with Sylvia. On top of getting everyone's costumes, on top of arranging rehearsals around fifteen different schedules, on top of everyone in the cast wanting a table for Mom and Dad and a party of sixteen, and getting the posters and programs printed and dealing with your manager. I'm a fucking wreck by the day of the show. But instead of sitting upstairs and putting on my costume and focusing on the show like everybody else, I've got to go down there a half hour before showtime to find that Sylvia has told the Universal people they're not on the guest list. Or she's stuck the Warner Bros. people next to the john, or given away Capitol's table. The other night I double-checked with Sylvia to make sure TriStar had a table. Yet there was none when the doors opened! Do you know who got it? Pat Rogers Andelman from New Line, because he's someone Sylvia wants to fuck. She wants all the suits going through her, not me. And I have to stand there and play footsie with Sylvia—not challenge her in front of these people—or she'll change tactics and screw us somewhere else. Do you have any idea how many people are pissed off by the end of the show?"

She was getting hysterical. Loud, real loud. "And Sylvia wants some shit to smear on me just to discredit me a little so she can be the big points person, the hub of everything, and your good fucking buddy Lisa Roberty walks up and says, 'Duhhh, hey, here, rub this all over Winnie.' I wish that cunt would have kept her big fucking mouth shut. Sylvia never had anything on me. Now she does."

"So, I'll stop writing . . . what the fuck. It's not worth it."

"It's too late, Grant," she said, "way too late. Write her. Play the Psycho Ex Game, or she'll go crying to Kat and Kat'll tell Sylvia and Sylvia'll tell everyone. One way I'm an idiot who's letting it happen; the other, I stopped it because I'm threatened. Either way I look stupid, and that's what Sylvia wants. 'Discredit Winnie. Divide Winnie and Grant.' Everyone wants your play, Grant, and I'm the bimbo standing in the way."

"Winn, I'll write and tell her I ain't got the time. I really don't. I'll stop it. Winnie, I am so sorry. I had no idea any of this was going on."

Winnie looked out the window. After a few blinks she said,

"No. You didn't do anything. I want you to keep writing her. I don't want to give Sylvia the satisfaction of having made me a paranoid wreck. Play the fucking stupid Psycho Ex Game."

I insisted that I would put an end to it, but she dismissed me with a wave, asking for a cigarette, signaling for a truce. It was just as well. The truth was I couldn't stop writing this stuff. Soon after the game began in earnest, I found I was accompanied by a voice, ceaseless and barely above a whisper, like news radio muttering low in the apartment next door. Independent of my own conscious thoughts, it formed silent words on the tip of my tongue, like the whispering of a rosary where the seconds of my life were thumbed and described. I could feel its delight as it conjured memories both epic and inconsequential, dissecting and then transforming them from raw sensation into paragraphs. And although this seemed new to me, I had a sense that this voice had always existed, dictating to itself, charting the maps of my journey so far.

Now, just how in the hell was I supposed to explain that to Winnie? She'd only shrug it off as so much Ren Faire–type hokum.

So I kept quiet as we sat on the side of Sunset Boulevard for a long time. She settled down and I settled down.

"What should I do?" I asked.

"Well, just let Sylvia have her fun. She'll find someone else to pick on soon. She usually hits and runs."

"Okay, but what about Lisa?" We lit more cigs. It was nice. I liked sitting in cars late at night with her.

"Write her less," she said.

Chapter 17

LISA

Dear Lisa,
Last night I thought the following:
You had a tale of old ladies on the beach. I had one of old people in the next apartment. Two stories that had a link, no matter how small, about the workings of two nuts in two different psycho wards.

How alike were they, really? How much did your P.E. have in common with mine? Like dream images, what are the collective symbols in these two nightmares?

See if you can do anything with this new variation.

MATCH GAME P.E.
Roger and Judy (some incidental shit from the worst year of my life)

Psycho Ex was working as a bartender at a strip club. She complained that I never took an interest in her friends. So she arranged for us to have dinner at the home of Roger and Judy. Judy was a stripper and a junkie. They were pals.

We went to their converted garage and sat down to dinner. Roger, who earned extra cash by testing new drugs from illicit labs, ate dinner with his hands. There was a lot of rice. It was messy.

Judy had twin three-year-old girls. They were anger-filled monster children who behaved a lot like Patty Duke in *The Miracle Worker.* Thwarted over some trifle, the kids would throw tantrums and scream till they were purple and gasping for breath. Roger and Judy just looked at the kids, shrugged, smiled, and said nothing. At last Judy piped up, "You know, I know I should correct them, but then I think, Look at the mess I've made of my life. Who am I to tell them what to do?"

Later, P.E. took me aside and said, "Roger was trying to impress you, because he knows you've been around the world, and so he was eating with his hands because that's what they do in India."

Roger drove us home. But not before taking P.E. and Judy down a dark street in a dangerous part of town to score drugs. Now that the gals were carrying heroin, Roger floored his beater and we hit Sunset Boulevard at fifty. While I gripped my knees, Roger entertained us with the details of the chemical compounds and thrilling psychological distortions of the new drug he was testing. "Whoa, I'm pretty toasted," he said, after realizing he'd just run another red light.

MATCH MY SCORE

	Points
Enduring awful friends	75
Eating rice with hands	50
Screaming purple brats	75
Feebleminded, frightening statement made by parent	150
Hubby testing new covert drugs as day gig	100
And then driving the car	100
At 50 mph on populated surface streets and running red lights	200
To score drugs in a slum	100
TOTAL:	850

Dear Grant,
I love the P.E. Match Game. I already have the perfect entry.

MY PSYCHO DINNER WITH P.E. FRIENDS

Psycho Ex and I didn't really have many friends, apart from the posse of folks he always puts in his movies, because, like every good narcissist/borderline, he found almost everyone too annoying or threatening. However, there were a couple of cretins he liked to hang out with that he'd known since junior high. To briefly acquaint you with the cast, they included Fred, an unemployed golf pro/actor who was usually on Quaaludes, and Sam, a security guard who had such bad obsessive-compulsive disorder that he had to turn his wallet over ten times in a row before he could pay for anything. Rounding out this mutant trio was

Roy, a dermatologist who'd been arrested a couple of times for shoplifting car parts.

On the occasion that I am going to tell you about, Fred's long-suffering wife, Charlene, invited us all out for a little birthday party she was throwing herself at her favorite restaurant. Charlene had a very bad eating disorder and was constantly enrolling in programs to help control her bulimia. But in honor of her birthday, and much to the displeasure of the restaurant, she brought a large cauldron of three-cheese lasagna and another one of bread pudding that she had made at home. She felt these dishes were too fattening for her to eat. So she asked for seven plates and doled us each a large portion, requesting that we describe the deliciousness of eating her cooking. This was her birthday present to herself.

From the moment we sat down, I could hear the buzz, buzz, buzz of "Nick Blake, Nick Blake" being whispered under people's breath like the sound of circling mosquitoes. It was only a matter of time until someone holding an envelope or a menu or an item of clothing, on which they wanted a signature, would appear to say, "I'm sorry. I don't mean to interrupt you . . ." Which always struck me as ironic, since that was precisely what they did mean to do. Dining out with Nick was a nerve-racking two-edged sword. If no one came over, that signified to Nick that his career was over. But if they did, they might say the wrong thing and upset the ecosystem.

Sensing Nick's growing angst, Sam decided to distract and cheer Psycho Ex the way he always used to back in junior high . . . by taking off his shoes and socks, putting his bare feet up on the table, then making loud rhinoceroslike snorting noises. This made P.E. and Roy laugh so hard they could barely sit up. Roy was blowing snot bubbles as the wives and I sat quietly in painful embarrassment, eating lasagna and sipping their chardonnay. After a big round of Birthday Praise for Charlene's Lasagna and Bread Pudding, I was no longer hungry. Nevertheless, we all had to order a dinner to keep the restaurant management happy. Everyone, that is, except the birthday girl, who ordered only iced tea.

When the entrées arrived, Psycho Ex was not happy with his pesto langostino. He wrinkled his nose and then turned to me and said, "Taste this stuff and tell me if you think it's gone bad." As in "If I have to spend the evening with food poisoning, you better fucking join me." A ridiculous premise but . . . even crazier . . . I did it. I, the royal food taster, took a bite and then turned to him and said, "It tastes okay. You're probably just reacting to the pesto sauce they put on it."

P.E. looked at me and glared with icy rage. Then he didn't speak to me or look at me for the rest of the meal. However, once we got into the car, he let the floodgates open. "You think I am so fucking stupid that I don't know what pesto sauce tastes like? How fucking stupid do you think I am?" Which soon morphed into the litany of my flaws—my crazy mother, my castrating nature, how I made a fool of him, etc. etc. etc.—and continued until we went to bed.

SCORE	Points
Enduring awful friends*	150
Enduring loud unfunny snorting noises while viewing feet[†]	100
Force-fed fattening food so Wifey could stay on her diet	100

*I had three full sets of them
[†]two rice-eating equivalents

Willingly tasting potentially poisonous shellfish	300
And being screamed at about my personality flaws for forty minutes	250

TOTAL:	900

NEW TOTALS: Grant 1,350   Lisa 1,630

How do you like that? Look who's still ahead. Well, I'll be. Looks to me like I'm winning winning winning winning winning!

P.S. Just a question about the rules: What do we do if we can't find a similar action? Is there a way for one of us to change the topic?

Dear Lisa,

I think anything that matches is okay, because that makes the maze more challenging, but let's say it's at least got to match a noun or a verb. For example, "dinner" or "friends." Denise Lightcap, a former friend of mine, was the worst conversationalist I ever met. If you spoke about the Loch Ness Monster, she'd return with an anecdote about door locks. Therefore, Lightcap's Parallel is continuing the story on the thinnest link. So if one has to rely on a Lightcap's Parallel, one is fined 50 points.

Although I do not mean to give you the impression that you have any kind of an edge, it occurs to me that maybe you suffered more every day with your Psycho Ex than I did. He kept you off balance with hit-and-run tactics. I wonder if you stayed as long as you did because it was so hard to get your bearings.

My P.E., on the other hand, came into my life as a listing ship. World-weary but consistent. Soft. Sweet. Funny. Occasionally I would get a glimpse of her amorality, but I could soothe myself by thinking she'd been on the street since she was fourteen and hadn't had the breaks I had. These flashes would fade in time, and we'd go back to normal.

Dear Grant,
I want to make sure I understand the sequence of events correctly. You slept with P.E. the same night you met her?

Lisa

Chapter 18

GRANT

Dear Lisa,

No. I did not sleep with P.E. the same night we met. What kind of a cad do you take me for? I slept with her twenty-four hours later.

We met on a Thursday evening at Zuzu. It was near closing, and I was the only customer left. The receptionist, who guided me to a closet, instructing me to lose the coat and shirt and don the smock, said, "Jane will wash your hair." As this was my first visit to Zuzu, I found it kind of disorienting. When I looked up I caught a shadow of a woman coming from behind a curtain. I think about that moment now. It was the last time I wouldn't know her. Is there something one can sense of another's soul in those first moments? I can't tell if that one quick glance said, "Sex! Sex! Sex!" or "Impenetrable malicious darkness." Whichever, I got a strong message.

"Over here," she said, offering a seat. She was beautiful, so much so I looked away. She was wearing a tight New York Dolls T-shirt and jeans. My mouth went dry, my pits got wet. As she rinsed my hair and massaged my scalp with shampoo, we talked about hair dye. What the fuck did I know about hair dye? But the subject didn't matter. We might have just been reciting multiplication tables, for all the listening we were doing. I was leaning back, eyes locked, mouth moving, thinking, Yeeow! Sad eyes! Tough! An adult! Late thirties? Mid-thirties? Endearing slightly buck teeth, blue eyes with the smallest hint of bags underneath. Weird accent! Canada? Boston? Are those really big boobs? They are! No. They are not. Oh wait they are . . . sorta big.

She was thinking, Oooh, a multisyllabic word. A smarty. Midwest flat A. Sad brown eyes. Naïve? Polite? Tight-pants cock bulge or big-cock cock bulge?

An uncomfy silence, and as I stood up and thanked her, with my hair dripping wet and a towel draped around my shoulders, I felt like a dork. Then: "Well, got to go. Nice talking to you."

About an hour later, after I was dyed and clipped to a perfect muss, I went up to the register, paid, tipped, said thanks, and left.

I should have known something was up by the way the two counter girls and two guys who cut hair stood there with her, beaming.

I walked outside thinking, What nice people, and I heard her voice behind me. "Hey!" she said. I turned, smiled. I was thinking I must have forgotten something.

"Ya wanna meet me after work for a drink?"

I felt like I had been punched with a big boxing glove full of feathers.

That was the first time in my life a woman, let alone a sultry, sad-blue-eyed one, had said that. Sure, I had heard every other type of come-on and pickup line before. But none of it was half as hot as "Ya wanna meet me after work for a drink?" It was so, how do I say? So goddamn grown-up. It spoke to me of black silk stockings, Cadillacs, and Aqua Net. Wind Song, stiletto heels, and black brocade girdles. It was *Perry Mason* early-sixties sex, a pickup line Jack Lemmon might have fielded in *Divorce, American Style.* It was sex that started with a Manhattan, then moved on to sirloin steaks.

That was the moment, right there, that I passed out of the bush leagues of my twenties and into the majors, like in the verse from "It Was a Very Good Year" that Frank didn't record. The better-left-forgotten verse between his "city girls" at nineteen and his "blue-blooded girls of independent means" at thirty-five, when Frank was twenty-nine and had a go with world-weary reduced-to-retail rock molls with bad drug problems. Not a very good year at that.

Okay, so we met for drinks at a bar down the way. She came in and, kapow! She looked great. She had put on a fresh coat of makeup and changed into a long skirt and a black bustier. The only jarring note was the six-inch tattoo of Anubis giving me the chicken eye from his perch on top of her breastbone. But the fact that she had spritzed on a perfume that made my head spin made it easier to overlook. It was expensive grown-up perfume. I was floating like Bugs Bunny, ears back, mesmerized by a snaky cloud of musk, with an index finger beckoning me onward, seduced by the exotic rhythms of cobra-charming music. You got to remember, this was Melrose Avenue, 1984, when the choice of scent was oil: patchouli oil, sandalwood oil, frangipani oil. Melrose gals wore oil because oil said "I'm not like my mom in San Diego." However, conversation was hit and miss. It reminded me of the *Monitor* and the *Merrimack:* subjects seemed to strike and then roll off our hulls. Subjects I offered didn't really connect with her, and vice versa.

She held forth on the significance that Anubis—the Egyptian jackal god, guide of the dead, and unfortunate name of her first band—had for her. As she talked, I wondered how anyone could make a lifetime commitment to a single image. If I had done that at the wrong times in my life, I'd either be covered in pictures of Bonaparte, the 1967 Eldorado, or hobbits. But as things continued, we managed to get out the facts: She moved around a lot as a kid, starting in Canada and then ending in Philadelphia by way of New Orleans and Boston. She was in bands. She was a singer. I was in bands. I was a singer. She had been fucked over by the industry. I had been too. She was single. I was single. She worked Melrose, I worked Melrose.

But though I tried to make her laugh, I didn't get a giggle. So after a while, I didn't care much for this "drinks after work" business. It reminded me of speech class. I thought I bombed.

When we left the bar, it was still light out. Late afternoon in late May, nearing summer. Dreamsicle sky with a hint of blueberry. I said I'd walk her to her bus stop.

This went better, as there was more to be distracted by outside. I fished around for artsy talk, seeing what she knew. I dropped some painters' names: Gustav Klimt and Egon Schiele are always good. A little off the beaten path but accessible. When both got crickets, I tried early modern: a little Miró? Again, crickets. Other topics of interest also got either a nod or a shrug.

So I decided to match her sphinxlike demeanor with a

sphinxlike demeanor. We walked in silence for quite a while. Surprisingly, all the discomfort ceased. We might not have had much in common, but we seemed perfectly at ease saying nothing. We strolled along the lush back streets of Hollywood, past quaint stucco houses and flawless lawns. Conversation was reduced to pointing at picturesque details. "Nice house." "Big tree!" "See that cat sleeping in the window?" "Oh! Yeah!"

And then back to silence.

Near her stop at Highland and Santa Monica there was a Naugles. I asked if she cared to partake of some fine dining—my treat. She laughed and said yes. We sat facing each other, and once again conversation was strained. Man, I didn't know what to make of her. She was impenetrable: husky voice, faraway manner, poised. We smoked and we talked about the usual stuff—school, bands, crazy parents. We gave Cliffs Notes about our romantic pasts.

I was mystified, fascinated. She was close. She was far away. She'd lean in, warm and intimate. She'd lean back, aloof. She'd smolder, then freeze. She'd guffaw, turning stone-faced soon after. A will-o'-the-wisp giving me just enough to chase after, pulling me in far enough not to feel too lost . . .

I yakked, trying to find more common ground. She nodded and spoke in short, well-placed sentences. A wry comment now and then, followed by watchfulness.

I felt foolish. Like my mouth was a tiny, festive pink-and-white theater where my monologues died and my clown act bombed. Then I began to understand the way she looked at me. It implied that what we said wasn't important. Bands, cities, jobs—who cares? Who we are is all that matters.

Of course, now I realize that what was really going on was she was blasted on drugs, projecting that cheap junkie omnipotence Anne Rice cleverly captured and cashed in on.

We finished up by talking about how we were both lousy at relationships. She admitted she was a bad girlfriend, and I admitted I was a bad boyfriend. I didn't give it much weight. After all, people always say that. They do. But in this case, it was right.

The sun had set by the time her bus pulled up. People in line were boarding. We lingered. I wanted to kiss her, but I knew it would probably lead to sex if she kissed back. No good. My apartment was a pigsty. Now it was her turn to get on board. It was now or never. You know the symptoms: aching groin, rapid heartbeat.

What did the rock god do? I put my hands behind my back and thanked her for the lovely evening. I stepped back. The door closed, and off she went. I walked home.

I found out later that she did want to kiss me. She later admitted that she "really, really" liked me, but when I didn't kiss her, she liked me even more.

It was a sweet sexy moment. She was hot and sad, a deadly combination in the world of codependency.

So the answer to your question is, I didn't sleep with her until the next night. And that night she commented that my place was a pigsty, which was a disappointment because I had, in fact, cleaned it up for her. So I guess I should have just kissed her at the bus stop and not been such a goddamn gentleman.

Grant

I felt hot and sticky, guilty and fearful, like I did when I was six and my teacher Sister Clemencita, the baby-talking first-grade nun, phoned my dad to complain about my lack of mathematical ability, sloppy desk, and poor penmanship. Holding the phone as she spoke, my father had turned his eyes on me and glared: Manson eyes, I would tell you today. I stood there in front of him in my PJs, fingers twisting. The good nun was only trying to help. She didn't hear the thump of his fist slamming into my chest, or the bump of me landing square on my ass on the other side of the room.

That was the first time I got beat up for school issues, the beginning of a fine tradition. And now, standing in my own living room in front of Winnie, four decades later, I felt ashamed all over again, as she read my latest Psycho Ex entry out loud.

" 'Are those really big boobs? They are! No. They are not. Oh, wait, they are . . . sorta big . . . oh! A smarty. Midwest-flat A. Sad brown eyes. Naïve? Polite? Tight-pants cock bulge or big-cock cock bulge?' "

Winnie looked up from the sheet she was holding, blinked coldly, and read on.

" 'It spoke to me of black silk stockings, Cadillacs, and Aqua Net. Wind Song, stiletto heels, and black brocade girdles.' "

"Okay, Winnie," I sang.

" 'Dreamsicle sky with a hint of blueberry'? Oh, brother!" Winnie put down the print-out. "And by the way, Grant, in case you've forgotten, I wear the Melrose gal's choice of scent: oil! I don't like 'grown-up perfume.' It smells like Sterno."

"Winnie, I was just fucking around with words," I said. I could feel the big punch coming.

"What you have here is a road map to your cock. 'Here, Lisa. Here are the things I like,' " she chided in a snotty tone. " 'I like sixties underwear 'n' I like big beehive hairdos 'n' pointy bras 'n' grown-up Sterno perfume. I can do wild sex, but I'm sensitive enough to please you if you wanna cry big hot tears.' "

"Well, why didn't you say something, Winnie? I figured you'd read it. I figured you'd say something if you didn't like it. That was the arrangement, right? I was just telling the story of a very confused woman and a very confused young man."

"Grant, you are confusing a very confused woman. *Godverdomme!* What is Lisa going to think?"

I felt a big whoosh of rage. "*Godverdomme* yourself. I didn't send it to titillate her, for chrissakes!" I shouted. "I sent it because it was a great goddamn detail. A one-night stand with scars on her fucking arms cries after climax! I'm supposed to leave that out lest Lisa get all hot and bothered over me screwing a junkie?"

"Yes!" Winnie screamed. She screamed it long and loud, dragging out the scant vowel sound so all the world could hear. The cats flew out of the room. The guy doing vocal exercises next door stopped.

We stared at each other, breathing hard. Winnie's eyes glowed black and hateful. It was the Claudia episode all over again. It was my dad with Sister Clemencita.

I felt sick, guilty, and dirty. But for what? For writing about my fucking life? Why must I defend that?

"I'm not trying to fuck Lisa Roberty, for chrissakes. I'm just writing!" I yelled. Locking and loading her return volley, Winnie took a deep breath. The phone rang. We looked at it. The machine clicked on and we listened.

"Hey, lovebirds!" It was Sylvia. "You'll never guess who is asking about you and your musical. Ya sitting down? Ya ready? Nick fuckin' Blake!"

Chapter 19

LISA

D ear Grant,

Upon rereading your story, I couldn't help but notice this little sentence: <<She admitted she was a bad girlfriend, and I admitted I was a bad boyfriend. I didn't give it much weight. After all, people always say that. They do.>>

I have a surprise for you. People do NOT always say that. What people always say is "I had to get out of there because my ex was crazy." People usually present themselves as the sane but beleaguered survivor of a crazy mate. Hey, if you don't believe me . . . check out this game we're playing.

But here we have you two not just predicting but laying the groundwork for the rest of your time together. And neither of you the least bit worried. You know, I have found that a really clear picture of how the whole relationship is going to play is usually available on the first date, if you can just turn the hormone level down a notch and listen like an impartial observer. Which, of course, almost no one seems to be able to do. People do not want to believe their own ears when they have the hots for someone.

Dear Lisa,
If I look back at P.E., I see that all the elements of destruction were there, like a genetic code, like a seed, from our first meeting on. Weeds will grow into weeds. Never roses. Tomatoes will always be tomatoes, never oaks. Everything about Jane was there from the beginning. She was a nasty, life-choking weed. Why did I think she was going to blossom into a bed of petunias?

Now I continue with the theme of dealing with annoying friends, and I attack:

BRANDON

Hoping to get out of the strip clubs, Jane married a young strip club patron/mill worker named Pat when she was in her early twenties. They had a son named Brandon. When Brandon was one and a half years old, Pat vanished into the land of ne'er-do-wells, and Jane raised Brandon alone, under the worst of circumstances, for a couple of years. At that point, Pat's sister Dorothy stepped in and offered to take the child. This arrangement was fine with Jane because Dorothy had married well and had a big house in Montana. Dorothy understood that Jane was struggling with a drug problem. "It'll be better for him this way," said P.E. According to Jane, they had an understanding that she would get off drugs, get her career going, and then come back for Brandon. When I met her, Brandon had been waiting for eight years. But now that P.E. and I had been together for a year, the security of our domestic life made her nostalgic for her son. After renewing her bonds with Brandon on the phone, she asked if he could stay with us for a week. I said fine.

It was wonderful to see this gentle motherly side to P.E. reveal itself. See? I thought. She's got so much good in her. Life had been tough, but now things were good. It seemed like the dark days were over.

Soon enough, I got home one evening after rehearsal and there in our two-room apartment was a skinny, nervous eleven-year-old boy who looked a little like his mom, eyes darting toward his feet, blushing. Dorothy had dressed him up in Montana semiformal wear: acid-washed jeans, expensive running shoes, and a T-shirt. He was very shy. This was a lot for him: away from home, Hollywood, Mom, and now me, Nosferatu the Rock Godlet, strolling through the door. He was very unsure of himself. Putting myself in his position, I knew it was best to treat him like an adult, so I kept my opening greetings short and friendly. He seemed to relax a little.

Over the course of a day, he settled in, but even in that short time, I noticed that he was needy, desperate for his mom. It broke my heart a little to witness the burgeoning young man give way to the child who ached for her. He followed P.E. around our tiny apartment like a baby duck. It was very sweet and sad at the same time. I was also touched by Jane's patient and affectionate behavior toward him. It was something I wanted to encourage for both of their sakes.

For a few days, the three of us had a little family. Dinners, long walks around Hancock Park looking at swanky homes. I told silly stories and sang dopey songs. We all laughed. It was certainly the nicest family I had ever been around. Or was it? The truth was, soon after she made the arrangements for Brandon to visit, she also invited Varla, her old friend and junkie cohort from her first band in Boston, to come and stay with us, too. If there is a bond stronger than motherly love, it must be rock-moll sisterhood. You should have seen these two, looking like Morticia Addams and Lauren Bacall on a bender.

At first Varla gushed over Brandon, but she then soon got down to biz with P.E. All the news of their Boston crew: who's sleeping with who, who's dead. Who OD'd. Brandon and I sat and listened to fifteen glorious years of punk-rock gossip.

It hurt me to watch Brandon's forehead knit as he tried to comprehend why his mother went into the bathroom normal and came out later pale and clumsy and whiny. I understood, but I certainly wasn't going to tell Brandon. Once Varla was in town, Jane confided in me that she really needed a break because Brandon was getting on her nerves. Could I take the kid for the day? Could I watch him the next evening while they hit the town? Tomorrow night? Please? She hadn't seen Varla in years. Please? Come on!

I was dumbfounded. Brandon was only staying for two more days. But I agreed and did what I could. One evening I took him to a Slowly I Turn rehearsal. Even though the guys were great to him, I knew he felt like he had been dumped by his mom. The last night I took him along to an art opening and showed him how to look at paintings. Later that night P.E. and Varla came back from the clubs wasted. There were more stories, more rock tales, more yarns about wild times and crazy boys.

I sat there listening and wondered if they were aware how Brandon was hearing these tales: "These are the reasons why my mom left me in Montana. The boys Mom is talking about are way more important than I am."

The next day Brandon was off to the airport. We three rock ghouls walked him to the gate. Although he struggled, he couldn't help crying as he hugged his mom goodbye.

On the cab ride home from the airport, Psycho Ex turned to me and said, "You were so wonderful to him. You know, he never really had a father. Thank you so much." I was genuinely touched.

She then added, "I just hope you know that kid is gonna go home and yak his little pea-brained head off about you, and Dorothy is gonna dump him on your fuckin' doorstep one day soon."

"She's fucking right, you know," added Varla.

SCORE	Points
Watching naïve son try to comprehend mother on heroin	100
Watching son try to make up for ten missing years by hugging, touching, kissing his mother, only to become second fiddle to Varla	100
Brandon carrying the burden of kid logic: "My mom abandoned me because I was unlovable. She doesn't want to be with me now because I am still unlovable"	100
Further kid logic: "Varla is a superior person. She inspires my mother's respect"	100
In spite of all that, Brandon still hugs his mom for a long time and cries at the airport	175
Listening to rock gossip	50
Having P.E. thank me for how great I was to her kid, only to use that as a big club to hit me over the head with and blame me for the mess we're	

in now because we may have to actually take care of the kid one day	100
Listening to a mother refer to her own child as "pea-brained" and as "that kid"	200
P.E. referring to the mother-and-child reunion as "the kid getting dumped on our doorstep."	250

TOTAL: 1,175

TOTAL pain suffered by Brandon: Beyond value

I was so unnerved by this story, I didn't even hear the phone ringing. Now it was eleven in the morning, and I had been sitting there reading and writing e-mails since six. I knew what I was really doing was delaying the start of my day. I was trying not to think about last night. Trying not to remember how I had stood expressionless by the side of the stage, covered from head to toe in goose bumps caused by the bad comedy being generated as they taped "my script."

"There's the writer over there," the noisy stand-up comic/hypnotist who worked as the show's warm-up guy said to the twelve rows of tourists and homeless people who had received free passes to the show. "Lisa Roberty! Come out and take a bow."

"Don't blame me. I didn't write it," I shouted to him.

He laughed, and immediately afterward there was a big burst of audience chuckles. "She's so modest," said the warm-up guy. "Give her a nice hand."

"Seriously, I didn't write it," I said again, over their moderately enthusiastic applause. Next thing I knew, three network executives came up to me, one after another, to congratulate me. "Great script," said Mike Novicki from Fox, who had developed a show with me a few years before. "It's nice to see you back at the top of your game."

"I only have about two lines in it," I said to him. He looked at me with blank but cheery eyes, squeezed my hand, and encouraged me to come pitch him series ideas.

"Hey, nice work, congratulations," said Brent and Robby, two of the chubby baseball-cap-and-football-jersey-wearing writing staff boys, on their way to the craft services table for Milk Duds.

"You guys wrote more of it than I did," I said.

"Didn't you write that bit with the plant?" said Robby.

"Yeah. I wrote one line in thirty pages," I said. "I guess I must be the luckiest girl ever!"

"Hey, great joke," he said as they grabbed handfuls of Red Vines and trail mix. I gathered up my purse and coat. I wasn't supposed to leave before the taping ended, but I planned to sneak out. I doubted anyone would notice.

But of course I got caught. As I approached the door, Mark Eden came up and whispered to me that I should meet him in the conference room when the crew had their meal break. In that moment I was overcome by an enveloping feeling of defeat. I had started writing when I was thirteen because it seemed like a place I could go to have my own thoughts. Now, in one fell swoop, I had created a life for myself where neither writing nor love had any meaning. And if I had eliminated them from the list of things that I believed in, what was I planning to put in their place?

When did I turn into someone who was willing to stoop this low? I was thinking as Eden grinned at me. Seems like I can remember a time when the members of the opposite sex with whom I had intercourse pretended to care about me a little. When did nothing at all become my gold standard?

And how did an e-mail correspondence turn out to be as close to a heterosexual experience as I could come? Of course, it fit right in with everything my brother and I always did: first wasting time trying to be intimate with a person who couldn't be, then finding intimacy with someone who just was not available. What a couple of bruised-up and broken-winged sparrows we had turned out to be.

I called up my friend Robinson. "I told you about this e-mail correspondence, right?"

"The musician guy."

"Right. Can I ask you a question? Do you think the fact that I hear from him so much indicates there's something going on?"

"What do you mean? You mean romantically? I don't know. I would say he probably has some kind of amicable feelings for you, yes. But with e-mail, you can't tell. He could have a million e-mail relationships full of some degree of something going at the same time."

"I wrote to this one guy for years," said my friend Kat. "You remember. The eyeglasses buyer? He used to tell me all his problems. We used to discuss his childhood. I thought we had grown very close. I knew about all his difficulties and issues with his mother. And then one day my e-mails started bouncing back, unopened. Never heard from him again. I went through a ton of withdrawal and depression. In fact, to tell you the truth, it still kind of pisses me off."

It suddenly seemed to me that God was speaking through Kat. How much closer of an analogy did I need? So, sensibly, I took the expansive view. Grant was not a solution but a marker, a pie chart of what had been missing in previous relationships where no time had been taken getting to know each other before establishing the nightmare of sex and bad behavior that would tear us asunder. I had never been close to someone first. I had been operating under the bewildering assumption that closeness was the by-product of sex, born in the chemicals of the afterglow. Grant was providing a spreadsheet on how to proceed differently. This alone made our correspondence valuable.

Putting those concerns aside, I wasn't sure how to retaliate after the upsetting story about Brandon. My Nick problems seemed pretty silly by comparison. For a minute I thought of fighting fire with fire, so I started to improve upon my story about Nick and his imaginary but beleaguered foster kids: Jocelyn and Micah. Poor little Jocelyn and the asthmatic reaction she had to all of Nick's screaming. I started to feel bad for her, which made me wonder how I could have such strong feelings for someone I just made up. And then I realized that was kind of the problem I had with Nick. Which gave me an idea of what to send next. So I sent the Crab Story.

Dear Grant,
I am going to use as my starting point a line from your last one: "Life had been tough, but now things were good. It seemed like the dark days were over."

SURF AND TURF

It was 1991. Psycho Ex and I had been sleeping together for about eight weeks when I went out on an interview to do punch-up on a little independent film called *Camp Catastrophe*. As usual, they were bringing in a female writer to try to make the shallow female characters in the script seem vaguely human.

I had just settled into my temporary office when the director handed me the cast sheet. Midway down the list was the name Nick Blake, the man who had been in my bed the night before. My jaw dropped. I had told P.E. about my new job. But he had given no clue that he was also going to be involved. Looking back now, I think he never said anything because he was pissed he hadn't been hired as the director. He'd just been given a small role similar to his famous dumb man on campus character from *Halloweenies*.

Meanwhile, I was so crazy about him that I started punching up and enlarging his part until pretty soon it was twice as long. Eventually, it morphed into the part of the head counselor, which got him so much attention that it turned his career around.

About a week into shooting, I got a call from P.E. to come down to the tiny trailer that was his dressing room. His voice was strained and furious. He led me into the bathroom, closed the door, and opened his shirt to show me a pride of crabs crawling through his chest hair.

I was horrified. I'd heard tell of crabs but had never actually seen them before. I offered to run out and fill the prescription he had already gotten from his doctor for Kwell shampoo.

"While you're at it," said P.E. as I was leaving for the pharmacy, "why don't you go through the telephone book and figure out which of the guys in the greater Los Angeles area that you fucked is responsible for this."

I was stunned. I hadn't been involved with anyone else since I'd met him. I'd never even thought about it. I was a bitch in heat.

As I drove, I was scanning the Rolodex in my brain for who could have given me crabs. I couldn't remember having been with anyone. But I must have been. Otherwise, where would I have gotten the crabs? I stopped by my house and examined myself. I didn't have a single crab.

Well, I thought, maybe they jump from one warm body to another, like fleas. I must have given P.E. all my crabs.

When I handed him his Kwell, still feeling guilty, I said, "I swear, I haven't been seeing anyone else since we started going out. And I don't have any crabs." Now I was wondering if maybe I did have crabs but for some reason just couldn't find them. Could they be hiding? Was it possible I had slept with someone but, due to repressed-memory syndrome, I couldn't remember?

"Fine. Whatever," he said, turning away and then walking back to rehearsal. Neither one of us ever mentioned it again.

When I looked at how far Brandon had put Grant ahead in terms of points, I knew I had to do some fancy scoring to stay competitive. I did what had to be done.

SCORE	Points
Being accused of something I didn't do	100
Believing that there was some way I might have done it and actually inventing explanations to prove him right	300
Running out to get his prescription filled after being falsely accused	200
Continuing to help him punch up his part after all this	200
Never actually accusing him of anything back	150
TOTAL:	950

NEW TOTALS: Grant 2,525   Lisa 2,580

Dear Lisa,
As a satisfied user of Kwell, I wonder why it never dawned on you to ask where he got them, since you didn't have them. Were you afraid to?

Were you just too happy in the spring of love?

Do you go back to this story and see that all the pieces were right there before you? A very standard tactic: projecting your infidelity.

I was just remembering how Psycho Ex told me, before I left on tour, "Don't get a disease. Don't fall in love. And don't get caught." Sounded like a world-weary joke until I realized she was giving herself permission to do the same.

So how did your P.E. get away with not mentioning it again?

Dear Grant,
Well, I knew where he got the crabs. One of the other actors on the set had joked to me that he'd seen P.E. hanging out with a large-breasted female extra. (They migrate to Los Angeles every spring to nest.) So I kind of guessed that she was the crab-boat operator. I also knew there was no way to get P.E. to admit it. He had already denied everything. Looking back, the way I made it through eight years of playing Gaslight with P.E. was to let things drop. A lifetime of living with my similarly inclined mother had trained me to think of crazy fights as unwinnable. But what's really scary was how I had such a sense of original sin that I figured I must have been guilty when I knew I wasn't.

Dear Lisa,
I'm very sympathetic to your position here. But what did you do with all that anger? I filled four notebooks full of rage-filled chalk drawings. I look at them now and think, Poor sap.

Dear Grant,
I have a very hard time getting to rage. I always assume that maybe I've done something wrong and then forgotten about it. And I've been like this for a long time. Once, in high school, my mother caught me in our backyard making out with a boyfriend. Out of all the reactions she could have had, the one she picked was to cry hysterically. Later she lectured me: "I told you not to get emotionally involved."

And I thought, Okay. That sounds right. But if I don't get emotionally involved, what am I supposed to do instead? Though now that I think back on her behavior, she was more emotionally involved in everything I did than I was. And hahahaha, you are not fooling me with your false-sympathy move. You're trying to draw me into some kind of pathetic reverie by getting me to reconnect to a time when I was a big wimp.

I was about to push "send" when I started worrying: Is it okay to be telling all this personal information to Grant Repka, someone I never even see occasionally? Why do I think I can trust him? So I added, "P.S. Do you think you guys might want to come over for dinner sometime?"

Ten seconds after I sent it, I heard "You've got mail." So much for bedtime.

Chapter 20

GRANT

D ear Lisa,
I advance by matching your thread of an unresolved infidelity.

"VENUS"
This story kills me. It's a hard story to share.

Chris was the handsome, brooding junkie member of Slowly I Turn. He was the band's wild man. For example, one night after a show when I was riding home with him, Psycho Ex, and a gaggle of other gals, he ordered the car to stop so he could pee. He got out, then he jumped on the trunk of the car and pissed all over the back window, laughing maniacally. And dig this: All the gals in the car were laughing hysterically! Chris could pull off antisocial stunts and be thought of as funny and sexy, though a similar act would have gotten me arrested. Why that is remains one of life's great mysteries.

Chris got me into Slowly I Turn and then fought me every step of the way. For the four years we worked together, he barely spoke to me. He shrugged. He grunted. He and I did not get along.

Chris had a song on the first LP called "Venus." The original title was "Venus de Milo," of all things. I liked the tune and the feel but was uncomfortable singing his words. Something about bones and skeletons, bats, and velvet. "Near the tomb beneath the dead you pulled me down," it went. Before we recorded it, I asked Chris if he would mind me tweaking the lyrics a bit to match my own lyrical voice.

"No fuckin' way," he snarled. I shrugged and went along. I was the new guy.

P.E., on the other hand, thought "Venus" was the best song on the album.

"But it's just Chris's gobbledygook."

"So what? It's my favorite. Get over it."

Cut to: Montage of four years of touring. I'm singing "Venus" in Italy, in NYC, in Berlin, Oslo, Sydney. Every time I sing it, I think the same thing: Just what the fuck is this shit about? I overcompensate in performing "Venus" by putting a lot of meaningless zing into my rock-god antics during it.

Cut to: Three years later. By this time, Chris has been fired from the band. I am walking with my manager's secretary, Karla, down Sunset. She used to be pals with P.E., but they had a falling-out while I was on tour. Anyway, out of the blue, Karla asks, "How's her drug habit these days?"

Nobody had ever asked me about Psycho Ex's drug habit before. I didn't think anyone knew. For the next hour and a half, I unloaded. I couldn't carry this around inside any longer. And Karla was more than empathetic. "I never understood how you stayed with her after all that 'Venus' business," she said.

"Venus" business? What . . . "Venus" . . . business?

"I thought you knew," she said hesitantly.

"Knew what?" I demanded.

"The song is about an affair she had with Chris."

"Who told you? How do you know?" I gasped.

"She told me. I was over at your house while you were on tour. When we were listening to her tapes," Karla said. I felt the world spin around my head as the years of singing, sweating, watching Jane standing in the wings blurred by me. "Best song on the album. It's my favorite. Get over it," said the echoing sound track.

For weeks I obsessed about it and wondered: Did they exchange winks while I faced the crowd? Did they laugh?

Flashback: Jane says to me, "Let's go to the cemetery. I wanna show you Tyrone Power's grave." The cemetery is just a few blocks from our apartment. We go. There Ty sleeps. A white marble tomb at the end of a reflecting pond nestled in a long deep sunken garden.

"Near the tomb beneath the dead you pulled me down. You did it good. Yeah, you did it good," went the song.

SCORE	Points
My gentility unremarked upon, my rapier wit ignored, while handsome Cro-Magnon man pissing on car is considered sexy	100
My manager's secretary and therefore every other secretary and all of their boyfriends as well as my manager and everyone he associated with in the community of my record label knowing what is going on except me, the dashing lead singer with the rapier wit	550

Having to sing a song called "Venus" (de Milo) in the first place	200
While using rock-god antics	250
With added meaningless zing	400
To sell song where I am unknowingly announcing to the world through Gothic imagery that the woman whose rent and bills I pay is fucking the Bronze Age Homo erectus heartthrob next to me	500
TOTAL:	2,000

Dear Grant,
BOY OH BOY. That she used you like a chess piece is chilling. Give me her current address, and I will go kick the shit out of her. I took a fighting class once. AND I take a lot of vitamins. She's a junkie. She's probably pale and wan. It won't take too long to demolish her. I'll be back to battle in twenty-five minutes.

Dear Lisa,
Yes, it's humiliating. Even today I find myself a little chilled that I could inspire people to hate me so. But I'm sorry, P.E. was no wan junkie. She might separate you from some of your favorite body parts, then sell them to a research lab for a few bags of dope.

Dear Grant,
See, it isn't about YOU. Except that you were there. The children of narcissists turn out a little like a guy who pays a lot of money for an ugly designer suit, then thinks it's his fault that it doesn't look good on him.

Now I continue your thread of being lied to and trying to answer the eternal question "What the fuck is this shit?" with the story of:

PSYCHO EX AND THE TERRIBLE ILLNESSES

Psycho Ex was a panicky hypochondriac. When he wasn't worrying about the dissolution of his film career, he liked to spend leisurely hours reading the *Merck Physicians' Desk Reference*. Every time he found symptoms that matched his own, his skin would get damp, his heart rate would soar, his face would grow pale. He would be sure he was dying. In the time I had known him, he was able to overlook his many troublesome indicators of glowing good health in order to diagnose himself with everything from sickle-cell anemia to Tourette's to macular degeneration.

On this day, as we drove to work together, he felt he had muscular dystrophy. My trying to talk him out of it made him punch the windshield of the car so hard that his knuckles began to bleed. He started to scream at me, "I am dying. My head is spinning. My eyes are swollen shut in their sockets. I can't even swallow, let alone talk." He got himself into such a state that he pulled the car onto the soft shoulder of the freeway and got out. "I'll just fucking hitch-hike in to work," he said, starting to walk. I pointed out to him that if he was dying, it might not be a good idea to walk the twenty miles to work. This, of course, made him angrier.

I got behind the wheel and began to drive the car slowly behind him. This was both dangerous and illegal. When he finally got back in the car, he insisted on driving again. He never spoke another word until we got to the set.

I went immediately into my office to do my work but was too rattled to concentrate. A few minutes later, he came in, closed the door, and said, "You want to know why I was so upset? How about if I just came back from the Ryerson Clinic and they confirmed that I do have muscular dystrophy. How about that?" Then he stormed out.

They were going to start filming in a couple of minutes. I had some pages I was supposed to turn in. But I couldn't work. I was devastated.

I got in my car and went to a liquor store to buy a bottle of vodka. I couldn't handle this sober. The enormity of him actually having one of the diseases paralyzed me. I started thinking, Oh my God. If he was a handful when he was well, now he'll be impossible. And once he's an invalid, I can never leave!

Soon I was drunk, sitting in my trailer, trying to determine my next move. Should I get on the Internet and research health options? Should I contact alternative therapists? I was overwhelmed. So I went down to the set to check in on him. And there I saw Psycho Ex in the middle of directing the big macaroni-fight scene. He was laughing; the cast was laughing too. He was giving notes, impressing everyone. A good time was being had by all. The scene they were doing went so well that he got a spontaneous round of applause from the crew.

Dizzy, I went back to the trailer. In a few minutes P.E. joined me noticeably more upbeat. "Uh, they didn't actually say I have muscular dystrophy at the Ryerson Clinic," he volunteered in an offhanded way. Then he turned and went back to the set.

SCORE	Points
Risking my life by following a crazy person along the soft shoulder of the freeway	100
And then relinquishing the car to him	300

Buying a bottle of vodka at nine A.M.	400
Panic and empathy for a sick person	500
And being dead drunk at ten A.M.	200
Then watching him laugh as he directs the throwing of macaroni and cheese to a big round of applause as I am heading for a hangover	500
Being this upset, drunk, and hung over at ten A.M. all for NOTHING	500

TOTAL: *2,500*
NEW TOTALS: Grant 4,525   Lisa 5,080

"Well, I liked that one," said Winnie as she worked to apply plastic fingernails to her own bitten ones. "You gotta admire his sadistic streak."

"Hey, Winn, I've been meaning to ask you," I said, sensing that Winnie had begun to accept Lisa a little more. "Is it okay if we take Lisa up on her invitation to come to dinner? I really should say something to her, one way or the other."

"Well, she's got her foot in the door. She might as well come in. It's what she wants," said Winnie, slightly exasperated. "It's her big move to get close to you."

"It's just an invitation to dinner! Jesus! We had dinner with Fricke the other night and he's your fucking ex."

"Grant, that was a birthday party. There were fifty other people. Besides, Fricke and I only spent two nights together. He's barely even an ex."

"Okay, okay. Well, what should I tell her, Winnie?" I said.

"Let me sit down. I'll tell her," said Winnie, taking my seat at the computer and beginning to rapidly type, despite the fact that only three of her plastic nails were actually glued into place.

Dear Lisa,

Thank you for your invitation to dinner. We would love to take you up on that at some point. Unfortunately, right now we are both very busy with work and do not have any time. However, if you are in this part of town, please call and stop by for a cup of coffee. We would love to see you. Evenings are best, late evenings are better.

"There," said Winnie, smiling broadly as she pushed "send," "I got us out of going to dinner. And offered her coffee at an hour when she won't come. So everybody wins! Now let's check the story you're going to send her."

I began to read. "And now I continue with your thread of being manipulated."

PSYCHO EX MOVES IN

It was summer 1984. I had my own place, and I liked living alone. One of the pleasures of finally living by myself was renewing my friendship with The Teacher. We had known each other for years, and had always been a little in love. She now lived in NYC and, like me, was recently single and making the dating rounds. "Dating" is a little mild; we were rooting like pigs enjoying that filth fest that once followed every long-term commitment that fizzled. We became very close by phone, sharing the grisly details of our love lives, laughing, snickering about this lover and that, giving them loving nicknames like Mr. Salty Mouth, Ribs, and Ms. Whiffy Pits. After months of talking it seemed to make sense that we spend some time together. So we made plans for me to visit her in NYC. We didn't talk about romance, but then again, nobody said it couldn't happen. Maybe it was finally time.

Soon after The Teacher and I made our plans, I slept with

Psycho Ex for the first time. The next day I called The Teacher and astounded her with tales of the slash marks up and down a lost soul's arms.

What I didn't tell Teach was that I kinda liked P.E. and that we had continued to sleep together all that week. Hey, what's a week? After all, she was about to leave town. I planned to miss her and write her a beautiful ballad in E minor. We said our goodbyes. But to my surprise, she was knocking on my door the very next day. Now she was NOT leaving town. Why? Because she had made a choice between me and her career, and chosen me. Uh oh. I remember trying hard to look pleased, forming what felt like a very glassy smile, but thinking, People who fall in love that quickly aren't really in love. Of course, I paid no attention.

P.E. was renting a room from a gay couple. But now that she was NOT leaving, I felt it was important to let her know that I was still getting over a recent violent relationship. I needed and demanded a lot of time alone. I also let her know that a trip to see The Teacher in NYC was already in the works. She asked me if The Teacher and I were lovers. I told her no, just old friends. It was technically the truth, after all; The Teacher and I had not even broached the issue.

The day before I left for NYC, as I was packing, I answered the door, and there was Psycho Ex on my doorstep with a pile of clothes. The gay couple had kicked her out, and she was hysterical. She had no place to stay. A cab out front was waiting with a trunk full of her things. Crying, she demanded I help her unload the cab and let her stay for a few days. This came at me all at once, one day before I was scheduled to leave.

I should have said no. But turn down a damsel in distress? "Okay," I said. "Just a few days." I gave her a lecture about how much I wanted to live alone and how much privacy meant to me. She nodded. "You must have a place when I get back," I said, hoping for some reason that she'd be out by Monday. The next day P.E. escorted me to the airport, grilling me about where I was going to stay. I fibbed and told her I would be staying at my sister's. Suddenly my life had gotten very complicated.

When I got to NYC, The Teacher and I devoured each other within seconds of my arrival at her place. So much for pacing. This turned into a week of rampant sex.

At that point, Winnie stopped me again. After much back and forth, I agreed to change "devoured each other within seconds" to "began our affair immediately." "Period," said Winnie. "Get rid of rampant sex." I nodded. Then I continued.

Now let's step back and examine my predicament. A junkie alone in my L.A. apartment—practically a stranger—blew the first rule of war. "Secure the home base." If she found out I was sleeping with The Teacher, she could wreck, slash, and steal everything, in revenge.

On the other hand, if I told The Teacher that I had been boffing the sad junkie all this time and now had her living at my place, this would ruin the chance for our friendship to possibly blossom into love. To say nothing of the lectures I would have to endure about how I was backsliding into my old self-destructive patterns.

Single-man logic, third, dictated that what I did was neither woman's business. Technically, I was in the right. Yet it all felt so very wrong. So I followed the Slowly I Turn Thirteenth Commandment: Thou shalt lie.

I told The Teacher that I was going to my sister's place every evening to call L.A. and catch up on daily band business. When I got to my sister's place, I waited for P.E. to call collect, and when she did, there I was at my sister's, just like

I said! But P.E., being no dummy, began to insist that I call her in the morning. Okay, I figured. I'd call her when The Teacher stepped into the shower.

After a week of museums, galleries, and great filthy squirty sex with The Teacher, it was over. On the plane, I proudly thought to myself, This playboy stuff is easy.

"Grant, stop it," said Winnie, rolling her eyes impatiently. "You can't say 'filthy squirty sex.' No wonder this cunt wants you to come over for dinner."

"I was going to include the phrase 'Geyserlike explosion of female ejaculate,' but I toned it down," I said.

She laughed. "I thought we agreed we weren't going to talk about sex."

"It works into the story, Winnie," I pleaded. "Just let me keep going." She sighed and shrugged as I resumed the narrative.

But when I got off the plane, there was Psycho Ex, who had suspected everything. There was something in my voice, in all those calls, she said, that had tipped her off. I denied everything. But meanwhile, although she had made no move to find her own place, my apartment was now immaculate. She had scrubbed and scoured my dingy cave and transformed it into a home.

After my return, The Teacher didn't understand why I wasn't calling her every night. Calling her from pay phones, I used the Slowly I Turn rehearsal lie, but that was temporary at best.

A few weeks passed. A letter from The Teacher arrived in which she informed me that she had noticed eight long-distance calls to my number on her latest phone bill. She figured out that I was calling the junkie chick, and that she was now living with me. Obviously, I preferred that sort of trash to her. She dug up all the horrible, funny things I had said about P.E. and threw them back at me. She also regretted every explicit intimate act we had performed together. And this letter was waiting on my kitchen table one night when I got home from rehearsal, already opened by P.E. And still there was no mention of Psycho Ex finding her own apartment.

So I said a silent goodbye to The Teacher, came clean to P.E., and sank into eight years of madness.

"Ugggh. I hate all three of these chicks," Winnie said, exhaling as she made a final scroll through what I had written. "All right. Well, tone down the 'filthy squirty sex' part and go ahead and send it. But for chrissake, first jack up your points."

SCORE	Points
P.E. on my doorstep with all her clothes, capturing my headquarters	2,000
Trying to fool both a summa cum laude and a vicious street junkie	100
The Teacher's unerring truths about what a jack-off I was	200
Giving all those funny junkie stories to a gifted letter writer who made explicit mention of the peccadilloes while graphically describing the degree of intimacy, passion, and eros we had shared in our week together, thereby creating a document that P.E. would read and quote many times in a snotty voice to get her way	1,500
P.E. opening a letter addressed to me in my house where she was a guest	500

And turning a wonderful romantic week in NYC
into a nightmare by her presence in my house   500

TOTAL: 4,800

Dear Grant,
Inconsistency Alert. You said we are allowed to question
points as long as we do it right away, so I'm wondering
about the fact that you gave yourself 2,000 points for finding P.E. on your doorstep. I agree it was awful that she
moved in without your permission. But let's look at your previous scoring of other traumatic events: P.E. bluffing while
selling drugs to Carlos earned you 10 points! Your whole
"Venus" story only came to 2,000!

   Also, why would you let a junkie move in and not make
some kind of excuse about why she couldn't stay? Just as
preposterous: How could you NOT know those calls would
show up on The Teacher's phone bill?

Dear Lisa,
Well, re: The Teacher's phone bill. I assumed that everyone
just left their bills in a pile, unopened, until the turn-off notices came. Like I did.

   Re: P.E. moving in. She knew I wouldn't ask a shipwreck
like her to live with me under normal circumstances, so she
fashioned an emergency. She constantly put herself in the
role of victim to gain an advantage. But hey, who am I kidding? I was hearing junkie snake-charmer music.

Why I thought P.E. acted crazy enough in this yarn to deserve 2,000 points

   1. I would never pass up being in a band just because I had
a nice week with someone.

2. I would never tell someone I loved her within that short a time.

3. I would never think because I loved someone that she loved me with the same intensity and therefore automatically owed me that kind of dedication.

4. I would listen very carefully, then offer sympathy and patience, if someone I loved told me that she was still recovering from a bad relationship and wanted to live alone. I would not think that because I was in love with her, she should drop her healing process pronto, presuming that what she really needed was a big shot of me!

5. I would never force myself into someone's home to keep her from falling in love with another party, then make demands as a guest in her house.

6. I would never open another person's mail.

Dear Grant,
Okay. Okay. I think 2,000 points is overkill, but I will let you keep them. Just be apprised that I will remember this new baseline when I am scoring myself in future stories.

"Yeah, so you can take fifty thousand points for a fucking water cyst?" Winnie shouted.

"Just keep reading, Winnie," I said.

And so I continue your thread of moving in.

I MOVE IN WITH PSYCHO EX

I was a new writer in town, with a brand-new fancy job, on the staff of the pilot for *Mr. and Mrs. Ed,* the short-lived attempt to revive the talking-horse show by giving him a wife and kids. It was an awful show, worse than awful, but I didn't care. I was no longer broke. And I was in love. Psycho Ex and I had been together for a year. Late every evening, I would pack up clothes, food, and incidentals and drive to his house to make him dinner and spend the night. We only lived about ten minutes apart, so I didn't mind the driving. I was crazy about him. Everything he did, including the way he did nothing, seemed significant and impressive.

At the year mark, Psycho Ex scored big by selling his self-financed independent film, *The Valedictorian,* to a big indie distributor. So suddenly he had some money and was advised to invest in a house. Prior to that, he had been living in a dilapidated single room that was dominated by a broken bed, which tottered like a restaurant table needing to be stabilized by sugar packets. The apartment was so void of every amenity that once, when I went to visit him, I found him typing a script by balancing his typewriter on the bathroom sink while using the toilet as a kind of a desk chair. And I haven't yet mentioned the shower, which required hip waders and typhoid shots.

One afternoon, out of the blue, P.E. informed me that he had spent the morning with a real estate saleswoman and bought a house in Santa Monica Canyon: a Mediterranean four-bedroom with a lap pool and a hot tub. He'd already gone down the street to IKEA and bought three rooms full of furniture. I felt a teensy bit excluded. I had fantasized that when things fell into place for him he would ask me to move in. Instead, he said nothing. Never even commented about how his new homestead had drastically changed the length of my nightly commute from ten minutes to an hour plus. No, P.E. still preferred that I continue to rent my mildew-scented bungalow in Van Nuys, a house that distinguished itself by having no heat anywhere except in the pool. It also turned out to be owned by a famous drug cartel . . . a detail I learned one evening when I saw my landlord's picture on *60 Minutes*. This underscored for me the notion that it was high time we move in together. But P.E. said no. And it was not until that moment that I really understood that he had no intention of ever normalizing or developing this relationship any further. So, although I didn't want to, I broke up with him.

"Arrrggggh," growled Winnie, "I hate this fucking woman."

"What?" I said. "What?"

"Don't you see how she is?" she fumed. "Nick's been living in shitholes his whole life. He finally buys a house and right away, the first night, she gives him an ultimatum that she's got to move in with him. 'Now! I want it now!' She doesn't give a shit what anybody else wants. And when she doesn't get what she wants, she breaks up with him." She thought for a moment as she continued to study the screen intently. "Plus, I love the way she just has to let you know that everybody she knows is on TV. Even her fucking landlord."

I was a weeping freeway hazard as I drove home from his house that night. But almost the minute I got home, he called to say that he'd made a terrible mistake. He did want me after all. He didn't want me to leave. I gave notice on my rental, said a sad farewell to the telegenic drug dealers, and by the end of the week, I had packed up everything I owned and moved into Psycho Ex's house.

It was all a very lovely scene of domestic tranquillity. For about an hour. Until I turned up the temperature in his refrigerator because I had noticed that the milk was full of ice crystals. Apparently that was the last straw. I hadn't asked his permission first. He told me to get the fuck out of his house.

My brain sounded like an air-raid siren as I put everything back into my car. I was back to my old sobbing tricks as I drove to the Holiday Inn in Santa Monica. There, to my surprise, I was the only one at the registration desk who was not dressed in a cheerleader's uniform for the big cheerleaders' international convention. As the evening progressed and I lay on the bed unable to stop crying, I could hear the soothing sounds of girls in the next room practicing their cheers: "Victory! Victory! That's our cry. V-I-C-T-O-R-Y!" After a couple of hours, I was so overcome with anxiety, grief, and blind hatred for cheerleaders that I found myself driving, zombielike, back to P.E.'s house to talk with him. It was a bad strategic move, but luckily, it turned out that by now he was full of regret. We had a tearful reunion. He asked me to come back. Of course I said yes.

The very next day, as a salute to our brand-new life, while he was out at three P.M. meeting with his agent, I went out and bought lobster and champagne. I had decided to have a special romantic celebratory dinner ready and waiting for him when he got home.

At eleven P.M. I heard his car pull into the garage. P.E. was too depressed and angry to even say hello when he walked in the door.

"What happened?" I asked, genuinely worried. "Is everything okay?"

"No. Everything is fucked," he said, refusing to look at me or at anything.

"Are you hungry at all?" I asked him. "I made a special dinner."

He shrugged dismissively and looked down. Undaunted, I led him by the hand to the candlelit table, sat him down, and gave him a glass of champagne.

"Prepare to be amazed," I said, trying to sound so upbeat that it might pull him out of his gloom. Then I put a plate of lobster down in front of him.

He poked it with his fork. "Why is it so greasy?" he said finally.

"Because the recipe said to drizzle it with melted butter. It's not actually greasy. It's swimming in buttery goodness," I said, sitting beside him and grinning proudly. Which was when, without warning, he picked the lobster up and hurled it across the room. "Perfect. Just fucking perfect," he said. "Just what I fucking needed. Greasy rubbery fucking lobster." Then he got up and went into the bedroom, leaving me to stare in shock at the big wet stain it had left on the far wall before crashing to the floor.

I sat still for a moment to see if anything else was going to happen. And then, without saying a word, I got up and cleaned up the mess.

The next day I got the name of a shrink from my friend Marc Robinson. I told the therapist that I had come to see him because I loved P.E. and I wanted learn how to make things go more smoothly. After I explained the difficulties we were having, the therapist looked at me solemnly. "If you ever want to grow emotionally, you are going to have to leave this relationship," he said.

I was dizzy with emotion as I drove home. That was not what I had wanted to hear. When I walked in the door, P.E. was waiting. "Where were you?" he asked me.

"I had an appointment with Marc Robinson's shrink," I said.

"For three hours? You talked to a shrink for three hours? You fuckin' the shrink now? Is that what's going on?" he said. He was angry, but under the anger I could see thinly veiled hurt and insecurity. I was looking into the face of a scared little boy who lived in constant terror because he could never be sure that he was really loved. My heart went out to him. I would show him he could trust my love unconditionally. I stopped seeing the shrink.

"Boo fucking hoo," said Winnie, fed up. "Lobster. Fucking movie people with their fucking houses in Topanga Canyon." Winnie started talking baby talk. "'Ooooh. I stopped seeing the shrink.' What did she take for that? Oooh . . . I knew it. A thousand points. I fucking knew she was going to do this. Look at her fucking score. This cunt takes seven hundred points for giving a blow job to a guy who is letting her live in his palace in Topanga Canyon, for chrissake."

SCORE	Points
Asked to make a nightly hour commute from a Mafia-owned dump	100
Being thrown out for thermostat touching	200
And then coming back	500
Standing in a line with cheerleaders during time of trauma	400
Paying top-dollar to listen to "V-I-C-T-O-R-Y" while sobbing	150
Concluding an inexplicable act of violence was somehow my fault	500
Being treated with contempt after trying so hard to please	500
Waiting, all dressed up, for six hours because I was being a good sport	100
Wasting hard-earned money on romantically associated food	200
Not having the self-respect to leave after that	500
And actually giving him a marital-relations job later	700

Firing the shrink after he gave me the right advice   1,000

Giving me a grand TOTAL of: 4,850
NEW TOTALS: Grant 9,325   Lisa 9,930

Top that, Mr. Wounded-in-the-Name-of-Love Musical Boy.
I'm WINNING WINNING WINNING WINNING WIN-
NING!

P.S. I may take you up on your invitation to stop by for coffee. So I hope you took that into account when you made
the offer.

"Oh, I cannot fucking wait, you fucking twat," Winnie said.

Chapter 21

GRANT

The waiter gave me a big smile. He had no idea who I was, but he assumed if I was with Nick Blake, I was fantastic, too. Then he took our order: two regular coffees and a slice of carrot cake with extra cream on the side for Nick. "Don't tell anyone. I'm not supposed to eat sugar or carbs." He winked, patting his gut. I nodded reassuringly, conspiratorially. Christ, we were bonding.

Like a lot of famous people, Nick was not as tall in person as he appeared on-screen. When he stood up to shake my hand, I was staring at the top of his head. I had heard that he was sensitive about his height, so almost without meaning to, I found myself slouching. Still, for kind of a short guy, his presence was enormous. By the light of day, in a near-empty café on Beverly, he was all the hacky descriptions I had read in magazines for decades. His hair was indeed "jet black" and "tousled carelessly." His "crooked grin" was in fact "boyishly disarming," as advertised. Either nature or plastic surgery had airbrushed his face. He was a man time forgot. Yes, he was overweight by ten or fifteen pounds, but he had so much charm that he made it look good.

In his presence, it became clear why he was America's Best Pal. He was the nice guy down the block, your kooky, irrepressible cousin, your nutty college buddy. He was like a little boy who had been given the magic snow globe that contained the world—and it made him a strange mix of old and young, of exuberance at possessing it and exhaustion at the sheer weight of it.

We had been chatting nicely when his cell phone went off. He apologized, saying, "I need to take this one, and then I'm turning it off." Add "considerate" to the hacky adjectives. I gave him his privacy and looked off at the traffic. It being L.A., there was always something good to consider automotively; in the space of ten blinks, I spotted a Bentley, a pristine '65 Mustang, and the obligatory rock guy in a beat-up Coupe DeVille, its torn vinyl roof flapping in the breeze.

Our waiter stood nervously in the wings, trying not to watch our table, trying to figure out what additional services to offer to get more Nick Time.

Like the waiter's, my third eye was still on Nick. I studied the tone of each single syllable he grunted, rummaging through the vocal minutiae for clues that might speak volumes about the man.

I thanked Christ for the correspondence with Lisa. She had armed me with an arsenal of information. I had come into this meeting ready. When Nick and I shook hands, I knew somewhere behind those gleaming eyes lurked a megalomaniacal monster capable of throwing lobsters at walls. But none of our letters had prepared me for this. No wonder Lisa had rolled over for him. This was akin to the Lincoln Memorial getting up and extending a massive mitt. There was also something about him that had me opening up my box of toys, spilling them all out. Giving anything for more of that crooked, boyishly disarming smile. That must have been what hooked Lisa: I had made a sad, lost boy happy. I had done a good deed. I wanted to do it again. Again and again.

He cupped his hand over the cell phone and rolled his eyes, pantomiming the person on the other end yakking and yakking. I made the same face back, and he made the ain't-we-naughty look. We were bonding again.

Knowing better than to try for more, I looked away again and took in the cars: A vaguely familiar Silver Lakey–looking girl chugged by in an art-chick car—'62 Valiant, faded red, with a gaff-taped convertible roof and standard zebra seat covers. What was she doing on this side of town? What was I?

I had caught only a glimpse of her, but even at forty paces, I could see her face dotted with the silvery zits and metallic pustules of way too many piercings. Her green shaggy hair said she was a distant cousin of my tribe: the Arty-Rock Clan. I thought of a hipster evolutionary chart. Starting off as pretentious midwestern art-school kids, they crawl out of their abusive homes, advancing to modern overdone cool Kats 'n' Kittens scrounging in the big city. The species takes a large leap forward to Successful Artist, standing erect. Ending here, at the ultimate peak of perfection—billionaire Nick Blake, with the world on hold, in cotton Dockers and a blue button-down shirt.

Then I thought about all the agents, actors, actresses, investors, writers, and cameramen who wanted him at this very moment. Their need created a ghostly presence at our table. Hollywood wasn't at his feet, it was in his lap, like a ventriloquist's dummy. But, unlike the rest of them, he had come to me. I owned something he wanted. He had seen my show and laughed himself silly. "This is my next movie," he'd told Sylvia.

"Okay," he said now, "right . . . okay." I could hear the cadence of the phone call coming to an end. He laughed politely. "All right—bye." He clipped the phone shut. All business now, he turned and said, "God, I'd like another piece of carrot cake. But I guess I shouldn't. So where were we . . ."

"We were talking about who would play Tommy Lee," I said, slouching in my chair, trying to equalize our heights so as not to replicate the Lincoln-Douglas debates.

"Right! Hugh said he'd love to do it."

"Hugh?" I urged him to fill in the blank.

"Hugh Grant," he said, scraping the bottom of his bowl of cream and crumbs with his spoon. The way he said "Hugh Grant" so nonchalantly caused two separate reactions in me. I split in half: the whore and the anarchist. The ho was willing to lie down and get fucked. The punk was snarling at the president of the millionaire actors' club, attempting to protect my artistic integrity. The ho just wanted out of the poverty that had accompanied it. "Well . . ." I said, pausing.

"Well what?" said a voice in my head. "Well what, you starving, obscure asshole middle-aged rocker on his last breath? Nick Blake has descended from Olympus to discuss casting for your movie. You say 'Gee, Mr. Blake, I think Hugh Grant is an outstanding choice for Tommy Lee.' "

"That's right!" shouted the whore, dancing in joyous circles. "Suck the man's dick!"

That was when, in an unguarded moment, the anarchist stepped forward and took over for me.

"Well, Nick," he said out loud, "my idea was for Tommy to be played by a complete unknown: chiseled, handsome, so people project onto him. A Broadway leading man. If people saw Hugh Grant, that's all they'd see."

"Hugh Grant would bring in a fuck of a lot more people than a faceless actor," Nick said, nipping off the end of a complimentary blue corn chip.

My anarchist got tongue-tied when challenged. "Suck his dick, sugah," shouted the ho. "Quick! Suck the man's dick, and let's get rich!"

"That's a great point, Nick," I said, shifting gears so quick I could hear them grind. "I didn't think of Hugh Grant because, well . . . he's not from my world."

"Oh." Nick waved that away, giving me his grin. "You'll be part of that world soon enough. Did you know Hugh's got a great singing voice?" Nick zeroed in with the eyes. "He does. And his name brings a lot of money for production."

"Great!" I said, overcompensating with great dollops of excitement as the anarchist gave me the finger. I suddenly felt depressed. Jesus Christ. Hugh Grant singing? What was I doing here? Did I just roll over? Was I supposed to back down? I saw the Silver Lake Art Chick now driving in the opposite direction, heading home. Was it my imagination, or did she just look at Nick and me and sneer? If she didn't, she certainly would if my movie starred Hugh Grant. I made a lateral move. "Let me ask you something, Nick. What if Tommy was played by an unknown and the rest of the cast were people of Hugh's caliber?"

Nick nodded, looking far off, suddenly distant. I couldn't tell if he was toying with my idea, or with the idea of getting up and walking away. The waiter refilled our coffees in the ensuing silence.

Nick came back from wherever he'd gone. "Another piece of carrot cake. You want anything?" he asked me.

"No thanks," I said.

"Johnny—Depp—said he'd love to do Tommy, but I see him as Nikki Sixx." He giggled as more carrot cake appeared. It felt like the sun had come out. "And you're going to love this!" Nick winked. He hunkered down and whispered, "Pam wants to play Pam."

Right on time, a car screeched. I had to remind myself again that these names were not the aggravating, pompous, self-worshipping show ponies who grin or weep on the *Enquirer* cover at the checkout stand. These first names—the Dannys, Demis, Jerrys, and Nicoles—were real people to Nick. They were his pals. They left silly messages on his machine and dropped by at Christmas. They were cherished employees who brought near-immeasurable value to his projects.

I also could feel Nick running hot and cold about me. And not knowing was part of the Nick Blake mystique. Did I stand up to him or let him steamroll over me? He was both a bully and a sweetie pie, blissfully happy one second and darkly morose the next. Did I deck the bully and gain his respect, or share my toys with the sweetie pie and collaborate? If I shared, did the bully lose respect for me? Lady or Tiger? Door number one or two? Come on, Repka. Call it right, and Gwyneth and Hugh and the whole darn gang would stand on the stairway to the stars, tossing dollar bills as you glide upward. Call it wrong, Repka, and the evolutionary chart is reversed. You go tumbling down ass over tits, back to Hipsterville, the place where all the good cool stuff is, except cold hard cash. The Silver Lake Art Chick picks you up out of the gutter and drives you home. The car smells of patchouli and armpits. Smeary, blurry angry rock sludge throbs from the busted boom box in the backseat. The broken plastic vibrates on middle C. The sun leaks through the convertible roof. The faux zebra-skin seat covers are damp and stinky. The backseat floor is stacked with the yellowed edition of the *L.A. Weekly* that mentioned her name, among eighty others who were at Beer Can Eggy's party, though they forgot to mention you.

What was the right choice, here? Pam wants to play Pam? Christ, Winnie plays Pam. Like a six-year-old choking down liver, I looked at Nick weakly and smiled.

"Great," I said. Man, oh man oh man—was I in over my fucking head.

Chapter 22

LISA

I had gotten so used to waking up at four A.M. to check for e-mails that I had ceased trying to sleep through the night. For the last couple of days, I had been fixating on Grant's invitation to stop by their house for coffee. Was this a real invitation? Or a thinly disguised rejection? He and Winnie being "very busy with work" sounded like a brush-off, like "no" with a qualifier.

For all the information going back and forth on the Internet between us, I was beginning to think this person I called Grant might not exist. That he was part of some kind of virtual-boyfriend software designed by a company offering single subscribers perfectly tailored daily e-mails from someone suitable but imaginary.

Which was partly why I was so curious to see

where he lived. I wanted to know what his living room looked like, what kind of coffee he drank, what kind of cups and rugs and art provided the ambience for our correspondence. I also wanted to talk to Winnie. Clearly, I hadn't understood her correctly. What was their setup that allowed him so much time to write to me? "They call it triangulation," Kat had lectured when I asked for an analysis. "When a couple brings in a third person to try and make a shaky situation more stable. It distracts them from their problems, gives them another focus." If I was the third leg of a triangle, what did that make me besides a corner table?

I had another reason. I wanted a reality check. Because, like it or not, Grant's letters were having a cumulative effect. Like the story about The Teacher: <<We shared the grisly details of our love lives. . . . We didn't talk about romance, but then again, nobody said it couldn't happen. Maybe it was finally time.>>

Wasn't that kind of like us? Was I the latest in a long unbroken chain of crushy correspondents? Was there always one on tap? If so, did he sometimes feel that way about me? Did I want him to?

One night I tried to have a fantasy about him before I fell asleep. I tried to conjure him walking in the door to my bedroom, a tall thin shadowy figure all in black. He lay down on my bed with me. Oooh, good so far. But when I tried to reel him in for a kiss, I couldn't remember what his face looked like. I tried to cut-and-paste in Grant's face from pictures on the back of his CD, but they were too staged, too hostile-looking, to use in a sex fantasy. Before I could even get the fantasy to first base, my imaginary Grant got up off the bed, stood far enough away so that he looked like the blur I see when I'm not wearing my glasses, and walked out of the room. Talk about X-rated Hot! Hot! Hot! Walked out on in my own fantasy. I was so pragmatic that even my fantasies had to have some plausibility. He was in a happy relationship, so why was he here? I tried to insert a backstory in which he was coming over to cheat just this one time. But as a writer, I knew this would only lead me to more pain, so I couldn't agree to it.

That was one more reason why I needed to pay Grant a visit. Observing male friends in their natural habitat was a time-tested, reliable way to kill a troublesome crush. It always served as a reminder that I got the best from them by keeping them at a polite distance. Love relationships seemed to be the place where perfectly nice men went to become nightmarish monsters.

I rationalized that I had errands to run in Hollywood, anyway. So I drove into town at about noon and did all the remotely important things I could think of doing. I stopped at the computer store and bought more RAM. I went to Home Depot and bought fertilizer and lightbulbs. I went to the Salvation Army to check for more recipe cards, and much to my delight, I found a bundle of about forty in a rubber band, stashed in the back of a water-stained copy of *The Joy of Cooking*. This made me so excited that I almost just scotched the visit to Grant, so anxious was I to go home and look for the face in Man-Sized Steak Salad. Double ditto for Oven Porcupines.

But I had driven all this way—hung out all this time. At about five, I dialed Grant's phone number and for the first time heard his answering-machine message: a woman's voice shouting the phone number. I found it a little frightening and quickly hung up. Then after a beat, I redialed. "Grant?" I said. "You said something about coming by for coffee if I was in the area, and I am. In the area. So I thought I . . . Maybe I'll call back." Now what? Give up? Call it fate and go home to make furious faces on Sweet-and-Sour Meatballs? I hung around in town a while longer, walking in and out of the little shops on Third Street, looking through racks full of clothes I didn't have the courage to wear and stores full of art I couldn't afford. On my way back to the car, I was approached by one of those aggressive homeless people who materialize seemingly out of nowhere. He was very close much too quickly. In a fear-based surge of adrenaline, I reached into my pocket and handed him whatever bill I could find, hoping to appease him so he would leave. When it turned out to be a twenty, the guy's face lit up. He was so delighted that he began to follow me. "Wow," he said, "I'm so happy, I'd like to eat your pussy!"

"Thanks," I said, sprinting toward my car, "but I didn't give it to you as a way to bring us closer." I was shaking when I got back into my car, then sad, then angry. I found myself sinking into one of my patented Fuck You days when I alarm myself by imagining that my eyes hold dynamite charges that can cause explosions wherever I focus. The guy in the NASCAR cap in front of me at the gas pump: *kaboom*. The yoga-mat-carrying girls in line for the ladies' room: *blam blam blam*. Look how fucking hostile you are for no reason, I scolded myself as I sat inhaling bus exhaust, my car stuck in gridlock that went on for blocks. Nothing bad even happened to you, I was thinking. Then I realized I was staring at an enormous photo of Nick! There he was, ten feet tall, grinning down at me from the back of the bus. I tried to switch lanes, but there was no easy escape, since the same handsome smiling picture of Nick juggling the planets of the solar system was on a giant billboard at the end of the block. There was also one at every bus stop bench in the city. NICK BLAKE: RULER OF THE UNIVERSE? they said. Apparently his new movie was opening this weekend.

The accidental intrusion of Nick into my day was nothing new. I was accustomed to finding him staring at me from magazine racks by cash registers, or from my perch on the Stair-Master as I gazed down at the gym floor where someone had dropped a newspaper. I would see him looking up from the coffee table at the hair salon or at the dentist. On a plane, I might be trapped with him on the in-flight movie as well as on the pages of the *People* magazine in the lap of the person sitting next to me. Used to it though I was, it still caused me to make those noises Curly makes in a Three Stooges film when he looks down and sees that his pants are on fire.

Finding myself in the middle of a brand-new Nick fit seemed a perfect reason to blow off the visit to Grant and head home. I would try phoning one more time, and if no one picked up, I would call it fate and start sake time early.

Chapter 23

GRANT

I t was rush hour. As I drove, inching my way home, I tried to think about the business that had just transpired. Nick, Pam, Gwyneth, Hugh, Johnny. Think! I said to myself. For once in your goddamn life, think! Do I hand this over to him, or fight for what I want? After all, *he* came to *me*! That doesn't mean anything if he owns the town.

But it was no good. I couldn't think, not in any useful way. I was damaged goods. A lifetime luxuriating in the arts had caused an overdeveloped right side of the brain. The left had atrophied decades ago. Thus, instead of pondering this potential life-changing opportunity, I found myself ruminating about Nick's big head. Hollywood might be a magnet for the lost, the abused, the beautiful, but most of all, it attracted the people with big Easter Island heads. Was this natural selection at work? With giraffes, long necks meant more leaves. In L.A., a big head meant more TV and movie parts. It struck me that in old sci-fi movies, big heads meant big brains. Now they just meant big plans.

Think, I said, shooing away the big heads. For once in your life. Think. But I couldn't. The Big Heads had me. It was at that point I noticed a faded alien sticker glaring at me from the van ahead as we inched down Beverly Boulevard: cold, slanted eyes and a thin, miserly librarian's mouth. It struck me that next to the smiley face, aliens' faces were the easiest in the universe to draw. As though nature, in her relentless search for perfection, had conveniently eradicated everything the average person finds impossible to render: noses, lips, eyebrows, eyelashes, eyes. Most telling were the hands, the bane of every artist—amateur and professional. Complex, subtle, expressive hands were reduced to three nasty streaks at the end of a silver sleeve. Aliens, in essence, looked like something drawn by God's little nephews on a rainy afternoon and taped to His mighty fridge.

The alien car jammed on its brakes. I jammed on mine, which jolted me out of my trance. Traffic back from the west side was murder. Everything in L.A. is twenty minutes away—it just takes an hour to get there. Nick Blake was burning in my stomach like ignored homework assignments.

The front door was open when I got home, and I heard music. I walked in and saw Winnie, in her black spandex tights, marching to the TV.

"Get out!" she shrieked, grabbing the mute thingamajig. I looked over at the VCR and saw a group of hunky guys and gals marching before a South Sea Island backdrop. Winnie jumped in front of it, screaming. "Get out." Winnie hated for me to see her sweating, looking less than perfect, and marching around the room like an idiot.

So I crossed the yard to the studio and, heading upstairs to my office, lay down on my bed where I lit a cigarette. In a few minutes, I heard the heavy stomp of Winn's biker boots. The studio door opened, and she clomped upstairs.

"Congratulations. Nick really liked you. Thought you had an instant rapport. He called Sylvia to tell her," she said.

"And Sylvia called you," I guessed.

" 'Nick was fucking blown away by Grant,' " said Winnie, imitating Sylvia's nasal voice.

"You're fucking kidding me. I thought I bombed with the guy," I said.

"You always think that," said Winnie.

I felt relieved, but I knew this wasn't quite right. "Early reports," I snorted. (Another war truism. "Things are never as bad or as good as first reported.") "Nick shows his love in a very odd manner," I said. "He acts as if he doesn't like you."

"Well, you should know that's true. It's everything Lisa has been saying."

I nodded.

"There's more," she added. "I just got off the phone with Barry, who just heard from Bobby Snuggs that you had coffee with Nick Blake. Sylvia, it seems, is giving everyone a full report on your meeting."

"What? Why?" I asked.

Winnie, winding up her pitch, explained, "Sylvia is a star fucker. And Nick Blake is as high as you can go. Nick wants your musical, so Sylvia's going to put herself right in the middle of it. I don't know what she's hoping for exactly: maybe a production deal. Maybe it's a weekend at Cannes. Unless she's looking for an eleventh-inning baby."

It became sickeningly clear. Since the meeting had ended an hour ago, Sylvia had alerted everyone in my cast and beyond. Now they were all at home doing crunches and making appointments to get their teeth bleached, hair dyed, and photos redone. Try as they might to stay calm, they couldn't help but see themselves as the exciting new stars of Nick Blake's *first musical.* So, with my songs in their hearts, they had called their agents and managers to give them a heads-up. Ballpark figures had been tossed about. Girlfriends, buddies, and even friendly enemies were alerted. This was the magic step to fame and fortune that they'd always known was up ahead, waiting for them. Provided, of course, that Grant and Winnie didn't fuck it up for everyone. I had a horrible hunch that this would all turn out badly. "Pincer movement," I muttered. "Austerlitz. Chancellorsville. The Schlieffen Plan. Cannea."

"They're all dying to be members of Nick Blake's posse," spat Winnie. I sat and let the terror of this intrigue paralyze me. "Which brings me to the other thing: Lisa called." Winn raised her eyebrows, boring a look into me. "She's in the area and wanted to know if we were up for coffee." I was happy to hear this, but I kept it hidden. "I just want to warn you," Winnie said, "don't tell her about your meeting with Nick."

"Why?" I protested.

"Just don't!" stressed Winnie. "If you get involved with Nick, I guarantee your pal Lisa will vanish. Right now she's a great source of Nick information. We may need it at some point."

"So I'm supposed to lie to Lisa?" I asked.

"No. Just don't volunteer the truth. Look, Grant, too many people know our business as it is. And besides, nothing's in stone." She thought for a moment, then added, "You know if Sylvia tells Nick Blake what you two have been writing to each other, you can say goodbye to Nick."

This was getting too complicated. I couldn't think about it any more.

"I better try to clean up around here," I said.

Chapter 24

LISA

G rant," I said, getting his answering machine again, "it's Lisa. Just thought I'd—"

"Oh. Hi, Lisa," he said, picking up his phone, his voice a little bit tense. I was struck by how unfamiliar he sounded. Then I realized I had heard him speak only once before, and it was on the night we met.

"Well," I said, "I don't know if you really meant for me to take you up on your offer to come by. But I need some caffeine, and I guess I don't have to tell you how hard it is these days to find a place that sells coffee in Los Angeles."

"I know what you mean," he said, laughing. Good. I had made him laugh. "Let me just check with Winnie. I'd love to see you. Call me back in five."

So I sat there in the car, holding the cell phone, watching the clock, feeling awfully tense about this perfectly innocuous get-together. The minutes on the car clock passed slowly. At minute four, I looked up and noticed that I was directly under another billboard of Nick. A Curly noise rose in my throat as I turned the key in the ignition and moved the car to another block. If Grant didn't pick up this next call right away, I was going home.

"Come on by," he said, after picking up instantly. "Okay, great," I said, and was overcome with a case of ice-cold jangly nerves the minute the call ended.

Lighten up, nutcase, I said to myself as I tried to decipher my Lycos map. If a simple house call kills a friendship, then so be it. You're wasting too much time on him, anyway.

Grant lived on a busy boulevard in the heart of Silver Lake, an area I began to like more and more as I noticed it had no billboards of Nick. Too many of the wrong demographic here, I guessed. Hipsters are too skeptical, I thought. That, too, made me happier.

Grant's house was completely concealed behind a big, ominous wooden gate. I parked out in front, then sat and reapplied makeup in my rearview mirror until my eyelashes were stiff enough to cause puncture wounds. After about seven or eight minutes of pointless, anxiety-based primping, I got up the courage to go knock.

And there he was. Grant Repka, a guy I hardly recognized. His hair was longer than I remembered. Handsome, I thought, and taller. A very nice height, I thought, a very sexy height. And then I hammered that idea flat before it could turn and bite me.

"Hi," he said, "come on in." He led me down a few stairs, through a wooded thicket, and onto an unlit path that led to the back door. Vines and branches hit my face. There were unidentifiable things to trip over everywhere. A hose? Wires?

A carburetor? A dog dish? I couldn't see where I was stepping, only feel a path that was strewn with objects beneath my feet.

The back door led into a tiny kitchen lit by only a candle. It was big enough for a table and a couple of chairs, but oh my God, what a mess. Straight ahead were four or five very full black plastic garbage bags stacked in a mountain, filled with clothes, shoes, magazines. Beside them were more of these things, loose on the floor as though they'd escaped. The sink was full of more dirty dishes than I owned clean ones. Everything smelled like unemptied cat boxes and overflowing ashtrays, with a slight overlay of Vanilla Glade. And something else. Was that smoldering plastic? Black bananas? Was this a house, a duplex, an apartment in a complex, or a rented room in someone else's house?

Grant was over at the coffeemaker immediately. I wondered if he was thinking, Please. Just take your coffee and go in peace.

I looked around. There were no gold records or musical instruments, just a few old framed advertisements on the wall. Mostly there were closed doors. One on my left, one on my right. Places Grant was not inviting me to see. Maybe after coffee there'd be a tour?

"Coffee-mate okay?" he asked, not waiting for an answer before filling the two cups he'd placed on the counter almost half full with the white powder poured straight from the jar. Of course I said yes, since it was a moot point. After which he added some coffee and stirred the mixture with a spatula handle. While I waited I petted the different animals who approached out of the blackness, drawn to the flickering candle like weary travelers to a campfire. Smiling, Grant brought me a thick brown mug with a chipped rim that had a cartoon of a little Swiss man on a mountaintop who appeared to be yodeling the logo "Woody's SmorgasBurger."

"Winn'll be out in a second," he said, sitting down with me at the tiny table. "So! Nice to see you. It's been a while."

We looked at each other and smiled. Did I look as unfamiliar to him as he did to me? He was wearing a black ensemble: boots, jeans, jacket, all black.

"I love your place," I lied. Well, it wasn't that I did or didn't like it. I didn't know where it was. Every door was closed.

"What brings you to this side of town?" he asked, lighting up a cigarette with the graceful economy of movement that said "constant smoker."

"Well, this and that," I said, starting to worry that he was annoyed I'd showed up. I sipped a little coffee. It was so strong I was suddenly very grateful for the protective coating the blanket of Coffee-mate offered my GI tract. "Whoa," I said. "This is quite a cup of coffee." He smiled again. Something about him, about his smile, made me happy, comfortable. I was glad to see him.

"Hi there," said a voice that I recognized from the answering machine. I turned, and through one of the closed doors came the always perfect-looking Winnie, her hair an architectural marvel, her makeup flawless. She looked lacquered and stunning, and she was carrying a stack of rented videotapes. "I'll be right back," she said. "I just have to drop these off."

"Come sit down for a minute," said Grant, as though there were another seat, which there wasn't. Winnie put her tapes down on the stove and hoisted herself up on the edge of the sink.

"Hi," I said. "What'd you rent?" I leaned over to read the titles. "*Return of the She Devils*. Wow, they're back and I didn't even know they'd left. And *Revenge of the Dead Girls*. Not just dead, but also pissed off. Bad combination," I joked. Winnie just blinked. "Beautiful films. I usually rent them at Christmas," I continued, trying for a save.

"So did we," she said. "That's why I gotta bring 'em back right now. They're way overdue."

She was dressed in jeans, platform boots, and a big white fur coat: one part rock star, one part porn star. In a way, her presence relaxed me. I really didn't have to fret about whether or not I looked okay. In a room with a woman like Winnie, I was invisible.

"Where'd you two meet?" I asked, and then listened to them finish each other's sentences as they told a story I couldn't quite follow concerning rock clubs I'd never heard of, people I didn't know, and a store on Melrose. When Winnie spoke, I found myself watching the way her lipstick didn't smear or melt. Not even when she sipped Arrowhead water from a plastic bottle. How did she do that? Was it tattooed on? I was surprised at how nice Winnie was. She seemed smart, witty, unflappable.

I am looking, I thought, at the perfect couple. How lucky for them to have met and connected. Was there anyone among the living who went with me as well as they went with each other?

As we continued to talk, she began to ask me a lot of show-business questions, mainly about negotiating business deals. Like I would have any valuable advice. Nevertheless, by now a second cup of Grant's dangerous coffee had me wired. I found myself holding forth: "I've found it was hardest to negotiate with people to whom I was close," I remember saying, not letting my lack of real information hold me back. I kept wondering how she and Grant had been able to handle the whole work/love thing with a success I could never manage. "Nothing like a little icy distance to make a business deal run more smoothly," I offered, pretending to know something but realizing I didn't. I was really just talking about Nick.

"Interesting," she said. "How?"

"Well," I said, "I guess it's the old 'familiarity breeds contempt' thing. You lose your leverage." The more I listened to my caffeine-powered mouth run on about things that depressed me, the more I felt my mood sinking. Why was I doing all the talking with Grant just a few feet away? I was eager to hear him talk. Great eyes, I thought, looking at him through a cloud of his exhaled smoke, hoping my face did not reveal anything crushy.

I wanted to stop. But Winnie had lots of questions. And I didn't want to seem rude, despite my sense that Grant was growing uncomfortable. What was that about? Had I come at a bad time? Was my depression contagious? Was I boring him? Jacked on coffee, I heard my mother's voice start haranguing me: "Don't overstay your welcome," she used to caution, and though I never quite figured out how to tell if my welcome was holding, it had made me permanently concerned that I had stayed too long everywhere. So I began to gather my things. "Well, I should get out of here," I said. "Winnie's got tapes to return." I got up to say good night.

"Aw. You're leaving so soon?" Grant said.

"Don't worry about it. What's one more night's rental?" said Winnie. "This is too interesting."

And still neither of them offered to give me a tour. This was the only time I had been to a house where I was trapped in one room with no explanation. Kind of the prisoner-of-war approach to entertaining guests. I never would have seen a second room if I hadn't asked, "Do you mind if I use the restroom before I drive home?"

"What? You mean now?" Grant said, as though this were the kind of alarming request that always threw him off balance. "Use the . . . ? Yes, okay. Let me . . . uh . . . Winnie?"

Winnie got up and ran out of the room through one of the closed doors, returning in a minute. "It's all yours," she said, pointing me toward a now-opened door. I got up and gingerly entered a very dark room that I might have called a bedroom, except that the bed was piled high with a structurally impressive pyramid of cantilevered stuff: a virtual clearance sale of sundry items like shoes, cleaning supplies, musical instruments, pants, shirts, coats, boxes, dishes, books, hats, pieces of the space shuttle. The floor was an obstacle course of more unidentifiable dark shapes: more clothes, dishes, shoes, mysterious things better left unidentified. There was almost no place to walk. If this was the storage room, the real bedroom was where, exactly? Somewhere behind one of those other doors? That had to be it. No one slept in this bed.

Like a moth heading toward the lighted room in the corner, I stumbled into a bathroom that had been leveled by the same tornado that had hit the rest of the house. The counter beside the sink was covered with cotton balls and bottles containing makeup, moisturizer, hair spray, mousse, glue, glitter, cologne, powder. Next to the toilet there were some towels in a damp pile, topped by magazines, shoes, panties, stockings, wigs, and a gray and white dozing cat, who looked up at me and said, "meh." Then the odd detail: a padded toilet seat. Like someone had a momentary delusion of sprucing the place up before hopelessness set in. To a person who fought and lost battles with messes on a daily basis, the sight of a place where the war was not even being waged was like a scene from my own worst nightmares: a terrifying vision of being out of control, of spinning into craziness. It was the one step too far that I had always feared when I looked out a high-rise window or stood on the edge of a cliff.

Too embarrassed to scream out for toilet paper, since I doubted there was any to be had, I quickly decided it would be easier to simply use the ladies' room at McDonald's on the way home. Not wanting to hurt Grant's and Winnie's feelings, I flushed the toilet and ran the water in the sink before I returned to the kitchen to say good night.

Oddly enough, I ended up hanging around for almost another hour before I actually left. It started with more of Winnie's questions, but this time I managed to turn them back on Grant, and he started telling stories. By the time I left, I was having a lot of fun.

I was kind of floating as I drove home. I liked Grant and Winnie. I felt lucky to have them as friends. I would have liked to talk to him more. But I was pleased that I liked her so much and glad she had been so friendly. What a great addition to my life I had stumbled into almost by accident. How lucky was I that he wrote to me every day?

By the time I got home, there was already an e-mail waiting for me.

Dear Lisa,

Thank you for coming by. We both enjoyed seeing you. Anytime you are out our way, feel free to visit again.

Grant

I sat down to answer him before I even took off my coat.

Dear Grant,

Thanks for having me over. I had a lovely time. And also thanks for the new coffee recipe. It never occurred to me that if I fill up most of the cup with Coffee-mate, I could save a lot of money on coffee.

I enjoyed spending time with you and Winnie, and if you don't mind me saying, I am very impressed by how you have been able to take the lessons you learned from Psycho Ex and apply them toward having an obviously healthy relationship now. It kind of gives me hope. Well, I guess I wouldn't go that far. But I am happy for you. You two are very cute together.

It was four-thirty A.M. I had barely sent off my response when I heard the nasal call of the Mail Irritant. The smug tone of voice he used when he said, "You've got mail," seemed to imply that he was surprised anyone was still writing to me.

Chapter 25

LISA

Dear Lisa,
I continue with your thread of waiting to see if anything else was going to happen.

SOMETHING IMPORTANT THE NEXT DAY
Jane and I have been together about two years. Soon after The Teacher episode, I am carried away by the demands of a professional recording career now thrust upon me. Slowly I Turn is anything but slow. The workload is brutal, the schedule demands fourteen-hour days filled with writing, rehearsing, gigging, arranging, and smoothing out the new songs. There are near daily meetings with our manager, weekly meetings with the label reps and press and art departments. Rehearsals are six nights a week. On top of this, there are scores of demo ses-

sions that start at noon and last until dawn. My future, along with the band's, is at stake. This is the make-it-or-break-it first album without Arvin Petro.

Jane now lived with me permanently. She never officially moved in. She just never left. That point, along with everything else, got sucked up into the whirlwind of Slowly I Turn.

Besides, by this time I had fallen in love with her. Life with Jane was a comfort. Those scars and needle marks were problems in her distant past. She was calm and affectionate, and she made me laugh with her deadpan manner. She was a rock veteran who understood the life and what it demanded. We never argued about it, like other musicians did with their lovers.

So life was extremely busy but rewarding. After a day of battling the label, or my band members, or playing the same song over and over, she was great to come home to. I found it touching to open the front door at two A.M. and find that Jane, willowy, raven haired, beautiful, had made fried chicken for a late dinner together.

A few times I'd come home early and find her, pale, slow, whiny, stooped, and prattling like an old woman. She had fallen off the wagon and was high. I knew there was no point in trying to use guilt on an addict, so I'd say nothing. Sure enough, come tomorrow, she'd be my sweet, funny Jane again. See? I'd think. A mere slip-up. No need to worry.

For all my efforts, we were very poor. Slowly was on an independent label, and my salary covered rent, food, and little else. Jane . . . well, she had a lot of jobs . . . and lost a lot. The poor thing was a runaway at fourteen, a stripper most of her life. She didn't seem to understand retail and its small paychecks and customers who didn't leave lavish tips. There always was some kind of fight she was having with her boss. At any rate, she never could quite make rent, so I ended up paying most of the bills with my Lowly-I-Earn salary. But I loved her. If I barked about money, she'd quickly remind me how she kept the place spotless and mended clothes, did the laundry, cooked. It all balanced out in a Donna—meets—Lou Reed sort of way.

At this time, our album, *Rah Mith Nith Nith,* was recorded, pressed, and shrink-wrapped. Slowly I Turn was about to embark on our first major U.S. tour. I was worried sick. All the bets were on Arvin Petro, none on me. Often I'd lay in bed, chain-smoking, going over and regretting every lyric on the album, damning myself for not working harder. A voice in my head—perhaps that of Coach Repka— chanted, "The critics are going to kill you." I worried so much that I got alopecia and lost a huge clump of hair above my left temple. I'd black it out with Magic Marker, which would drip black streaks down my face when I sweated onstage.

So, this entry finds me on a Friday. The big kick-off show was the following night in Chicago. The demanding schedule included an early morning flight and an after- noon of press before the show. *Billboard, Spin, Rolling Stone,* the *Chicago Tribune,* and a host of other music mags, fanzines, and college radio stations wanted to ex- amine the pretender to Arvin Petro's throne. This was my first foot forward, and I wanted it right.

That day was spent taking care of the last details. I looked forward to a quiet night with Jane. However, when I got home that evening, I found her extremely ill. She was chalk-white, and white-hot. She had been vomiting into a pan by the side of the bed, too weak to keep getting up. She complained of abdominal pain that got worse as the day wore on. I immediately called a cab and zipped her to a free clinic. There they probed and poked and quickly sus- pected appendicitis. They advised us to get to an emergency room right away. That we had to rush Jane to County Hospital was just awful, but her pains were getting worse. Another cab was called and we were off.

Once Jane was processed, she was whisked away. I trotted to the pay phone and called my manager, giving him a heads-up that tomorrow might get canceled if Jane's condition worsened. This of course would create a logistical nightmare and blow a year and a half's worth of plans, not to mention money lost. But what could I do? He did a great job of being supportive and controlling his urge to scream. He calmed me down and assured me Jane would be all right. At this point the plan was to wait and see. So I waited and saw the horror show in County's waiting room: gunshot victims, mugging victims, victims of stabbings and car wrecks . . . oh, it was Friday night out there, all right. Alongside youthful, bleeding hooligans, poor old yellowing people limped in, with gaping mouths, and eyes wide in fear or slitted in pain.

And everywhere, there seemed to be cops. Cops coming in or just going out. They escorted victims, they filled out papers and joshed with the staff like old pals. I watched as five LAPD officers escorted ten men in orange jumpsuits, all chained together. Every five minutes, some new crisis involving blood and/or brutality caused the whole place to go up for grabs.

After waiting an hour, I figured the place was busy. I called my manager again. He now had a plan. If Jane was sick, I could skip the press and just do the show. She should be okay by tomrrow, no? This would mean exchanging tickets with the other Slowlys, who were coming in later, letting them do the press. "Though," he warned, "the press doesn't want to talk to them, just to you."

So we agreed to wait and see . . . some more.

At an hour and a half I was beginning to worry about

her. At two hours I was getting panicky. I checked with a nurse, who told me over her shoulder that they were running behind. She added they would see to P.E. soon.

At two and a half hours, I had had enough. I marched over and explained politely but firmly that my girlfriend was very ill and I had not heard anything in almost three hours. "I want to see her now," I said. She directed me to P.E.'s cubicle.

When I walked in, P.E. sat bolt upright and screamed, "You got to get me out of here *now*. I want the fuck out of here!!"

"You're sick. You're not going anywhere," I said, surprised.

"Get me out of here now!" she shrieked, panicked. She was red-faced, hysterical.

"They're busy," I exclaimed. "Just hold on. I'll get the nurse."

"No," she said, frenzied. "Fuck the nurse, just get me out. Let's go!"

I looked at Jane, shaking my head, trying to understand. "What is this? You can't go," I said. "Settle down. It's going to be okay."

"It is not okay!" she said, slamming her hands down on the bed. "Get me my clothes. Now." Then she exploded. "I'm fucking dope-sick, you idiot. Do you fucking understand? Do you understand now, asshole?"

I must have been standing with my mouth open.

"Is this what you wanted to hear, you fucking asshole? You happy now? Huh? Are you?"

I stood there saying, "What? . . . what?"

"Just shut the fuck up and let's go!" she screamed, drawing the final word like a frantic two-year-old.

"What?" I still stammered. "Drugs?"

"Yeah. That's right. Drugs. I never stopped. Okay? There,

now you know. Okay? Can we go now? I hid it from you, 'cause you don't like it. Okay? Are you fuckin' happy now?"

All the questions rushed up at once: How much dope? How does she pay for it? When does she do it? How did I not see this? And for fuck's sake, why does she keep asking me if I'm "happy now" as if I did something wrong here?!

"Howdya howdya who who?" I stammered. By shouting I got it out. "How much fucking dope do you do?"

"Eight," she spat, like a spoiled, enraged child. "Eight fucking bags a fucking day—there, ya happy?"

We went back and forth like that. She wanted out. I stood fast—we were not leaving. Period. "They are going to see you soon."

I was her only hope at that moment. I had the money. I had cab fare. Only I could get her clothes, get her home, get her high.

Eventually, screaming failed her. She now put all her desperate hope into absurd bargaining.

"Just take me to Hollywood so I can cop. Okay? Please?" she pressed. "We'll come back, okay? Just to Hollywood and then back, okay?"

While trying to reason with her, I did some quick junkie math on the few facts she ever told me. Two years? Eight bags a day? The cost was staggering.

"So, call a cab, okay?" she pleaded. "Call a cab. I'm fuckin' serious, let's go."

"No," I said, "the doctor is coming. You're really fucking sick. You can't go."

"Then you go. You got money. Go call Ricky."

"Whaddya mean, call Ricky?" Ricky was our next-door neighbor, a twenty-something roadie, a metal fan, and a lughead who rode a motorcycle. Nice enough kid. He sometimes gave me rides. Occasionally we'd sit on his doorstep and bitch about the music industry. An inconsequential character, until now. "Ricky?!" I said. "What the fuck goes on when I'm not home? What else don't I know?!"

"Just fuckin' call Ricky and tell him what I need," she implored. "He knows where to go. Have him take you there then drop you off back here."

"You want *me* to do a dope deal?" I asked, dumbfounded.

"Just give Ricky one hundred and fifty. You got it. I know you do. Go with him. Do what I fuckin' tell you. Please, just get it and bring it back, okay?"

"Ricky's a dealer?"

"No, Ricky's not a fuckin' dealer. He'll take you there . . . just go."

The room reeled at the gravity of her plea. Many times in the past, Jane had commented how "cute" it was I knew so little about drugs. I recalled another time she and Chris were snickering, teasing me about what an innocent I was. Now tonight she wanted me to go to God knows where with Ricky the moron and do a sizable dope deal to soothe the habit she'd lied to me about for the past two years. My first dope deal, hours before the debut tour was to begin; that was what Jane wanted. Tomorrow I faced the culmination of a life's work; I would stand before the world floodlit by *Spin, Rolling Stone,* and *Billboard.* But wait, Grant, before you go, Jane wants you to do something illegal, dangerous, and incredibly stupid. Then you can put your best foot forward. My lips bobbed like a fish gasping for air, but no words came. I could not believe that she'd have me, the innocent, naïve drug virgin, jeopardize everything I had worked for so I could sneak heroin past the ranks of L.A.'s finest, who were stationed all over the hospital. She would do this? Ask this of me? My loving, gentle, mysterious, chicken-frying, supportive Jane Gray? She would risk my future and put me in that kind of dangerous position? Oh yes. She would.

"No," I said, trying to keep her soothed. "Just relax. The doctor's coming."

After more pleading and cursing, she gave up. Her face crinkled. Hopeless tears formed as she gripped the sides of the bed to control her pain and panic. Soon the nurse came in and prepped her for the doctor. She sat up and played her last card. Still crying, she blubbered to the nurse that she was a junkie. She begged for a painkiller in a tone that reminded me of myself as a child, squealing to my father to withhold a beating. The nurse was unfazed. "We have to wait for the doctor," she said.

I went back to the lobby and sat for a long time, stunned, looking back over the past two years. I recalled all the times I could have sworn there was money in my wallet, and yet there wasn't. The things that had vanished from the apartment. I thought about all those cash registers she manned, and all the jobs she got fired from. How did I not see it? The lightbulb went off: The times when I came home and found her high weren't the exception. *I* was the exception, because I was home when she didn't expect *me.* I didn't see it because, aside from a few exceptions, Jane Gray was consistently the woman I knew her to be. And if she was the same day after day, who would think to doubt her? All the loving adjectives I used to describe her—calm, affable, even-tempered—now took on a new and sinister shade. If all the reasons I loved her were manufactured, induced, and paid for, then who really was Jane Gray? I no longer knew. Had I perhaps just met her for the first time back there in that cubicle? That harpy would have sold my ass out for a mere whiff of dope.

Not too much later, I was approached by a doctor. "Are

you Grant?" he asked me. "She's got a hot appendix, and it's got to come out. We're going to have to take her up to surgery right away."

"Is she going to be okay?" I asked. "Is she in any danger?"

"No, she should do well," he said, explaining that the surgery itself would take about an hour. After that she'd be out for another four or five hours. However, she'd have to stay in the hospital for two days. I told him about the whole thing with Slowly I Turn, the tour, having to leave in the morning. He reassured me that this was a routine procedure. "But if she's got friends or family in town, maybe you should give them a call," he added.

"And what about her other problem?" I asked. "Can you give her something?"

"Well, I'm going to give her a pre-op," he said matter-of-factly. I didn't know what that meant. The only pre-ops I knew about were two transsexuals in San Francisco named Thumper and Beanie. The doctor read my confused expression. "I'm going to give her a shot of Demerol before she gets anesthesia," he said flatly.

"Well," I said brightly, "that should make her day."

He looked right through me. "We have to go," he said.

As angry as I was with P.E., I accompanied her gurney as she was wheeled up to the next floor, holding her hand the whole way. I couldn't help but feel terrified as I watched them take her off to surgery.

For the next hour and a half, I hung around the waiting room. During that time, I alerted some of her friends. In about an hour and a half, the doctor came out in his scrubs to tell me that Jane would be fine. "We got it just in time," he said. "It was nice and clean." I had no idea what he meant by that, but it sounded like good news so I thanked him. Then I quickly called Jane's friends back to make sure that they would look out for her. They assured me that they would be there when she woke up.

With that taken care of, I called my manager again. "It's on," I said. He was fast asleep but still greatly relieved, adding that he was glad Jane was okay. I nodded and grunted, "Uh-huh."

By now it was almost dawn. I took a cab home, picked up my bags, and headed for LAX. I was resolved to end this relationship.

SCORE	Points
Seemingly nice girlfriend actually an eight-bag-a-day heroin fiend	1,000
Finding out at County Hospital while she screamed loud enough for LAPD to hear	1,000
Having to wonder, even for a second, if it was maybe better she leave, cop drugs, and then come back	300
P.E. suggesting violently that I go to Hollywood and buy enough drugs to put me behind bars	1,000
And that I bring it back so she could do it there	200
All about twenty-four hours before my big debut	300
Bonus Points: The album bombed, the interviews didn't get me shit, and now I would have to hear, for years afterward, about how I abandoned her in the hospital	250
Being asked if I was "happy now" for discovering she was a junkie, when, according to her logic, if I had just helped her leave when she wanted to	

(despite her appendicitis and 103° temp), then
simply brought her back later, helped her reregister,
and sat out front waiting another three hours, I'd
have never suspected a goddamn thing   250

Coloring my head with a Magic Marker and
having it run onstage   150

TOTAL: 4,450

And while you mull over the points, here's a sidebar to
the story:

Cut to 1961: Little Grant and his twin sister, Joanne, are
grossing each other out by looking at the grainy photos of
brain tumors, amputated legs, and syphilitic noses in Mom's
nursing textbooks.

This isn't random gross-out. This has a point. They want
to get good and scared before they see THE LADY.

Once the twins are at a fever pitch, they close their eyes
and slowly turn the page. Counting one-two-three. They
open their eyes and behold her: THE LADY! She is horrifying: a simple line drawing of a woman with wild hair sitting
bolt upright in a hospital bed. Her eyes are wide with terror.
Her mouth is a perfect O, like a Fury. She points to some un-
seen, menacing object. A nurse runs to her aid.

The twins cannot read so they fill in the blanks with their
own sordid anxiety-ridden imaginations. The dull paper of
the book, the musty odor, only heighten their terror. The line
drawing is a frozen image from one of their shared nightmares, where the silence throbs and they wake, paralyzed.

Cut to 1985: Grant walks into the cubicle. P.E. gestures
wildly. He immediately thinks: THE LADY! Now he is the
nurse running to her aid.

                                                        Grant

My first thought: Whew, his fucking P.E. was a bottomless pit of point possibilities. I could see her trajectory, and it did not bode well for my potential victory in the P.E. Game. Nick lied and screamed, bullied, and once even threw his glasses against the wall until they shattered, while insisting that he had every kind of cancer. But in order to win the P.E. Game, I would have to revise Nick's murderous rampage from one victim to several, maybe over a period of years. I would also need a lot of specific, convincing details to substantiate my stories. I wrote down on my list of things to do: "Research methods of disposing of bodies." Then I wrote back.

Dear Grant,
That is an absolutely horrifying story. I can't believe you didn't see this coming for two years. How did that amount of money go missing without being noticed?

Dear Lisa,
Figure it this way: It's like anything you buy in bulk. When you buy heroin, two bags get you one free. Three get you two more free bags, etc. It rises in direct proportion. So, what you really need is a small daily supply of cash, which working a cash register easily provides. Before computerized cash registers, it was pretty easy to just pocket forty to sixty bucks a day. Then if you pool your cash with the other members of the Melrose Heroin-for-Lunch Bunch, you are now making a sizable purchase.

Dear Grant,
Thanks for the tip on heroin shopping. As the game heats up, I may need an addict in my corner. And since time is tight, it may have to be me.
        Meanwhile, I continue with your thread of Something Important the Next Day.

It was the end of 1994. Everyone I knew was always saying, "Come on! It's the nineties!" as a reaction to everything anyone did that seemed less than truly evolved. In the name of greater independence, I started writing a column called "Travels with Norm" for the *L.A. Reader.* In it, I would write about little trips around town with my dog Norm. It seemed to be going pretty well. There was talk of a book. Even more exciting, Norm and I got invited to judge a pet parade at the Visalia Onion Festival. Channel 9 asked me to do a report on it for their local weekend pop culture roundup. I know it might sound small-time to you, but I was very excited about it. It was going to be my first-ever appearance on television.

Meanwhile, P.E. was still reshooting some scenes on *Macaroni and Cheese Club II* in Toronto. On weekends I would fly to Toronto to stoke the home fires, then come back to L.A. midweek to work.

Which brings us to the night before the Onion Festival, when, unannounced, P.E. blew into town, on a forced break from filming. Chad, the kid actor who played the Macaroni and Cheese Club president, had pneumonia and was hospitalized for a couple of days. P.E. hated to have his work interrupted by life. So he was acting edgy and gloomy. As soon as he arrived, P.E. made plans to meet his junior high school buddies at a hockey game, then go to dinner. As usual, he didn't ask if this was okay with me, he just informed me that we were going. And me being me, I said, "Fine," even though what I really wanted was to stay home and prep for the Onion Festival. I didn't know how to say no to him.

P.E. habitually ran a half hour behind schedule. So we were getting into his new Jeep to head to the game only fifteen minutes before whatever you call the beginning of a hockey game—the puck-off?—was supposed to take place. The drive time alone was forty minutes, and of course, he was angry about this. But he was even more pissed off when, right before we backed out of the driveway, he noticed there was a smudge on his windshield. So he took off the vintage bowling shirt he was wearing—with the name WAYNE embroidered on the pocket—wadded it into a ball, wiped the windshield clean, then put the shirt back on. Oddly enough, when he looked down he now saw that this had added big grease marks to the front of the shirt. This made him even angrier, because now he was going to have to waste even more time going back into the house to change his shirt. "Fuck me. Fuck. Fuck. Fuck. All I want to do is go to a goddamn fucking hockey game, and now I'm completely fucked!" he screamed, slamming the car door as I followed him back into the house and watched as he stormed around like a chubby little troll, screaming about how there were never any clean clothes when he needed them, about how he was always fucked no matter what he tried to do. By now I was nervous, because I knew where this was all headed: to an attack on me that would probably make me cry. And I didn't want my face all puffy and swollen when I appeared on TV for the first time tomorrow. So I told him, "I better just stay home and work on my little report," thinking that if he went to the game alone, maybe the hours he spent with his buddies would change his mood. That made sense to me. I very calmly strolled into my office and sat down at my desk. I imagined that he would leave without me, swearing as he slammed the door. But instead he came in after me and pushed his beet-red face an inch from mine as he began to scream about what a miserable fucking cunt I was. His spit was hitting me. His eyes looked murderous. I sat expressionless, trying to disappear. I didn't want to get upset, so I was time-traveling, detaching, pretending to have no reaction. And that was making him even angrier.

We had indeed hit the point I had hoped to avoid, where he was listing all of my intolerable flaws, berating my crazy fucking mother and the way I always had to have everything my way. He was also saying scary shit about how if I left him, he would sue me. For just a moment, I worried that there might actually be some way to sue someone for having a crazy mother. Could she be considered an accessory after the fact? Finally he left, slamming the door so hard that it knocked over a lamp and a vase.

As soon as he left, I was panicky. I knew this fight would resume when he got home. It was just a matter of time. And he would keep it going until he made me cry. I didn't want to be exhausted and look like a prizefighter in my first and only appearance on television. I was secretly hoping it might lead to an opportunity to do more little reports—an opportunity that would be less likely if I looked like Mrs. Potato Head. So I called up my shrink. "Is there anyplace you can go and spend the night?" she said, after hearing about it all. I began weighing my options. I didn't know which motels in the area, if any, would take dogs, so I decided to call Kat, who after all is the queen of bad relationship behavior. Of course she understood and welcomed me. I packed a suitcase and spent the night on her couch. It was a landmark moment for me, because it was the first time I had ever put my own interests ahead of P.E.'s. I wasn't happy about leaving home under these circumstances. It felt really bad. But I didn't feel like I had a choice.

The next day, at ten A.M., I showed up to meet the camera crew in Visalia like nothing ever happened. Everything went very well. (Although I confess it occurred to me that if I had shown up with red eyes, I could have blamed it on the onions.)

Later that afternoon, when I got home, Nick was in front of the television watching football. He didn't look up. Never said a word. We didn't talk until six o'clock. Then I asked what he wanted for dinner. He said burgers. And I made them.

SCORE	Points
Sitting in a brand-new Jeep watching a bad situation escalate	500
As a man cleans a windshield with his own shirt	125
Then blames me for the dearth of clean clothes	125
Being screamed at for protecting my career opportunity	1,000
Unpleasantness and humiliation of having to leave home and sleep on someone's couch the night before I need to perform capably at a high-pressure new job	800
Okay, it wasn't high pressure, but it still mattered to me	200
Making burgers for the enemy	250
TOTAL:	3,000

NEW TOTALS: Grant 13,775   Lisa 12,930

I sent it off at six A.M., and then, unable to go back to sleep, I sat down with my food cards and began ruminating about everything. I was turning a big Cider-Marinated Beef Roast into a kind of a moody, angst-ridden all-meat version of Ernest Borgnine when I heard a fresh e-mail arrive.

Dear Lisa,
I just read your last P.E. story and here's what occurred to me.

Our Psycho Exes were the consistent ones, it was we who were all over the map. The real thrust of your story is the way in which he changed you.

I had my eyes open and got caught anyway. It sounds like you walked into your relationship, never suspecting what was going on inside you until you were in the middle of it.

I am wondering why your P.E. didn't just figure you'd be busy preparing for work and go to the game with his pals. It seems he was setting up this disaster.

Well, there it was again: Grant offering me empathy, seeming to feel concern. I reminded myself that even if I did maybe sometimes have deepening feelings for Grant, it was fine because he had been dropped into my life not as a romantic possibility. He was there as a template for a different kind of relationship. He was part of a very happy couple. And even if he'd been single, he was too obsessive-compulsive and far too adolescent, too out of control for me. If I ever found myself an available Grant type, I would definitely try for a tidier, more adult model.

Dear Grant,
I don't know if he intentionally set up disasters or just enjoyed them so much that they were, for him, like a bowl of mixed nuts to a guy drinking beer. Impossible to resist.

I guess my true blind spot was that I assumed growth was an inevitable part of life. I didn't believe that "no growth" was possible for anyone, year after year. I forgot that the rule "Things always change in time" only really applies in L.A. if you're a kid under seventeen or a mini-mall.

And then again, sometimes in a weird way I liked how Psycho Ex was so distant. I think I liked always chasing a truck down a hill. I got to be the well-intended person who was trying so hard. I got to be the one who appeared saintly and sane.

Lisa

After I pushed "send," I was still very keyed up. I sat in front of the computer for about an hour, just in case another e-mail arrived. While I waited, I started work on Pimiento-Glazed Bass, and almost immediately was able to find a perfect pimiento that looked like an angry mouth. It already had an internal shadow and a little speckling of white sauce suggesting teeth and a tongue. That's what I was doing when, at about ten o'clock, the phone rang. And rather than risk messing up my newest masterpiece, I let my answering machine take the call. It was Mark Eden telling me he had good news and bad news. The show had been put on hiatus. And "my script" was nominated for a *TV Digest* Award. I had a feeling that his idea of which news was supposed to be good and which was bad was 180 degrees from mine.

Chapter 26

GRANT

Y ou might say my world is upside down. Many have. In my world, L.A. is cool, if not downright chilly. There is a moon and no sun. There are always four open stalls at the coin-op car wash. Supermarket parking lots have hundreds of open spaces. Although Winnie can just drop off to sleep, at three A.M. I'm too wound up to rest. So I drive and think. I like being the only car on the road. That way I don't have to worry if anyone can see me lecturing myself in the empty passenger seat.

Not that I actually talked to myself per se. I talked to people who were no longer there; to the girls I should have kissed, and the girls I shouldn't have. I'd explain things I couldn't tell them at the time, facts they didn't know, so they would finally understand and forgive. If I'd been cruel to someone, I'd reenact it and correct it. I'd rage at tyrannical label presidents, club owners, old managers, and band members, vindicated at last. I even spoke to Arvin Petro. Other times my tone would be gentle, philosophical, as I played tour guide to my life's passengers, explaining how we all got to this point and why . . . for the ten thousandth time. For me, this was part of being a songwriter, always digging through the past. I never let go of anyone or anything.

If Winnie ever bugged the car, I'd be dead, because I often spoke out loud to Claudia. It felt good, like scratching a rash. I'd explain why I chose Winn over her, why I never called to say why, and how sorry I was that I had hurt her one more time. Though this never made me feel any better, I did it to feel close to her, holding on to our last remaining bonds, though they were only shame and sorrow.

Mind you, I loved Winnie. I was happy. The way my career had whooshed up had proved I had made the right decision. But at the core of the looming success, I'd find myself fingering the shreds of Claudia. Life with a near-perfect goddess like Winnie, who seemed to need no one and had a snappy answer and a solution for everything, got to be pretty damn lonesome.

I could survive. Like anything else, love had its trade-offs. Winnie wasn't going to sit on the couch, purr in a low voice, and talk about last night's dreams, just as Claudia wasn't going to get up onstage dressed like Pam Anderson and sing the aria "I'm Changing My Tattoo from Tommy to Mommy."

That's why Lisa was the perfect supplement, I thought. Everybody needed a friend, didn't they? Well, Lisa was mine. That she was female was the problem. But the old punk in me felt that was bourgeois horseshit, that men and women could be friends. That this Winnie and Lisa thing would smooth out in time. I could see it all clearly. I'd make music and money sharing my life with Winnie. And I'd never have to slow her down, because when I needed a sympathetic ear, there'd be my friend Lisa: a friend like Claudia was minus the cheating, the sneaking around, the betrayal.

When Lisa dropped by our house, my hopes were confirmed. The two of them got along easily, and without much help from me. Every time one made the other laugh, it was like church bells chiming. At the same time, I couldn't help comparing; Winn was stunning, Lisa was striking. Winn was charmingly overdone, Lisa was charmingly disheveled. Winn was an extravagant musician, Lisa an understated writer. Winn acted, reacted, and tossed out wisecracks. Lisa contemplated, probed, analyzed. Winn was bright and fiery, Lisa brilliant and warm.

Later, after Lisa left, I said proudly, "You two seemed to get along very well."

Winnie shrugged, "She was only being nice to my face." An hour later, when Lisa's e-mail arrived, Winnie read it out loud: " 'I am very impressed by how you have been able to take the lessons you learned from Psycho Ex and apply them toward a healthy relationship now. It kind of gives me hope.' Faint praise," Winnie said, biting her fingernails. "The dog could learn that much after being with a junkie."

"Oh, come on. It's a perfectly nice letter, Win."

Again she shrugged. "Lisa's trying to win me over to get close to you. 'You two are very cute together,' " she mocked, rolling her eyes.

"Are you always at war with everyone?" I shouted at the empty passenger seat as I headed down Ventura. My destination was Casa De Cadillac. Like rain in the wind, I smelled a record deal coming, so I wanted to see if there was anything worth dreaming about in the showroom. This attempt to cheer myself up turned out to be futile. "Jesus Christ, Winnie. You have a hundred people coming in and out of our house day and night! Drag queens and Drag Hags. Guys from your old band.

I counted three ex-boyfriends last month alone: Isaac, Chas, and Ben Fricke." Now I was on a roll. "You go where you want. You do what you want. You see who you want. And I encourage you. But all I have is you and the piano and the Psycho Ex game."

This was a little overdramatic, I knew, but not far from the truth. Being director of the musical put me in a position to keep my distance. In a cast full of stand-up comics and musicians, I couldn't be a goofball and then demand respect. Maintaining my authority meant the difference between a tight show and one that was a shambles. At the cast party, when Winn and all the gals stripped down and dove in the pool, black bras and panties shining in the moonlight, the rest of the guys joined right in. But when the girls from the chorus chanted, "Strip, Grant, strip!" I waved them away playfully and went off to smoke. Sorry. Beethoven, Napoleon, and Churchill didn't strip down to their skivvies and do a cannonball.

As I drove, I found myself fuming about the current windstorm. Lately, Winnie was starring in and also producing the Drag Hags, a male/female burlesque revue full of Silver Lake amateurs seeking the spotlight, any spotlight: part boys in drag putting it on, part girls taking it off. Winnie believed in centralizing power, so along with *Tommy! (Lee!)*, our home became the Drag Hags' main office. Lately the floor of the front room was carpeted with cheesecake photos of Winn and her girlfriends, in pasties and sheer panties. And as Winnie made a constant stream of calls to cast members organizing rehearsals, and auditions, her fellow Dragsters minced around my living room, transformed into high-heeled harlots in mink, fishnets, and push-up bras, practicing their walks and naughty yet cornball bits for the show. The phone trilled constantly. People were always at the door. My former bachelor pad had become a crossroads where gossip and intrigue collided with chaos.

This started early in the day and ended late at night. Winnie never slowed down, except to sleep for a few hours in her clothes. The next day it would all begin again.

By the time I drove past Casa De Cadillac, I found myself resenting Winnie. I barely even looked at the lot. For everything she had, for everything that we shared, she wanted me to nix my friendship with Lisa.

I was too disappointed now to talk to the ghosts. I drove a block farther. "Fuck that bourgeois horseshit," said the old punk in me. "Give it a little time. Winnie will come around. I ain't doing nothing wrong."

I flicked the turn indicator and headed back to Silver Lake.

Chapter 27

LISA

I almost didn't pick up the phone when I heard Eden leave that message on my machine. But when I heard him say, "The awards ceremony is Sunday. Let's go together," I figured I'd better.

"Why don't you just go," I said, surprising him mid-sentence.

"But it's your name on the nominated script," he said.

"You have my permission to put your name on it instead," I said.

"I don't get you," he said. "I thought you enjoyed working on the show."

"Eden, I've told you before," I said, "the reason I don't want my name on that script is because I didn't write it."

"Just come to the ceremony," he said. "We probably won't win anyway."

So I agreed, out of a vague desire to network. Then I sat down and read the story that had come this morning at five.

Dear Lisa,
I will continue with the theme of starting to separate your interests from those of P.E.

"HOW YA LIKE ME NOW?"

Psycho Ex was the singer in a band of sloppy Stones clones who aptly called themselves Personality Crisis. They got drunk, slung their guitars low, and posed like Keith. Their big showstopper was a song that P.E. wrote in her Boston years called "How Ya Like Me Now?," a dreary mid-tempo two-chord Velvets knockoff that they thought would get them a record deal. It contained lines that made me squirm, references to hunger, blood, and Seventh Avenue in New York City. To my ears not a great song, but regardless of what I thought, in our circle, when someone would solemnly ask P.E. to sing it at acoustic-guitar jams, it would be a sacred moment. Like saying, "Hey, Paul, could you do 'Yesterday,' " or "Hey Jimmy, do 'Stairway' for us."

Here's what was odd: She always sang it exactly the same. No left turns or new inflections. And at the end of the tune there was a little throwaway line, "Come on and cry for me," which she sang "Comowna kwa fuhmay." Even that was always the same. No impromptu heys or yahs, or even "Yeeeow, com owna owna owna kwaaa fuhmay baybee." But what the hell. It wasn't my song, or my band. I knew better than to comment.

Around the time of the hospital story, Psycho Ex was down in the dumps about her songwriting. She wished, she said, she could just sit down and write any old thing like I did. But no, she sighed, she had to wait for inspiration. Supportive boyfriend that I was, I pointed out that if she wrote every day for a year, she could have a lot more songs that were as good as or better than "How Ya Like Me Now?" She thought a moment, then shrugged. "Naahhh. I can't do it like you. I have to wait for it to hit me."

Cut to me, out on the road with Slowly I Turn, wistfully staring out the window of the Winnebago, revisiting that horrible hospital scene. I was thinking, I'm through with her. It's over. But also thinking, If I boot her out while I'm on the road, she'll steal everything I own. I'll wait for things to settle down when I get back, then end it. Close-up as I brighten, because suddenly it dawns on me: Hey, if it's over, that means I can fuck around!

When you're a touring band, you find that the more famous you become, the better-looking the groupies, male and female. At this point, the gay, straight, or bi members of the band could generally choose from a group of plump little Goths with black lips, whiffy pits, and bacteria-laden leather pants. The choice was further limited by the type of people who would put their mouths all over a stranger just because he's memorized some lyrics. I can remember getting onstage and my guitar player shouting off-mike, "You people are so fucking ugly I can't take it. Stop looking at me! Stop!" Not that we were in much better shape, in our stinky stage clothes.

So . . . there we were in Montgomery, Alabama, hanging out at the bar after our show, when I struck up a conversation with Jasmine. A very affable woman, she had spent time as a musician in Boston. I don't know why exactly, but I got an odd feeling when she said "Boston." "My girlfriend played in a band in Boston," I said. "Well, I know everybody in Boston," said Jasmine in that boastful southern manner. "What's her name?" When I said, "Jane Gray," her face lit up. "Of course I know Jane Gray—why, she used to do a song I wrote." For some reason I knew what she would say next, but I asked her anyway. "It's called 'How Ya Like Me Now?' " she replied. Still holding on to a shred of hope, I lied and said, "I think I know that one. How does it go?" And over the thundering dance music on the house system, she leaned in close and sang in my ear. Word for word, note for note, it was the first verse of the same song. Naturally, I wanted to find out more. So, without tipping my hand, I accepted her invitation to go to her apartment. I also liked her. She was a hoot. A political activist, she was sexy, smart, funny. I sensed that she was dangerous. That's for me!

We had marital relations. Even when you start the entwinement with "Sorry I'm on clap watch," there's still all sorts of great filthy stuff you can do. Hey. We were rock vets. We're a hearty lot.

In the bleary morning, as Jasmine was driving me back to the hotel, I asked her to send me a copy of her singing "How Ya Like Me Now?" "I'll let you know who sings it better," I said with a wink. That was catnip for someone as competitive as Jasmine.

In two months I was home. Jasmine sent her album and a gushy letter to my manager's office. And yep, there was "How Ya Like Me Now?," listed right on the sleeve. By Jasmine Harper, ASCAP. It was registered. In my manager's office I put it on and heard the same dreary song I never liked, note for note exactly the way P.E. sang it. At the end, Jasmine Harper sang the same little throwaway line: "Comowna kwa fuhmay." That scared me. I got a little chill. Psycho Ex didn't just steal, she copied. What scared me even more was that in all the years I'd heard her sing it, she'd never thought to vary a single note.

I sat on this for a few days. But I was greedy for more information, so I decided on a bold frontal attack.

"Oh hey," I said to Jane, "I almost forgot. I met a woman who said she knew you. Jasmine Harper."

"Oh, Jasmine. Yeah. I knew her," she said, a little too casually. We both agreed she was a very nice person. "Yeah, we played some of the same clubs together," she said, then changed the subject to dinner.

But I couldn't stop. I had to know. "Uh-huh. Sure. Fried chicken is fine. Hey, listen . . . she said the weirdest thing. She said she wrote 'How Ya Like Me Now?' "

"What?" she screamed. "She what? That's a fucking lie. I wrote that song. That's my fucking song."

"Okay. Sure. Fine. Cool off. I just thought it was a strange thing to say. Why do you think she said it?"

"I don't know what that cunt's trip is. It's a great song. Why wouldn't she want to say she wrote it? She probably wanted to fuck you. That's why. Did you fuck her? Is that it?"

I knew it had been a risk to bring up the name of a woman I'd had sex with. "No," I said. "But why would she lie about a thing like that when she knew I could ask you? It's too risky."

"Stop screaming at me. Believe whatever you want. But I wrote that fucking song. And I don't want to hear another word about it," said P.E., though I hadn't been screaming. She was doing the screaming.

We never did have another word about "How Ya Like Me Now?"

Epilogue: As it turned out, I was only home for about a month when another tour started. P.E. and I still hadn't broken up. But next thing I knew we were back in Montgomery, where I saw Jasmine again. This time I confided about my troubles with P.E. She was sympathetic and supportive and offered me her friendship. I, in return, offered her our tour itinerary, saying, "Give me a call sometime."

Over the next six months, getting me away from Jane Gray became her new political cause.

Days before the tour ended, Jasmine called me in Sydney, Australia, and said, "Guess what, shugah? I'm gonna meet yew at the airport when you get home. I'm gonna be your welcoming committee." When I told her that Jane was going to be there, she said, "I'm gonna get yew away from that awful woman." And then she added, "I've moved to L.A." I don't remember my exact response, except that it began, "Under no circumstances are you going to meet me at the airport, you fucking screwball."

Once back in L.A., I calmed Jasmine down. "You gotta let me handle this thing by myself," I told her. She accepted that to a point. But when she found out that P.E. was playing at a club, she called to say that she was going to that show. To cover my butt, I told P.E. that I'd heard Jasmine had moved to town.

"Oh," she said. She could care less.

At the show, P.E. and her band of junkies got up to play. Jasmine showed up about halfway through and sat down with me in the audience. She looked at P.E. onstage, and whispered, "Grant. She's sad. Is this what you really want?"

At that moment, P.E. looked up from the stage and saw me talking to Jasmine. I saw P.E. blanch, then turn to Kip and say, "No 'How Ya Like Me Now?' "

I watched Kip shout, "What the fuck? Why?"

"Just drop it," P.E. ordered.

After the show, P.E. walked past Jasmine, shouted, "Hi," and took off. If I hadn't known better, I would have thought it was the perfect time for P.E. to say, "So what's all this about you writing my song?"

SCORE	Points

That out of three and a half million people in
Montgomery, Alabama, I met the woman who
wrote the song P.E. was stealing. This fact
confirmed that P.E. wasn't just a victim to her
drug but was at heart corrupt. A fine line I would
not have understood had I not been standing in a
bar three thousand miles from home   500

Enduring yet another New York City street
reference in a rock song intended, as Gilbert
said, "to give artistic verisimilitude to an
otherwise bald and unconvincing narrative."
(A crime I have been guilty of myself, but those
are someone else's points in another P.E. game
where I, if you can possibly imagine such a thing,
am The Psycho Ex)   100

Enduring titles like "How Ya Like Me Now?"   50

Limiting one's sexcapades due to clap watch   300

Having to pretend that P.E.'s tantrum convinced
me that she was the author of "How Ya Like
Me Now?"   500

Jasmine stalking me, saying, "Guess what, shugah!
I'm gonna be your welcoming committee."   500

TOTAL: 1,950

I digested this story. The first thing I thought was: Thank
you, Jesus, for opening my eyes to the fact that Grant is not
really the sweet sensitive extension of my computer that I
imagine. He is, in fact, the kind of aloof and cold-hearted

touring musician who goes out on the road and has sex with groupies. This is just the additional information necessary to nudge a bothersome crush into its final death throes. I knew it was a little pretentious to presume, after a lifetime of turning my back on the church, that Jesus was suddenly taking an interest in my e-mails. Still, once again I was relieved that Grant was spoken for. No more out of the frying pan and into the even bigger frying pan for me. This latest story also bothered me, made me feel rankled and irritable. I felt I had to say something.

Dear Grant,

I hope this isn't the end of a fantastically entertaining friendship, but I am going to contest the following points:

<< Jasmine stalking me, saying, "Guess what, shugah! I'm gonna get yew away from that awful woman." . . . 500>>

I apologize if this hurts your feelings. But I wouldn't be a very good commander in general if I didn't call 'em as I see 'em. Seems to me she was your victim, not vice versa. You used her to get info about P.E. and alleviate your sexual frustration on the road. It seems like you were leading her on all over the place, taking her calls all around the world every night, flirting with her, confiding in her. But when she responded by wanting you, you were suddenly her victim. That don't wash. That, to me, is lying down in the middle of the freeway and saying you were the victim of crazy drivers. To say nothing of taking points for clap watch. How did that have anything to do with P.E.? Please don't hate me, but I don't think you get to take points in this game for "limiting one's sexcapades." You do not deserve points for having to curtail cheating due to paranoia regarding sexually transmitted disease. How does this not make you the Psycho Ex?

Now I'll sit here quietly while you punch the computer.

Dear Lisa,

No, no. I'm not upset in the least. The points you raise are good and reflect the general ugliness and insanity into which I was sinking. But let me clarify my reasoning about why I claimed the points. I liked Jasmine and the night I spent with her. However, I didn't want a relationship with her. Nor did I make any fake promises. When she asked if she could call me on the road, I had no idea that she meant every night. I figured once a month, or now and then. That she called me every night after spending a grand total of ten hours together (two nights at five hours apiece) certainly seemed like stalking. So in an effort to turn down the heat, I began not to take her calls. You might assume that I, the evil male, was leading her on. But I did no such thing. The big mistake I made was letting Jasmine in on my problems. I never imagined that she would quit her job and drive three thousand miles to save me from the clutches of the deadly Jane Gray, crying all the way to L.A. like Dick Shawn in *It's a Mad Mad Mad Mad World*. But when she arrived and found that breakups take a long time, she wasn't just mad, she was hopping-teary-insulted-disenchanted-eyeliner-melting-refusing-to-believe-it mad. Maybe even vengeful-hell-hath-no-fury mad. I was afraid of what else she might do: Call Jane? Write a tell-all note? Show up at my door? Shoot me?

And almost getting the clap from someone came as a result of discovering, just hours before I left, that my beloved was a hard-core junkie who was leading a double life the whole time we'd been together. Since the source of all that was Jane, I claimed 300 points. However, I have just consulted the rule book, and I see here that the use of Circumloquacious Projection (blaming another person for your own rotten behavior as a motive) results in removal of 25 percent of the points assigned. So I will voluntarily remove 75 points from that total, bringing the clap-watch points down to 225.

Finally, as far as lying down in traffic goes: Your P.E. punched car roofs, screamed through windshields, and left you on a dark road. The whole thrill of this game is watching two seemingly intelligent people lie down on the highway.

Dear Grant,
Okay. Keep your damn points.

I was trying not to be fixated by the place in the story where he said, "There's still all sorts of great filthy stuff you can do." That image had a hold on me and was creating a kind of low boil in the part of my DNA where my attraction to him was buried. From time to time, it would rise up like an unexpected flame in my gut, a specter that could overwhelm me, make me dizzy. Luckily, this same story had just taught me that the act of confiding meant nothing to this guy. I was in probable danger. So if I couldn't put the emotional reactions I was having to Grant back in the airtight containers where they had been previously sealed and buried, then it was time to call a halt to our correspondence. I had always vowed that I would discontinue it if it became problematic in any way. Maybe that moment was near.

Meanwhile, I saved his letter in "incoming mail," deciding to answer it later when I wasn't feeling quite so wound up. And I went out to try and find something to wear to the *TV Digest* Awards tomorrow. The show would be televised. I supposedly had to look nice, even though I knew from years of attending events with Nick that lack of fame made a person completely invisible at such events. Nevertheless, I went out trolling the mall for some kind of glamour wear, having no idea what that meant where I was concerned. I always envied the way that men got to rent a standardized outfit. But women were supposed to have an instinctual feel for these things. I wished I was brave enough to go to General Costume and rent a prison outfit with a set of leg irons. Instead, I ended up buying a plain black dress that I could hopefully wear again.

The so-called ceremony was scheduled to start taping at five. Eden showed up in my driveway at three, in the back of the limo the show provided for its nominees. The *TV Digest* Awards had to offer all kinds of enticements to get the nominees to attend. Thus the car was just a little bit longer than a city block and had a bar stocked with every amenity: liquor in all kinds of oversize cut-glass carafes, a hefty assortment of salty snacks, a television, a DVD player, an Internet connection, an aromatherapy kit, a library of CDs, a string of Christmas lights above the doors, an air-ionizing machine. The uniformed driver opened the door for me, and I crawled into the backseat, where Eden was leaning against the far door, drinking a water glass full of Scotch.

"What? No sauna?" I said, looking around. "No koi pond? No fireplace?"

"Hi, beautiful," Eden said. "Here. Drink up. No one should go to the *TV Digest* Awards sober." He had commandeered the carafe full of amber liquor so handed me a glass and a carafe full of clear. I made myself comfortable in the enormous black leather seat and as the car headed down my street I consumed about half a glass of gin in a single gulp. That was Eden's cue to try to rekindle what we once had, to the extent that we ever had anything. But sadly for him, away from the magic that was *You Go, Girl!*, he looked like a balding chubby guy in a rented tuxedo and running shoes. When he put his hand on my thigh, I started to laugh. "I'm afraid I'm two weaselly guys past my annual quota," I said, moving it off me.

"Who was the other one?" he asked, putting it back.

"You," I said, moving it off again, this time with more zeal. But at least now, after large quantities of limo hooch, we both were feeling giddy. He either didn't care or was too drunk to know if he did.

As we pulled up to the red-carpet area outside the Shrine Auditorium, I could hear a roar of "Cybill, Cybill, Over here!" from the crowd gathered across the street. Lo and behold! Cybill Shepherd exited the limo in front of us. As if to prove the award-show corollary to Newton's Third Law of Motion, there was an equally loud silence and hush of disappointment as we exited. I thought of how different things would have been if I had exited with Nick. Then I started to laugh, realizing I was crazy. Nick would never have agreed to attend the *TV Digest* Awards, and if he had he would have insisted we parachute in through a skylight.

By the time the taping of the ceremony got under way, Eden and I each had two more cocktails. This transformed the seemingly endless cavalcade of unknown supporting cast members who were there in lieu of some actual star who couldn't be bothered into a deeply hilarious Brechtian piece of theater of the absurd. Soon we both had succumbed to the kind of cumulative unstoppable giggling that used to overtake me at particularly solemn junior high school assemblies and religious gatherings. Thank God our category didn't come up until almost the end of the show. Because after the giggles died down, I really needed the slight amount of tension and curiosity about who would win our category to help me stay awake. My eyes were closing, my head falling forward spasmodically. By then I was so drunk that when I heard them call our names, I thought I was hallucinating. But if it was a hallucination, it was happening in a group, because the next thing I knew, Eden and the ten boy writers were all surrounding me as we were herded, like a flock of geese, onto the stage. The other writers encircled me, applauding, clearing a path to the podium for me to make my speech. I gestured no. It was too late. No one listened or moved. I had to take the mike. I didn't know what to say.

"I want to thank everyone connected with the show," I began, trying to find a way to prevail over this completely surreal moment. "And I . . . uh . . . well . . . I couldn't have written this script without the rest of these guys. Seriously. I couldn't have. In fact, I really didn't. This award really belongs to them. The only lines I wrote were the ones about the plant." And having said that, I stood back and applauded them, refusing to say another word, because I couldn't think of one. Eden took the mike.

"*You Go, Girl!* is thrilled to have been honored by all of you this evening," he said. "Especially in light of the fact that the show was just put on hiatus." He waited for some sound of audience empathy that never came. But never one to let circumstances alter his preconceived notions, he continued as if it had. "I want to thank everyone who worked on the show. As well as my wife, Elaine, and our three beautiful children, Ashley, Jake, and Ahmed, for all their love and support. But as I'm sure you know, it all begins and ends with the writer. So, most of all, I want to thank the ridiculously modest Lisa Roberty for her brilliant script. I think I speak for the whole cast and crew when I say 'Lisa, you go, girl!' " Everyone stood in a semicircle around me and applauded again as a woman in a strapless sequined gown handed me a ten-inch mounted crystal rhomboid. I looked at the joy-filled faces of my fellow staffers . . . and then realized I didn't recognize the ones closest to me. As I found out later, Brent and his writing partner, Robby, had gone to the restroom when our category was called, and their seat-fillers were onstage accepting their awards.

"I'm not kidding. I didn't write it. I only have about two lines in it, the bit with the plant and . . . oh hell, like you care. . . ." I remember mumbling drunkenly as I was drowned out by the bumper music they use to segue into commercials.

As we rode home down Sunset Boulevard in our big white limo, Eden was still happily swigging Scotch. I, on the other hand, was already nursing a hangover. Approaching the arc of Sunset Strip that is mostly music stores and clubs, we were soon trapped in a gridlock of unmoving cars. All around us were overdressed, overstimulated kids in search of nightlife. "Well, how do you like that, you network ass wipes? Revenge is sweet. We won an award for a show that's been canceled," Eden kept saying with increasing emphasis. To make sure his point was being made, he stood up, opened the limo's sunroof, and stuck his big bald head out. "Take that, you dumb motherfuckers! Not good enough to be on the fall schedule, but somehow good enough to win a fucking award! What other awards did you get tonight, you brilliant programming genius cocksuckers? Answer: NONE, you fucking morons. NONE!" he yelled as we inched along in traffic, surrounded on all sides by an unsmiling rainbow coalition of rage, drugs, and bass-heavy rap music.

"Eden," I screamed at him, looking around nervously, "stop it. One of these guys will think you're yelling at him. You're going to get us killed." Fortunately, all our potential antagonists had the sound systems in their cars up so loud that I don't think they could make out what the drunk white geek was screaming. By then Eden was so unsteady on his feet that I had no trouble pulling him back into the car. He tumbled down into the backseat as though he had no skeletal system, then he leaned over and put his head on my shoulder.

"Eden, sit up," I scolded.

"You know what? You're my soul mate," he said. "G'me a kiss."

"A half hour ago you were televised nationally thanking your wife and kids for all their love and support," I said.

"Ah, no one saw that. The fucking *TV Digest* Awards don't get any ratings," he ranted. "They'll be lucky if they get a two share. Anyway, we're separated," he said, gulping more Scotch straight from the carafe. "I'm hoping she'll hear about it and not go for spousal support. Lisa, listen. I want you to come home with me. Let's make this a perfect evening." Those were the last words he spoke before passing out on the enormous black leather seat as the carafe of Scotch emptied onto his cummerbund.

By the time the driver dropped me off, Eden was snoring. I was so glad to be home. As soon as I unlocked the front door, I headed like a lemming back to the cliffs of my little computer world, where I could get points for my pain and humiliation. Grant didn't even know about my nomination or the awards ceremony. I wasn't planning to tell him.

Chapter 28

LISA

D ear Grant,
I continue your thread of someone wanting
to rescue you from P.E.

OUT OF THE FRYING PAN, AND BACK INTO THE FRYING PAN

Macaroni and Cheese Club was in the last stages
of editing, and I was supervising the final cut. This
meant that the film's editor, Zack, and I spent long
hours together. We talked a lot, ate lunch and sometimes dinner together. There was some chemistry
building.

Psycho Ex had picked up on that and was doing
his part to make everything better by hardly speaking to me and then, at night, torturing me with his

paranoia. Zack became our main topic of conversation. I woke up to accusations that I was fucking Zack, and I was still defending myself against them as I fell asleep.

It's true that Zack and I had gotten close, but it was because being with P.E. had made me extremely needy. Nothing had ever happened between Zack and me. All we did was work. And talk. Until the last few minutes of the wrap party when we kissed goodbye. That was the first time I had empirical evidence that electrical voltage existed between us. I left the party in a state of vertigo, walking into walls. Fortunately, I didn't have time to contemplate all this. P.E. and I headed straight to the airport and caught a plane. We were home and hundreds of miles away by the next morning.

Next thing we knew, the film had tested well and gotten a summer release date. Instead of being thrilled, P.E. sank into hopelessness and insecurity.

"But the movie really tested well," I would say.

"Big deal," he would howl. "In this town, you're only as good as the thing you're doing right now. And right now I am doing nothing."

"But you've got a movie coming out in a couple of months," I'd counter.

"But I'm not doing anything right NOW. Why can't you understand that's all that matters? Everyone thinks I'm a loser."

A spiraling into terror over the fear that the movie was going to bomb because it was a piece of shit would follow. I would try to be reassuring. But don't forget, if it was a piece of shit, I was partly responsible. He was also attacking something I had helped create. This made me a very conflicted support system.

I was miserable and lonelier than I have ever been

alone. I thought about leaving but wanted to be around for the film's premiere. So I tried to roll with the punches, which were coming fast and furious. Then the word got to me through mutual friends that Zack, the high-voltage editor, was in L.A. seeking work. Next thing I knew, he started turning up wherever I was. At my gym. At the park where I took my dogs. At my friend's house for dinner. He was all sympathy and empathy and chemistry, which I, of course, found pretty appealing, since at home there was no affection at all. One night Zack and I went for a walk together. We kissed again, and he told me he loved me. He wanted me to leave P.E. This ended with some very hot making out that made me horribly nervous. I knew I was not in the clear emotionally from the commitment and loyalty I still felt to P.E. I was also finding the sexual heat from Zack hard to resist.

And then *Macaroni and Cheese Club* opened to mixed reviews but very strong box-office numbers. The financial success of the opening weekend alone meant P.E.'s career as a director was assured. But he was depressed because not all the critics liked it. "It's making money, and that's all anyone cares about," I would say.

"Everyone thinks I am a no-talent failure. Any moron can make money," he would counter.

About a week after the film opened, my mother had a colitis attack. I decided to go to San Diego to visit my family. When I got to the airport, Zack was at the gate waiting for me. His car was parked in the loading zone by the baggage area. He wanted to drive me to San Diego. I was weak. I craved a chance to be with someone who acted like he loved me. I said yes. On the way, we stopped in La Jolla and checked into a nice motel overlooking the ocean. It was part romantic, part terrifying. The more sexual we got, the more I felt like I was having freezing water poured down the back of my neck. I was a nervous wreck, worrying about P.E. finding out. I still hadn't given up on the idea of making our relationship work. I hadn't made a decision to leave him. I think that was the reason I finally had sex with Zack. I was trying to create a reason to leave P.E. by violating a basic relationship rule. Otherwise, it appeared there was nothing P.E. could do to me, no behavior so intolerable, that I wouldn't rationalize and put up with. However, once I had officially cheated, I knew I had to move out.

When I got home, I waited until P.E. was at a meeting. Then I packed my bags and put my dogs Juicy and Norm in the car. I remember feeling annoyed by how happy they were to be going for a drive. "No. It's not a walk, it's a breakup. They're not at all similar," I remember saying to them as I drove the packed car to my brother's house in Culver City, where I camped out while I tried to find a place to rent that took dogs. Every morning I circled rental prospects in the paper. Then I would drive up and down the streets, looking toward the sky to see where buzzards were circling. That was always the one house where pets were welcome.

By the end of the week, I had rented a horrid, barely ventilated little house not too far from my brother's. I moved in with no furniture, some unpacked boxes, a bed. And Zack seemed to be staying with me. But as sweet as he was, I kept obsessing about P.E. *Macaroni and Cheese Club* was a big hit and there were references to it everywhere. There were billboards, there were ads on those dividers that separate your order from someone else's at the supermarket. But it was the sound-track display in the window of the Wherehouse that got me so rattled that I rear-ended another car at a red light. That was frightening enough, but then two things happened in rapid fashion. First, I had an obscene phone call at my new house. "I am watching you," said a creepy voice with a cackling laugh, followed by quacking duck noises. I had never thought of ducks or the quacks they make as remotely scary. Now they were Satan's poultry.

Then I read that *Macaroni and Cheese Club* had been nominated for a People's Choice Award: for Favorite Comedy Motion Picture.

If I was obsessed with P.E. before, now I was really off the deep end. I found myself cruising past our—his—old house in Santa Monica Canyon. Almost as if I were sleepwalking, I found myself in a movie montage. A beautiful field of tall grass and flowers appeared in our living room as we ran toward each other in slow motion. I could hear oboes and cellos and seagulls and feel gentle breezes as we hugged and wept. A few days later, we went to that awards show together and won.

We were back in love and back on track, so I gave notice on my little house, broke Zack's heart by saying a fond farewell, and moved back in with P.E., lock stock and barrel, to be tortured for seven more years. And because the whole reunion had been my idea, I now had absolutely no leverage.

SCORE	Points
Being browbeaten for cheating I didn't do	500
Having to move out and then pay rent to avoid more screaming	1,000
And then getting a scary obscene phone call	100
Involving quacking	50
That made me so nervous I got into a car wreck	500

Because I was distracted by pictures of Nick in a store	75
Turning my back on a wonderful guy who seemed to love me in order to go back to the same situation that had driven me out in the first place	900
Forced into a movie montage	25
TOTAL:	3,150

Grant 15,725   Lisa 16,080

I sent it off at midnight, then took a bath to wash off any lingering traces of award-show microbes and fell asleep in the tub. When I awoke at four A.M., rather than go directly to bed, I turned on the computer. An answer was waiting in my mailbox.

Dear Lisa,
I disagree. Making out is one thing for pimply teens, but for pockmarked adults, making out is KWIF (kissing with intention to fuck). Furthermore, I feel that your definition of cheating/adultery is disingenuous. The generally accepted definition of cheating is doing something you would shoot your mate for doing to somebody else.
      So, okay . . . P.E. is tormenting you. Got it. I certainly understand your chemistry with Zack. People become close working long hours together. It's natural that he offered you support. But I have to question the points about being unjustifiably accused of cheating when you were, point of fact, cheating. Something was going on, and P.E. picked up on it. Anyone would have reacted the way he did. So clarify that and you can keep those points.

                                                                Grant

P.S. Didn't that spook you out when Zack arrived unexpectedly and met you at the airport? To me that sounds like he's a S-T-A-L-K-E-R.

No point in trying to go back to sleep now. I wrote back at four-fifteen.

Dear Grant,

<<KWIF (kissing with intention to fuck)>> only applies to men. I know a lot of adult women, myself not among them, who would make out with a guy but not consider having sex with him. "I'll pretty much make out with anyone, but that's as far as I go" is how one of them put it. I have one friend who doesn't even consider first-date naked hot-tubbing to be a promissory note. So you have to re-initial this behavior as OHKWNPITDAE (one hot kiss with no particular intention to do anything else).

In the P.E. story I am telling, it was definitely OHKWNPITDAE. I had the kind of sad desperate hots for Zack that can only be produced by fighting in the trenches of an unwinnable war. I was full of WWII "Anne Frank and Peter in the bunker" feelings about the guy. And the fact that P.E. was hammering me about stuff that hadn't happened only made the fantasies more florid.

The point is that nothing took place until the goodbye kiss. It was meant to be a peck, but it accidentally turned hot. And only Zack and I knew. P.E. had no idea. He was on the other side of the room, schmoozing and being schmoozed. Of course, afterward I obsessed about that kiss all the time. The next thing I knew, Zack was staying at a hotel near my house.

But I don't think that made him a stalker. I think he was in love with me. And he had that crazy rescuer impulse that never works for anyone.

Lisa

In the name of staying up, just in case an answer was on its way, I made myself a cup of tea. By the time I had finished deciding whether I wanted caffeinated or herbal, honey or sugar, black, a little milk or nondairy creamer, there was something waiting in my mailbox. A bolt of tingly energy went through me. Grant and I were synched up. It was the middle of the night, and we were online at the same time. I found that strangely thrilling.

> Dear Lisa,
> Regarding OHKWNPITDAE. I think what you were talking about is actually called WNPITFBISAWLTSC (with no particular intention to fuck but it sure ain't writing letters to Santy Claus). You still didn't explain why P.E. shouldn't have been upset. Also, Zack moves to your area, shows up at the airport unannounced, and, to use your very own words, "was in love with me" and had a "crazy rescuer impulse," and he's not a stalker? Haven't you been reading my letters? Stalkers always own you. They always want to save you.
> Grant

I wrote right back.

> Dear Grant,
> P.E. shouldn't have been upset, because he didn't know about any of this. Even after it was over and he and I were back together, I denied everything, thinking no good could come of any admission except a lifetime of punishment and revenge.

I got a letter back almost instantly.

> Dear Lisa,
> So, you're saying that P.E. shouldn't have been suspicious because he had no way of knowing you were making out with a guy you had no intention of sleeping with—until later?

That's still really funny. Convince me that P.E. didn't sense some kind of sparks. Maybe you broke the Three Times a Day Law.

Dear Grant,
Re: the Three Times a Day Law. I am holding my breath waiting to hear what this is.

Dear Lisa,
The Three Times a Day Law: Never mention anyone you have an innocent crush on more than three times a day to your significant other. Once, maybe. Twice, you're pushing it. And three . . . you're in danger.
     The Shampoo Law, on the other hand, needs very little explaining.

Dear Grant,
Re: P.E. not being suspicious <<because he had no way of knowing you were making out with a guy you had no intention of sleeping with—until later.>> I still don't get why this is funny. Just because you see some chemistry between people doesn't mean anything has happened. Isn't every office a cauldron of flirtations? What reason did P.E. have to be suspicious? There was nothing going on except some oblique flirting. Okay, maybe there was stuff going on in my head. But otherwise, I was totally faithful.
     Re: the Shampoo Law. I guess I should take a run at this. Is it "If you were fucking around behind someone's back, at least take a shower before you come home"? Or is it "Don't let someone you were fucking around with leave his shampoo in your shower"?

I couldn't turn off the computer. This was as much fun as was available to me in any corner of my life. And it was kind of turning me on: all this talk about infidelity, showers, fucking around. Titillating, but I knew it meant nothing personal. Until this:

Dear Lisa,

WHY WHAT YOU WROTE AMUSETH ME

Let me see if I can follow what you're saying. You claim that P.E. had no right to be mad about something he didn't know about, although had he known, his rage would have been completely justified. However, until his suspicions could be confirmed, his pained outbursts amounted to nothing more than an irrational if not childish display. My my my. W. S. Gilbert would applaud your logic.

The Shampoo Law: You were close. It's this: If you are two-timing someone, always keep a bottle of the same shampoo you use at home in your paramour's apartment. Just tell Ms./Mr. Dirty Secret how much you love Walgreen's Extra Cheap and Pungent shampoo and he/she will buy you some, just like your favorite coffee.

While we're on the subject of lying, here's a story you might like: I was about eight. My sister and I were staying at Grandma's, and for some reason, we'd forgotten our toothbrushes. So we brushed our teeth by putting toothpaste on our fingers and rubbing. As we were kids, we thought this was great fun.

Cut to: home, a few nights later. "Time for bed. Kids!" says Mom, "Go brush your teeth!" Still thrilled by the finger method, I put toothpaste on my finger and rubbed. More fun! For some reason, Coach Repka came in as I was leaving and barked, "Ya brush your teeth?"

"Yes," I said, then immediately felt guilty because lying was a sin. I also knew that if my father checked my toothbrush and found it dry, he'd kill me. I felt guilty and wor-

ried, so I went back in the bathroom, figuring I'd set everything right, like the nuns said, if I told the truth. "Hey, uh,
Dad, I didn't brush my teeth with a brush. I put toothpaste
on my finger and—"

He was on me like a leopard. "Liar!" he screamed. "You
little fucking shit!" he roared as he kicked and punched and
pushed me into my bedroom. What I recall next is him deep
in my room and me trying to break loose and run out. Just
as I made it to the door, a huge book exploded next to my
head on the wall. Boom! And I mean BOOM, hurled with all
the impact you'd expect from an ex-pro-football player.
BOOM! Missed me by inches and would have taken my
head off. The book was in pieces. Worse, it wasn't my
book, it belonged to the library; after the screaming subsided, Coach Repka ordered me to pick up the pages and
the broken binding. "You're gonna pay for that goddamn
book," he said.

To tell the truth, I felt very guilty as I trudged to the library with the broken book and my birthday money, which
I hoped would cover it. I brought the pieces to the librarian
and said, "I'm sorry, ma'am, but this book got broken. I
have the money for it right here."

"How did this happen?" she snapped.

"My dad threw it at me," I said.

I swear I thought she was going to ask why I had made
him so mad. But she didn't. Instead she took a deep breath.
I remember she looked away, then I watched as her face
softened. "Never mind, honey," she said. "You don't have
to pay."

Grant

It came over me all at once, like a jolt from a stun gun: Oh shit.
I think I'm in love with this guy. Reading about his childhood

anguish made me feel protective, made me ache for him. "But what do you love?" I asked myself.

"Well," I said, "the way he opens up and tells me about everything. How could I not have feelings of love for him?"

Which was when it occurred to me. Duh! He's a fucking songwriter. Misery with a melody is what they do: Seducing an audience with romanticized pain. Realizing I was just being manipulated gave me back my perspective. It brought me back to my center. And kind of pissed me off a little.

Dear Grant,

The thing that amuseth you: I guess it is pretty funny. Maybe the reason I am even defending myself is because I had so many years of being accused of things I didn't do that it seemed incidental that there was actually a little just cause at long last. It occurred to me after P.E. and I broke up that I'd had more intense crushes on people when I was with him than I've had since I've been single. It's weird how it's possible to be lonelier in a relationship than you are when you're actually alone.

Okay. I am obtuse. I don't get the Shampoo Law. What is the thing you were trying to cover up by having a bottle of shampoo in his/her apartment? I mean, I know you said you were two-timing her, but what does the bottle of a particular brand of shampoo have to do with it?

I don't know if this rule works for women with men, as I have yet to meet a man who made a note of my favorite coffee or shampoo.

My Shampoo Rule: After giving your dog a bath, remember to remove the bottle of flea-and-tick shampoo from the showering area. Do not assume you will read the label when reaching for something to wash your hair with during your next shower.

Coach Repka: I love how, although he took no responsibility for wrecking a book or assaulting his kid, you were punished for a toothbrushing irregularity. Coach Repka is in a hideous class all his own. Tell me where he lives, and after I am done punching out P.E., I will stop by and hammer him, too.

Dear Lisa,
Re: Coach Repka. As a six-year-old, I would set up an altar in the living room made of a stack of books topped by a statue of the Virgin Mary and flanked by rubber grapes and wax fruit and pray for God to stop the beatings and the terror and just take me. If my mother had walked in she might have thought, "How cute! It's Little Father Repka saying mass," never suspecting I was offering myself up as a sacrifice. When it was clear that God wouldn't answer that prayer, I created an elaborate fantasy life where I was a general fighting grand, desperate, and bloody battles.

Dear Grant,
That is one of the most relentlessly depressing childhood stories I have ever read. However, I must say that in the midst of all that gloom, the part about the rubber grapes and the wax fruit really brightened things up.

One other thing: Since you have a rule for everything, I am wondering if you have a rule about sleeping with someone on the first date?

Dear Lisa,
I'm a musician. You should rephrase that question to: Do you have a rule about dating someone after you slept with her?

Chapter 29

GRANT

I was being pulled by my hair back into my past. To Lisa, this was a game for points; to Winnie, I was showing off for another woman; but to me, I had inadvertently stepped onto a road of words that would lead me back to a place where opportunity met my mental illness like a sledge-hammer greets an anvil. A moment where my victimhood revealed itself for what it was: cowardice. I could never justify, only explain, how I had allowed so many awful things to happen to so many people. Forty years ago, a speed-crazed high school coach took a wire coat hanger and beat his five-year-old so badly the kid secretly prayed for death. By the time the kid was thirty-nine, there'd be a lot of blood, a suicide, grieving parents.

It all might have happened without me, true, but the fact is it happened with me. In order to forestall a little personal pain, I underwrote the destruction of others.

So I walked into the studio and took another step on the trek back.

Dear Lisa,
I am continuing the thread of the story where, after the wrap party, you and Nick packed up and flew home.

WE FLY HOME

1986 was a great year for me professionally. The Slowly I Turn album was released to a great fury of love Arvin, hate Grant.

In that year, I was barely at home. We worked nonstop. Every night I had to sell the band and myself. We toured Europe and sold out everywhere. We were gaining momentum. We traveled as far north as Tromsö, Norway, and as far south as Perth, Australia. In five months of touring, we had about three nights off. We were dirty, stinky, and tired, but progress was being made.

The tour was extended when our song—that is, my song—went to Top Ten in Australia. We flew coach through the Chernobyl cloud and were escorted by fighter planes over the Holy Land right after Reagan bombed Libya. To top all this off, my song was on the in-flight music program! "Here's a song that's going up the charts in Oz," said the DJ, "by a group of survivors, Slowly I Turn." Survivors!

When we got to Australia, we were big news. Front-page stuff! Okay, second-page stuff. For a few days. But what the hell . . . we had a bona fide hit. The hotels were better, we were fed and feted. There were girls and press and parties and TV shows and, strangest of all, teens at the airport holding teddy bears and roses. So, you get the idea:

Life was really good. We had worked hard for a long, long time and the payoff seemed at hand.

After five months, the tour was over, and we flew home. I was ten pounds lighter than when I had left, and miracle of miracles, I had made money. I had twenty-five hundred dollars in my pocket, a lot of money for me. It meant clothes, a trip to the dentist, maybe a beater car.

Jane met me at the airport, and we had a nice evening together. The next day, still jet-lagged and road-weary, I began to make plans for my twenty-five hundred dollars. But there was a problem. Psycho Ex told me that one half of six months' rent was due. Yes, my manager had sent in *her* share every month, and that kept the landlord cool. But P.E. had told the landlord that I would pay *my* share when I got back. This was all news to me. Kiss one thousand dollars goodbye. "Some people don't get flown around the fuckin' world" was her logic. Besides, she had gotten fired again. Okay, so skip the used car. I still have fifteen hundred dollars, but . . . not so fast. She also didn't pay the phone bill. The bill owed, plus a charge to restore service, was three hundred dollars. "But I had my manager advance you the money," I said.

"It was too late," she said. She had to eat, didn't she?

Ricky, our junkie roadie neighbor, had installed a phone in his name at our place for her to use by stealing a credit card from his roommate, Duke. Reading between the lines, I sensed that some kind of Byzantine dope deal went with this, the structure of which I couldn't begin to understand. However, the upshot of it was that Duke had found out that his card had been stolen, and if I didn't pay Duke his money back right now, he was going to call the cops.

"Hey, we talked every night when you were on the road," P.E. explained. "You knew I was making those calls, and you never said anything." After I railed at her about not only stealing someone's credit card but making me an accomplice, she yelled back, "Listen, pal. How do you think I fuckin' manage while you're gone? This is what it takes."

Cost: seven hundred dollars. Now I'm down to five hundred bucks. Oh well, I think, at least I'm gonna save my teeth.

"Don't forget, this month's rent's due," she says. "You're gonna have to cover me again. Five hundred bucks. And I forgot to tell you, they're gonna turn off the gas tomorrow." So I'm broke in thirty seconds.

I gave you such a long buildup so you might understand the emotional effect this had on me. I didn't mention that I was deathly ill through the Australian leg, or that our plane fell about two hundred feet over the Pacific. So understand that my song being a hit and the money we made were a great source of pride, the reward for a lot of work, and time, and danger. But the story doesn't end here.

The following day, I paid all the bills, and now I had nothing. I was still horribly jet-lagged, and now I had to figure out how to get food for us and the cats. I walked down Melrose to Chimera, where I'd worked on and off since 1982. "Lee, I need to work. I need cash right now. Today," I told the owner. Poor Lee. I put him in a bad spot. He knew how well we did on tour and didn't want to see me like this.

"Well, uh . . . the only thing I have right now is . . . uh . . . I need someone to sweep the sidewalk and gutters. It's a mess out there," he struggled to tell me. I looked out front by the bus stop and could see cups and cans and free newspapers all over the place by the city trash can. "I'll pay ya forty."

So, thus ended my world tour. That's me . . . Rock God . . . on Melrose with a big push broom and a shovel. That's me, Rock Star with the hit ten thousand miles away, picking up soda cans and popcorn cups and stuffing them in the trash can, then jumping up and down in the can to compact all the crap. The sun was going down. People were headed home. There was lots of traffic. I swept and shoveled and jumped and thought about those fans handing me roses and teddy bears only four days ago.

SCORE	Points
My hard-earned, well-deserved fortune wiped out in sixty seconds	1,000
Humiliation at having to sweep gutters and jump up and down in a trash can during rush hour on L.A.'s then most fashionable street	1,000
Four days after I got home from a hit tour	500
The uncomprehending rage that I would have to do this while P.E. could get free rent and phones and cash	1,000
Minus Lightcap's Parallel for flying home	−50
TOTAL	3,450

Dear Grant,

Wow. Couple nosy questions: What did P.E. do that she got fired from? Five months is a dangerously long time to leave even a sober, serious, stable relationship. When you left a wacked-out woman to go on tour for five months, what did you imagine would be going on in your absence?

Then again, you were "dating" on the road, and she knew it, right? So was knowing that little detail fueling a layer of resentment? And maybe partially responsible for the whole "I'm a basket case, take care of me" thing that she was doing? And if I'm not being too cruel and naïve here, how is it that you, a Rock Star, come back from a

world tour, and all the money you have is twenty-five hundred bucks? That sounds low to me. No offense. When you
made the decision to go back to Chimera for forty bucks,
was there a conversation in which you told P.E. she better
go get a job, too? Or is this the prequel to the "I'll go suck
dick" story? Did you yell at her when all this happened, or
was she so out of it there couldn't be any back-and-forth?
What did SHE say about the fact that you had to take that
garbage-jumping job?

Dear Lisa,
Of course there was yelling. But talking to Psycho Ex was
like talking to a shrewd child. You get tired of explaining to
your mate, "If you got a job, Jane, and combined your income with mine, we could maybe have a car or see a movie
and not worry when rent came around." The shrewd child
would accuse me of being unfair.

"Well, you're just lucky," she would say. "People give
you money." Then I'd be off explaining that no, they didn't
give me money; they advanced it against future earnings.
"Same difference," she'd say.

She would entangle me in that nonsense instead of the
real issue at hand, which was, of course, how her heroin
habit was destroying our life together. Exasperated, I pulled
out a pencil and added up what she got while I was on tour.
"Combined with the rent, the phone, the cash from my manager," I said, "you made about five thousand dollars off this
tour, just for staying home, while I, on the other hand, only
made nothing." I saw a faint smile cross her face, then fade.
As for P.E. getting fired, her employment always followed
the same trajectory: She'd make a good first impression,
work hard, get elevated to an assistant-manager position.
Soon after there'd be a fight with the boss because he
turned out to be an asshole. And out she'd go. I would sit

with her and explain the hard facts of working for minimum wage: "You have to toe the line. He's the boss. You have to learn to be more patient and forgiving. You get more flies with honey than you do with vinegar."

"That's what my mother always used to tell me," Jane said. "And you know what I'd say back to her? 'Who wants flies?' "

A few years ago, Winnie ran into a mutual friend of ours who had sold records with Jane at a store on Melrose. "You're going out with Grant Repka?" the friend had said to Winnie. The guy then remembered Jane and described her as the junkie chick they fired after they found her dying in the bathroom with a needle in her arm. I, of course, had heard a completely different version of the story where Jane got fired because the boss's wife was out to get her.

<<How is it that you, a Rock Star, come back from a world tour, and all the money you have is twenty-five hundred bucks?>> I think you confuse Rock Star with rock star. One has a hit, the other plays music and is the featured performer. Slowly I Turn was on an indie label. Our record budget was eighty thousand dollars per album, a mere pittance in the Reagan years. I got two-fifty a week while I was recording, which came from whatever was left, split five ways, after the manager took 20 percent, and the lawyer 5 percent, the producer got his fee, and the studio got theirs. When that money was gone . . . back to working retail at Chimera.

While I was on tour, I got a fifteen-dollar per diem. Meanwhile, my manager kept the money I earned from the shows and sent it to P.E. to pay my share of the rent. Of course, there was always some sort of emergency with Jane, so I'd have to call him and have an additional check made out to her. She finagled a princely sum of money that way. That's what I meant when I said she made five thousand dollars. The twenty-five hundred I made on that tour was the only time I ever made any money off touring. The European leg of our tour was a big success, but because our label had so little faith in Slowly I Turn without Arvin, they undersold us to the promoters. So we got nothing. It's a hard thing to take when the fans are climbing up drainpipes to meet you, in the dressing room, and the promoters are the only ones who get paid. When we had our hit in Oz, our management finally woke up and cut us a good deal. So that's how it worked out that I made any profit at all.

Rock Stars who have big hits have a coterie of things like wardrobe assistants, personal assistants, handmaidens, gofers, and lickspits. We, on the other hand, traveled with two roadies, and a tour manager who doubled as a sound guy. Trust me, I know there are other bands who dream of having even that much. Under these conditions, we seldom had time to wash clothes. We'd carry three bags: one for what was clean, one for what was dirty, and the last containing the awful, cheesy, briny, B.O.-ridden flashy stuff we'd wear onstage. Backstage you could hear us screaming as we got into our damp duds.

Here's another difference: When you're a Rock Star, you pull into town and stay a few days. When you're a rock star, you have to keep moving. It's too expensive otherwise. That's why, in five months, we had pretty much no days off. We were either playing or on our way to the next place. You know all those images from rock videos where the stars are looking wistful and weary out of the tour-bus windows? Picture me in a Euro truck/van holding an umbrella because the roof of the van is leaking. Look up to the front seat, and there's our roadie, manually operating the broken windshield wipers as we head down the Alps into Italy. Is my face sad and pretty? Am I wan and wistful? No. I am blank, and my face is slack. My mouth is open. No romance, just dull dumb numb exhaustion. Here's an exciting day as a rock star with a small r: Leave Vienna at dawn, arrive in Munich at nine P.M. Get on a plane and fly to Oslo. Get on another plane and fly to Tromsö, six hundred miles from the Arctic Circle. Now get on a small prop plane with seventy-five Euro/Norwegian rock types and fly to Lakselv, a couple hundred miles away, for an outdoor rock festival. Arrive at four A.M. with the sun at high noon and sleep for an hour. Get onstage and jump around in the subarctic wastes, take a bow, then get on prop plane and return to Tromsö, fly back to Oslo, board plane, get back to Munich and get stuck in rush-hour traffic. Arrive two hours late, set up your gear, and play for an angry impatient crowd, who assumes the delay was due to your American laziness and rock star arrogance. From Munich to Munich—a perfect circle, in twenty-four hours. That's why I would hit the roof when P.E. tried to guilt me with "You're lucky. You get to travel. People *give* you money."

As far as your other question—regarding the effect this had on my relationship—be patient. It is part of the rich fabric I am weaving.

Dear Grant,
I kind of understand. I have been on a couple of book tours that were ridiculously hectic. Nothing remotely like what you described, but I've had days when I had to get up at five A.M. and board a plane (seated between two people who were both eagerly competing to see which of them could get me to take their cold with me onto *Good Morning America*). Then afterward to fly to another city in order to arrive at a TV station for an interview at eight, where the interviewers would not only not have read my book but would only want to talk about how great it must be to know Nick Blake. After which I would have to sit in rush-hour traffic to be back on a plane at six o'clock to get

to a radio interview that evening at nine in order to pro-
mote a bookstore appearance the next day in the desperate hope that more than four people might show. Four
people, I might add, who would have turned up to ask me
if I could introduce them to Nick because they wanted to
show him a screenplay.

On an evening like this, I would morosely observe myself
walking through the dappled light of a big airport all alone,
pulling a wheely suitcase, and begin narrating my life in the
third person. "As she boarded the human conveyor belt that
took her through the endless neon-lined corridor of the
Chicago airport, pulling all her belongings behind her, she
ached for someone to talk to. It was a Friday night, and
though the idea that she was headed for a radio interview
had sounded good when she first heard about it, in person
it all seemed hollow. She was alone. She was so very
alone."

I guess maudlin self-pitying monologues that involve
dappled light are one problem you don't have when you're
traveling with a band. Although bad poet's disease can certainly strike anywhere, in any occupation.

But your schedule sounds like a real nightmare.

Lisa

Dear Lisa,
Your scenario is the one that sounds like the nightmare. I
love touring. I love hotels, movement, rushing through air-
ports. You develop a great bond with your crew and band.
There were in-jokes, stupid road songs, and indescribable
memories. I mean, there were only five guys in the world
who would know what I meant if I said, "The Hissing
Woman of Amsterdam."

However, imagine moving a movie production down the
road every night for five months. Tempers would flare, per-

sonalities clash. But you build up this great immunity to dis-
aster, to fear, to work. It gets to be like Vic Morrow in the
Combat! TV series. "What's the plan, Sarge?" "Kill Krauts.
Keep movin'."

Dear Grant,
Surprise air raid. One good "we fly home" deserves another. Now:

WE FLY HOME

It was 1994, and P.E. was in Toronto making *Macaroni and
Cheese Club II,* living in a rented hotel suite. He was under
so much pressure, as he was contractually obligated to direct his first big studio sequel, that he didn't seem to want
much to do with me by the time I saw him. So I began flying
back to L.A. on Fridays, taping a travel piece on Saturday
for the little local show I was still working on, then flying
back to Toronto. This way I still had a foot in both worlds.

On this one particular Friday, my show was on hiatus,
which is what they call a snow day in television. P.E. was also
not shooting because this time an important cast member
had to go to a funeral. Only such dire circumstances could
have inspired him to agree to fly to Minnesota to attend his
parents' fortieth-wedding-anniversary party. I agreed to go,
too.

As we were packing in our hotel room, the TV was tuned
to *The Oprah Winfrey Show.* On it was a discussion of
abusive marriages. I was only half watching until P.E. came
out of the shower, furious because he had been forced to
curtail his shooting unexpectedly. Making grunting noises
and a face like a gargoyle, he pulled the shade off the lamp
on the dresser and began to bend it like he was creating a
balloon animal. As he did this, a printed checklist of symptoms for gauging whether your spouse was mentally ill ap-

peared on TV. Oprah read the list out loud: "Controlling, jealous, flies into unpredictable rages." It was like she was Miss Nancy from *Romper Room*, watching us through the television. I half expected Oprah to say, "And I see Lisa and Nicky. Now, Nick, you straighten out that lamp shade and put it back where it belongs, mister."

By the time we were ready to leave for the airport, a huge freezing ice storm had begun. P.E., predicting that bad weather would mean traffic tie-ups, did not have the patience to wait for the hotel staff to call us a cab. Instead, he put on a slicker and ran to the parking garage to get our rental car. I was to wait, curbside, with the suitcases. He would pull up in front. Fine. Except there were no parking spaces at the curb. His only option was to double-park. And when he did this, there was a small but deep lake of slushy, muddy rainwater in between the curb and the door of the car. As I was wearing a brand-new pair of three-hundred-dollar light brown suede high-heeled boots, I didn't want to step into that deep puddle and stand there long enough to lift and load two moderately heavy suitcases. So I hesitated. P.E. began to honk and gesture. He pushed the passenger door open from the inside, yelling at me to put the suitcases in NOW so we could leave. "I can't," I tried to yell over traffic noise, miming the reason. He looked at me with exasperation. Then he got out of the car and walked around to where I was standing. Furious, he picked up my suitcase and heaved it in the car himself. "Get in," he said.

"I need you to pull the car up to the corner," I said, "I have on suede boots." He was beside himself at the inconvenience of moving the car a few feet forward. Once inside, he screamed at me nonstop all the way to the airport about how I never did what he asked, how I always had to have everything my way. "This crazy man you see before you is totally a product of trying to deal with your stupid fucking shit!" he raged. During all this screaming, I sat quietly, wrestling with the question you were probably about to ask me: Why was I still there? Well, for one, it wasn't always like this. Just when I would be packed to leave, things would greatly improve. P.E. responded better to the ends of ropes than the middles. Next thing I knew, he would be charming and funny and sweet, and I would remember why I loved him. So I would think if I just played my cards right, things would be transformed. My parents didn't walk out on each other in situations like this. No, sir. We all stayed and clawed and bit and made puncture wounds, because we all understood that hostile behavior was the currency of love. On a more practical note, there was also the question of timing. Deep down, I secretly believed that when the new movie came out and was a hit, gratitude and happiness and a new sense of security would change P.E. for the good. I thought that the sweet but wounded little boy who tugged at my heart strings would blossom into a sweet loving guy I could adore. This really didn't seem like an impossibility.

Moving on. One of the really great things about traveling with P.E. was that we always went first-class. We were just finishing up our hot hors d'oeuvres when a woman in a short wool suit came up to ask for an autograph. She was very sorry to bother him, but despite her sorrow, she had a lot of specific requests. "Would you sign one to my mother? And another one to my aunt Jeanne? And this one to my friend Bonnie, who really likes you." She was flirting with him, posturing saucily with her hands on her hips, then playing with her hair. I considered giving her hate vibes but decided to rise to the occasion and so pretended to be reading as P.E. signed and signed. He was very polite but all business. After he finished, she stared at him and said, "You know, all my friends think you're hot. But seeing you in person, I'm not that impressed."

I looked at her and understood her delusion. She thought that by saying this awful thing, she was somehow etching herself into his consciousness. No common fan, she. This was her Hepburn-and-Tracy "meet cute."

Now it was time for me to begin to radiate hate vibes. "Lady," I wanted to say, "not only did your ploy not work, you just wrecked my fucking weekend." Instead I just gave her a look that felt like it could start fires. After she left, I had to spend the next hour reassuring P.E. that not only did he not look awful, he was handsomer now than he had been in his twenties. He was not short and fat. He was solid, like a weight lifter. She only said all that stuff because he was so attractive. When we landed in Minnesota, airline personnel, having learned that P.E. was on board, met us at the gate. They gathered excitedly around P.E., carrying his belongings: his flight bag, his golf clubs, whatever. I trailed behind the group, lugging a suitcase.

We got to the hotel with an hour to kill before his parents' party. For that hour, P.E. sat silently in front of the TV, watching reruns of *Green Acres*. Then, ten minutes before we had to leave, he disrobed to take a shower. Naturally, we arrived at the party just as everyone was finishing dinner. "You can see they all hate me," he whispered as we sat down in the chairs they had saved for us at the end of a long banquet table. We only stayed for about an hour. At which point P.E. told his parents he had to split, despite the fact that they begged him to stay. But no, he couldn't. He had a busy schedule. He was sorry, but we had to run.

"I told you my parents hated me," he repeated several times as we rode back to the hotel in the taxi. He was irked that no one at the party had said anything about his recent successes. Especially not his father and his father's business partners, none of whom had ever thought he'd amount to much. So we went back to our hotel room, where he watched ESPN the rest of the night, while simultaneously studying the Merck manual to see if he had Lou Gehrig's disease. I knew better than to argue.

The next morning we got up at noon and flew back to Toronto.

SCORE	Points
Oprah reads nutcase list as lamp shade is bent into a balloon animal	300
Screamed at for not standing in a five-inch-deep mud puddle	1,000
In new three-hundred-dollar boots	500
And having flown across country for this	500
Trailing behind with my own suitcase while P.E. has help	100
Then making P.E. feel better about an asshole fan	300
After pretending to read while she acted like I didn't exist	100
All of this to be late to a family party where we stayed only an hour	100
In order to rush back to the hotel room to discuss amyotrophic lateral sclerosis	500
TOTAL	3,400

Grant 19,175   Lisa 19,480

Dear Lisa,
On the surface, I would say the scores were about right. The puddle bit is so much like Coach Repka. It's sadistic and

parental at the same time. You deserve all those points. But on closer examination, these questions arise.

Lugging luggage: I expect the man to carry the heavy bag and open doors for the lady. The man must provide assistance for his girl, if for no other reason than he loves her. Why didn't he ask someone to help you if he didn't want to do it himself? Then again, why didn't you ask him to help you? Were you again hoping he'd notice your plight and show you he cared?

If I was being an insensitive clod, I'd generally get A) direct confrontation, B) womanly wiles, C) withholding of womanly wiles, or D) quiet-girl-pouting face. Out of those four, something would work. Did nothing work with him? Please clarify.

Dear Grant,
Psycho Ex was not a "That's my gal" kind of a guy. Affection was not his strong suit. That made us a good match, because I was brought up not to really expect any. I think I had trained myself to believe that anger was as strong an indicator of feelings of love as considerate behavior. And as for hoping he'd notice my plight and show he cared, I may have been doing this but was only vaguely aware of it. I didn't realize then that rescuing only works in an animal shelter or a rip tide. And as far as << A) direct confrontation, B) womanly wiles, C) withholding of womanly wiles, or D) quiet-girl-pouting face>> goes, I have just one question: Did any of this stuff work with Coach Repka?

Dear Lisa,
I never put on something slinky for my dad. Maybe I should have tried it.

                                                                    Grant

Chapter 30

LISA

I was becoming concerned about my e-mail compulsion. When I wasn't checking the computer, I was making notes. Or obsessing about where this whole thing with Grant might be heading. I began reading compilations of famous letters, looking for parallel situations and possible outcomes. The closest one I could find was a correspondence in the late 1890s between George Bernard Shaw and an actress named Ellen Terry. True, Grant Repka and George Bernard Shaw were clearly not two peas in a pod. Still, the whole thing rang a bell for a couple of reasons. When it began, Ellen Terry worried that if she and G.B.S. actually spent time together, he would be disappointed in her appearance off the stage. As they continued to write, she became "determined to avoid meeting at any cost," going on to say, "You have become a habit with me, sir. And each morning before breakfast I take you like a dear pill." So there she was: insecure like me, obsessed like me. A compulsive letter writer like me, trapped in a crushy but doomed correspondence. When she died, after twenty-five years of writing to each other, they still had never spent a single moment together. Later, when people nagged G.B.S. about the fact that their romance existed only on paper, Shaw said, "Remember that only on paper has humanity achieved glory, beauty, truth, knowledge, virtue and abiding love." Of course, with e-mail, there was no paper. Maybe that was what was holding Grant and me back from achieving more of the high-minded things on that list. Not only had we peaked with truth, I doubted that I could hold Grant's attention for twenty-five years unless I freshened the game up with a couple of new psychos.

Then there was the uncomfortable fact that only I gave a shit about our abiding love. He had a full dance card. Otherwise, our trajectory had now been revealed to me. And I have to confess I found it depressing. Maybe we were to the point where this was becoming too sad. Maybe it was time to stop writing. What was there to be gained by being pulled in any further? I had made my decision to stop. And then I got this:

Dear Lisa,
I continue with the theme of the question you asked: "Why was I still here?"

I FALL OFF THE MOUNTAIN: or, Never make a major life decision while rolled up in a terrified ball on the bedroom floor

I had more success than I had ever seen: a sell-out world tour, a hit in Australia! Groupies! Fans! Strippers! Euro TV and magazine articles! And more: romance! While I was on tour, I met a lovely woman in Switzerland named Jenna.

I liked her so much we planned to meet in NYC on her next vacation. So. A hit! A new girl! The world practically at my feet!

I had only one unpleasant thing to do when I got home: get rid of P.E.

It wasn't as if I didn't love P.E. I did. But I had been betrayed, lied to, stolen from, hustled for the last time.

During the tour, P.E. had hired a new guitarist. I had caught the strong whiff of a crush when she phoned. I told you about this guy before—Kip Kinches. She couldn't stop mentioning him. Kip had a Mazda RX-7. Kip had a big-screen TV. Kip had a house in Venice. Kip was real cool. Kip couldn't wait to meet me. She maintained they were only friends. Whatever, I thought, you can go off with him when I get home.

When the plane touched down in June, my plan was to break the news. I had the cash to get her a place. I could do that much for her.

But once I was home, P.E. once again drained me financially. And there I was sweeping the gutter outside Chimera.

However, I didn't really mind, because I was on a huge upswing. I was making a conscious effort to rise to the occasion of living. "Demand more of yourself, and life will make bigger demands! Spiral UP for once, Grant," I said to myself, and I felt like I was glowing inside. I knew my life was beginning again. I had only to walk away from Psycho Ex.

But now that I no longer had the cash to make this exit smooth, I would have to do it the old-fashioned way: Tell her and wait for her to clear out. It took about a week for me to get up the nerve. Then I did it nice and gentle. I was respectful but kept to the facts: "You are an addict. I am not. Although I love you, it won't work. I would like you to leave as soon as possible."

P.E. was shocked. She pleaded and cried. But I couldn't be moved.

We talked for hours, to no avail. I told her she could stay until she found a place. When it hit her that I was serious, she howled like a wounded animal. Then she started to get street-fighter mad, tough, steady. "I don't believe this," she said. "Just because you went around the world, now you think you're some big rock star. I'll give you another week to change your mind. You think hard about what you're throwing away. Because once somebody hurts me, I never come back." I told her that was sort of the idea.

For a period of about three weeks, she slept on the bed and I on the couch. Every night she pleaded, "This is silly. Get into bed." But I didn't. And it was tough. Every day we talked. She said she hated heroin and really wanted to change. She wanted another chance. It was too little too late.

I wasn't home that much. I was away writing songs, because after two years of "Where's Arvin Petro?" the band was finally making headway. If we could deliver a great second album, we could recapture the U.S. market and save the band. So it was imperative that Slowly I Turn have hits. And I believed that there were hits in me. I couldn't wait to get all my ideas down on paper. I needed a place to write, make noise, and not bother anybody at night, so Lee gave me the keys to the storage room above Chimera. Every evening I'd walk to Chimera and start the music at sundown. I'd be there till five or six A.M.

I wrote about everything. It all came pouring out: joy, misery, anger, stupidity, sex, Broadway, rock fast, rock slow, sad rock ballads. I was a writing machine. One night I wrote six songs, not all of them good, and walked home singing as the sky turned orange. God, I was happy.

Jenna and I were exchanging letters, which came to my

manager's office. She had friends in NYC who had asked her to house-sit their penthouse. So I was moving not only forward but upward. The world seemed to be throwing itself at my feet.

Which brings us to week three. P.E. was still at my house. "How soon are you going to leave?" I asked. "Soon," she said, but she was dragging her feet. She still wanted me to stop all this, have fun, meet her friends. When I said no, that I had to write, I was thinking, Jenna! Hits! Penthouse! P.E. warned me again: "Once I go, I never come back." I was assuming that she and Kip would get together when she moved out. It didn't matter much to me.

One night at about ten-thirty at Chimera, there was a banging at the door. It was Heather Connelly. She and I used to work together right there, selling artsy toys and novelties. She was a bright, bony girl who looked like a very pretty yet sleepy pony. We had always been kind of crushy, but I wasn't available. I respected Heather because she had kicked heroin, gotten twelve-step sober, and even put herself through law school. I was proud of her. So there we were, having a happy reunion on a Saturday night, when it dawned on me. "Heather, how did you find me?"

"I was driving around and stopped by your place. Jane told me you were here," she said.

"Oh. So you know Jane and I are breaking up."

"I heard."

Here was Heather, smart, sexy, successful, sober, single, and kind of sniffing around. And P.E. had sent her to see me? That was not like P.E. at all. I asked her, "How did Jane act when you showed up?"

"She was nervous. I got the impression she thought I might be you."

"Why would that make her nervous?"

"Well, she was with Kip Kinches."

"Wow. Really? Do you think they were screwing?" Why was I asking these questions?

"No. It looked like they were watching TV. She introduced me to him. She said, 'Grant's at Chimera. I know he'd be happy to see you.' "

I'm thinking, Kip Kinches is cooling his heels in my apartment, watching our shitty little black-and-white garage-sale TV? Why not go back to his swanky place? Why send Heather, a single, interested woman, over to your man who is single and interested?

Then I get it. P.E. introduced her to Kip to make sure that the info got back to me. She was saying, "Hey, go screw the sleepy pony. I got my rich cool boyfriend now."

I found myself very irked by this. For almost six months, I had needed nothing from P.E. except freedom. Now I found myself obsessing on this one point: How can she show me so little respect as to entertain her next boyfriend in my home? Just beneath that righteous indignation, in my psychological swamp, was insecurity, doubt, inadequacy, the very beast of my childhood. He didn't rise with a roar, he came on like a poison gas, a deadly superintelligent *Star Trek* fog that surrounded me with an irrational feeling of terror. He whispered, "Because you are not worthy of anybody's respect, you are easily replaced, easily forgotten." That's what happens when you tell your kid, "We should have left you to die in California" and "We're gonna dump you off at the orphanage."

Heather talked me through this. "I know junkies. Jane needs someone to take care of her. She knew her days were numbered with you, so she cultivated Kip as a backup plan. If she loses you, she still has him. He's a local star. She needs his money and status. Let her have him. It doesn't matter."

She was right. The cloud passed. Heather stayed till four

A.M. If there was romance in the air, I killed it. Still, we had a nice time. But when we said goodbye, the prospect of being alone scared me. I had this thing in my gut, glowing like a mini–Super Ball. Ten thousand pounds of compressed space-age rubber and fear. It made me jumpy, distracted, agitated, depressed. What was I afraid of? Was it natural male territorialism? Was it the finality of the breakup hitting me? It wouldn't let me go. I was worrying about it like an aching tooth, touching it every few minutes to see if it was still sore. Yeouch. Yes. Still there. I tried to start writing again but was too distracted. I accepted this as natural. It would pass. When it was time to leave, I didn't want to. It was nine A.M. on a Sunday, a horrible hour. Bright, hot, and getting hotter. Still, with the sunlight I was out of the dark. I had been tested and passed. I was feeling peppy again. P.E. and Kip? Who cares? I got the whole world waiting in Zurich! NYC! Hits! Songs!

I boarded the bus and headed home, still resolved to lay down the law when Psycho Ex woke up. I should have known I was on a manic upswing by the way I sang "Breaking Up Is Hard to Do" a thousand times as I rode across town. I forced myself to stop before I got to our apartment. I didn't want to wake P.E. up whistling that song. I unlocked the door and looked toward the sleeper couch. For the first time in three years, no Jane. Just the sleeper couch folded up with the shitty garage-sale TV on a stool in front of it. Yeeow.

I once knew an old lawyer who had a stroke. He said the stroke felt like someone snuck up behind him and hit him in the back of the head with a two-by-four. That's what it felt like: kaboom. Up until this very second, I had no idea how deep and sick my love was, and in that sickness how strong, how deep, how persuasive, my repetition compulsion. I can sit here now and label it with popular buzzwords like "codependency" or "fear of abandonment," but at that moment it felt like getting caught in an undertow. I felt like I was going to die. I think of it now as dropping fifteen thousand feet in a second. Of making a 360-degree turn, in reverse, into a brick wall. It really took about an hour. A long, slow descent, thought by thought, down to the brink of a nervous breakdown. Something in me was pulling me back to her like a magnet. I saw all sorts of fuck-you notices around the apartment. Things she knew I'd see. Toothbrush missing, fuck you, Grant. An empty hanger in the closet, what was there? Aagh, I remember. Her one good blue silk nightgown. The nightgown that, in the relationship, said, "My lust is big. I desire you to take me gently, slowly, with candles 'n' things." Gone. Fuck you, Grant. Overnight bag gone. Fuck you, Grant. Go fuck the Pony Girl. I got my cool boy now. Do I have to tell you how I got into our bed and how the blankets and sheets were rich with Halston, hair spray, and her scent?

That's when I started breaking down. How do I get you to understand that while there was every reason to laugh her off and start a new life, I was overcome by a sudden, inexplicable need to get her back at any cost. I went, in an hour, from a confident, whistling man to a confused, terrified little ball on the floor. It was so painful, so devastating, that I stayed with her for the next three years, in mortal fear that I would break down and never again get up.

The hardest question to answer is: Why did you stay, Grant?

I stayed because I liked being the smart, capable one, the one she needed desperately. And though I'm embarrassed to admit it, now that she had gone off with a man who had all the advantages, the illusion of my superiority vanished. Now I was looking into the void: the suicidal, chain-smoking, pray-to-God-I-die, self-destructive pit my father dug for me. Sometimes I think I may have picked her, lived with her, encouraged her, and pushed her out just to experience this moment. If this was repetition compulsion, I was not only reliving the abuse but finally experiencing the awful moment they really did dump me off at the orphanage and leave me to die in California. I did not matter. But I had mattered to her once. I wanted to matter again.

As I sank lower and lower, I could not believe that my life would ever be as good again as it was with P.E. In that little ball of pain, I had flipped over to seeing it from her side. I had never been there for her. I had always been aloof. I had kept my love conditional. I had punished her for her habit. Suddenly, she was a misunderstood saint. But I would change. I would gladly and willingly put down my defenses, be an attentive, loving, boyfriend.

Better than that, I thought of a real smart deal that I hoped it wasn't too late to offer. Because our phone was disconnected again, I ran out of the apartment to a pay phone on the corner to try and find her. Every conscious fiber in me said, "Stop. Do not do this." But the sane side watched helplessly as I ran, like an idiot kid running back into a burning house to retrieve his favorite toy. On my way out of the building, I walked past Ricky's apartment. I could hear the sounds of Metallica coming out of his living room. I knocked on the door and heard him yell, "What the fuck?"

"Oh, hi, man," he said when he saw it was me. He looked like he had either just gotten up or never been to bed.

I didn't really know how upset I was until I heard my own voice demanding to be heard over his Metallica album: "Where's Jane?"

"Whoa," he said, stepping back with his hands up in surrender. "Rules of the road, man. See no evil. Speak no evil." Mystified, I demanded that he explain what he meant. "I don't want to get in between you and your old lady," he said. Now I was really thrown. Get in between? What did he know? Instead of inquiring calmly what he meant, I heard the pitch of my voice rise even higher. "What the hell is going on?"

"Grant, lissen, man. There ain't nothing going on between me and your old lady," he confided in a brotherly sort of way. But feeling that he was on the hot seat, he continued to elaborate, hoping to defuse the situation by placing his cards on the table. "I tell you, man, I ain't been laid in months, and when you're on the road and Jane comes over here saying, 'I'll do anything to get high,' I gotta tell ya, man, guy to guy, bro, the thought has crossed my mind . . . But I could never do that to you, man." Unsure I was convinced, he added, "Besides, I'm so fucking strung out, I don't think I could even get it up, anyway."

P.E. had once told me that as a stripper, she had learned "you get more from a customer if he *thinks* he can fuck you." Now I stood there watching that philosophy at work on Ricky. Just what I didn't need now was more painful, incomprehensible intrigue. I shooed it away. "When was the last time you saw her?" I barked at him.

"Dude," he said, hands up again, "she called me last night like always. I went over there like always, did some business like always. I hung with her and her guitar player, had a cup of coffee, watched a little *Letterman*, and split."

"Did they tell you where they were going?"

"Didn't think to ask, man. None of my beeswax," he said.

Completely panicked, I really overreached. "Did you see them leave? Did you overhear anything?"

"Dude," he said, peeved, "hey, I might be a fuckin' asshole, man, but I ain't no narc, and I ain't no fuckin' Peepin' Tom. You better get a fuckin' grip, bro."

I went to the pay phone on the corner and called all her

girlfriends, looking for her. No one knew where she was. I left the phone-booth number in case they heard. Soon the phone rang. One of P.E.'s girlfriends had spoken to P.E., who said she had merely been out to breakfast with her chubby, harmless bass player. It didn't scan, but I let it lay. She'd be back at one o'clock to talk to me.

Now I had nothing to do but wait, and smoke, and poke around the apartment. I was greedy for any indication of how far this had gone. I did something I shouldn't have. I looked into her diaries. And found a lot of love lyrics and poems. She never wrote love lyrics. Not this mush. I also found directions to restaurants, notes, unfamiliar numbers. It was more than I wanted to know. I put them down. They were evidence of the depth of the life she had been living in my absence. She hadn't been pining for me. She had been making plans. She had a whole support system set up, and she had been thriving. Life for her had been good.

Around one-thirty I heard high-heeled boots clicking down the sidewalk. I opened the door. It was P.E. And P.E. was not pleased. "I told you not to do this. Now you've fucked everything up!" This was not a happy reunion. I had wronged her, booted her out, when all she had ever done was love me, put up with me, live in this shithole, gone without, endured alone. She had forgiven me for The Teacher. And I had the gall to kick *her* out?

In our discussion, she freely admitted that something was brewing between her and Kip. It was only a friendship until I pushed them together. Now she had feelings for him.

If I brought up drugs, she didn't want to hear. "I don't need an antidrug lecture from you. I have a life now. Anyway, my drugs weren't a problem till you found out I *did* drugs," she said.

I refused to see how hopeless this was. I had no high ground. I had pussed out in front of her girlfriends. I had asked her to come back. And yet, like King Lear, I thought if I gave away gladly, I would get love and understanding in return.

I had failed to persuade her, so I had to offer her something. My big plan, which I had hatched while I was rolled up in a little ball, was that I needed to treat her drugs like any other problem: kidney disease, cancer, depression. And I would try to help her. "Take time off and kick," I told her. "Quit your job, and I'll support you. I'll accept your drugs if you try to kick." She must have been laughing inside. God, I was easy.

Seeing I had gone this far, she got indignant. "What about my band? You pushed me into having feelings for Kip. I looked a long time to find a guitarist like that. So just because you fucked up everything, I'm supposed to kick him out now?"

I told her that Kip didn't have to quit as long as he was a gentleman and respected that we'd worked out our differences. Again, I asked if she and Kip had spent the night together. She said, "No. I was packed and heading to Venice in his car when I broke down crying. He drove me back to John the bass player's apartment. I spent the night on the couch."

Certain things didn't add up, but if I pointed them out, she'd start yelling, "I had every right to fuck him. You pushed me into this" in that do-you-want-me-to-leave-again tone. And I'd back down.

So! No rent, no job, no guilt about drugs, AND Kip! I gave her the farm, and the game was lost.

At first we kissed and made up, and the breakdown feeling subsided. We spent all our time together, screwed all the time. She seemed happy. I was happy. I was once again the romantic boob I had been with other girlfriends. Flowers, notes. It was good to be that guy again and yet the radioactive mini–Super Ball was glowing again. I had a sense that she was not the same old gal. It seemed like the harder I tried, the more she pulled away. Not in feet or inches but quarter-inches, just enough to make me queasy. That's why, later in the week, when she said, "You know, I liked you better when you weren't here all the time," I was devastated.

"But . . . but . . . but turtledove, isn't this what you always wanted?"

A week later, she was set to rehearse with Kip for the first time since the bustup. She hadn't talked to him about "IT" yet, but she would tonight. I told her I would like to meet Kip as soon as the smoke cleared.

Later that night we began to screw. P.E. goes for me in a big way and doesn't want anything for herself. Lay back, baby. It's over in a big loud flash. I'm thinking, Man, this girl really digs me. And she digs me so much she does the same thing the next night. All for me. Hey, ain't I the lucky guy? Guess what? Three times lucky. However, by the fourth night, I am finding it a little odd that she still doesn't want me to do anything to her. And on the fifth, it dawns on me that she's not getting me off, she's getting me over. When I ask her about this, gingerly, she tells me that sex doesn't mean that much to her. After three years of nasty notes and calls and orgasms after which she weeps, this is real news to me. She says, "When we first met, sex meant a lot. But now I'm used to you. I don't need it as much." I went off on a long sputtering defense better suited to a Woody Allen movie. "It?" I say. "I'm not talking IT. I am talking US, because screwing says a billion things that words can't."

"Well, I'm not like you, I guess," she says. "I just like sex once or twice a week. That makes it nice. That makes it special."

"What, nice? Unlike all the unpleasant orgasms? I mean, I understand pacing, but why dictate how many times is good?"

"That's just the way I am."

"But you were never like this. What about last week?"

"I was just trying to make you happy. You seemed so . . . I dunno . . . weird."

"Oh," I said. And now I really died. Easily forgotten, easily replaced. And now she was rationing sex. That discussion went back and forth, building, until she shouted that she had warned me that once someone pushed her away, she never came back. "So, I'm back," she said. "You got that much. But don't expect me to fuck you anytime you need it." Now it seemed like she'd come back just to punish me. I remember thinking, Maybe she fucked Kip at rehearsal. Maybe she's fucked out? If I was obsessive before, I was insanely so now. Last week she was fine in bed. Come rehearsal with Kip, everything changed.

I began to notice something else, too: the pat on the back. If I held her, I'd feel her tapping my back affectionately. People of the same sex do that, moms and sons, a male friend and a female friend. It's a social signal that means "Time's up! No boners, please!" She never did that before. Now she pat-pat-patted me all the time.

As the month went on, the big wide open world I had thought was mine vanished. I fell deeper and deeper into her world, trapped in some kind of tide I couldn't pull out of. I was dead inside, crushed, defeated, confused, and fragile. That was the state I was in when I met Kip and saw all the jewelry I had bought her hanging on his gorgeous chest, along with my earring.

"Here you go, ya big baby," she said when I asked for it back.

And that's how I entered the second half of the Psycho Ex

years. For the first three years, I was in control. The second half of the story is about me getting my marbles back. And now the game really begins.

EPILOGUE

In a fog, I wrote Jenna a letter, explained what had happened, and never heard from her again. I never did write that hit. The second album bombed. The band eventually got dropped. I tried to keep writing, but for lack of a better phrase, the joy was gone. Life was rotten. I was paying all the bills, and sex had lost all its spontaneity.

On this night, I was determined for her to face one goddamn night without heroin. She knew I had forty dollars in my coat. She took a bath and pulled out the sleeper couch. She wore a T-shirt and panties to bed. She had no drugs. It was going to be a long night.

"I need drug money," she said. "Give it to me. Now."

"No. One night. Just get through one night," I said.

"I can't," she said.

"Yes you can. I'm here."

She went ballistic, lunging at me full force, screaming like she was being murdered. She took down the bookshelf. She threw a can of pennies at me. I ran into the bathroom. Then I remembered I had left my coat out there. I ran out to get it and found her back in bed. I put my hand in my coat. No money. "Give me my money back," I said.

"I don't have it," she said, lying there in her T-shirt and panties, nothing in her hands. Her shirt was flat. She mocked me like a nasty kid.

I looked at her and figured, It can't be far. I was gone only seconds. "Lift the pillow."

"Oh. Is the big Rock Star's billion dollars under the pillow? No! See? No billion dollars, asshole."

I scanned her from the face on down. Shoulders. Hands.

And then . . . at her panties, I looked back up at her face. She looked at me deadpan, but around her left eye, almost imperceptibly, a tiny muscle moved.

Oh God, don't tell me . . .

SCORE	Points
For even having to wonder for a second whether she had hidden any money in any kind of cooch proximity	500
No sex unless Mr. Heroin said it was time	500
Stealing money	500
Screaming, smashing, throwing	500
Not just asking her to come back, but offering her incentives and rebates to do so	10,000
TOTAL	12,000

What I learned about breaking up:

1. Go out and screw cute singles as soon as you define the relationship as being over. If you broke up once, even if you do go back it's only a matter of time till you break up again. And when everything is gone, only one thing will remain: the undying thirst to know what Heather the Pony Girl looks like naked.

2. Change the bedding. On your first night alone in the former marital bed, strip the sheets and pillowcases, and douse the mattress with your aftershave. Use only fresh towels.

3. Never make a major decision based on anything you thought while rolled up in a little ball on the floor.

Chapter 31

LISA

I was getting confused. I was a little too excited now when I turned on the computer. Since that was a couple times a day, I was starting to carry Grant and his stories around with me. They filled me full of empathy, and though I tried to deny it, there was some of George Bernard Shaw's "abiding love." But it was love that made me nervous. Love that reminded me of someone coming up and tapping me on the back, then acting like he hadn't done anything when I turned to see who was there. When I read about Grant's panic and terror, I wished I had known him back then. I wished he could have called me and I could have talked him through it. Of course, I probably would have been just one more woman whose advice he ignored. He might have called me a stalker. Worse, I'd have wound up with a snotty moniker, starring in one of his painful vindictive songs.

I sat down to respond to his lying-in-a-ball-on-the-floor epic. Rereading it, I saw this for the first time:

> And that's how I entered the second half of the Psycho Ex years. For the first three years, I was in control. The second half of the story is about me getting my marbles back. And now the game really begins.
>
>   Grant

Jesus Christ, I thought when I read that, you mean he's just getting started? HOLY FUCKING SHIT, after all this, he's only now at the beginning?

The more I read his stories, the clearer it became that in order to win the Psycho Ex Game, it would be necessary for Nick to become not just a murderer but a serial killer. The details of his misdeeds would have to be suitably grim. I wrote "Research methods of grisly murder" on my list of things to do. Thankfully I wasn't picked up by the police for questioning at any point during that day. Some district attorney would have been able to make himself famous just by getting ahold of my to-do list.

It was time to counterattack. Grant's theme seemed to be humiliation and degradation. I couldn't begin to approach his attack by *Star Trek* swamp gases. The closest I could come was the time I sat frozen with terror, phoning Nick at four different numbers for twelve hours in a row. That was pretty painful. I hated remembering how I lay there in bed pushing redial, many, many times an hour for the entire night, ice water in my veins as I listened to the phone's empty ringing in four locations. The following morning, my heart was in my throat when I heard the phone ring. How sad and weird it felt, because it wasn't a relief to get a call from Nick. "Hi," he said brightly, like nothing was wrong. Except for the sound of planes taking off behind him.

"Where are you?" I asked.

"Home," he said casually.

"Oh," I said. "Remind me, when did we move to the airport?" My voice was agitated.

"Well, I can't be honest with you, because whenever I tell you the truth, you just get mad at me," he said. My stomach was quaking. I hung up the phone and changed my number. For a guy as telephone-dependent as Nick, I knew that would have its effect. That was the day I learned to be more afraid of the phone. That was the day I started screening calls.

Dear Grant,

I continue your theme of . . . well, I don't know how to label it, but I am referring to the part where you said, <<Sometimes I think I may have picked her, lived with her, encouraged her, and pushed her out just to experience this moment.>>

I FALL OFF THE FREEWAY

When P.E.'s fourth movie (*More Macaroni and Cheese*) started production, he asked me to help out. I was reluctant at first, because of all the troubles we were having personally, but he seemed so sad and worried. He wanted out of the *Mac and Cheese* franchise, even more since the last one had been panned. However, he was contractually obligated. I hated to see him in such a state of agitation, so I agreed for a couple of reasons. 1) He offered me a producing credit on the film, which would be done as three segments. 2) One segment would be my baby. This seemed like a good career move. 3) Since my asserting more independence hadn't been the answer to our problems, I was back to telling myself, after years of evidence to the contrary, that working on something of mutual interest might help. By spending so much time apart, we were growing distant. Maybe this time it would work for us, like it does for you and Winnie.

But once work began, P.E. and I were in a lot of turmoil. I was very confused. When I was around him, he acted like he felt suffocated. But when I was away from him, he acted like he had been abandoned. I couldn't leave. I couldn't stay. I was paralyzed. I went into therapy twice a week.

Meanwhile, I was trying to do a big job with zero confidence. The filming on my segment was to start early on a Sunday morning at a soundstage in Ventura, about an hour away. At home, things with P.E. were tense. He was very short with me. Snippy. He'd speak to his friends on the phone but ignore me when I asked him questions. He'd turn up the sound on the TV when I talked. And when he treated me like that, instead of getting angry, I got very uncentered, almost disoriented. I didn't know how to *be* in the world. I didn't know what behavioral correction on my part would change things. I was so consumed with worry and fear about the state of our relationship that I took a wrong freeway exit and got lost on the drive home from Ventura the first night of work. Familiar landmarks looked unfamiliar. It was about two in the morning, and I was panicky, dissociating, lost on a road I should have known. I could have stayed the night in Ventura. Everyone else working on my segment was spending the night in a nearby hotel. But I had wanted to touch base with P.E. I wanted to see him. Make sure things were okay. Find out if I could get him to do something reassuring. Even though, by the time I got home, it was three-thirty and he was asleep. We never even talked. A minute later it was sunrise, and I had to get up and go back to work.

It was a gray day, foggy and misty but not raining. I was

very aware of a jittery feeling as I got on 101 North in my Jeep at six A.M. Thinking I was going too fast, I put my foot on the brakes, and the car began to fishtail. I know you're supposed to turn into a skid to straighten the car out, but on that two-lane section of highway, it was counterintuitive to turn the steering wheel toward oncoming traffic. The next thing I knew, I was living inside of the longest three seconds of my life. The car began to spin, then went up onto a small embankment and came scooting back into the road on its roof. The sound of scraping metal was thunderous. When the movement stopped, I was upside down in the middle of the freeway. In a flash, all those times I had heard "over-turned vehicle on 101" came back and meant something for the first time. So there I was, suspended by a seat belt, wondering, Do I still have limbs? Teeth? Am I damaged but so much in shock I can't tell? Luckily, because it was six A.M. on a Sunday, the lack of traffic allowed the car behind me to stop without plowing into me.

A guy got out of his car, asked how I was, then called 911. After I figured out how to unhook my seat belt while upside down, he helped me crawl out the back window. An ambulance, fire truck, and police vehicles all showed up pretty quickly. The Jeep was totaled. They made me take the ambulance to the hospital. I was X-rayed, but except for some blood on my face, I was intact. All four of my earrings were still on. Once that registered, about a second later, I called a taxi to take me to the set.

When I arrived, I looked very dramatic in my blood-stained shirt. I was starting to feel sore, but I was glad to be there, because everyone treated me like a conquering hero. It was so pleasant that it occurred to me I might have had more success in life if I had only been in horrible accidents at key moments.

We filmed until about eleven at night. Everything went

okay. At some point, someone on the production staff called P.E. to let him know what had happened. Later, when I called him myself, he barely said a word. Finally, it was time to go home, after a stressful but productive day. My body was aching in all sorts of places I didn't even know I had. My production manager called a taxi for me.

The lights were out in the house when the taxi pulled up. Inside, P.E. was in bed. When I opened the door to the bedroom, he woke but lay still. He didn't turn on the light. He didn't say hello or ask how I was. He didn't even say, "Is everything okay?" or act mad and growl, "What the hell happened?" He just lay there and said nothing. By the time I woke up in the morning, he was at work. He had left no note.

I now realized that all the unnatural twisting and turning that came from being in a capsizing car had caused a lot of pain in my abdomen. It was difficult to sit up or lie down. Laughing was out. Fortunately, nothing was funny.

When I finally got up, there was nothing to eat in the house. So I phoned P.E.'s office and asked if there was someone who could pick up some food and aspirin and bring them by. This irritated P.E., who pointed out that everyone in his office was WORKING. He suggested I call a cab to take me to the store. Since I didn't have any cash on me, that was out. I lay around depressed and hungry for the rest of the day. When I had to call up my shrink and cancel my appointment, I told her about the accident. She was horrified, sympathetic. "Don't be a martyr," she said to me. "Let him take care of you." I remember thinking, Doesn't she listen when I talk?

Fairly late in the evening, P.E. came home after having dinner out with the cast. I was lying in bed upstairs. "A bunch of people in the cast bought you cards and stuff, but

I left them in the restaurant," he said. Then he went down-stairs to watch TV.

SCORE	Points
Going to work for P.E. again when I knew better	1,500
Then feeling so nervous I got lost and turned over a car	5,000
Coming home only to have him ignore me	3,000
No food and I couldn't move	1,000
"Everybody got you cards, but I left them at the restaurant"	1,000
"Let him take care of you" from shrink	1,000
TOTAL	12,500

Grant 31,175 Lisa 31,980

Chapter 32

GRANT

I had just left a big Drag Hags party. The guy we all called Stu Lovesya, the benign fan of absolutely everyone, had loaned them his house. They charged five dollars at the door for unlimited cheap beer to raise funds for their next show. There was a large turnout: a houseful of hundreds of Silver Lake hipsters. When I got there, Winnie was at the front gate, taking bills. I pecked her on the cheek, then moseyed over to Russ Bublis, a porno director and a fan of mine. We stood outside talking about his new adult film, *Mali-Booties*. Obscure sixties garage-band records played loudly as people milled around on the lawn and inside the house. After a few cigs, I heard the music stop and the DJ make an announcement of a special Drag Hags performance. A cheer went up when the DJ put on some loud surf crap from the *Las Vegas Grind* CD. I looked toward the house. There, framed by the picture window, was Winnie, frugging in emerald-sequined panties and pasties. The crowd inside roared. Friends, acquaintances, and total strangers crushed toward her, standing just inches away. Her body was glowing red-hot in the makeshift floodlights. I watched in awe as she frantically raised her kid-gloved arms and shook her substantial boobs, sneering with a practiced sassy expression. A hundred throats, male and female, roared, "Yeah!" Outside another crush of people made a beeline for the doorway to get inside and join the action.

"Jeez!" I said. "I thought she was doing the door."

"Looks like she's doing the room," Bublis laughed.

I'd never had a negative reaction to her burlesque dancing. I'd always seen it as a naughty, glamorous lark. I took it for granted that the Drag Hags were some nebulous form of Performance Art, in which enlightened women could don high heels and push-up bras and still consider themselves staunch feminists. But as I watched Winnie in Stu Lovesya's living room, it struck me that in the presence of his ratty couch, his fish tank, and his family photos, her brand of Performance Art was suddenly crossing the line into Bachelor Party. If it was art, it sure looked like a titty show. The moment struck me as a scene out of one of Russ Meyer's movies. I had been cast as Norman, the quiet fuddy-duddy husband, helplessly watching as his oomphy wife peeled at a suburban swap party.

As I watched her, sweating and naked in public, and listened to men around me judging her physical attributes, I had an unexpected question: Is this right? It arrived filtered through thirty years of Liberal Bohemianism, and purified by sensitive male introspection. By the time it exited from my depths, it had been reconstituted into the laughable but enlightened question: Am I wrong to feel uncomfortable?

Winnie was bending low and shaking her boobs in the face

of a couple who squealed as if a clown had hit them with a shot of seltzer. I wondered, Was I supposed to be aroused? If I was, then she was failing as a Performance Artist. Not forgetting to mention that if I was indeed aroused by my future wife exposing herself to a crowd of drunks, then I was little better than the pathetic Cro-Mags who wrote lurid, boastful letters to *Hustler.* On the other hand, if I didn't find this sexy, then her Performance Art was succeeding, but her titty show was a flop. Oh! I was so confused! When one of her pasties flew off and I heard a chorus of male voices roar in unison like they do when the Yankees or one of those baseball teams wins whatever it is they're supposed to win, it led me to wonder: If Winnie was allowed to strip for men in the name of art, why was I forbidden to write to another woman in the name of literature? That is, if stripping could ever be called art or the Psycho Ex Game could be called literature. At that moment a low gong went off deep inside me. Watching Winnie up there, I had a sense that something wasn't right. It was time to secure the home base. Solidify things with Winnie. Winnie hated the Psycho Ex Game. So it was time to end it. But not without winning it first.

I looked at Winnie as she danced, making flirty faces, and thought of her as a fire. Everyone was illuminated, and everyone got about as close. I couldn't help thinking that despite all our talking, and all the business we did together, the crowd at the party knew her about as well as I did.

I felt that it was time for me to go. Winnie was having a ball. It was her night, her show. She didn't need Norman hanging around.

Instead of taking my regular route home, I made a left off Sunset and twisted around a few side streets until I found myself in front of the Spanish-style stucco apartment complex where Jane and I had spent the final year of our relationship. The last act of my Psycho Ex Game took place here. I pulled over and lit a cigarette.

Looking back and forth from Ricky's apartment door to Jane's, I was hoping to jar a memory. But nothing needed to shake loose. I remembered everything. How could I forget? I could see TV lights flickering in one window and the homey glow of a table lamp in the other. I wondered if the people living in those places now had any idea what went on in their apartments ten years ago.

When I got home, I knew Winnie wouldn't be back for hours. So I sat down at the computer to wrap up the game.

Dear Lisa,
I'm tired of this game. And this correspondence is destroying my life with Winnie. It is time I make my last move. So I'm going to push everything forward three years.

RICKY

It's 1989, three years later than the last story I sent. By now I had left Jane a bunch of times and come back a bunch of times. There were many tearful promises. I even went to Al-Anon, to hang out with people like me who hung with people like Jane. I finally got away for good when P.E. shot up our last twenty-five dollars. I left her penniless! That would teach her! I got my own place and slept with a fan the first night there. A new life dawned. Until I found that Jane hadn't been chastised and wasn't even begging me to come back. Instead, she was getting back on her feet without me. And so the whole cycle began again, with the added treat that I now was paying rent on two places.

While I had been gone, two Narcotics Anonymous strippers in our building took pity on Jane and got her a job tending bar at Chubbie's, a low-rent strip club. The job was Jane's to keep as long as she attended NA meetings. Fortunately for her, she didn't have to be clean, because she could slip through the NA loophole: "Just keep coming back, high or not." Now that she was working and there was some money coming in, she and Ricky went on a tear. I watched as Ricky lost his car, then his bike, then his records, and still the heroin came. Jane got strong on the stuff, Ricky got weaker.

Heroin shrinks the world: where you can go, who you can see. Jane and Ricky were now a global population of two, with me as a visiting dignitary and the dealer as God almighty. They'd pool their money to buy drugs, then ride the bus together back from downtown with their little balloons of dope. When they got back to her place, I'd listen to them bitch and yell at each other like an old married couple.

"Ricky," she'd whine, "what the fuck ya doin' in the bathroom, already?"

"Fuck you," he'd croak back. "I'm taking a shit, whaddya think I'm doin'?"

"Well, come out, I gotta use it," she'd bleat, higher than the moon.

"Crumpets sold us bullshit," he'd moan. "I'm not even getting straight. I got fuckin' ripped off."

"Fuck you, Ricky, Crumpets doesn't sell shit. Anyway, you fuckin' ripped me off yesterday. That stuff you bought was bullshit," she'd reply in junkie slow mo. Back and forth they went with this witty banter, sounding like William Burroughs's single misguided attempt at producing a sitcom.

Little by little, it also became apparent to me that Ricky was in love with her. The things he said, the way he looked at her, the hostility I felt directed toward me. Now that his world had shrunk all the way down, I was standing in between him and the last woman on earth.

By the time this story takes place, Ricky's long-suffering roommate, Duke, had booted Ricky out, so Ricky was homeless. He was sleeping on couches, storing a duffel bag of clothes in Jane's closet, begging a shower now and then. But as long as he continued to steal gear from bands and from the studio rental services he worked for, he had something Jane wanted, so she would tolerate him and continue their partnership. However, he was rapidly deteriorating. And she was growing abusive and intolerant. She'd still take whatever he offered, if it could get her high, then dismiss him until tomorrow, when she'd need him again. At that point our evening would begin. She'd bitch about Ricky until she nodded out in front of the TV. On this particular night, Jane came back from their drug-buying trip alone. "I played a joke on Ricky," she said as she walked in the door. "He couldn't wait to get home to shoot up, so he did it in a bathroom downtown. Then he passed out on the bus ride home, so I left him there." She added, "Ha ha ha," like a snotty kid.

"That wasn't very nice," I told her. "He'll wake up a million miles away with no money."

"Fuck him," she said. "He's a creep."

We both assumed that Ricky would show up at the usual time the next day. But he didn't. Jane was dope-sick and getting frantic. I, of course, gave her money to buy her drugs and keep her sane. Another day passed, and the same thing happened. Still no sign of Ricky. I paid for her drugs again, and after she shot up and felt omnipotent, she bitched about what a baby Ricky was for making such a big deal out of her little joke.

On Monday I picked her up at Chubbie's after her day shift. Together we headed back to her place. It was one of those perfect spring days in Los Angeles, breezy clear sky, late afternoon. Like the day we met. We turned the corner up her street, and there was Duke, Ricky's former roommate, looking at the sky and screaming, "WHY'D YOU DO IT IN MY HOUSE, MOTHERFUCKER?"

Concerned, we ran up. "What's wrong, Duke?"

"He did it in my fucking house," shouted Duke, coming close to me. "Right in my house. He did it in my house."

"Did what?"

"Right there. I open the door, and the motherfucker is right there. You motherfucker. Why'd you do it in my fucking house?" he said, spinning around again, screaming skyward.

"Duke, who?" I demanded.

"Ricky!" he said. He was hysterical. "He broke in and got my gun. Blew his head off. Fuckin' take a look for yourself! See?" He pointed, and there in the doorway, just inside, we could see Ricky sitting with his legs spread, a shotgun between them. No head. Pulp. Blood and brain matter everywhere.

"You motherfucker!" Duke screamed again. "In my house. In my fucking house. Right where I'd find you. Fuck you, Ricky. Fuck you, motherfucker!"

P.E. whispered to me, "Keep Duke cool. Cops are gonna come. I'm gonna see if Ricky left anything behind. You know, so they don't bust Duke. Tell him it's gonna be okay."

Good idea, I thought, so I put my arm around Duke, who was now alternating between rage and incoherent muttering, and said, "It's gonna be okay. It's gonna be so . . . so . . . great." P.E. went up the stairs. I heard the door close with a sharp click. And I thought, Click? The door goes click? The door is open, there's a dead guy behind it, and now it's closed? Click? Let me tell you, it's hard to comfort a hysterical neighbor while simultaneously wondering what your girlfriend is doing behind a locked door in an apartment with a suicide, one of the many options being rifling through the pockets of a headless corpse. It's hard, but it can be done. I had my arm around Duke and turned to look at the closed front door. If Ricky left anything behind, she could sure use it. Right then I knew . . . she was in there going through that . . . thing's pockets.

In a few minutes, the LAPD showed up. Some neighbor had called. Those two cops talked to Duke, and then more cops showed up. They were followed by the ambulance and the crime-lab guys. I heard Duke repeat his story over and over again, getting exasperated, yelling, "Look, man, I didn't fuckin' kill him, okay?"

The cops went about their business, taking pictures and whatever they do. Jane and I stayed with Duke, trying to comfort him. Over the next hour, his tone went from rage to remorse. He felt terrible for kicking Ricky out. Ricky was his friend. They'd been through a lot together. Sure he was a fuckup, but . . . At this point, Gayle and Sandi, the two NA strippers who lived in the complex, came over to join us. When Duke explained what had happened, Sandi said, "Whoa, Duke. You got to get a white witch in here. Suicides are very angry spirits, and they don't leave. You need someone to get this place really cleaned out and tell Ricky's spirit, you know, to head to the light."

Duke stood motionless, listening, and then shouted, "Fuck you! That's bullshit, man. When this is over, I'm gonna throw one big fucking party to salute the memory of Ricky fucking Bock!" Sandi felt Duke hadn't really understood her helpful suggestion, so she repeated herself, explaining in greater detail. Duke, pushed to the limit, repeated what he had said at top volume to the night sky, until a cop told them to knock it off.

Later, they carried Ricky out on two stretchers. One had a black bag for the body; the other, a smaller bag, was for the rest of him. I listened as the last cop explained to Duke that they got all of Ricky, and the bone in the kitchen belonged to Duke's dog, so don't worry. Then the cops turned to leave. Duke said, "Wait a minute—this place is still full of fucking blood."

"Oh, we don't clean that up," said the cop.

"Who does?" asked Duke.

"Not us," said the other cop, getting in the car.

The night ended with Duke standing on the sidewalk screaming to the exiting squad cars, "I gotta clean up this shit? Me? I gotta do this?" He again turned skyward and cursed Ricky.

The next day, word came through the grapevine that there'd be a memorial service on Tuesday. The morning of the service, of course, first P.E. had to get her day's drugs. The front doorbell rang. It was Ricky's replacement, her new junkie butt boy, a guy with a car who could take her downtown to buy drugs: Chris, onetime Cro-Magnon sex god of Slowly I Turn. My old bulimic junkie guitar player, Chris, the guy who wrote the song about fucking P.E. in the graveyard. He looked like shit. It had been two years since we kicked him out of the band. He was wearing a raggy suit full of what I assumed were bulimia stains. They were foody-looking.

Here was the plan: P.E. and Chris would go downtown and cop, then come back and shoot up. Then we would all go to Ricky's wake together.

"You got to be ready when we come back," she said to me in a severe tone of voice, sternly lecturing me like she was my mother.

When we walked into the white marble chapel, it was full of mourners. There were two hundred people: rock goons and rock molls, bands and band girlfriends, has-beens, never-weres, never-really-trieds, roadies, bouncers, rock journalists. I looked around at the throng: that one—junkie; that one—dealer; those two—junkies. Him? Drunk.

Her? Speed freak. Him? Cokehead. All dressed in leather, lace, big hair, black hair, red hair, green hair. All in bands or linked to bands. The chapel was like an ornate alabaster vase containing a nightmarish creeper with black leather limbs and flower tops of green, black, and traffic-cone orange/red. Two hundred variations on Keith Richards and Anita Pallenberg, or Sid and Nancy.

In the middle of all this sat Ricky's parents, puffy, middle-aged, and looking like they didn't know what the hell had hit them. Dad was in a suit, Mom in a Sunday-best dress. They looked like two glazed doughnuts in a box of spiders.

Because we were among the last to arrive, we paraded through the group already seated. Oddly enough, there were three empty chairs waiting up front. God had reserved ringside seats. The casket was closed.

A progressive, swingin' Catholic priest conducted the service, tap-dancing around the fact that suicide was a damnable offense. He said he personally believed that God was far more forgiving than all that. Very sweet, but then again, Ricky's parents were right there. What else was he gonna say?

Oh, how Jane cried and cried. One would think she'd lost her best friend. One could almost forget she had left him alone on that bus when he had absolutely nothing left and nowhere else to go.

In 1986, when I met Ricky, he had no habit. By 1989, he'd have no head.

As I looked around, God, how I suddenly hated this romantic, teetering-on-the-edge-of-self-destruction, Dionysian horseshit. I suddenly hated Morrison and Joplin and Brian Jones. I hated Jimi Hendrix. I hated Keith Moon. I hated any famous beautiful corpse with a fat bank account that made death look good. At that moment, I hated Iggy Pop. I hated Lou Reed. Fuck you, Keith Richards. Fuck you, John Bonham.

I hated all those millionaire rock gods with their armies of lawyers, label ass-lickers, and sycophants who kept them afloat and helped them make self-destruction look like a lifestyle, a fashion choice, an accoutrement. I realized that I was just another one in a generation of idiot white kids who grew up respecting these millionaires the same way earlier generations stood in awe of industrialists like Ford, Rockefeller, and Carnegie. Their heroes fought at Normandy and went to the moon. Most of my generation ended up doing nothing except buying the clothes, getting the haircut, and doing the drugs so we could look as if we'd made it. Ricky's death secretly satisfied all of us. He reminded us of just how dangerous this rock life was. And danger substituted for purpose. Excitement was mistaken for accomplishment.

As I sat there and listened to the priest blab on, I knew Ricky's parents were watching a long reel of black-and-white family movies in their heads: the beginning so perfect, so beautiful, the ending shattering and making no sense. "When did all of this start?" they must have been asking themselves. "What could I have done? How did this happen? Who are all these people?" Could they even begin to imagine my role in all this? Should I go up to them and introduce myself and say, "Hi, I facilitated your son's suicide. See that woman over there? I paid her bills. I bought her drugs and kept her going. Provided her a safety net so she was free to reduce your son to two bags of pulp."

I now had a very clear picture of what my life had degenerated into. There I sat between my junkie girlfriend and my former band member, whom she fucked behind my back, in his cheap suit full of vomit splash. He sat there beside me guilty of having written a song about their affair and thinking it was good fun to have me record it and then sing it to audiences around the world. Before us was the closed casket of a headless kid whose pockets she had picked. For all the sick people in the room, I was the sickest, because I had managed to destroy myself while being completely sober, cognizant, and in control. I was there as proof that drugs were just the tools of self-destruction for the unimaginative.

Had I hit bottom? I suppose I had. Funny thing about the bottom: It's not nearly as romantic as they paint it. You actually sit there feeling very dirty and extremely stupid.

SCORE	Points
	Zero.

Although I could collect one million points. (And, if you need me to tell you what they're for, two million.) I would not feel right taking points for someone's tragic death. So the score is actually: minus 50 points for Lightcap's Parallel.

Grant

I put the letter into "drafts," planning on proofreading it later.

It was still early, so I got back in the car and headed to the Empire. I was feeling grateful. Compared to how things used to be, I had a great life now. Might as well go enjoy it.

Chapter 33

GRANT

T uesday at one-thirty A.M. Turning north onto Fairfax. Pulling into the alley behind the Empire, I saw the clot of stand-ups catching a smoke in the darkness. Three of them were in my play—Bobby, Brian, and Barry. The rest were club regulars. As I walked up, they all greeted me, mimicking Bobby's melodious cadence: "Hellooo!" Bobby was top dog of the stand-up pack. "Hellooo!" I mimed back as I was hit by a wave of goodwill. Even the ones who rarely spoke to me looked at me with a smile and a twinkle.

I went inside. I could tell by the small amount of dish clanking that business was slow. I waved to the cooks, and they waved back. From behind, someone grabbed my arm.

"Hey, man!" It was Barry, who'd followed me in. "Nick Blake, huh?"

Putting my fingertip to my lips, I winked cartoonishly. "Shhhhhhhh." He winked back. But inside my skull, a million lights went off: sirens, bells, and the screech of a bird at night. Just like Winnie had predicted. Everybody knew about Nick.

In the glow at the bar, Karen O'Malley sauntered up, stood in front of me, and looked me up and down, nodding. At the bar I noticed a couple I didn't know, pointing toward me and whispering. Bells were continuing to go off, lights popping in my skull. The kitchen doors opened behind me, and I heard Sylvia's nasal growl in my ear, "Nick Blake loves you."

If this had been a car wreck, which it eventually was, this was the moment when, going through the intersection on green, I would have noticed a dark speck out of the corner of my eye. In no time at all, that speck would turn into a black Escalade going ninety, with the whole LAPD in pursuit.

"Come on upstairs," said Sylvia, and we went back through the kitchen, the comics cracking wise about Sylvia's miniskirt and thigh-high boots as she went up ahead of us. Brian looked at me, eyes wide, as he sucked in a chestful of air and shouted, "We won't tell nobody we're all going to star in Nick Blake's next film!"

Bobby, taking the cue, played Moe: "Quiet, numbskull, don't ya know we ain't s'posed t' tell no one?"

I laughed off the horseplay while, inside, up went a red flare of rage. Then I had a small epiphany. Laughing on the outside, demonically murderous on the inside; that's how a stand-up comedian feels every minute of his life. Again, as Winnie had predicted, the result of Sylvia telling everybody everything was that every comic in my play thought he was going to be in Nick Blake's next film, a huge leap forward on the Hollywood Board Game.

While the comedians bad-mouthed other comedians, Sylvia leaned in close. "Nick Blake thinks you're a fucking genius!" she said, placing an ashtray in front of me. I looked behind me to see who she was talking to: a classic move I had learned from the comics. With them, it always got a laugh. With me, nothing.

"Where's Winnie?" she asked.

"Drag Hag rehearsal," I said as I watched Sylvia grow uneasy. Sylvia was a no-bullshit New Yorker. Winn stripping in public was, to her, well, stripping in public.

"Hey, who's the guy singing downstairs?" I asked, controlling the subject before it went somewhere I didn't want it to.

"Noah," said Sylvia. "Oh, he's fucking great. He's like a *GQ* model. He's twenty-five, and his lyrics are like if Joni Mitchell had been screwing Allen Ginsberg. People are saying he's the best new songwriter here. And you know what? He's funny as hell. Last week he had Warners out. He . . ."

This was meant to hurt a little, and it did. I had been sucked into that familiar painful vortex of insecurity, the wasted years scrolling past. I was young, handsome, and funny as hell once, twenty years ago.

When Sylvia sensed she had tapped enough sore spots, she changed tactics. "Nick was impressed by your ideas. He says you two saw things alike."

"Yeah," I said, forcing a smile.

"You know," she leaned in and whispered, "if Nick finds out you and Lisa have been swapping stories about him, this whole thing is going to fucking fall apart." I must have looked shocked, because she broke out laughing and slapped her thighs. "Oh Christ, you should see your face. C'mon, your secret's safe with me, you big pussy." She stood up. "Come with me downstairs and let's watch the next big thing take off."

The kid was good, he had a voice like an angel. Here was the guy every college girl who gained twenty pounds her frosh year was going to fall in love with. So later, as I pulled the car out onto the empty street, it all seemed painfully clear to me: Without this musical, you are headed to the poorhouse. The days when you were young enough to write like Noah are past. Even if you could, what nineteen-year-old wants a man in his mid-forties? No, my dear Grant. This is it. This is the door that opened, and Nick Blake is welcoming you.

I drove home with a bad feeling. Everyone seemed to know more about my business than I did. Nick had been hanging out at the club, and now he and Sylvia were friends. And that warning about Lisa and the e-mails? "Your secret is safe with me"? No secret was safe with Sylvia.

"Sylvia and Nick are tag-teaming us!" shouted Winnie as soon as I ran it all by her. "Sylvia's winding the cast up. I knew this would happen. And we haven't even begun to make a deal with Blake yet."

"Yeah. How do we handle this?" I asked.

"Be real careful. That Lisa stuff was a warning," she cautioned.

"Well, I better just come clean and tell Lisa what's been going on," I said.

"NO!" said Winn. "Don't come clean. She'll just clam up. When she hears you're in bed with Nick Blake, she won't talk to you about him anymore. We might still need her for a little more information. Here's what you do: Ask her about him indirectly, theoretically. Something like 'If one is negotiating a business deal with a big fucker, should one stand up or roll with the punches?' Lisa will naturally draw on her experiences with Nick. She probably has some good insights. And then . . ."

"And then?"

"Then you have to knock off the correspondence. Look, if Sylvia ever plays the Lisa card, it would be better for you to tell Nick you used to write to Lisa than for him to find out that you two are still writing."

The sun was about to come up. We had been talking about this for three hours. Almost obsessively, Winnie and I traveled down these dark paths together. And like always, despite what we had promised, it was the only thing on our minds after sex. It was also on mine during it.

Dear Lisa,

Do you mind if I ask you a business question? A high muck-ety-muck A-list asshole bastard has expressed interest in making my musical into a film. He is famous for being a bully. The question is this: In your vast experience, do you think it is more to my advantage to stand up to the A-lister, or roll along with whatever punches may be in store?

Chapter 34

LISA

 wrote him back immediately.

Dear Grant,
Re: Your business question.

Well, I don't know if I am the best person to ask. But since you did, in my vast experience I have noticed that if someone wants to do business with you, whether he's a bully or simply a greedy pain in the ass, he will find a way to make it happen. If we're talking bully, we may be talking narcissist. And if we're talking narcissist and you go belly-up too quickly, he will cease to think of you as a force of any consequence. A narcissist will jump your boundaries and kind of annex you as a territory, but without the rights of a full state, like the U.S. did to Puerto Rico or the Philippines. You will become an extra star in his constel-lation, void of individual rights, no longer a separate set of concerns at all. So you have to make your boundaries clear at the outset.

My advice, for what it's worth, is hang tough in the be-ginning and see how it goes. If you are too tough, and Mr. A-list Bigwig Asshole gives a real shit, he will make a counteroffer. And if he doesn't, you are better off not being consumed and digested by a narcissist anyway. If you don't believe me, go back and read "I Fall Off the Mountain," which, if memory serves, I believe you wrote.

Strangely enough, "no" can sometimes be an aphro-disiac in a negotiation. I remember that I used to be able to make P.E. come toward me when I would lie next to him in bed and vibe a wall of hatred.

But enough about me. I wish you the best of luck. Who is this muckety-muck of whom you speak so highly?

Lisa

I was pleased and proud to have helped my good pal Grant out of a difficult situation, although I wondered if I had really helped at all. Following advice from me, a woman who got confused picking a dressing for salad when offered too many varieties, was at best a questionable course of action.

It took a couple of days for me to understand that every-thing had stopped. After all, the letters could come at any hour of the day or night. So only after I had checked my e-mail every hour on the hour did I understand that there had been a total cessation of letters from Grant.

Of course, my first thought was that something was wrong. He was ill or had been in an accident. Maybe he spilled a glass of water on his computer and was technologically disabled. Or could he have left town without enough time to tell me? Since the letters had begun, I had gotten between one and five a day, every day. Neither flu nor dental work nor lack of a topic had kept the e-mails from their appointed rounds.

It was alarming to see how off balance their absence made me. I got edgy, sad, needy, and anxious. I held off as long as I could, and then, Monday morning, the first thing I did was write.

> Dear Grant,
> Hey—did you get my last e-mail? I haven't heard from you, so I'm thinking something got lost in the transmission. Here it is again.
>
> Lisa

I re-sent my last letter. Still nothing. The following morning I wrote again.

> Dear Grant,
> Where are you? Is everything okay? I'm beginning to worry. If there's anything you need, please feel free to ask.

I waited twenty-four more hours, trying not to check my e-mail more than five times an hour. In an attempt to distract myself, I went through most of the rest of my recipe cards. Hawaiian Spareribs came out worried and fretful, the Scandinavian Fish Scallop anxiety-ridden. I was working on a depressed and agitated Lamb Shanks in Red Wine when I couldn't take it anymore and actually phoned Grant's home. The answering machine picked up. That meant his house hadn't burned down. I didn't leave a message. Instead, I sat back down and did a very wistful Sauerkraut Casserole (with sausage) and a disoriented Hamburger Pie. Then I wrote a third time.

Dear Grant,
Is something wrong? Did I say something to upset you? You
know I would never do that intentionally. Was the business
advice I gave you a disaster? Did I cause you to lose your
upcoming fortune?

I got a letter back three days later.

Dear Lisa,
Thank you for your concern. Everything is fine. I'm really
sorry I haven't written, but the show has been taking all my
time. Next week's show is a big one. I hope to see you
there. Got to run.

Grant

It hadn't even occurred to me to be upset with him. But this
pissed me off. After constant daily communication, he suddenly disappeared for days and then all he had to say when he
reappeared was "Got to run. Grant." Without offering an explanation? Without acknowledging the gigantic break in the
pattern? After dragging me through a blow-by-blow detailing
of his every painful moment from early childhood to the present, all he had to say was "Got to run"? I didn't know how to
respond. Well, I did, but I didn't feel like it was right to be so
hostile. So I wrote him back.

Dear Grant,
Oh . . .
Lisa

It was only when this also went unacknowledged that I really
got a sinking feeling. I don't know if it was quite as over-
whelming as the glowing mini–Super Ball of fear, or the *Star
Trek* gases from the psychological swamp. Maybe I just wasn't

as quick with hyperbole. But I was really queasy and upset. I had never been through withdrawal. That was how it felt. Did everyone connected to Grant wind up a junkie?

I accepted that he suddenly had more pressing obligations. Fine. But to pretend that no real explanation was needed after so many daily e-mails? That was just painful. My recipe cards offered me no solace or escape. In fact, I couldn't even focus on them. Instead, I started sake time early.

I had to keep reminding myself that I had done nothing wrong. To be sure of this, I repeatedly reread the advice I had given him. Had it been bad advice? Had I maybe ruined his life? I continued going back and rereading the last few weeks of letters. Had I not reacted properly to a previous story? Had I said something inadvertently mean or inappropriate? Had I caused him financial ruin?

I called up Kat, because I thought of her story about an e-mail relationship that had ended abruptly. "I told you," she said. "This is just what always happens with them. They're a false read. Always."

"You still have no idea why the glassblower stopped writing?"

"None. They just stop at some point. It's a question of when."

"Huh. Could be he's got a new person he's writing," said my friend Robinson. "Or could be the chick he lives with put her foot down. My wife wouldn't have tolerated anything like that for very long."

"But she never had any problem with you and me being friends," I said.

"Well, not now. But she did at first. When you and I were working together, she felt threatened and gave me a lot of shit."

"You never told me that. So Sara hates me?"

"No, she doesn't hate you now. But we went around and around about it in the beginning. I had to convince her I didn't find you attractive."

"So you and Sara have had conversations about my physical shortcomings?"

"No. Come on. I didn't say that. Don't make this a bigger deal than it was. I'm just saying I bet that's the reason your buddy stopped writing."

"You don't find me at all attractive? What about me is so awful?"

"Stop it."

This also pissed me off. If Robinson had ever indicated that there was a problem with him and Sara, I would have backed off instantly. Same with Grant. Fuck them both. So much for nicely putting my heart back into its former condition again.

The thing that bothered me most was how I had misread the signs. What I had seen as laying the groundwork for a lasting friendship through a growing intimacy had been more of the noxious atmospheric gases that were the building blocks of most friendships in L.A. It wasn't as if I hadn't been through it a dozen times before. L.A. friendships were frequently just a facsimile. They often came apart without warning. The confusing part was that they included elements that looked an awful lot like friendship: dinners, parties, personal soul-baring, lengthy phone calls full of shared confidences. They all added up to a Bizarro World replica, similar to real friendship except for the goatees and the beret.

And that, I guessed, was what had happened with Grant. Just another callous Bizarro World friendship replica, nothing more insidious. But nevertheless, pretty heartbreaking.

And then I got a call from Nick.

I hadn't spoken to Nick in four years. I didn't expect to speak with him ever again. Unlike some people, I didn't keep a coffee klatch of old lovers. Large chunks of my past were stored in airtight, leak-proof containers in the basement of my brain, where they couldn't be accessed. There was only so much hurt I could effectively process, and it seemed to me that the present offered a more than adequate supply.

When I heard Nick's voice on my answering machine, the reaction I had was physical. I felt sweaty, flushed, and a little nauseated.

"Lisa," he said, "hi. It's Nick. I wanted to talk to you about something. Do you think you could call me at your earliest convenience?"

I picked up a magazine and began to leaf through it to prove to myself that his call had no effect on me. But it had made me so amped, so nervous, and agitated that I couldn't translate English into English. "Hi. It's Nick," he had said. Like we had just talked earlier in the day.

I paced. I stared. I went out to the store but came right back without parking and going in. And a couple of monthlong hours later, I called him back.

"Nick. Hi," I said, trying to sound casual back. "It's Lisa, re-turning your—" He picked up. From the moment I heard the slightly mournful tone in his familiar twangy voice, it was my instinct to try and cheer him up. "Everything okay?" I asked.

"Oh, sure," he said, pretending it was a casual reunion. He asked about my mother, my father, my brother, my nephews, my dogs. He wanted to know how the car was running and if my knee was still bothering me. It was the most personal and most un-Nick-like list of questions he had ever posed. I hesi-tated at first. I had my doubts about his ability to listen to the answers. Sure enough, as soon as I launched into the details of my brother's divorce, Nick cut me off. "That's too bad," he said. "Well, you're probably wondering why I called. An inter-esting project has fallen into my lap. I'm thinking of buying the rights to a musical."

"Really?" I said. "I never imagined you in *Oklahoma!*, but now that I think about it, I guess I'd go see it."

"Much as I've always wanted to play the lead in *The Pajama Game*, that's not the direction I was thinking of going in yet, Lisa. Ever been to that club the Empire? I know you're not too big on clubs. . . ."

When he said "Empire," I felt like I'd been kicked. "Actually, I have been there a few times," I said, now doubly agitated, waiting for the other shoe to drop.

"Well, you know how I've been looking for something that takes me in a whole new direction? Or maybe all that happened since we last spoke."

"I read that *Ruler of the Universe* is doing great," I said quietly, refusing to offer enthusiastic praise.

"Yeah. Big fucking deal, though, you know? What else is new? I feel like it's more of the same, like I'm on autopilot." He paused, probably expecting me to jump in and reinforce him with a big hearty "No, no, your movies are so GREAT!" I considered it progress that I wasn't willing to play along.

"Anyway," he said, "there's a musical they put on there about Tommy Lee and Pam Anderson. It's better than it sounds."

"Oddly enough, I saw it," I said, suddenly very still, feeling like someone was sneaking up on me with an ice pick. "Grant Repka's play."

"What'd you think?" he asked.

"Great," I said. "I liked it a lot."

"Yeah, me, too," he said, pleased. "I've had a couple meetings with him."

"You and Grant Repka had meetings?" I said, strangely out of breath.

"Yeah. Nice guy. Pretty down-to-earth. Nicer than he looks," said Nick, as if he had any functioning understanding of "down-to-earth." "We really hit it off. He seemed to like my ideas. I think it's going to be a lot of fun.

"See, here's the thing," he said, after a medium-sized pause when I kept quiet because I was speechless. "I'd like to see if I can pull off the kind of thing no one would ever expect of me, you know?"

"Huh!" I said, because I was stunned in such a wide variety of painful ways that words failed me completely.

" 'Huh' like how?" he asked. " 'Huh' like you think it's a horrible idea? 'Huh' like you think it'd fuck up my career?"

"No, no, not at all," I said. Nick's career trajectory was the last thing on my mind. My mental computer screen had frozen and was shutting down. "You want to play Tommy Lee?" I asked him.

"Well, that neatly brings us to the reason I called. I don't know how you'd feel about this, but I was hoping maybe we could work together on it. We were always a good creative team, and this would be quite a stretch for me. I was thinking maybe, if I bought the rights, you could rewrite it with me in mind. I would like to play David Lee Roth."

I was in such stimulus overload, I couldn't actually speak.

"Well, that's just the sort of rousing support I was hoping for," Nick said in a nicer tone of voice than he would have used if we had been living together. "I take it that your spooky silence means no?"

"No, no, not at all," I said, trying to fill my voice with a cheerful energy that I didn't feel. The part of me that had said yes to *You Go, Girl!* was now hounding me to keep my options open. "But Nick, I saw the musical. And I don't remember anything about David Lee Roth."

"There's a good reason for that," said Nick. "It's because he's not in it. But he should be. I've always wanted to play a guy like that. Big hair. Tight pants. Insatiable chick magnet. No one expects to see me singing and being a sex god. Ha! Can you imagine? There's got to be a way to add him. They're both from the same eighties rock thing, right? They probably knew each other. Or at least met. And if they didn't, we can figure out a way that they meet. Even if it's by telepathy."

"Maybe, depending on my schedule," I said, hedging, ashamed to observe the "award-winning" writer of *You Go, Girl!* sniffing out a paycheck. "I'd like to think about it for a minute. If that's okay. When did you want to do it?"

"Right away," Nick said. "Production should start almost immediately. It's the next thing I'm planning to do."

"Well, do you mind if I look into my availability and get back to you?" I said, knowing all too well that I had nothing planned until the end of time.

"Sure, will you call me tomorrow? I think we're going to make them an offer this week, and you know me. If I'm going to do it, I want to get going yesterday."

It's hard to describe how I felt after I hung up the phone. For the first minute I thought, Say yes. Take the job and work for Grant from the inside, help protect him from Nick. For the next minute I thought I might start crying. But instead of getting sad and self-pitying, I surprised myself by segueing into anger, then resentment. Why, after telling me every detail of his life, did Grant never mention meeting with Nick? Nothing ever just slipped his mind. He remembered his life with his idiotic Psycho Ex in microscopic detail. And he certainly hadn't been too busy cleaning to write and tell me. So why didn't he want me to know? Was it because, with that final piece of business advice, my usefulness to him as a connection and an informant was completed? Was that possible? And if it was, goddammit, how sad. Though I deserved it. What was I thinking, trusting a guy who could give his girlfriend money for drugs? He had drawn me a vivid portrait of himself as someone who shouldn't be trusted. And I had ignored it. How humiliating for me, that I had been confiding in him with such ridiculous candor because I had been totally blinded by a crush. I had been a fool in my relationship with Nick, but at least then I had been young and naïve. This betrayal was worse. At least Nick, in his limited way, had actually cared about me. Nick's bullying and sadism felt like a mother's warm embrace compared to the way I had just been used by Grant.

I wondered if he had mentioned our game to Nick, if the two of them were now setting me up. It couldn't be a coincidence that Nick had called right when Grant's writing stopped. What else didn't I know about my own fucking life?

Chapter 35

GRANT

W inn was asleep. It was four A.M. My day was three hours away from ending. I was numb from rehearsal, ears sore, tongue-tired from giving orders. My lungs ached from the four packs of cigs I'd wolfed down during the day.

I went into the studio, opened up my laptop, and went straight to a file of porno. I scrolled past a Roman phalanx of amateur shots. Jeez, had I really downloaded two thousand of these snaps? I roped 'em in and tapped twice, and they whizzed by me. Once they'd stopped, I filed through them. What, I wondered, did all of these gals have in common? You would think my tastes would have gotten more bizarre as I got older. But no. There were no strapped breasts festooned with pushpins. No chains. No one hung upside down with a ball gag. The opposite. It wasn't the moments of penetration or orgasm that my libido went looking for. I was drawn instead to hundreds of soft come-hither smiles, the eyes deep, knowing. The unifying fantasy? The women all seemed to really like me. Sad, Grant, really sad. I looked at one of my favorites; she was dark-haired, maybe ten pounds over, early thirties. A mommy with a dresser behind her, the middle drawer open. Some shirt or sock hanging out, and on the top, perfume, deodorant, hair spray, the obligatory wooden box for jewelry. A basket of dirty laundry. She kneeled on a bed. I knew that type of bed. I'd moved hundreds of those when I worked for Super Howie's Furniture. I knew those brass knobs were plastic and the black metal posts wouldn't last five years. Everything about her world said underpaid, overworked, in debt, fucked up, undervalued. It said Kmart and ninety-nine-cent store. The walls were white, artless. And yet, there she stood in the middle of this hopeless mess gloriously naked, wearing only a devilish smirk, her blazing blue eyes intoning, "Let's play."

I looked at her and sensed that beyond the first rush of lust was loneliness. What kind of pervert was I? Was she more real than the supermodel next door?

Winn was a lot of fun. But Winn at a party was the same as Winn in your bed. Winn never changed. Winn was constant as a ruler. There was no Secret Winn that she only revealed to me. If there was, it was in the work she did, in the weight she carried. But in all the time I'd known her, and loved her madly, she'd never once looked at me like this slatternly woman in the shot. Devoured me with her eyes. Purred when I touched her.

Still, sex with Winnie was fine, and our life was great. But I felt bad about Lisa. I understood that curtailing the correspondence kept us both out of the line of fire. But business aside, I should have just come clean and said, "Lisa, out of all the things that could have happened, Nick Blake is in my life." If she blew me off because of that, then so be it. But Christ, I should have given her the courtesy to let her make up her own mind based on the facts. However, that would have been pushing the buttons with Winnie. In fact, without Lisa's letters, we were getting along again. Yet I felt resentful. I had successfully maintained a friendship with Lisa that had never degenerated into a sex exchange.

"I'm not writing to her vagina," I yelled once.

"But that's where she's sticking your letters," she screamed back.

That was all over now. In the back of my mind, I wondered if Winn was right. "You tell Lisa things you've never told me!" she once said. And it was true. The weight of that truth floored me.

In the meantime, Nick Blake at the center of our lives solved that problem. Winn and I were back where we were before this game started: talking business, discussing the cast, Sylvia, and now Nick Blake and The Film. Winnie was in control again.

Though I thought it was too bad that we didn't have Lisa to help us steer through the rocks that loomed ahead. And what rocks they were. A second meeting at Nick's house had Winn fuming. When she mentioned that Bobby Snuggs was perfect for the role of the fat asshole manager, she got that glassy-eyed, vague nod from Nick that I recognized as the same faraway look I had seen at the first meeting. I knew that in his mind, Bobby and the others in my cast had already been axed or reduced to walk-ons.

Even worse, Winn didn't like Nick. She felt that he always ignored her. Strangely enough, I heard Winnie confiding to her friend Mitchell that Nick didn't like "real women." "He likes skinny little chicks, anorexic chicks. And guys who want that really want guys," she said. When I pointed out that he had spent years with Lisa, and she was nothing if not a tall, well-shaped woman, Winn brushed that off. "Yeah, she's also a doormat," she said.

At the Empire, people were being very nice to me. A little too nice. Comics came up to me like trick-or-treaters, smiling, expectant. The cast members were thrilled to be associated with a guy who was the apple of Nick's eye. The other club regulars looked at them with envy. Nick had added Sylvia to his A-list golf crew. He'd even gotten her into the Oscars. Most important, Nick's celebrity crowd started to hang out at the Empire: full-time. When a disappointingly underdressed Nicole Kidman came up and lightly touched my arm, asking, "When is your next show?" it took me a while to realize who she was.

Soon the whole inner circle at the Empire began every sentence with "Nick says," "Nick had," or "Nick wants." Names like TriStar, ICM, CAA, and United Talent had replaced the old musicians' concerns, like Warner Bros., Capitol, MCA.

My whole life, I had yearned for a major-label record deal. I had wanted that fat advance to pay off the IRS and finally buy a car that ran. I wanted that awful, bone-crushing power of a corporation behind me. However, record deals were milk money compared to what I was hearing about movies.

Now, at last, every record-company president was calling my manager. They all asked about Nick. The labels dropped everything to meet with us, to take us to dinner. We said expensive; they got us very expensive. The *L.A. Times* ran a blurb that was picked up by AP and radio because it was such perfect on-air filler. When Robin Quivers read the blurb, Howard Stern, who hated both Nick and musicals, gave it two seconds of commentary. "Stupid," he said.

At meeting number two, sitting in Nick's kitchen having coffee, we had sketched out the movie in the loosest sort of way. Of course, his kitchen cost more than my mother's home, and we were overlooking two acres of garden, grotto, and pool-with-an-island on which there stood a bamboo tiki bar. We were both animated and cracked each other up. Well, he cracked me up. It was impossible to make him laugh. He seemed unreadable, unknowable. At times effusive, other times cold, indifferent. A new man every ten minutes. I still wasn't sure if I liked him.

There were dark clouds, too. He had given a blank look to many of my casting suggestions, the same one he gave every time Winn added her thoughts. I suspected these were not accidental emotional slipups. I was being reminded to read his face, and thus his mind.

Nick had formed a beachhead in the Empire and was firmly planted in my camp as a hero, a savior, and a liberator. And we hadn't even begun to make a deal yet. It soon became very clear that Sylvia and Nick had sprinkled Hollywood Dream Dust in the eyes of those around us.

Nick had Winnie and me surrounded.

It was a real dumb-ass time for us to stop speaking to Eva Braun.

In the few hours we had to ourselves, Winn and I continued to fret and discuss Nick, and try to anticipate every move of Sylvia's. Our home, ever filthy, was a hothouse where fear blossomed into conspiracies that ripened, then rotted, and fertilized a crop of suspicion, doubt, and persecution and ultimately harvested hatred. Winn and I were back on track, bonding again.

Chapter 36

LISA

I really fretted for the next twenty-four hours. About Nick's job offer, yes, but more about the fact that I had misread my relationship to Grant. How was it possible for me to be stupid so repeatedly in only one lifetime? I fretted so hard that I got a backache and a rash on both elbows. I made an appointment to talk to my shrink, Johanna, who I hadn't seen in three years.

"You must be furious" was what Johanna said when she heard about the Grant betrayal. She often said things like this to me, because over and over she had watched me continually speed past the Anger exit, only to get off at Depression and Logic by mistake.

"Yes. I must be furious," I said, staring at my lap in controlled misery.

"I think it would be a good thing for you to say something to your friend Grant about this," she said. "Make sure you've got the story straight. It's good for you to practice speaking truthfully on your own behalf."

"And what do you think I should do about Nick and his job offer?" I asked.

She looked at me and rolled her eyes. She knew I knew how she felt about Nick. She was a Holocaust survivor. She didn't believe in expecting people to change much, except for the worst.

By the time I got home, Nick had already left a message on my machine. "We're going to make Grant an offer this week," he said in that warped growly baritone voice. It was a voice by which I used to be able to read his moods like a nurse reads a sphygmomanometer. Today he was happy, which for him was like mild irritation is to a regular person. "Then I'll be in a position to make you an offer," he continued. "Here's how we'll proceed: Grant's doing another performance at the Empire, end of the week. Go down and watch it with an eye toward a rewrite and a way to add David Lee Roth. I won't be there, but TriStar will. We've got a table. Brad and Jennifer will be there. He's interested in playing Tommy Lee. Jen might want to do Heather Locklear, how great would that be? Sit with them."

In minutes, my backache returned and my neck got tight and unmovable. Was there any possibility I could survive working with Nick again? I had survived *You Go, Girl!* Nick's movies paid better. But could I put up with the glaring, the pouting, the tantrums, and the insults? Could I eat shit from Nick without the pretense of everlasting love? Well, sure I could, but should I? A smart person would just take the money and run, make a tidy bundle doing the least amount of work possible. Then, as soon as the depression lifted, use the handsome profits on home repairs. And, if there was some left over, perhaps become a heroin addict. Might be really worth it if I could be sure the word would get to Grant. And how did I feel about rewriting Grant? Did he even know the extent of the rewrite being planned? He wasn't stupid. Maybe he was in on it all. He would be damn lucky to have me at the helm of his rewrite. I could fight for him, consult with him on Nick's changes. A total stranger would care only about pleasing Nick. But if our whole friendship had been a ruse, why would I bother? Fuck them both.

What really hurt was that for some reason I had thought this thing with Grant wasn't just another fraud. I had been in a manic upswing because he seemed so interested in me and spoke with such seeming candor. I had desperately needed something to be different. This was all that was available.

I sat down and replayed Nick's message. Just hearing his voice gave me the shakes, almost as if the room temperature had dropped. At the same time, it made my abdomen burn. My body was screaming at me.

So now I was supposed to call and make an appointment, get all dressed up and drive across town to Nick's new office. I would introduce myself to the newest receptionist, who was almost certainly blowing him. She would look at me with icy paranoia. Then Nick and I would share an awkward hug and pretend to be such good old friends. All I would have to do was figure out a way to seem enthusiastic at the prospect of working for a year on something that could add luster to Nick's career. Unfamiliar as I was with anger, I suspected I was feeling it now. I sat down at the computer and wrote to him instead.

Dear Nick,
I am terribly sorry, but I won't be able to take the job you have offered. Just listening to your voice gives me a back-ache AND a stomachache.

Best wishes, Lisa

Then I replaced the second sentence with "It appears I have other conflicting commitments." I pushed "send" and sat there in shock at my boldness. But almost immediately, I was haunted by the feeling that I had once again chickened out. So I opened up a blank e-mail and began to write.

P.S. Just hearing your voice gives me a backache and a stomachache. I also got rashes on both of my elbows.

I pushed "send" again. And it was sake time.

Chapter 37

GRANT

There was a fresh layer of snow on the ground. The air smelled clean, cold. The world was silent. Lisa and I looked at each other. There was a second, a beat, that was profound. She stepped forward for a kiss. I drew her in and then, fighting it, gently pushed her back. "I don't think we should be doing this," I said.

That's when I heard the thumping, fast, growing louder. I heard a door slam, and the winter field shattered. Winnie charged up the stairs screaming, "Goddamn fucking whore!" In my semiconscious state, eyes stinging, nauseated from having woken only an hour after falling asleep, I heard myself yelling, "What? What?" as Winnie stood over me shouting, "Fucking cunt, fucking goddamn whore!"

I felt guilt, panic, fear. The dream . . . did she

know? But wait . . . I pushed Lisa away! No. What am I thinking? "What?" I shouted, finally coming into the present.

"Your fucking best pal, your e-mail buddy Lisa Roberty, has been signed to rewrite your fucking musical for Nick Blake. I was wrong about your friend Lisa," Winn shouted. "I thought she wanted you. She didn't want you. She wanted your work." Winnie turned and clomped back down the stairway, slamming the door behind her.

I lay there trying to figure it out. To tell the truth, in my sleeplike state, Lisa's involvement didn't seem like such a bad idea. She was someone who liked the show. She also got me. That was a plus, not a negative.

Nick had come to me out of the blue via Sylvia and the Empire. Why couldn't it have been the same for Lisa? Maybe Nick had just called Lisa out of the blue because she was good at what she did. But to Winn, Lisa's manic persistence in writing me had always been suspect. "She knows your past, she knows your thoughts, she even knows your dreams. That woman is now completely inside your head, and she knows how to work you." If I followed Winnie's logic, Lisa had lured me into false friendship, and God knows what she would do once I had signed a contract with Nick.

I heard the clomping of Winnie's boots climbing up the stairs again. I heard the downstairs door open. "And don't forget," yelled Winnie, "you also just sent that whore your life story. She's got years of material now!" The door slammed.

Chapter 38

LISA

T hat Friday night, I got dressed up in the same goddamn pin-striped suit I'd worn the first time I saw that godforsaken homage to Tommy Lee. But this time there was no tableful of people waiting for the world's least easygoing, least confrontational female human. I was on a mission.

As usual, Sylvia offered a warm greeting. "I've got a great table for you right up front," she said graciously. When I told her I would rather stand by the bar, she gave me a knowing wink. I ordered a sake right away and started to drink. Across the room was a coven of comedians I knew, all hanging out together. They waved, but I didn't go over. I didn't have the patience to stand there and listen to them all try out bits.

In the center of the room, I could see Nick's

table, minus Nick. It was hard to miss, since it was the only one sporting Brad and Jennifer.

I enjoyed the show in spite of myself. But this time, I was distracted not with fantasies of Grant but with near-psychotic embarrassment and anger. Yes, anger. There it was after all. Watching Grant charm the crowd with the same apparently superficial magic he had used on me pissed me off. How many sociopaths could one city or one life accommodate? It almost seemed like they were transported from some underground breeding center, numbered upon arrival, and, in numerical order, given a Lycos map to my house.

Chapter 39

GRANT

W innie, Justine, Jamie, Brian, Barry, and the rest of the performers on the crowded stage swept their hands and pointed to me. I rose from the keyboard, and as one, the crowd stood up and cheered louder, if such a thing was possible. I don't know what my face did, but my soul's jaw dropped. I swept my hand back, acknowledging all of my cast. A month and a half of working, rehearsing, perfecting, and now a home run. Nick Blake's interest had brought every corporate bastard in town. If this reaction was any indication, we would soon have a bidding war. At last I'd have a little power and a lot of money.

The cast walked out into the crowd, toward the back of the club. I followed, saying, "Thank you! Thank you!" into the blur of faces and clapping hands. I saw key players from my life: friends, fans, people from meetings, my manager and lawyer. John Turturro gave thumbs-up. "Thank you! Thank you!" I said, making my way back to the kitchen door in the rear, where Sylvia stood waiting to escort me backstage. Ten feet away, "Thank you! Thank you!" Still cheering. Smiling faces. I smiled back. And then I found myself looking at Lisa Roberty, dead on. I felt a stab of fear, like I was seeing an ex. Then a flash of anger. I smiled. "Hey!" I said. She glowered back.

Chapter 40

LISA

I don't know if Grant saw me standing by the bar during his performance. But when he came offstage doing his patented "thank you thank you" thing, he sure did. Oh, he was so very humble and grateful. Look how appreciative and gracious! As only a narcissistically disordered sociopath with borderline tendencies can be.

When he saw me staring at him, grim and unsmiling, it was great. I'd never seen an expression like that before. In the space of a few seconds, I watched it morph from innocent delight and elation to horror and fear before it receded into some kind of a generic cover-up mask.

"Hey," he said, with what passed for a sweet smile, as he walked right by me on his way backstage.

"Go run in the dressing room and hide," I muttered, "you porno-addicted personality-disordered phony rock-has-been dickhead. You big fucking liar." I almost said it out loud.

Chapter 41

GRANT

Fifteen people in a tiny dressing room full of after-show chatter, the guys pulling off their shirts, the ladies in a curtained area laughing. People talking about what had happened on the third verse of . . . and in the middle section where . . . and then during the dream sequence . . . I sat, smoked, and drank coffee that Sylvia brought up for me as the cast left in groups.

They congratulated me, and I them. Everybody was thrilled. We all knew this was a done deal. Last to go was Winnie. "You were great," I said to her.

"You, too," she said. "Did you see our good pal right there by the door?" I nodded. I was feeling too good to let it bother me. Besides, Winn had called Lisa "our good pal." That was an improvement. For the past week, she had been "your good friend, that fucking cunt Lisa Whore Roberty." Things were looking up.

Chapter 42

LISA

After the show, I stayed seated at the bar, clutching my sake, watching the people in the audience file out. I waited alone, in uncomfortable and very prescient silence. After a few minutes, Grant reappeared from backstage. He definitely saw me, raised his eyebrows, smiled, and offered a jaunty wave. "Perfect. Now you're off the hook!" I wanted to call to him. "You only wrote to me several times a day for months and months, you duplicitous social-climbing pretender. But thanks for the wave. What a nice touch!" Where did the people of Los Angeles go to learn how to conduct these one-dimensional friendships? There had to be some rule book I had missed that they had all memorized.

I watched as Grant was greeted by a couple of guys from his show. They all headed out the back door to smoke. I could hear them talking and laughing. How convivial. Ah, the good-natured joie de vivre among phonies!

I waited a few more minutes, giving him a chance to reenter his body after the high of performing. I drank another sake. By the time I got up the courage to go out there, his pals were waving good night. "Lisa, hi," said Kevin Beezer, the guy who had started all this with an introduction. "Great show, Grant. Congratulations. See you tomorrow," he said, and headed for his car. I could see that he had picked up my uneasy vibe.

Now Grant was standing by himself, back against the outside of the building. He cleared his throat, but before he could say anything, I cornered him.

"Do you have a minute? How about I just assume that you do. Because there's one teensy thing I need to know," I said to him, louder and more forcefully than I had intended. The sake had turned up my volume. "The whole idea of writing to me, all that soul-baring and pretending to confide, was just some kind of weird ploy so you could weasel some details about Nick?" He blinked and looked surprised. "I guess you just forgot to mention to me that you two were in business," I said even louder. Now I was yelling at him. "An oversight. It slipped your mind. You're a busy man. You've got a musical to run, not to mention a house full of garbage bags to stack. I'm sure it's just a coincidence that you stopped writing when you were finished pumping me for information."

"Pumping *you* for information?" he said. "How about you were pumping *me*? The way I hear it, the only reason you wrote to me to begin with was so you could be first in line to do a rewrite of my play for Nick. What an amazing coincidence now that it's actually happened. Why didn't you mention that he asked you to rewrite me?"

"Where did you hear that?" I said, shocked.

"Everyone knows. Once I heard that you were doing the

rewrite, I didn't trust you anymore. You're just trying to take over my musical."

"WHAT?!" I was screaming now. "Why the fuck would I want to do that? Christ. Take over your musical? That's all I fucking need."

"Because you, uh . . . I don't know. It's what I heard from someone," Grant yelled back.

"I'm not even doing the rewrite. I couldn't face working with Nick again. As you probably would have guessed if you ever read any of my letters. The only reason I even considered doing it in the first place was some kind of misbegotten desire to protect you. But now you're on your own, pal. And just because I'm still a nice person, I'll give you fair warning. Nick wants to play David Lee Roth." And then I stalked off. I was red-faced, teary-eyed, and my heart was pounding. I was so out of my mind, dissociating so hard, that I had completely departed my body. When I say I was beside myself, it wasn't just a figure of speech. I think I actually was.

"David Lee Roth isn't even in my fucking musical!" I heard Grant yell as I turned the corner.

"Guess again!" I yelled back.

Chapter 43

GRANT

I got spooked when she walked out into the alley. She stood there just outside the circle, glaring at me. Stalker, I thought. Then it happened out of nowhere. One second I was saying "Ta-ta" to the comics, and the next, Lisa was nose-to-nose with me, hissing about Nick Blake.

I know it sounds crazy, but, stalker or not, she was thisclose. And she was red-hot. I could smell the Chanel just burning off her. She practically had me pinned in a corner. I always prided myself on being an elevated kind of guy, but I wondered, Is this how she looks when she's all turned on?

I gathered my thoughts, stuffed my cock back into my id, lit a cigarette, and withstood the barrage of Hollywood bullshit. Then I watched as she turned around and clicked away in her heels. She didn't

quite know how to walk in heels that high. Her toes were pointing out. That tiny, insubstantial fashion flaw made my heart
bleed. She doesn't know, I thought, and I wanted to protect her
from that and show her how it should be done.

At this, I felt guilt, as if I had betrayed Winnie, and so I tried
to sew up the breach with fresh anger: Winnie's anger. I was
not going to be bullied by some A-list ass-kisser. I heard Winnie's words: "She needs your credibility. It's the one thing you
can't buy in Hollywood."

So as Lisa clomped away, I shouted at her back: "Hypocrite.
A-lister." I reached for "hack," but put it down at the last second. She had already spun around, stunned. I calmly pointed
out that it was common knowledge she was rewriting my play.
That she had basically seduced me into trusting her and then,
having failed to fuck me, fucked me. Which is when she went
off like Donald Duck strapped to a big red rocket that was
aimed at me. She charged. To tell you the truth, I was only
good for that one opening shot. When she demanded I substantiate my claims, I forgot everything. How did that conspir-
acy theory go again? Shit. I had screamed it to myself so well
just the night before in the car.

Then she dropped the bomb. She wasn't working on the
film. Work for Nick? Didn't I read her letters? But she wasn't
done. She fired once more.

"David Lee Roth is not in my musical!" I bellowed.

She had done me a favor and given me a glimpse into the
mind of Nick. For that little bit of compassion, perhaps the last
left in her, my head spun and my heart squirted hot, drippy
puppy love. Her ass looked great as she walked out of my film,
my musical, and my life on rickety high heels. Pulled into the
void created by her sudden absence, I now really wanted to
work with her.

Chapter 44

LISA

I could hardly drive home. I was vibrating like a tuning fork. All I could think was that the reason I had been making a left turn before I got to Anger all these years was because of how horrible being angry made me feel; like I had a black mark on my permanent record, like I had gotten an F in conduct on my report card. By intentionally contributing to the craziness, and even fanning its flames, I had also lost the coveted title of Completely Blameless. But worse, another friendship had fallen off the vine before it ripened, and now lay rotting on the ground, full of worms. The whole thing had been soiled, transformed into something infected and dark that could never be resurrected. Goodbye to one more ridiculous attachment with no chance of long-term dividends. And hello to figuring out how to wean myself off an enormous dependency on e-mail. Its importance had grown to such an extent that it was almost a roommate. I had become accustomed to checking it every time I passed my computer. More likely than not, something would be waiting. It was a full-service time-killer, an always available companion, even in the middle of the night. It would not be an easy hole to fill. Any replacement had to have that same obsessive-compulsive potential. I had to find the e-mail equivalent of Nicorette gum.

I tried reading but didn't fall into the right book. I had more success with gardening. In a big burst of sadness, I dug up a lot of my yard, then planted seeds and a number of smallish rose-bushes. But staring at the moist ground waiting for plant growth was a little slow. So I went to a psychic Kat had recommended. "She's so accurate it's frightening," said Kat. But she said that about every psychic in her never-ending attempt to find someone who would hand over a perfect future. The woman turned out to be a Jamaican hippie in a floor-length skirt and cowboy boots who worked at a new age bookstore. "My spirit guides say no. You will not hear from him again" was what she said when I asked if I would hear from Grant. As for whether we might patch things up: "You have finished the karma you began with him many lifetimes ago in ancient Egypt." Final, but not very comforting.

Later that day, I was back to recipe-card faces. Spareribs with Onion Sauce became a plateful of nervous guys with chattering teeth. A giant sheet of cookies called Fattigmands Bakkelser lay side by side, worried and ill at ease as they whispered to their fellow dough twists. Convenient Oven Meals stared out from their separate pans, anxiety-ridden. Stuffed Cabbage Rolls regarded each other with hostility and suspicion.

The next thing I knew, I was typing Grant's name into various search engines. That had to stop. I'd been jerked around by him since the fall of Rome. It was time for a different approach.

A brief perusal of Internet chat rooms proved that strangers with whimsical pseudonyms were not my cup of tea. Then a phone call to Kat yielded the e-mail address of Ethan, her former bass player. I learned that he had just been forcibly ejected from a lengthy marriage. "He kind of liked you, hon. He asked about you," she said.

"Why'd the marriage break up?" I asked.

"They just grew apart. They'd been together since high school," she said. Which I guessed was longhand for "He fucked around on her." But I recalled that he and I had some chemistry. Whether Ethan was sane seemed beside the point. I needed something new to worry about. I e-mailed him.

Dear Ethan,

I got your e-mail address from Kat, who told me that since I saw you last, your marriage fell apart. I am terribly sorry. It must be a very painful time for you. I hope this doesn't find you cowering in a closet, unable to get out of bed. Not that I mean to imply you sleep in a closet. Although if you do, believe me, I am not one to judge.

You know, it has been my experience that extreme situations like these call for extreme measures. Which is why I would like to invite you over for a tasteless, nutritious dinner. It's not what I'd call a permanent solution to your problems, but it's the best I can offer at this time.

Lisa Roberty

I sent it off. Then felt so anxious, I picked up my food cards and started to work on Shrimp Creole, which turned out wryly amused. Baked Swiss Steak looked almost hopeful. Seemed like a good sign. Later that day, I got a response.

Dear Lisa,
Sure. How about tonight?
Ethan

As a correspondent, he was no Grant Repka. But where had all those long-winded letters full of pointless confessions gotten me? I wrote right back and told him Wednesday night was better. I needed a couple of days to strategize. I liked Wednesday because it was a day that held no preconceived expectations. And I wanted to try out my new interpersonal-relationship plan. The idea was to replicate the appealing slow stroll toward intimacy that I had fooled myself into believing my correspondence with Grant provided.

Now I spent hours poring over the recipe sides of my food cards, trying to remember what I knew how to cook. "When do you usually eat dinner?" I asked him in my follow-up e-mail.

"Well, I usually wake up at about five," he wrote back.

Wow. An early riser, I thought, pleased until I realized he meant the afternoon.

"This week my band is playing every night at the Tool Shed. I'm done by about eleven. So let's say midnight, to be safe."

"Sure. Midnight is fine," I wrote back, demonstrating that I hadn't changed as much as I had imagined. I was usually in bed by eleven. But unwilling at this point to debate timetables and logistics, it was easier to just take a Vivarin and roll with the punches. If things worked out, I would take a stand later.

I ended up making pasta and salad at eleven P.M. A mental checklist cataloging good signs and bad ones began to form as the evening proceeded. Ethan was on time. (A good sign.) He brought me a present: a CD that his group, the Jazzenovas, had just finished. (Very considerate.) He was an appreciative dining partner who ate without making negative comments or expressions of disgust. (Good sign.) He was handsome. I liked his long hair, his callused fingers, his wiry body. (All good.) We seemed to have a pretty easy time talking to each other. Maybe not as easy as it was with Grant, but then again, Grant didn't really talk, he wrote. That was very different, as everyone had been pointing out from day one. Ethan also brought flowers and a bottle of drinkable wine. (Good sign.) He helped clean the dishes off the table. (Good sign.) He talked incessantly about his recent breakup. (At least he took it seriously.)

We sat opposite each other at my dining room table as he stared at the wall above my head and made a circular jogging track through the details of his failed marriage. "But how could you not see it coming?" I asked him.

"Well," he said, "I knew she was in a bad mood. But I thought things might get better. I didn't know we were all the way to the last straw."

As I listened patiently, trying to be empathetic, I found myself drifting back to Grant's tales of Psycho Ex. Now I was sorry I'd never had a chance to hear her side of it. I kind of wanted to buy her lunch. I wondered if he had betrayed her, too. How great would it be if he heard that the two of us were hanging out together? What if I was teaching her about narcissism, and she was showing me how to dye my hair and do a drug deal? Best of all would be if I could sell a movie script based on her life with Grant, but told from her point of view. Ha!

I shifted my attention back to Ethan, continuing to offer a sympathetic ear, not an easy thing to do at three A.M. as the stories started to get a little repetitive. I was afraid to blink. Any eye closure could lead to sleep.

When the evening ended, we didn't have physical contact. We were in agreement that it was a bad idea to jump into anything too quickly. I was more than willing to give Ethan recovery time. We did make another date to get together after his show on Saturday night. He finally left my house at four forty-five A.M. By then I was so wired on Vivarin and black coffee, I couldn't fall asleep. That was when e-mail withdrawal hit like a ton of bricks. Somewhere, Grant was awake, maybe at his computer, but not writing to me. I knew it was for the best. But just to make sure, I checked at five and again at six.

Saturday night with Ethan was enjoyable enough. I caught a nap from nine to midnight and so was a bit more awake during the continued recitation of Ethan's marital tragedies. I served chicken marsala with porcini mushrooms at two forty-five A.M. But during dinner, I began to notice that when he told his stories, he always told them the same way. The later the hour, the more of a challenge it was to pay attention. Still, I was patient. Ethan was an emotional guy. He seemed to be trying to assimilate and learn from what had happened. (Good sign.) Maybe he didn't know he was asking the same rhetorical questions over and over: "How could she just up and leave without even warning me first? How could she just turn her feelings off? Why did she make all these life-changing decisions without giving me a chance to talk to her about them? Are all women like that?"

In the interest of variety, I tried to rephrase my identical answers. It reminded me of the way I used to rephrase grade school reports that I had copied from the *World Book Encyclopedia.* "No, all women aren't like that." "Women aren't all like that, of course not." "On the contrary, you can't make generalizations like that about an entire gender." But the more we cycled around on the same few points, the more I wondered if it mattered what I said. I started suspecting that perhaps the wife's "surprise" departure had been preceded by a thousand unheard ultimatums.

Playing shrink and parent was a difficult way to kick-start a new romance. But I decided to think of it as an adjustment period during the tedious task of building intimacy. Once we built a modest foundation for a structure, I supposed we could add on a new rec room or a second story. Maybe he was sensing my frustration, because on our third date, he did something endearing. He showed up at midnight dressed in a tuxedo jacket. Instead of coming inside, he told me to go put on a coat. Then we drove about forty minutes up to a clear spot in the San Gabriel Mountains to watch the Leonid meteor shower. "This might be the most romantic thing anyone has ever done for me," I said as we sat down on a blanket on a hillside. It was a perfectly clear night sky, ideal for viewing between two and five shooting stars a minute. It was legitimately thrilling.

"Well, then, I probably shouldn't blow the romance for you by mentioning that what you're looking at is the earth plowing through meteoric debris," he said. "Like a shitstorm in outer space. In West Africa, they actually think of meteors as solar poop. Outer-space excrement."

"You can't blow it for me," I said. "I've never seen a meteor shower before. I love that you even thought to bring me here."

"I'm really glad you're having a nice time," he said, putting his arms around me under the pretense of keeping me warm. "I probably also shouldn't mention that almost all the ancient civilizations thought of meteors as portents of disaster."

Portents or no, the shooting stars had worked their magic. It turned into the night we went to bed together. It was also the first night I didn't check my e-mail.

Chapter 45

GRANT

I was worried about David Lee Roth. If Nick was going to write him into my musical, God only knew what he'd do to poor David. "Dude, don't let Nick make me dance with my feet inside no two wastepaper baskets," David's soul seemed to beg from the astral plane. David was referring to the "Singing Janitors" number from *Mac and Cheese Club II*, Nick's desperate sequel.

"As one musician to another, I promise to fight for your integrity," I said.

This was the result of a great deal of anxiety. Nick and I had now met a number of times, swapped ideas, sketched things out, and decided to take the step of making the deal that would get this thing rolling. Once Nick had sent a short form of his intentions to my lawyer, a big powwow was scheduled. Jack, my manager, suggested we all meet at his house for a pre-meeting meeting.

Jack was a thickset mid-forties music-biz veteran with a reputation for being a cold-blooded bully who used the widest definition of entertainment law. We met in his vast, moderne, single-level fifties Bachelor's Dream Pad on Mulholland. Inside, jagged shapes in chrome abounded. Even the candy dishes, filled with his favorite—Jordan almonds—were blade-like. You could poke your eye out all over the place.

Jack ushered Winnie and me into his living room, where we were greeted by Earl, my lawyer, already seated. The lights of the San Fernando Valley twinkled below as we sat in four vintage Barcaloungers facing one another. With knees up and feet out, I didn't feel like we were on official business; more like we were gathered three hundred years in the future for a group root canal.

"Here's the story," said Earl, pausing. "It's pretty cut-and-dried. Nick owns you, your play, your music, and your idea. You are to have no input, and from what I can gather, no writer's credit."

Winnie shrieked. " 'Based on a story by'?" I asked.

"Not here." Earl winced. Winnie gasped.

"What about the sound track?" I asked.

"Well, that's Nick's, too. All money received from the record company goes to pay for the sound track," said Earl. "The way this is worded, this is Nick's record."

"Do I get to work with the producer and arranger?" I asked.

Earl shook his head. "No."

"Can Grant visit his music on weekends?" Winnie sneered.

"What about my cast? I asked Nick to guarantee that if they don't keep their original roles, they'll still be prominently featured."

"Nope. Not here," said Earl, blushing. "Ultimately, you surrender the culmination of your life's work for the all-in price of fifty thousand dollars." He put the paper down. "This is real shit, you guys. I'm sorry." A heavy silence hung in the room. "Oh, wait! One more thing!" Earl giggled. "Nick owns your play for the next five years. You can't perform it without his permission. If he does give permission"—Earl smiled—"you can only perform it in its present condition, and I quote, 'in an Empire-like environment.'"

Winnie saw my brows knitting. "It means, Grant, Nick doesn't want you to preview all the wonderful new improvements he's going to make," said Winnie, her voice full of contempt, "but you can still do your inferior original version as long as not too many people ever get a chance to see it."

The three of them were now sitting uncomfortably upright in the Barcaloungers. Earl interpreted the legal points one by one as Jack added punctuation by shouting, "Of course! Of course! That motherfucker."

I made an honest effort to follow, but I began to drift. I was thinking two things: first, of Jane Gray, who had said, "When ya move into a new part of town, always let the dealers rip ya off the first time. That way, they show ya who's boss, and you show you're willin' to cooperate. It just works out better in the long run." The second thing that came to mind was the day I first saw an ancient black-and-white photo of a group of semi-pinheaded people in a family album. "Mom, who were these people?"

"Oh!" she chirped proudly. "Those were all your great-aunts and -uncles from the island." The island meant the family seat: a tiny gull-stained rock in the Baltic. I looked at them, studying their weak chins, bulging foreheads, and slitty eyes. Inbred, I thought. Fucking each other for centuries. I had an epiphany of sorts: I understood that most of my life's woes were not caused by failing to concentrate, or by lack of focus, but were the result of generations of inbreeding. I was congenitally stupid, and therefore, life went completely over my head. In situations involving more than basic colors and primary numbers, I was lost. That's why what Nick was offering sounded pretty good to me. Fifty thousand was fifty grand more than I had in my pocket. Take it, let's go. I'm inbred, I thought. I won't suffer, as I lack the intelligence to comprehend anything better.

Jack spoke my name and brought me back from my family seat. "Grant? Your thoughts, please . . ."

"Okay," I said, hoping to catch up. "So what do we do?"

Jack looked shocked. "Grant! Have you been listening? You created it. You wrote it. It's your work." He nodded, as if encouraging a baby to walk. "Right?"

"Right," I said. "And so?"

Jack's eyes and hands implored the ceiling, presumably asking God to give him a little more patience with me. He was shouting now. "*And so* we tell Nick Blake that you are to contractually participate creatively and financially in the sound track. *And so* we tell Nick Blake he's to contractually state you are a creative partnership. *And so* Nick Blake has to define your credits, as well as take care of your cast."

"You're yelling, Jack," I said.

"*And so* Nick Blake has to pay, like everyone else in this fucking town," he concluded.

"How much?" I asked.

"Lowballing and figuring it's going to be a fifteen-million-dollar Nick Blake film," said Earl, pausing to do some mental math, "we would be more than reasonable to ask for five percent of the budget. An all-in price of five hundred thousand dollars."

Stunned, I whispered, "Nick Blake will never go for that."

Jack laughed as he threw a handful of Jordan almonds into his mouth, crunching aggressively, managing to speak through a thick mash of pastel candy coating and nut meat. "Nick Blake fucking better go for it," he said, shoving aside a wad with his tongue, "if he wants this as his next fucking movie."

. . .

In the song "Dead Man's Curve," either Jan or Dean recounts the final moments before the fateful crash in a middle-eight recitative. If that song were about my life, I would say, "The last thing I remember, Doc, I entered United Talent—UTA. All the agents were smiling my way . . ."

Winnie, Jack, Earl, and I were ushered into the United Talent Agency conference room: standard landing-deck-sized table, standard black leather chairs, standard breathtaking view of L.A. designed to remind one just how high up we were, and how quickly one could fall.

Nick sat at the center of the long table, nursing a water by himself. To the far left was a small coven of his boys, the Home Team. Presumably the other end of the table was for us, the Visiting Team. After handshakes, introductions, and courtesy-drink orders, one of Nick's guys offered the Official Welcome, confirming how excited they were to be involved in the project. Nick nodded. Now it was our turn.

Earl acknowledged the great opportunity and honor that Nick Blake was offering. "But," he added, "we need to define, if not redefine, a few general issues." Nick's guys smiled, murmuring, "Of course, of course," as Earl handed the meeting over to Jack. From that point on, it was a slaughter.

Jack had arrived in UTA's lobby wrecked. He was puffy, red, his eyes were gummy. I feared drugs, but as it turned out, some Californian species of weed had inflamed his sinuses and had filled his head with mucus. He was slow, peevish, bloated. In a word: gross. He reacted like a drunk being denied car keys when I told him he might want to go home and rest. And once he took over, he coughed and hacked, harrumphed, snuffled, blew, and sucked snot all the way through. The room watched as Jack's hankie went from virtuous white to defeated gray in only a few juicy blows. Phrases like "deal memo," "gentlemen," and "money and rights" dripped out of Jack as "deo bebbo," "gentle ben," "bunny and rides."

Nick's tycoons, comfy in their healthy, glowing skins, tried hard not to be repulsed. Each time Jack made a point, he over-compensated by turning up his natural arrogance fifty degrees, then leering with an expression that asked, "Ready for more, you cocksuckers?" This might have worked on the low-level MBAs, reformed groupies, ex-bouncers, and club scum who run the music biz, but not here. These were movie people, and that meant the Cultural Elite. They wore cream-colored pants and had a deep understanding of which books they should have read. They dealt in millions of dollars every day. They'd seen bums like us come and go. It was bad enough that we were up-pity poor people making demands. But with Jack leading, we were seen as diseased ingrates staggering up from steerage, de-manding equality.

The real issues were money and rights, bunny and rides. Nick wanted all the rides and offered only token bunnies. My manager was willing to concede rides, "widdin dreason," pro-vided we got "bore bunnies, alod bore bunnies." If we didn't get bunnies, then it stood to dreason, we'd get rides. Nick could get one or the other, my manager said, "bud nod bode."

In response, Nick's team murmured in cottony country-club tones. In so many words, their message was "Nick fucking Blake is offering you the chance of a lifetime. Take it or take off."

Exasperated, Jack went for the personal approach by de-scribing the shithole I lived in, my tax problems, and the crappy car I drove. Not knowing what expression to wear, I felt that nodding grimly acknowledged the hopelessness of my in-competence, while smiling seemed to imply a workmanlike pride in my own limitations.

"I simply want to see Grant raised to a level to which we all are accustomed," Jack concluded, on the high note of an unexpected sneeze.

There was silence in the room. While making me out to be utter scum, Jack had introduced a much needed note of compassion. If this were a sitcom, the usually chipper theme song would play soft and sad. Nick and I would hug in slow mo. "Hey! My allergies are gone!" Jack would say, followed by canned laughter. Then the theme song would get zippy as the credits rolled.

But this was far from a sitcom. After Jack was allowed enough time to wipe his nose, one of Nick's boys said, "We feel we are taking care of Grant by giving him a role in a Nick Blake film where Grant's music is the focus . . ." He looked at Nick and shrugged, as if to say, "What is it these people don't understand?"

My manager would not be cowed. "Let me point out that your offer fails to reflect that this is a competitive environment," he insisted in head-cold English.

In the center of the room, two large hands slammed down on the table. A sudden, brutal fanfare announcing that the real Nick Blake had arrived.

"Competitive fucking environment?" he shouted. Down came his hands again. "Competition from who?"

"Nick," Jack said in a wake-up-and-smell-the-coffee tone, "this isn't the only offer we have on the table."

Nick pushed himself up. "Well, fuck you!" he shrieked, spit flying, his red face going purple. He quivered and splattered abuse around the room, then turned and exited, propelled, it seemed, by a rocket blast of four-letter words. Agents, secretaries, and staffers in the outer office buried their heads in their work as Nick flew by and then vanished, still screaming, into the maze of the corporate hive. The meeting was over. So, too, I feared, was my future.

Afterward, as Winnie, Jack, Earl, and I sat in a nearby restaurant, I felt lost, depressed, defeated. It hurt to imagine what a celebration this dinner might have been had all gone well. As they griped and snickered over Nick's tantrum, I blurted out, "What the fuck went wrong?"

Eyes rolled. Winnie groaned.

"Grant," whined Jack, "knock it off, okay? Nick was trying to punk us, and I wouldn't be punked, okay? You got to stand up to these fucking monkeys. This is how it goes: We're positioning. They're posturing." He was explaining slowly, patiently, as if I had to hear every word in order to understand. "They will call back, trust me. Everything is fine. For chrissakes, stop worrying."

I wasn't so sold on Jack's cockiness anymore. For one thing, I had noticed that away from Nick's daunting presence, his debilitating allergies had suddenly vanished.

■ ■ ■

"What does your fucking manager think he's fucking doing? Nick is fucking furious," Sylvia said. "For fuck's sake, Jack was bragging that you were taking other offers."

"He wasn't brag—" I tried to say.

"He was, too!" Sylvia cut in, rewriting a moment she didn't witness. "Nick said you were all acting like a bunch of dangerous amateurs. I told him I would talk some sense to you."

Winnie and I had stopped into the Empire later that night. It was now after hours, and the gang of regulars were just warming up. Under the guise of showing me a vintage Rickenbacker guitar, Sylvia had lured me into her office, then pounced. I was berated in the name of Nick while I was stuck sitting on a couch with a broken spring, sinking me lower than I already felt. As Sylvia reapplied her lip gloss, she shook her head. "Blowing it for fucking money," she said, disgusted, as a raucous laugh busted out downstairs among the loyal regulars around the familial hearth of the Empire bar. "You know what we ought to do?" she said, brightening. "Randy's having a get-together at his house on Sunday. We can meet there, have some dinner with everyone, and then just you, me, and Nick go off and talk. Nick will say what he wants, you say what you want. No lawyers. No agents. No managers. No Winnie. We'll keep it informal."

"No Winnie?" I asked, stunned.

"Well . . . she can be there if she wants," Sylvia stuttered.

"If she *wants*?" I asked. "Does Nick not like Winnie?"

"Oh no. No. He thinks she's great. He really likes her input."

I had been around long enough to know that no men of power think anyone is great, nor do they value input. While Sylvia prattled on, I marveled at how Winnie's intelligence, creativity, and drive had threatened the great Nick Blake. I felt a glow of pride. However, it fizzled right out when I realized that without her, Nick and Sylvia considered me a pushover. Worse, this attempt to divide and conquer was so clumsy, it could only indicate to what degree they thought I was a chow-derhead. The sad, chickenlike faces of my ancestors rose up from my subconscious, gazing at me with empathetic pity. When I snapped back, Sylvia was looking at me, lips pressed, angry, waiting for a response. Anything I said would be tossed around on the Empire Playground. So I played it safe and de-flected. "I'll talk to Jack," I said.

Sylvia leaned in close. "I'm just trying to help you, here. Nick is fed up." Her voice dropped to something a little less than a hissing menace. "Do you think your cast is going to stick by you if Nick Blake walks? Do you?"

I shrugged.

"If you don't have Nick, and no film, and no record, and no cast, then what the fuck do you have, Rock Star?" She leaned back.

I nodded. I got it. Do it Nick's way, or lose everything. I suddenly felt enormous empathy for her ex-husband.

At that the kitchen door downstairs swung open, and up the stairs charged Winn, Randy Randall, and a host of others singing, for some deliriously funny reason known only to themselves, the theme song to *Maude*. Sylvia broke out laughing and waved them in, the very portrait of good cheer.

The next afternoon, Jack called our home and asked for Winnie. "I fucking knew it," she said, handing the phone back to me once Jack was done talking to her.

"Guess who called and wants to see a response to their deal memo?" Jack taunted. "I guess Nick settled down and came back to earth."

I was happy now. Relaxed. Crisis averted. I wrapped my arms around Winnie's ass and lifted her up while she shrieked for me to put her down.

"I told ya not to worry! See? See?" I said repeatedly, knowing that would drive her nuts.

Later that evening, I was working with two members of my cast, Justine and Lolly. I was unveiling my gift to them: a bittersweet duet between a young groupie and a threatened rock wife, herself a former groupie. However, instead of attacking it with enthusiasm, they were giving me some resistance. "Guys, something's wrong here. What's up?" I finally asked.

"We would like to say that we think you should take less money and do this deal with Nick," blurted Lolly, just this side of snotty.

"It's really a no-brainer," Justine added, nodding. It was a perfect moment for a spit take.

"And you are one hundred percent certain that when I sign this, Nick Blake will insist you be in the film?" I asked.

"Nick said we will be prominently featured," Justine assured me.

"When did you see Nick?" I asked cautiously.

"At the Border Grill," said Lolly proudly. "We ran into Nick and Sylvia and they bought us all lunch."

"I see," I said, my queasiness confirmed.

"You should just let Sylvia do this mediating thing," Lolly admonished.

"Yeah, well," I said, attempting to appear kindly, wise, and paternal, "we should all just step back from this. You know what they say about friends and business."

"Oh, I always do business with friends!" Lolly smiled.

"You guys are way too worried about money," Justine jumped in warmly, batting her big vacant eyes. "I've always found that it's better to take a little up front and a lot on the back end."

Lolly nodded. This from a team who had been aping Céline Dion in a Tustin Holiday Inn a year ago.

"Duly noted," I said politely. For Nick to have lured Justine and Lolly, the most gullible, naïve women in my cast, into doing his dirty work for him was a stroke of sheer evil genius. Now it seemed to be Nick who had their best interests at heart, not me.

"It's really not about the money!" chirped Justine.

●●●

That Monday, our response was faxed over. Now there was nothing to do but wait. While the war clouds gathered, I took meetings with Warner Bros., MCA, Capitol, DreamWorks, and more. The name "Nick Blake" opened all doors. After twenty years in Hollywood, I was finally in demand.

Later in the week while Winnie was out rehearsing with Mitchell on a Drag Hag spot for the S&M Ball, Jack called with good news. "Nick's people said they see no problems coming to an agreement with us," he said.

"Take that, Sylvia!" I shouted, dancing around the living room, scaring the cats off the bed. I congratulated Jack on his acumen and on the progress we were making. The moment he and I hung up, the phone rang.

"Nick wants to talk with you," said Sylvia furtively. "He's crushed by this response your guys sent. Nick was sayin', 'Why's Grant doing this? I don't understand.' So he wants you to call him."

"Oh, for fuck's sake!" I shouted. "He wants to talk to me, and yet I got to call him?"

"Just passing on the word," Sylvia said.

It was midafternoon. I hadn't eaten, and five cups of coffee were churning in my stomach. It was time to stop this horseshit and meet Nick head-on. "Just keep the subject on the creative," I chanted to myself as I dialed.

"Hey Nick!" I said optimistically when he answered. "Sylvia said you wanted to talk? What's up?"

"Hey Grant," he said, sounding a little glum. I heard him pausing, looking for words. "Look, I feel like we've gone way off track here. The managers, the agents, and the response they sent. I hate those fucking people. They always complicate things. It was better when it was you and me talking."

"Yeah. It's a complicated business," I said dryly.

"Not really," said Nick. "Not if you just keep the costs low, and the suits stay out of your fucking hair. Trust me."

"I do," I said.

"Do you? I get the feeling you don't," he shot back, suddenly spooky. This was a side I hadn't seen yet; the sullen, manipulative kid.

"Well, I do, Nick, I certainly trust you artistically," I said. "The business stuff I don't really understand, so I have my guys to explain it to me."

"You know," he said, brightening, "I was thinking maybe we should just let Sylvia handle all this. No managers. No agents. Just you, me, and Sylvia, and Winnie, if you want her to be there."

This again. I'd had enough. "Nick, can I talk honestly?"

"Go on," he said.

"I'm gonna put all my cards on the table." I paused, gathering my thoughts. "Nick, I have been living hand-to-mouth for decades. Now I finally have a property that's valuable. I've worked on it for eight years. Under all the silly shit about Tom and Pammy is thirty years of experience making music."

"Yeah," he said. "It's great. That's why I love it."

"Thank you. So here I am. I owe the IRS. I rent a crappy little shack. I got a seventies Lincoln that stalls in left-hand turns. I'm over forty. I want to buy a house and a car that runs. I want to be paid, like everyone else."

"Whatever," Nick pouted. "Why all this crap about money? I just hate to see it all get bogged down in money."

An infuriating thing for a wealthy man to say to a poor one.

"I'm looking forward to a great collaboration here," I said, repositioning. "But at the end of the day, it's going to be your picture. So when I need some consolation, I want to be able to say, 'At least I got paid well.' " I was trying for honest bonhomie, the rough-and-tumble approach.

"What?" said Nick, his voice a few decibels lower. "I'm not sure I like that. What does that mean?"

Somewhere in his past, I sensed a drunk mother who had talked to him this way. Oh fuck, I thought, how could he not see my point of view? I'm fucking poor! His fifty grand, minus taxes, minus manager's commission, minus rent and food for two people, meant I'd created a major motion picture for one of the biggest directors in Hollywood, and thus the world, for what I made selling windup jumping penis toys at Chimera in 1983. Why was I supposed to be the only person in the United

States of America who didn't care about money? How had I become some kind of a national test case for working for love? So I tried again. "Well," I said, "you and I are naturally going to have our disagreements, and since you'll have the last say, it will make my life easier if I can come home and know I got, y' know, a fair trade."

"Why disagreements?" he asked.

"Because you are Nick Blake. You are the master here. You have your own ideas, and naturally, I won't agree with them all. I mean, maybe I will . . . but the thing is, I more than know what value you're bringing to my project."

"You're talking to me like I'm a child," he said, sounding a little bit insulted.

"Sorry. I didn't mean to! I am way over my head here," I said. "Look, Nick, I really don't feel comfortable talking about money, either. Just think of our counterproposal as a starting point. We will continue to negotiate until everyone is happy, okay?"

"Okay, I think I understand now," said Nick. "I'm glad we talked."

"Well, good. Me, too," I said. I put the phone down and saw that I had smoked four cigarettes during the call. Two sentences were going round and round in my skull. "I'm not sure I like that" and "You're talking to me like I'm a child." An old garden hose dripped poison into my stomach.

When Winn came in from the Drag Hags rehearsal, I explained what had happened.

"Of course he got upset," she said, sounding tired and bored with it all. "He's Nick Blake. He's always right. Why would you ever disagree with him?"

Later that night, I went out for a drive, using the hypnotic grid of the San Fernando Valley to induce autopilot and give myself room to think. I found myself missing Lisa. I felt like driving over there and telling her everything. After the phone call to Nick, I had turned on the computer and looked through her old e-mails. In a file I had saved, I found what I was looking for: "My shrink used to say, 'With Nick, you are either part of the pillar of support or part of the abyss around it.' " In other words, what I had thought was horse-trading was, for Nick, what? Humiliation? Was Lisa saying that if I didn't say yes, I was *insulting* him? Was that how this worked? And if that was the case, the real question I was facing was this: Should I just go along with Nick's program, or take a chance and stare him down? Hollywood wisdom told me to attach my nose to Nick's butt, no matter what the financial or spiritual cost. Let Nick take you to the heights and don't ask questions. On the other hand, school-yard wisdom dictated that if the bully aggressively moves on your sandwich, you deck him, then afterward you become pals and share.

On top of that, I was one of the last remaining members of my punk-rock class of 1978. What the hell did I tout all that new-wave/punk bullshit for—go unwashed and unfed, drag all those band members and girlfriends along—if not to piss off people like Nick Blake?

Heading down Lankershim Boulevard, I was shocked to discover that a whole section had vanished. My band used to rehearse in a storefront down here. Now entire blocks of withered businesses had disappeared. A sign declared it THE NOHO DISTRICT OF THE ARTS. I wondered how a city could first rip down the only buildings artists could afford and then designate it an art district without an actual art scene to back it up.

A theater, a coffee shop, and a tattoo parlor stood out like three gold-capped teeth in an otherwise empty mouth. Wow! When did all this happen? Or was I living in the Stone Age? Maybe this was that crazy new go-go world I saw flashing from TV screens, the world that answered my question "When does shit turn into art?" with "Right now, jackass!" and "When does that art turn to shit?" with "Just did, Grandpa." A world proclaiming that art and commerce were like peanut butter and jelly. A world that said my seventies punk ideals with regard to Nick Blake were as current as raccoon coats and ukuleles.

As I drove on, the years and the list of debts scrolled by. If you are about to leap into the big time, I thought, it's because you are standing on a mountaintop of failed ambitions, busted plans, dead bands, and weeping girlfriends; the sum total of the faith and toil of others. You also owe the universe hundreds of thousands of dollars in bummed cigarettes, back rent, and dial-'n'-dash phone calls, Grant Repka. You, sir, have fucked up a lot of lives in the name of your uncompromised vision. You lived under a card table in an eight-by-eight rehearsal room and ate Cremora when there was nothing else. Back then you were ready for a fight. Well, here's your war. It's just too bad this moral dilemma didn't come when you were young and re-silient, spry and frisky, brainless and twenty-two. Fuck it. Stand up to Nick Blake and face the consequences; there's no other way.

I steered the car back toward Silver Lake. Besides, for chris-sakes, it's not the first time he's gotten a counteroffer. It'll be all right.

. . .

"Grant," Nick said, "I just don't see this happening. I'm gear-ing up to do *Winter Formal*, and I just don't think it's the right time. I'm just too busy at the moment."

The demands of his current picture had never been men-tioned before. What new twist was this?

"There is not some way to make this work?" I asked.

"I don't think so. I'm not sure anymore. I really loved this project, though," he said wistfully. His tone was sad. Was he opening a door?

"Tell you what, Nick, think about it. Give it another day,

then call me," I said, wondering if that was the right thing to say.

"Okay," he said. He never called back.

■ ■ ■

I didn't go to the Empire for a week. When at last I did, I was shocked to see that the frost had set in. Instead of getting the usual warm welcome, I was greeted by polite, glassy smiles and darting eyes. The in-jokes and repeating gags that once bound us had disappeared. I understood. This was the result of the Empire Spin. According to club wisdom, I had thrown away everybody's chance of a lifetime because my ego was out of control. All *I* cared about was money. Nick was the innocent multimillionaire powermonger, and I was the big bad penniless musician who had broken his heart.

Christ, I was Out Crowd! Me! I was no better than Bobby Snuggs's ex-girlfriend! I felt myself blushing hot and red. But I brazened it out and took my spot by the kitchen door in the Cool Kid Corner. Fuck it. That night I shared the space with three uneasy members of my cast. Before we could even pretend all was well, Sylvia walked up and whispered something to them. They giggled. All eyes darted toward me, then looked away. Man, things were bad. Then Sylvia suddenly charged into the kitchen. Through the portholes, I saw that Nick had arrived. Sylvia rushed up, gave him a big hug, and escorted him quickly upstairs. I knew I had better leave.

So I said goodbye to those around me. "Good night!" they all said a little too brightly. Only a week before, they would have protested and said, "Aww, c'mon! Stay!" I returned their stressful smiles and left through the back door.

Out in the alley, Brian and Barry, my favorites from the cast, were having a smoke. They waved me over, cheerfully, thank Christ. I lit a cig and chatted. I hadn't taken but two drags when the back door flew open, and out walked Nick. Our eyes met. "Hey, Nick!" I said.

"Grant!" he said, surprised, smiling. And then he got dark. "How's business?" he said over his shoulder, walking away.

" 'How's business?' " scoffed Brian once Nick was out of range. "What a jack-off. What the fuck is that?"

I shrugged, but I understood. Nick knew I was dead in this club, and he was letting me know it. And I supposed if Nick Blake can get ya killed in a club, then you're dead all over Hollywood.

Chapter 46

LISA

W hen it became obvious that I was poised on the precipice of sex with Ethan, I initially worried that I was compromising my goal of a slow, careful stroll toward intimacy. Then I realized I had never really quantified what I meant by "slow." The fruit fly, with whom we share almost an identical genome sequence, goes through a whole life cycle in a week: larva, pupa, fertility, the works. After that, it gets one more week to look around, have a few laughs, and that's it. Over and out. So an argument could be made that a month—which was how long I had known Ethan—could be a lifetime. In that time, I'd learned that he was a sensitive, creative person who had taken his last marriage seriously. I knew he repeated himself a lot, but I didn't expect anyone to be perfect. I knew what I was doing.

However, during the sexual act itself, as I stared up at the bug-eyed hormone-driven grimace he was making, I realized that comparing myself to a fruit fly was a bit of a stretch. I actually had no idea who this guy was.

On the plus side, sex with Ethan was more imaginative than it had been with previous boyfriends. Well, almost anything would have been more. But with Ethan, it was good even at the beginning, when "Am I touching you in the right place?" and its partner in crime, "How okay is it for me to tell you where the right place is?" were still unspoken. If it involved sex, Ethan was fine with it. And after Nick, this was a relief. Nick's critical nature made me too paranoid to experiment. I never purchased lingerie, because Nick would have looked at me skeptically and said, "What are you supposed to be?" But Ethan thought I looked hot. And even that much positive reinforcement caused such a huge expansion of my personal confidence that it almost made up for the fact that when we weren't having sex and the topic wasn't his breakup, we didn't seem to have much to say to each other. Sadly, there weren't any more meteor showers scheduled for viewing in our hemisphere for months.

But there were other signs of progress. On our fourth weekend, he asked me to come down to the Tool Shed to see his group perform. In honor of the occasion, I went to Trashy Lingerie and purchased a particular garter belt and stockings that he had pointed out as his favorite in a catalog. Afterward, I managed to slide the whole works up under my skirt while seated in my car in an isolated parking garage. Only then did I learn that the garters on the belt were either defective, or my feminine powers of comprehension were. I couldn't make them attach to the stockings.

But aha! I noticed that the stockings themselves had big wide banded elastic tops. So why would I suspect that they would drop below my knees the minute I got out of the car and gave the keys to a parking valet in front of the Tool Shed? And with such a rapid speed of descent that I found myself walking in tiny baby steps, knees together, like a cartoon of a person who had to go to the bathroom. Suddenly I was a bad *Playboy* caricature, a dumb girl with defective underwear elastic. I had no choice but to sit down on the edge of a planter box in front of the club to consider my next move. Since I was no longer ambulatory, my only option was to kind of scoot around from place to place on my butt until I arrived at the most isolated spot available. Which, as it turned out, was only a few feet from the least isolated spot available. At this point, dignity was basically out of the question, so I pulled the stockings off entirely, pretending I was invisible.

I don't know if the curse of the meteors had anything to do with it, but that was just the beginning of an evening of unpleasant surprises. The second one came when I walked up to the front door and learned that Ethan hadn't put my name on the list. "I'm the girlfriend of one of the band members" didn't even register on the face of the dull-eyed guy whose list did not contain my name. So I paid for a ticket. They seated me in the back at a table full of drunk fraternity boys. Happily, when one of them passed out and fell to the floor, the other two felt they'd better take him home.

The third surprise was that I couldn't begin to fathom Ethan's music. It was the kind of improvised jazz that features twenty-minute solos on an upright bass. I never much liked the song "Would You Like to Swing on a Star?" but their fifteen variations on it made me miss the irritating original. Hopefully, I reasoned, I would grow to better comprehend and even love this music as I grew to better comprehend and love Ethan himself. He seemed so accepting of me, I thought. I certainly owed him that much in return.

And, in the way that the universe likes to be ironic, this was the evening that Ethan's unquestioning acceptance of me ended. It started when he came up to greet me at the intermis-

Merrill Markoe and Andy Prieboy

sion, apologized about the table mix-up, and brought me backstage. After a big kiss, he took me into the dressing room and
pushed my hair around so it was messier. "Take off your jacket
and join the human race," he said, pulling off the top of my
pin-striped suit. "You look like you're going to a funeral. Just
the sweater by itself is better."

Who is he making me into? I wondered.

After the show, we went back to my place, where, at three
A.M., I took a Vivarin so I could be awake enough to cook and
listen to the tales of a marriage torn asunder. Tales, I might add,
that were word for word the same as they had been the last time
I heard them. Odd that when he played music, he improvised.
Not so when he told stories. It was starting to remind me of that
old vaudeville routine where a guy in prison cannot hear the
words "Niagara Falls" without launching into the same emotionally deranged anecdote about shooting the man he'd found
with his unfaithful wife. "Niagara Falls! Slowly I turned . . ."
And then a light went on. That had to be where Grant's band
had gotten their name. I didn't know why I'd never thought
about it before. I wanted to write and tell him. A fresh wave of
Grant nostalgia came over me as I remembered how he used to
ask personal questions. That was when the universe, still pursu-
ing an ironic theme for the evening (unless it was the meteors
after all) struck again.

"So, what did you think of the show tonight?" Ethan asked
me.

"Great. You guys were fantastic," I said, because after all,
there wasn't another right answer.

"Looks like the House of Blues is going to book us," he said,
pleased.

"Excellent! The House of Blues is great! I loved it the time
Kat and that music-critic guy, what'shisname, who she was seeing after she broke up with the glassblower—Garland something?—we all went there to see Freur."

"Who the fuck is Freur?" he asked, suspicion creeping into his voice.

"They did that song 'Doot-Doot'!" I said. "They were big in the eighties."

" 'Doot-Doot'?" he said, starting to get pissed off. "Fucking 'Doot-Doot'?"

"What's wrong with 'Doot-Doot'?" I said.

"What's wrong? Apparently you're trying to tell me that the House of Blues will hire any fucking piece-of-shit act."

"No! Not at all! I always loved 'Doot-Doot'!" I said, surprised, and not understanding. I sang him the little piece of it that I could still remember. " 'What's in a name? Blabbity blee / Blabbity blah / Memory fades / Doot-Doot.' It was such a sad little song," I said, hoping that at least he understood I only mentioned it because I liked it.

"So what you're saying is, it's too bad we don't have a pathetic eighties hit to milk forever, huh?"

"They weren't pathetic," I said, quickly losing track of what we were talking about. "They were kind of ahead of their time."

"Coming up next at the Wisconsin Dells, the Jazzenovas opening for . . . for . . ." Ethan said, really angry now. "For Katrina and the fuckin' Waves!"

"That is not at all what I was saying, not at all." I got up and started clearing the dishes, just to change the energy. "I don't get how you pulled all that out of a comment in which the only sin I committed is that I liked a song that you didn't like." I walked into the kitchen and was beginning to load plates into the dishwasher when I heard what sounded like a door slamming. But how could that be? I thought. Who'd slam a door over "Doot-Doot"?

"That music-critic guy told me that Freur was one of the bands that started the whole techno thing . . ." I was saying, still trying to make things okay, when I realized Ethan had indeed slammed the door behind him. My impulse was to run after him and apologize. I got as far as the landing outside my front door when I heard his Honda start up and race out of my driveway. I realized that I had no idea what I was apologizing for, so I forced myself to go back in the house, sit down, and have a glass of sake. Then I made a list of all the precedents and eerie facsimiles to this fight that I could recall in my past. After a second and then a third glass of sake, I took Ethan's CD off my CD player, where I had been meaning to listen to it, and to his handsome, ferretlike face in the cover photo, I sang, "Blabbity blee / Memory fades / Blabbity blah / Doot-Doot, Doot-Doot." I imitated the synthe-sizer falling-bomb sound at the end of the last "Doot" as I dumped his CD in the trash. And then I went to bed.

Ethan called to apologize the next day. I didn't take the call. I had decided to cut my losses rather than play through another sand trap. As I listened to him record the message on my an-swering machine, I just continued finding places to put eyes on a platter of Medallions of Beef with Sauce Béarnaise. But I was really hit with a sense of loss. Now I had not one abyss in my life but two: the big one that used to contain Grant, and the much smaller, shallower one that used to contain Ethan. Was I only attracted to impossible narcissists and therefore doomed to relive these identical scenarios forevermore, like "The Rime of the Ancient Mariner"? Was I stuck in some kind of karmic wheel of love with the insane? And if so, was there any way at all to ever make things work with the nutty people I loved?

Books, I thought. What is needed is more psychological re-search. So I went online to type "narcissism" and "borderline personality" into the search engines of the different book-sellers. And that was the only reason I saw the e-mail from Grant waiting for me. I had stopped checking my e-mail en-tirely. It was too painful.

Chapter 47

GRANT

W ithout the halo of Nick and his film offers, the whole furor died down. The record labels lost interest and so did everyone else.

I filled the hours sitting down and tweaking the play, finishing a song, editing out a chorus, adding a bridge, anticipating that things would be back on track soon. However, within a month, some key members of the cast pulled out, politely, apologetically. They just didn't have the time anymore, what with auditions coming up for pilot season.

While most of the cast was disappointed with the turn of events, the most experienced among them had seen other projects fizzle and so shrugged it off. It was Justine and Lolly who were truly angry. They now saw me as the man who canceled Christmas.

"It's really not worth our time anymore," said Lolly. "You guys shouldn'ta acted all big 'n' all."

At this point, it was no longer comfortable hanging out at the Empire. Nick and his team had become fixtures there. Winnie and I heard about the parties, and the big wingdings up in Sylvia's office after hours. We both pretended it didn't bother us when word got to us that Randy Randall was asked to compose the sound track for Nick's new movie, *Winter Formal*. I wasn't nearly as bothered about it as Winnie. Winnie was enraged.

Times were rough, but Winn and I had weathered bad patches before. What the hell, I thought, we'll get through this one, too. With the house quiet now, I put my arms around her and said, "Fuck Nick Blake. As long as I have you, I'm a success," hoping to get something equally as drippy and encouraging back. She just smiled, nodding.

A couple days later, Winnie dumped me and my sorry-ass hyperbole. Well, she didn't out-and-out dump. Winn wasn't like that; I had to pull it out of her. "Come on, tell me what the fuck's up?" I said to her over and over as she looked off. I had gone through this countless times with her through the years. Every fight we ever had started with fifteen minutes of coaxing her to talk. Strange behavior for a woman who always had something to say about everyone around her.

One moment I was yelling, "What the hell is the matter with you?" Then, the next thing I knew, she said, "I want to break up. I want to move out."

I sank into a chair. From somewhere I heard my voice say, "Oh."

"Great. I thought I'd never have to go through this again," I heard myself add from far away. I didn't think she was serious. But she insisted it had been over for a long, long time. "Who is he?" I asked her.

"No one," she said. "I just feel I've given so much to you

and the band . . . and you know, forty isn't too far off and . . . I'm not sure if I want to be here. The only way to know is to step away from it. I want to have my own life. I want to drink."

That didn't make any sense. "You want to *drink*?" I asked.

"Yes. I want to get drunk. To drink."

"So go drink!" I said.

"I want to drink and not have to come home."

"Oh. . . ."

The next week was a miserable blur. I recall jumping around the living room and pointing to all the things I had just bought her, or encouraged her to buy on eBay, and screaming one word over and over again: "*userous!*" Which I'm embarrassed about now, because I found out that it didn't mean what I thought it did. I was just looking for a stronger word than "user." Even then I knew that shouting "USER! USER!" in my living room would sound pathetic. I should have just kept my mouth shut.

I remember this period like a blizzard, the snowflakes being countless isolated incidents of unrelenting pain. In that storm, things come in and out of focus. I recall asking her why, if she was so unhappy, she didn't tell me in time for me to do something about it. But I can't recall her exact response. Just more cold. And why, I demanded, did she keep spending my publishing money buying herself stuff if she knew it was going to exit the premises? When she answered with something that sounded like double talk, I was hit by another Arctic blast. I was blinded, lost. From far off, it seemed I could hear my voice bellowing, "Who is he? Who is this fucker?"

"No one," she says. "There's nobody." And then it all gets fuzzy again, letting up a little to reveal me crying my damn fool head off. When the storm finally dies down, I see myself sitting on the couch with Winnie and talking for another week. We unplugged the phone and sweetly, patiently, reviewed the misunderstandings and accumulated hurts of eight years together.

However, it became obvious that we were at cross-purposes. I was talking to clear the air. She was talking to clear out.

What surprised me was how vividly she recalled pinpricks, slights, and screw-ups from years gone by, things I thought I had made good on. Apparently no apology, no redemptive gesture, gift, or sacrifice had ever made a difference. To Winn, any offense was permanent. It could not be erased. It had always just happened yesterday. One by one they had piled on top of one another to create a burden she could no longer bear.

Eventually I came to accept her version of the end. We would stay friends and work together. "That's where our real love is," she said.

After that, we didn't argue about who kept what. It was all pretty obvious. I would keep the books on Napoleon, classic cars, and military history. She would keep the books on strippers, pin-up models, and fetish wear. How easy it was to separate her things from mine was a testimony to how specific and different our interests were.

We spent the final two days in a slightly anesthetized state, running errands, resigned and yet somehow buoyant. The shock had passed, the bad news had been digested. And to be honest, it didn't seem so bad. Maybe it was because she hadn't left yet that I was optimistic.

Or perhaps it was the manner in which we were communicating. Whichever, now that there was technically no relationship that could be jeopardized, we were free to crack wise, say what we felt, and ask questions that would have once been thought inflammatory. We laughed a lot, exclaiming, "I didn't know that!" and "Why didn't you ever tell me before?" If this was any portent, then Winnie and I weren't ending; we were heading into a brilliant new era. We'd be like Tsarina Catherine and Potemkin, advising each other on all kinds of chicanery. We'd nod to each other across future stages, bonded by destiny, unbeatable as a team. We'd chide each other for our horrendous tastes in groupies. This could be fun, I thought for a moment. I can live with this. Maybe we would never be husband and wife, but we would be something that suited us better: band members. After all, anyone can be disloyal to a spouse, but only a fool fucks over his band.

Which is why I felt no shame when later I decided to ask her to stay one more night. "Come on, Winnie, I'm not going to make a play for you," I said as she dumped a drawer full of foundation compacts into a cardboard box.

"No, Grant. I'm sorry. I have to be alone and think." She opened another drawer and rattled through it.

"Think about what?" I asked. "It's over. What's to think about?"

"Grant!" she pleaded mildly, as more compacts clattered into the box.

"Just one more night, Win. I mean, out of . . . of respect."

She opened up the lipstick drawer and, without so much as looking, dumped what must have been two hundred tubes into another box.

"Or . . . or sorrow, or something," I said.

She was now on her knees, digging deep into a shelf, tugging at a litter of red falls that had become entangled. She shook her head, wadded them up. "Duck!" she said, and pitched them over my head and out of the room.

"I mean . . . we'll give ourselves a big finish, you know? A send-off. That's us, right?"

She nodded and turned toward another drawer. This one wouldn't open. She stuck her hand in and dug out fistfuls of eyeliner, mascara, and eye shadow, chucking them in with the rest.

"We can drive to the ocean and watch the sun come up and say goodbye. You know?" I continued. By now the drawer was empty enough for her to yank it, but it got away from her, crashing down onto the tiles.

"Shit, shit, shit!" she screamed. "Grant. I told you I need to be fucking alone. Whaddya think? This is easy for me?"

"Okay!" I said, backing off. "Sorry." She nodded and, after scooping up the fallen eye makeup, emptied the two fingernail polish drawers and the one full of junk jewelry with no problem. After which I helped her carry everything out to the Electra. She was heading to Mitchell French's, where she was going to camp until she found a place to live.

We gave each other polite pecks, and she promised to call me tomorrow.

At that point, I didn't fuck around. I followed my own rules. I stripped the bed and washed the towels and sheets and anything that might have Winnie's scent. For the next three days I swept, vacuumed, and continued my campaign to somehow eliminate years of animal damage and street grit and general mayhem. Then I spent the two following days moving everything of Winnie's across the way to my dormant studio, where, I told her, she could pick it up when she found a place.

Once I moved all the layers of Winnie's thrift store stuff, dirty panties, girdles from the thirties, brassieres from the forties, fifties high heels, sixties high heels, seventies platforms, faux furs, real furs, wigs, coats, and her collection of fifties and sixties detective magazines and girly magazines like *Swank*, *Cad*, *Rascal*, and *Knave*—not to mention her Art Deco dresser and matching vanity—waiting for me under it all, like a nicely preserved archaeological site, was the quiet, comfortable home of the guy I was before I met her. Before the Empire, before the musical, long before Winn, I had worked to make this wee cabinlike apartment look like a small gentlemen's club. I dug out my old framed battle paintings and hung them. I repositioned the lamps till the room glowed red and warm like candlelight shining through a glass of claret.

It took me another day to rearrange the furniture and reclaim the territory. That accomplished, I found myself hungry for progress, so I called a club that had made overtures awhile back and booked a series of shows.

Right around that time, as a perk, I got a call from Beer Can Eggy and Stu Lovesya, offering to treat me to dinner the following week. As social whirls go, it really wasn't much, but I was grateful for the start.

The day of the dinner Winnie arrived a couple of hours after she said she was going to, driving a small U-Haul. I was relieved to see she was alone. I had spent the previous night worrying about standing by while a flock of tittering Drag Hags emptied my house of the last vestiges of a love that was supposed to last a lifetime. All told, the move took about four hours. I was pleased that it went pretty easily, as long as I kept my mind focused on the task at hand.

Afterward Winn and I had a quick cup of coffee and chatted about the upcoming shows. Then I escorted her to the truck, gave her a friendly hug goodbye, and watched her speed off.

As I turned back toward my house and began to open my front gate, my neighbor Cole ran up. "Dude! Dude! Whoa! I saw the truck and I went, 'Whoa, is she out of here, man?' You guys split up?"

"Yeah," I said.

Cole stepped back, shaking her head. "Whoa, man, I am sorry, Dude. She was beautiful, man."

"Yeah." I nodded. "Thanks, Cole," I said as I turned back to the gate.

"Yeah . . . that's why I thought something was funny," she said, slapping her thigh. I turned around and looked at her, confused. Cole stepped back in that manic way she has. "Man, I'm sorry, but I thought I saw some bullshit goin' down."

"What do you mean?" I said.

"Hey, it's like we say: 'I watch out for you and you watch out for me,' right? Right?" I nodded, waiting for her to get to the point.

"So, it's about like two, three weeks ago, and I'm like getting home from the club late, on accounta I dance in Torrance on like Thursdays, right? So I pull into my place in back, and I see this Cadillac, and I think, I don't know this car.... Cos, you know, I gotta think like that cos I'm a woman, and I'm alone, right? And some fuckin' lunatic could follow me home from the club sometime. Right? Anyway . . . At first when I see the guy in the car, I think it's you. Long-haired, thin . . . right? And I'm thinking, Whoa, did he get a Caddy? But then I think, No way. Why would he be parkin' way the fuck back here? He always parks in front of his house. But check this out, sitting there with him I see your old lady. At first I think, Well, whatever. And then she like waves at me so I wave back, right? And that's when I see that the dude she's with isn't you. And I think, Whoa, is this some bullshit, or what?"

"You sure it was her?" I said, suddenly feeling sick.

"Dude, you kidding? Who looks like her? Plus she waved to me."

"Yeah." I was reeling. "Uh . . . what color was the Caddy?"

"It was night, man, something dark. Hey, listen, I don't want to start nothing, but I just thought you should know. In case she's trying to pull some shit. I mean, if they were just friends, why park the fuck back there at three in the morning, except that it's dark? That's what I was thinking, know what I mean?"

"Yeah . . ." I said.

"Awww, shit," she said, stepping back, shocked. "I fuckin' bummed you out! Dude! I am sorry!"

I thanked her for watching out for me and said I had to go. Stu and Eggy were due to pick me up in an hour, so I hurried back into the house to shower and change. I tried not to think about Cole's news, but my hands were shaking as I got undressed. It was impossible to imagine Winnie sneaking around. I began desperately spooling off possible explanations based on a paucity of fact. On top of this was the persistent feeling that Winn would clear it all up just as soon as she got home.

"Winnie's not coming home, you idiot," I said to the blur of my reflection as I stepped into the shower. To maintain some kind of control, I tried to reduce my growing panic to a manageable essence. But the truth was I had no idea what was going on. Any explanation was possible.

"I know fuck-all about what you did, where you went, or who you knew, Winnie," I hissed, shaving with jittery hands. That afternoon, I hadn't asked who was going to unload the U-Haul, preferring not to know. But now Cole had put a form, if not a face, on the mystery mover on the other side of town: a musician. For a second I saw Kip Kinches standing, legs akimbo, my dragon head earring dangling from his godly chest.

This was all too familiar. I thought I had gotten away from Jane Gray, but perhaps this was her revenge. Over the chasm of decades, I could hear her chanting, "Ha! Ha! Ha!" in that vindictive playground manner of hers.

■ ■ ■

Like Bonaparte returning from Elba, I began my new life with a ragtag crew. Instead of a thousand loyal Old Guardsmen, I was flanked by Jamie, Russ Bublis, Beer Can Eggy, and Stu Lovesya.

"Gentlemen, I want to toast my first night as a new man." I raised my coffee cup, and as glasses clinked I sang a tune I made up in a manic mood swing on the ride over.

> *"My refrigerator's lookin' kind of gross*
> *And I'm eatin' lots of tuna and toast.*
> *And I ain't no slave to a shower or a shave.*
> *Hey, I'm a single guy again!"*

Jamie laughed and said, "Your refrigerator couldn't be any worse than it was when you were with Winnie."

"Yeah," said Bublis. "And you look like you just shaved, plus your hair's still kinda wet."

"Mere corroborative detail," I said, explaining how I had just spent my first week as a bachelor thoroughly cleaning the place. Then I begged them, for the sake of my sanity, to leave Winnie out of the rest of the dinner conversation.

"No shit," said Stu. "She really fucked you, dude."

"Why, thanks for your support, Stu," I replied.

"We all knew Winn was out for herself, but man . . . She was strident! She took you down!" chimed in Beer Can.

"Yeah. Okay," I said, getting queasy again, hoping to get off the subject. "I really didn't see it coming."

Jamie slowly dug his finger into my elbow. "Neither did Fricke."

"Fricke?!" I said, my heart suddenly pumping.

"We thought you knew. . . ." said Stu Lovesya.

Fricke was a guitarist friend of both Winn's and mine from the old retail days. They had dated a long time ago, and as was the case with a lot of her exes, they had stayed friends. It was par for Winnie's course. Fricke was one of the twenty or so people—male, female, gay, straight—who had called regularly to invite Winnie out to one fab thing or another. Somewhere in that sprawling group of friends, he'd snuck in and, apparently, made his move.

I was speechless. I hadn't suspected him. I broiled, thinking of all the times he called the house. "Hey, Fricke! How ya doin'? How's song-writin'? . . . Good. . . . Yeah, I'll get her." Nice enough guy, if a little dull and whiny. One of those musicians who was forever joining bands and then quitting them a few months later because the band let him down. I guess I never thought of him as Winnie's type.

But my gracious dinner companions could list a score of Drag Hag parties, out-of-town shows, and clubs all over Silver Lake where they'd seen the two of them together. On nights when I had stayed home writing songs, or the goddamned P.E. Game.

"Oh, God, they were carrying on for ages," gushed Jamie. "I thought you had an arrangement or something."

"Nobody ever has arrangements," I said, suddenly furious, "except nudists, old hippies, and sheikhs."

Jamie patted my wrist compassionately. "Well, he got his. There must be some satisfaction in that."

"Who got what?" I implored.

"Fricke!" Jamie laughed. "She got rid of him as soon as a position opened up in a better firm." The guys all laughed.

"But . . ." I said, trying to keep up, "but we've only been broken up two weeks. She only just moved her shit out today!"

"Grant!" Jamie said, digging his finger in my thigh. "We're talking about Winnie here."

"So she dumped me for Fricke and then dumped Fricke?" I said. "For who?"

• • •

"Randy Randall!" I screamed. Three hours later, and I had yet to simmer down. Outside my Lincoln, Burbank slept as I swept past. It was the third or fourth time I had gone through this rant.

"What right did you have to make decisions about my future if you weren't in it for the long haul?" I railed at the empty seat. "If you had just said, 'Grant, I'm fucking Fricke,' I'd have fired you all and signed with Nick!" I shouted, storing that unexpected rhyme away for a snotty song I planned to write.

I drove on in silence, spent.

If Winn was indeed such a cutthroat, I absently wondered, who would she set her sails for once Randy had outlived his usefulness? There was no one bigger at the Empire than Randy Randall.

Except for . . . Nick Blake. The implications hit me so hard I sat through a green light. "Holy Fuck," I said.

. . .

I got home that night and lay down, sickened by thoughts of her screwing these yutzes while my life was coming apart at the seams. And then it hit me. I recalled our final night. How she couldn't stay because she was so upset that she had to be alone. But the truth was, she had to be with him. She needed the comfort of Fricke . . . or was it Randall? Or was it somebody else? As I lay there I thought of drilling a quarter-sized hole in my temple, attaching a silver garden hose nozzle, and turning on the faucet and flushing my brains away, like Grandpa used to spray dog shit off the sidewalk.

An hour later I got up off the couch, turned on the computer, and wrote:

> Dear Winnie,
> I will no longer be needing your services professionally.
> As always my best to you and your family,
>
> Grant

For the next three days, Winnie called and left enraged messages on my machine: indignant, furious, insulted. At every turn, she railed at me as though I were an uppity underling. I guffawed when I read an e-mail that said, "I will not tolerate this behavior!" Apparently from her point of view, she was the only one who was allowed to dissolve ties, and like something out of the P.E. Game, I had no right to be mad about something she didn't think I knew. To my delight, Winn was now chalking up quite a few P.E. points herself.

And then there was silence. She gave up.

A week later, when it all died down, I sat down and wrote another e-mail.

Chapter 48

LISA

What you and I have in common" was the subject. I stared at it for a few minutes. It was the first letter from Grant in a couple of fourteen weeks. Not that I was counting.

I studied the subject before I opened it. Bet you anything it's more shit about Nick, I thought. All the money in the world that he fucked Grant over, and that's what we have in common. Well, tou-fucking-ché.

I opened it up. And there were only two words: "I'm single."

I sat and stared at it for a while. It was hard to take in, almost as if it were written in a foreign alphabet. I was having so much trouble comprehending its meaning that I felt woozy. I had to call someone. I called Robinson.

"I told you that girlfriend of his was pissed off," he said.

I called Kat. "Honey, that's too weird," she said. "Whaddya think you're gonna do?"

"Well, I guess I should call him," I said. "He probably needs a friend now."

"A friend?" she howled. "Some fucking friend. Honey, did you or did you not tell me the last time we talked that he fucked you over? Aren't you the one who said that the whole premise of your friendship was false?"

"Well, in a manner of speaking," I hedged. "Whatever we had died pretty hard in the wake of the Nick shit. But you know, I still have feelings for the guy. And I've heard about what he's like in a breakup. He might be lying on the floor, choking on swamp gas, with a radioactive Super Ball in his stomach."

"I have no idea what that means," Kat said, "and I don't much care. So he chokes on swamp gas. Fuck that shit. Not your problem."

I paced around. I drank some coffee. I went out into my yard and pulled weeds. I sat down and drew a nervous face from the crusts and raisins on Swedish Limpa Bread. And then I went over to the computer and wrote him back.

Dear Grant,
Is this some kind of joke? Are you setting me up to make me look foolish for some reason? And second of all, as far as "what you and I have in common" goes, where do you get off just assuming that I am single?

I am inviting you over here for dinner, because I would like you to explain to me what has been going on. Pick a night. Any night.

Lisa

Dear Lisa,
No. This is not some sort of joke. And no, I am not setting you up. And I am sorry for just assuming that you were still sin-

gle. Did you get married? If so, congratulations! I would love to come to dinner. I look forward to explaining everything to you and your new husband. Is tomorrow night okay?

Grant

Dear Grant,

Yes. I got married several weeks ago to Johnny Depp's brother, big-band leader Dickie Depp. He's older but still very vigorous and alert. And he's really good with meats.

Okay. Maybe I am still single, but I didn't like the way you took it for granted. Tomorrow night is fine. Have you had your morning coffee by eight at night? What sort of food do you eat, anyway? Any dietary restrictions?

P.S. I noticed that in your extremely cryptic e-mail you failed to congratulate me for winning the P.E. Game. I was never clear on whether or not there was a cash prize, or just some valuable merchandise. Nevertheless, I might as well get this out of the way right now: YAY I WON I WON I WON I WON!

Dear Lisa,

No dietary restrictions. By the way, I'm a big Dickie Depp fan. I'm sorry you two couldn't make it work.

Don't worry about cooking for me. I smoke so much I can't taste anything, anyway. Eight is fine, but I might be a little late because I probably will just be waking up. Looking forward to it.

Grant

P.S. Find attached a little P.E. story that I was saving for the proper occasion. It's called "Ricky." *Bon appétit.*

Chapter 49

LISA

W hen the phone rang, I was still dizzy from that ghastly story about the suicide and the funeral. Nevertheless I tried to put on a sultry but nonchalant voice, just to let him know I didn't much care if he had decided to cancel. An attractive gal such as myself had a schedule too hectic to keep up with.

But it was Eden. "So, revenge is sweet," he said. "You win an award, and the network suddenly wants you back. They ordered six *You Go, Girl!*s for mid-season. And I'd like you to write as many of them as time will allow."

"Thanks, but I really can't," I said.

"Why not?" he argued. "You have a better grasp of the show than anyone."

"Eden," I said, "here's what I suggest: Since

you're going to change every single word of every first draft anyway, why not let the homeless write all your first drafts? That way they'll get a paycheck and health insurance. And you'll be a cultural hero!"

After he hung up, I chanted, "Nicely put my heart back into its former condition again. So pleasant again I can become," hoping to cleanse any remaining *You Go, Girl!* particles from the ether. After exhaustive thought on what to serve for dinner, I decided to make the one and only recipe that came up when I Googled "Napoleon recipes of": chicken Marengo, invented on a battlefield by Napoleon's chef. At the risk of appearing to be trying too hard, I also bought a CD called *The Sounds of War*, in order to provide some dinner ambience. Many of the cuts, like the Uzi assault rifle, were not appropriate for the late eighteenth century. But just in case things grew uncomfortable between Grant and me, I figured the CD would offer a useful distraction.

Grant was just a few minutes late. He had warned me he was keeping weird hours and moving kind of slow. I had a hard time believing my eyes when I opened the door and there he stood on my very doorstep. He was once again wearing all black, as though dressed for his own funeral. He looked sad and disheveled, tired, and somehow shorter, as though he had been defeated and surrendered, then imploded. I told him I was sorry about Winnie. He shrugged unconvincingly. So I went into high-energy hostess mode and started offering him food. He seemed to cheer up a bit at the idea of chicken Marengo.

We talked over dinner to the sounds of battle noises, which Grant promptly found too loud. I got up and turned the volume down, too nervous to eliminate the sounds entirely. Track twenty-three, explosions with falling debris, segued into twenty-four, a nuclear explosion: a fitting sound track for the details of Grant's newly decimated life. I remembered too well how unbalanced, how physically devastating, it was to have someone you had relied upon, good or bad, suddenly gone. Of course, there was some unsettling post-Ethan déjà vu when Grant kept asking, "Why didn't she say something in time for me to try and fix things?" The sound of a falling projectile echoed behind him.

"I don't know," I said. "Seems like there's a lot of that going around." There were pistol shots and the grunting of men in a fistfight. A trumpet played "Taps."

Since the best way to help someone through something painful is through distraction, I changed the topic to something worse. "What happened to you and P.E.?" I asked him, raising my voice so I could be heard above the whistling sounds of surface-to-air missiles.

"Well, after Ricky blew his face off, things got really bad. Do you mind turning that down some more?" he asked over machine-gun fire. "Jane and I broke up and got back together about twenty times. I'd come back only to hear Bugs Bunny in my head screaming, 'What am I doin'!?' as the cycle started again."

"Wow," I said, shaking my head. "You know, the more I hear about this happy little relationship of yours, the more I get a hunch that you may be pulling ahead in the points."

"Nah. I don't want any points. I deserved it for coming back so many times," he said.

"I have to confess," I said, "I was starting to wonder which of the two of you was really the crazy one."

"I definitely was," Grant said. "I guess the good news is that I was able to transform my death wish into a desire to write light musical theater." He got up to help me clear the dishes.

"So—how did you finally get out?" I asked, putting some water on for tea.

"Like any recovering hophead, I found the time I could stay away got longer and longer. During those periods, I began to see other possibilities that didn't include rolling up into fetal positions on the floor. After seven years with Jane I had actually forgotten that people occasionally aspire to things besides getting away from pain. So I ultimately stopped blaming her for everything, left, and stayed gone."

We sat quietly for a moment,

He paused to eat a few bites of the napoleon I'd served him for dessert, then said, "Where were you heading with your stories about Nick?"

"Some other time, if you don't mind," I said, winking. "I can't take any more gore right now." I invited him into the living room for some post-dinner distraction. "I have a movie I think you should watch," I said, putting arguably the worst comedy ever made, *Hardly Working*, into the VCR. Jerry Lewis's study in narcissism and egomania seemed like the perfect capper to the P.E. Game. So we sat down on the living room floor, in front of the fire and the VCR, to watch the bloated, aging Jerry Lewis successfully woo a woman with romantic techniques like shoving an entire water glass into his mouth. When Grant groaned, I found myself wanting to reach over and take his hand. What's the worst that can happen? I argued with myself. If he's offended, I'll pretend it was a nurturing, compassionate gesture. And we can nicely put our hearts back into their former condition again. Unless, of course, he finds it upsetting. And thinks it has undermined our friendship. So I sat frozen, overwhelmed by feelings similar to love. Whenever they arose I made an effort to push them away.

It's not *that* kind of love, I was quick to remind myself. He's only here because he wants and needs my support. But, what do I do with these feelings I have for him? I wondered, realizing they were starting to become compulsive and obsessive. I wasn't watching the movie. I was watching Grant. "Follow your own advice," the answer came back. "Distract yourself. And do it *now*."

Focusing with renewed intensity on the grisly antics of Jerry Lewis, I marveled at how he was able to make a woman glow with desire by destroying her car. Could that work? Should I go out and break Grant's windshield? Would that help him to see me in a better light? As I looked over to see how Grant was reacting, I was hit by another wave of astonishment. After all this time, he was right here. Right on my living room floor! Another swell of desire crashed over me. Now I was becoming consumed with the idea of stroking his hair. So you stroke his fucking hair. So what? I argued with myself. It's just hair stroking. Not date rape. The worst thing that can happen is he says, "Leave my hair alone." But I knew that would kill me. So I sat, paralyzed. The molecules in the space between us had grown to the size of golf balls. There was nothing to do except pretend amusement as Jerry Lewis destroyed a gas station, pumps and all. I had to give him his due. Who else would have been capable of imagining that a frightening display of violent incompetence in the workplace might make a woman fall deeply in love. Which is when I realized that it had certainly worked for Nick.

And still I didn't make a move.

Chapter 50

GRANT

I couldn't find solace in the rage and informality of rock. From Lennon to Strummer to Cobain, the slang, the anger, the dropped G's all seemed out of place and naïve. The informal lyrics reminded me of teens wearing sweaters and slacks to a funeral. It lacked respect, and refused to acknowledge the enormity of my unexpected loss. Thus, out of countless songs that might offer solace, there was only one that truly hit home. It was 130 years old and barely under a minute long. The operatic grandeur matched the magnitude of my devastation. I'd wait until the hurt became unbearable, and then I'd play the song loud enough to scare the gangstas on the next block.

The hour of gladness is dead and gone
In silent sadness I live alone
The hope I cherished now lifeless lies
And all has perished save love, which never dies.

I always had a crush on Katisha, the aged, love-starved matron in *The Mikado*, rejected by a younger lover. I empathized with her now. Like her, I was old, plain-faced, and delusional. So much more than romance had perished.

The last time I had seen Winnie, I stood by as she dumped our seven years into a city garbage can. Happiest when busy, she did this in a chatty, friendly manner. For her, she was lightening her load, yet as she did so, she added to mine. I hurt as she threw out the silliest objects, crap that had sat stacked in piles. Magazines from the fifties, bags of clothes, things I had tripped on and cursed. Things that had made the backdrop of our life, she disposed of without a thought.

"All has perished," I sang quietly to myself as I watched her.

Winnie had coldcocked me. I simply didn't see it coming. When I broke up with Jane, there had been a landing system forming. So many knew of my troubles with her that by the time it was over, a small, loving group was waiting with open arms. Most understood the damage that Jane had wrought, and were kind enough to keep it all friendly, simple, and nasty. But not this time. I had been too busy, too secure, to even consider a second string.

So it was hard to know what to feel with Lisa. I thought of her as brassy. But I had only seen her in public, on guard. Now she was soft-spoken and relaxed. When we sat down on the floor in front of the TV, I got a pang of fear: Was eros in the air? Then I relaxed. I wasn't going to make any move here. And having read her e-mails, I knew she wouldn't, either. I felt safe.

The Jerry Lewis movie went on forever. A few months back,

Winnie and I would have laughed ourselves silly. But now the last thing I could enjoy was watching an aging greaseball flailing pointlessly. I related to him too closely.

I had built a steel wall around Lisa for so long that when she reached over and touched me, I was mildly horrified. I had grown to like her as a friend, had come to rely on her objectivity. At first, when she put her arm around me, I wanted to say, "Stop. Stay like this. Don't let's kiss. Kissing leads to sex, and sex leads to calling the next day, and that leads to setting up more sex, and then later, commitment, and the next thing you know, you'll want to leave me so you can strip in public."

I could feel her moving in, her face getting closer to mine. I kept shrinking into my chest. Jerry Lewis was talking with a mouthful of doughnuts while the tinny *Hardly Working* theme provided the sound track. Oh, Lisa, if you kiss me, you discover the man without spell-check and worse. Kiss me and meet the chain-smoking, self-involved porno fiend.

I knew if we kissed, she and I would no longer be friends, but something complex and fragile. But most of all, after losing Winn, I wasn't ready to lose Lisa.

Chapter 51

LISA

I put my arm around him. When he didn't move, I froze. A wave of anxiety hit me. No reciprocity, just like the first time with Nick. Learn your lesson, I said to myself. Leave it right here and escape with your dignity. He's letting you know he's uncomfortable. Do more, and face humiliation and rejection.

So I withdrew my arm. It's okay, I calmed myself. It was just a gesture of affection. Nothing wrong with that. No harm done.

We sat side by side on the floor, leaning against the base of the couch as the horrible movie refused to die. Even during the credits, it continued on and on with an endless series of theoretically hilarious outtakes. Grant shrieked in agony and held his head as the simple but terrible flute-filled movie score played under the credits. "Well, you were right. That was really awful," he said finally. I nodded proudly.

We were talking again. He was letting me know he still liked me. I was relieved. And so, for the next hour, we continued to talk as we watched the fire with more interest than we had the movie.

"I never thought I'd be here with you like this," he said at one point.

"Me, either," I said, wondering if this contained a subtext. I couldn't help thinking, It's four A.M. And there's an adult man next to me on the floor, showing no signs of wanting to leave. Could I be reading this wrong? Is it possible that after all those years on the road, and all those girls coming on to him, his approach to seduction is to simply make himself available, like a dessert tray?

I debated this with myself for a while. He hadn't moved when I had touched him before. But had anything changed? I was starting to drive myself crazy. So I took another risk and put my arm through his. And when that seemed okay, I leaned my head on his shoulder. My backup plan was to claim that I was comforting him, like a caring friend.

With that, he began to deliver a speech about how he didn't know if he was ready. He felt too damaged from his breakup. The wounds were so fresh. When he said that, I remembered again how painful, how disorienting, a breakup can feel. His home life had just vanished, along with all his predictable routines. I moved away from him again.

"I don't want to be just another fucked-up guy in your life," he said to me.

I thought about that for a minute. He was right. It was much too soon. The last thing either one of us needed was more heartache, or another poorly conceived, badly constructed, and misguided attempt at a love relationship. What we had with each other was preferable. It was solid, reliable, painless. We were friends. And it was a friendship that, with the proper tending, might really last.

"I understand," I said. "And I don't want you to be."

Then I lost control of myself and I jumped him. What the hell, I thought, I have enough goddamn friends. And friendship is just as fucking unstable as love.

Chapter 52

GRANT

J ust as the last notes of *Hardly Working* sounded, it happened. She pounced. To my surprise, the old rock slut in me awoke. I liked the way she kissed. She made my head swim, and I forgot where I was. I liked the way she smelled of Chanel and the woodsy Topanga air. As we rolled around in the blue light of the video, I became aware that a melodic line from *The Mikado* kept repeating: "I think I am sufficiently decayed." Katisha again, the long A of "decayed" jumping up about seven notes. The melodic snippet repeated endlessly as Lisa and I kissed.

Chapter 53

LISA

I can't believe it's you," I remember saying as I ricocheted back and forth between dissociating and feeling overwhelmed by lust. I could feel that he also was zooming in and out of the kiss: there for a moment, then gone, and in a few seconds, back. But I had made the commitment and decided to see it through. Soon I was deep into it, then lost in it. I had never ignited with someone I actually knew pretty well first. Guess it had to happen sooner or later.

Somewhere midkiss, another wave of anxiety washed over me. The reality of what was taking place startled me. What had I done? Had I just opened the door to another complicated nightmare? I was so used to thinking about endings before beginnings that I was already wondering which one of us would be the new Psycho Ex.

When he left at sunrise, I was in shock. I felt like I had when I flipped the car over on the freeway—separated from myself and unhinged. I couldn't sleep. I couldn't sit still. It was the wrong time of day for sake. I was much too tired and much too wired to try and read. So I sat down at the computer to write him an e-mail.

Dear Grant,
Just thought I'd write you a note to let you know what a nice time I had this evening. And how glad I am about the way things turned out. I had been trying in vain to figure out what to do with all the feelings I

And then I pushed "delete." Fuck this, I thought. I'm not rolling over for this guy. Besides, if I reveal myself to be too eager too soon, Grant will think I have P.E. potential. I started the letter again.

Dear Grant,
I couldn't stand the idea that I conceded the P.E. Game without ever having revealed the truth of what really happened with Nick.

Then I saved the letter in a folder and lay down on the couch in my office to think. What to write next? How to win in one easy e-mail? Maybe now was the time to make up the story of Nick's murderous spree. And even better than the random killing of strangers, how about if I said that he killed my crazy mother. He had always hated her. What if he finally couldn't control his rage? And then something else occurred to me. Maybe the Nick/murderer card was one I didn't need to play. So I sat back down at the computer to start another letter.

Dear Grant:

I had a lovely time with you this evening. And I hope you are feeling okay.

I was very touched that you didn't take any points for that grim little story about the guy who killed himself. However, something else occurred to me. Since you didn't take any points for that poor suicidal soul and his tragic funeral, I have no choice but to conclude that I am still WINNING WINNING WINNING WINNING WINNING WINNING.

Chapter 54

GRANT

It was almost dawn when I left and got onto the Pacific Coast Highway. To my right was the Pacific Ocean; the sky was turning that rich dark blue that I wished would never change. Katisha's seven-note jump was still in my head. I cued up the CD player and turned up the volume and sang along.

> There's a fascination frantic
> In a ruin that's romantic—do you think you are
>   sufficiently decayed?
> To the matter that you mention, I have given some
>   attention
> And I think I am sufficiently decayed.

I was giddy, high on an upswing of sex and my consummated crush on Lisa. Everything seemed clear. Solved, simple. The sun was due any minute. As *The Mikado* thundered from my car speakers, I found myself laughing at Gilbert's timeless, eloquent cruelty. I knew my patterns, though. This joy wouldn't last. I would get home, collapse, and mourn Winnie for years. Winnie, on the other hand, would have a ball. One day she'd marry rich and jet around the globe. She would always assume that the men she broke up with were fine with it and that they, like her, had run their course. She would always want to be the boss, and then, like Bonaparte in Egypt, would duck when the game went awry, somehow landing on her feet if not the throne. I felt the heat of both anger and envy, as if oily rags were smoldering just above my stomach. Winnie would do quite well without me.

But today I had kissed Lisa, and I almost called her, of all people, Claudia, who had always harped at me about intimacy in a way that made me gag. Maybe I was old enough now to let down my guard a little. Yes, maybe now I had lived long enough; maybe I was sufficiently decayed.

As Katisha's song looped in my head, I looked out at the ocean. The sky was losing its bruised color and taking on the lighter powder-blue tones. I recalled an exchange from *The Mikado* that seemed apt. Hand-wringing and weak, Koko declares, "I dare not hope for your love—but I will not live without it. Accept my love, or I perish on the spot."

He was the very voice of my overblown state at the end of every relationship, obsessive and despairing. I filled my lungs with tobacco smoke and tried to remember Katisha's response. When I did, I delivered it to the empty passenger seat with full nineteenth-century bravado.

"Go to! Who knows so well as I that no one ever yet died of a broken heart!"

ABOUT THE AUTHORS

Emmy Award–winning writer MERRILL MARKOE has authored three books of humorous essays and the novel *It's My F---ing Birthday*. She has worked as a radio host and a TV correspondent and written for television, movies, and a delightful assortment of publications. She lives in Los Angeles, if you can call that living.

ANDY PRIEBOY has written and recorded with Wall of Voodoo and produced three solo albums. His musical, *White Trash Wins Lotto*, is currently in pre-production for a 2005 run. Emmylou Harris, Linda Ronstadt, and Concrete Blonde are among the artists who have covered his songs. He lives in Los Angeles.

For more information about the authors, visit www.thepsychoexgame.com.